"Eclectic and tear   ..al and lyrical by

...PH...DI AN...   —in
fact a dazzling polymath... ...ons of geology, hunting, popular
religion, immigrant history, and frontier economics at his disposal—
Matthew Neill Null is bound to become one of the most admired
and influential fiction writers of his generation. He is the only writer
I know—besides Edward P. Jones in *The Known World*—who has the
chops to represent the American past in a way that is richly credible for
its period and yet is stylistically daring, even experimental."

—JAIMY GORDON, author of *Lord of Misrule*, National Book Award Winner

"In one of the most assured debuts of the year, Matthew Neill Null
tells the story of an American tragedy that began when Union soldiers
from wealthy Eastern families first saw West Virginia's thousands of
acres of nearly impenetrable virgin forest. *Honey from the Lion* brings
to mind the literature-as-history triumphs of E. L. Doctorow and
Denis Johnson, yet Null is specific unto himself. His compressed, lyrical prose penetrates every darkness and wheels through time like a
soaring bird."

—JAYNE ANNE PHILLIPS, author of *Lark and Termite*,
National Book Award Finalist

"*Honey from the Lion* is provocative in its exploration of transgression
and redemption and exhilarating in its lyric evocations of this rugged
American landscape. Matthew Neill Null establishes himself as a perceptive seer of haunted souls and as an astonishing stylist."

—LAURA VAN DEN BERG, author of *The Isle of Youth* and *Find Me*

"*Honey from the Lion* is a magisterial achievement, suffused with the
Faulknerian values of love, honor, pity, pride, compassion, and sacrifice,
concerning nothing less than the cohesion of an American civilization.
Matthew Neill Null is a brilliant writer, and his first novel is a gift."

—ANTHONY MARRA, author of *A Constellation of Vital Phenomena*,
National Book Award Longlist

"Matthew Neill Null writes with great originality about a place, West
Virginia, that his singular vision has made universal. He illuminates the
mercenary side of American history—its rapacity and greed—and also
the resistance and protest that this novel itself so eloquently represents."

—ZACHARY LAZAR, author of *I Pity the Poor Immigrant*

HONEY FROM THE LION

MATTHEW NEILL NULL

LOOKOUT BOOKS
University of North Carolina Wilmington

This book is a work of fiction. Names, characters, places, events, and incidents are products of the author's imagination or used in a fictitious manner. Any resemblance to actual persons, living or dead, or actual events is entirely coincidental.

First printing, September 2015
ISBN: 978-1-940596-08-2 | E-BOOK: 978-1-940596-09-9

Cover illustration by Alexander Heaton
Back cover image © Kevin Russ
Interior design by Abigail Chiaramonte, Katie Prince, and Bethany Tap for The Publishing Laboratory
Title page lettering by Katie Prince

LIBRARY OF CONGRESS CATALOGING-IN-PUBLICATION DATA
Null, Matthew Neill.
Honey from the Lion / Matthew Neill Null.
    pages ; cm
ISBN 978-1-940596-08-2 (acid-free paper) .
1. Young men—Fiction. 2. Paper mills—Fiction. 3. Logging—Fiction.
4. Interpersonal relations—Fiction. 5. West Virginia—History—20th century—Fiction. I. Title.
    PS3614.U8644H66 2015
    813'.6—dc23
                                2015014289

Lookout Books gratefully acknowledges support from the University of North Carolina Wilmington.

Printed on FSC-Certified paper by Thomson-Shore in Dexter, Michigan.

15 16 17 18 TS 4 3 2 1

LOOKOUT BOOKS
Department of Creative Writing
University of North Carolina Wilmington
601 S. College Road
Wilmington, NC 28403
lookout.org

For the land and the people

Then went Samson down, and his father and his mother, to the vineyards of Timnath, and behold, a young lion roared against him. The Spirit of the Lord came mightily upon him, and he rent the lion as he would a kid, and he had nothing in his hand. But he told not his father or his mother what he had done. And he went down and talked with the Philistine woman, and she pleased Samson well.

And after a time he returned to take her, and he turned aside to see the carcass of the lion. Behold, there was a swarm of bees and honey in the carcass. And he took the combs in his hands and went on eating, and came to his father and mother and gave honey to them, and they did eat. But he told them not that he had taken honey from the lion.

—Judges

THE ABSENTEES

CONFLICT BEGETS COMMERCE, and theirs was the American Civil War.

Kennison Mountain, billowing white with chestnut blossoms. Petals clung to the coats of soldiers. If you touched a branch, the blossoms fell like snow. In forty years, a blight would wither the chestnut trees and end white summer forever. By then, Eugene Helena would be a minority whip, an arm-twisting U.S. senator, and nearly vice president but for a sliver of votes.

But now, in July of 1861, he was a young infantryman with little more than a bellyful of green apples, a pain in his heel, and a question as to the whereabouts of the just and righteous God he'd

learned of in Sunday school. Why create the world only to excuse yourself from it?

He kept this thought to himself. The confetti of blossoms was no comfort.

Nor to Shelby Randolph, his roommate and club rival, who had been talked into enlisting, out-debated one more time. No one hated soldiering more than he. Randolph cursed and blasphemed to the point of giving offense. Gnats drew to his eyes and mouth—he left off swatting at them, because Helena wasn't. The third one, Cleve Baxter, the boarding school dunce, followed close behind on the thin and rocky trail.

Randolph told him to back off and not tramp on his heels. If Baxter did it again, Randolph would be forced to bawl him out in front of God and everyone. Baxter was teetering now on the rocks.

They were children, really. None of these three New Yorkers— or any of their company—had been south of Philadelphia before the war began. On a trail no more than a deer trot through laurel, the greenbriers tugged buttons from coats and gave the men's skin red little licks. The New Yorkers panted like dogs. Their sweat burned in the cuts. They crossed the mountain's girdle of red oak. Gained elevation. The air turned coolish and right for pine.

The forest opened in big timber. Ferns and the smell of water and a lush handsbreadth carpet of moss. They could breathe.

Admiring the waxy rhododendrons, Helena couldn't know he would die of this place.

When they made the summit of Camp Spruce, Helena asked, "What is that—all that blue? Are those buildings out there?"

Helena had mistaken the creeping mist for factory smoke.

"Ain't tenements." Their laughing guide—a local hunter hired by chance on the pike—swept a hand across the horizon as if to strike it from the earth. Waves of ridges and hogbacks, gnarled valleys and backbone peaks, boulder fields and rivers of flagged pine. Here, the dregs of Europe had scratched a toehold; it was the first place they'd come to that no one made them leave, that no one else coveted. The native people were long gone. A place the indentured fled to from the coast, coloring their hair with bone char and shoe polish, inventing names. And then the circuit riders followed.

The guide took off his felt hat and used it like a bandanna to swab his brow. "A hundred miles just like it," he said. "Indians called it the Shades."

Helena, the garrulous one, forever questioning the guide, said he believed it. Randolph and Baxter sidled up. They followed Helena always.

"Struggle through them laurel hells and tell me different," the guide said as if Helena had not agreed. "Not me. Takes a cleverer foot. A deer can't wade it."

Randolph was listening close.

"Why has it not been cleared?" Helena asked.

"Ah, they clear a little to farm. Slashes now and again."

"The ground's not fertile?"

The guide pulled a briar from his vest. "Witch you up a little corn. Won't take cotton nor tobacco nor nothing."

"Indians?"

"Only one I ever seen was on the backside of a penny. He did not put a scare in me."

"You say the people are trash?" Helena asked.

The guide nearly bit off his pipe stem. "I'm proud to be one," he said.

Randolph blushed on Helena's behalf. He pretended to rummage through his pouch for bullets and shot patches.

Helena took a chance: "I meant the black Irish," he said coolly.

"Ah," said the laughing guide, "not many of them."

Proving why Helena was admired for his grace. He could mend any break. Randolph hated him for it.

This was the Mountain Campaign, the war's first year and its most maddening. It made for an ambiguous setting, here in the western mountains of Virginia, claimed both by the United States and its rebels; even the mayors weren't quite sure which government they belonged to, which flag would get you shot.

In some towns, the Confederate sympathizers were rounded up and arrested; in others, the Federal. In Camden-on-Gauley, the Presbyterian church quit meeting during the war, believing that, as the deacon said, "The less said, the better." The land was still Old Virginia on the maps, but that meant nothing now. The New Yorkers—Watertown boys all, except for Baxter, the misplaced Manhattanite—fought under a brigadier general named Milroy, who had been told to snap western Virginia from the Shenandoah Valley like a withered limb. They must overtake the Staunton–Parkersburg Pike. They must.

Randolph said, "My God, imagine the timber."

They linked arms and failed to encircle a spruce that disappeared in the green oblivion above. The guide watched this spectacle, laughing in his husky, crowish way. Finally the bugle called them back to camp, but they had gotten a bit lost and found their way blocked by a fallen tree as long as seven train cars. Randolph slapped the trunk. Its roots clutched rocks the size of rams.

Late now, they got a cussing from General Milroy. They talked most of the night about these lands, when they should have been twisting up quickloads for armory-bright Springfield rifles. Randolph fell finally asleep to dreams of milled boards. When he woke, he could see nothing through the fog, not even their own guidons, but then a molten sunrise spilled into the mountains as if tipped from a jug. He heard a whistling volley. Then another.

"Buckle down!" came a shout down the line.

A dozen claps like distilled thunder. They'd camped on the wrong side of the mountain, exposed themselves. Air jumped with earth and roots and glittering mica.

Stricken, the general swatted at his boys with a saber, asking, "Are you froze?"

Baxter fell, burying a splinter deep in the ham of his hand. He put it to his mouth to suck, and a sabot round tore off his ear. Blood spilled like a sash down his shirt. Helena dragged him into a gulley, an episode that would be reported in memoirs of war, while others stood gawking.

The battery turned their hasty fort to a mash of pulp and bone.

Everyone ran. Branches fell. Grapeshot sang its wild notes. A man shot in the teeth covered his mouth with his hands as if to keep from blurting a secret.

Ledger columns: killed, wounded, gone missing. This day: five, seven, one.

Baxter earned a trip to the Cumberland hospital. Randolph could hardly contain himself. Oh, how he admired that docked ear. "I may not soldier again," Baxter said mournfully.

Helena patted his hand and assured him that the nation would find some use for him.

Helena's very touch was anodyne.

In his report, the brigadier general wrote, "Our nest became too hot to hold us." To his wife, "Nothing lost, nothing gained but rocky ground not level enough to shoot dice upon." That summer and fall, a third of the company would die or desert. Would he lose his commission?

Their guide, more to the point, said, "They went through us like a dose of salts."

Yet the Federal campaign succeeded. Winter came and let them wreck hot-blooded slavers in the snow. It was a rout, a wonderful thing. Randolph said, "You are watching the withering away of the party of Jefferson and Jackson." The disagreement, Randolph ventured, would end in a month, and Baxter would miss out on the war. The laughing guide asked would he like to wager.

NOT A MONTH ON, Randolph lost his silver coin.

Gritting his teeth, he was reminded of this twenty-five years later, when the New Yorkers returned to Kennison Mountain. Where was that guide now? Dead, Randolph believed—or hoped. Now let him spend his coin. Let him laugh.

The going up the ridgetop was just as rough as he recalled, these irregular chunks of stone that suggested a trail. This time, they brought along champagne coupes and wives. They were dressed in civilian clothes. Helena liberated a bottle from the galvanized bucket of pounded ice. His wife brought out glassware from a wicker basket plaited with red ribbon. She wore the prettiest butterfly choker and floated to her husband's drifting touch. Everyone smiling into one another's sweaty faces, joy-drunk. Gaiters, neckties, shining ankle-high boots. Bosc pears, sheep's milk cheese from Spain. Helena leaned over and tweaked Baxter's ear, which had healed over gnarled, like a woodland mushroom. To do it, he had to reach behind the flowing Dundreary whiskers Baxter affected to hide the deformity, and Baxter socked him gently back. The return to this place from their youth encouraged horseplay, even in such serious men, even in Randolph. A cork popped into the weeds with a gush of froth.

They owned all they could see, except a wedge of Jump Mountain. To the ladies in riding coats, the place was pretty but didn't look like much. Green upon green. Could you call these roads, this sucking mud that stole your shoes? They kept such thoughts to themselves.

No one noted the irony in traveling so far to celebrate a land from which they would mostly absent themselves. Not even Randolph, the lawyer, who styled himself a bitter collector of ironies—for him, they unlocked the human heart. Helena and Baxter never saw Kennison Mountain again.

"I dreamt of this place," Randolph said. "It haunted my very dreams."

Three years later, in 1889, the New Yorkers incorporated Cheat River Paper & Pulp. The Company, they called it among themselves. They were no more villainous than any human child who has ever drawn breath. Yale and Exeter men, their grandfathers had made money from shipyards and the Middle Passage; their fathers were speculators and textile merchants; they would make their mark in timber and coal. They didn't gaze sidelong to Europe as their fathers had. Surveyors were sent to measure the parcels, and notes came back in one excitable gush, outlandish numbers— wild outbursts for such prudent fellows—claiming trees that rivaled the cedars of Lebanon, swearing the Alleghenics richer than Cyprus. The country was a child's sloppy painting of green: spruce and fir in the highlands, hardwoods in the foothills and on the flanks of mountains. Turn it brown, move a mile upriver, repeat a thousand times. Plenty of river for steam engines and mills, and coal all around, in-state no less. God had been felicitous in the placement of water and stone. A favorable tax scale and a young state government so keen for commerce, keen for leaders. The chief surveyor wrote Randolph, "All through the environs are men willing to work. Unbidden, they approach to ask when do the agents come a-hiring."

It was, for the most part, Helena's money. Everyone knew it. But Randolph took the lead. He set his jaw, set to work.

1889: Block deeds.

1891: Lay the Cheat River mainline.

1892: Construct the sashmill, hire the first thousand to the satellite camps.

The few residents welcomed the saws, selling rights to vast tracts with little ceremony and a little profit. The land, when cleared, would amount to free newground with none of the work, the land agents said. The plow shall follow the ax and, as we know, rain follows the plow.

Contracts of onionskin were signed by jug-eared farmers who grinned over the paper bills, building them into small, sloppy mountains on their kitchen tables—once the agents left the houses. Their wild glee gave the children a fright. Wood spurs jumped off the railroad mainline every day, blooming like cracks in bone china, finding every secret hollow. Helena liked to say, "The meek shall inherit the earth but not its mineral rights." Later, another robbed him of this aphorism and made it his own. The cities and the ghettos would buy what they were selling—and always would. In decades to come, when someone praised the prudence of municipal bonds or precious metals, Randolph would chant, "Land, building materials, and fuel. Land, building materials, and fuel." You can't chew a gold coin, he said.

Rich years. Their names recommended to the state legislature. Friendships, children, cabinet positions. This was long before the passage of the Seventeenth Amendment. Helena—then Baxter, on the joyous occasion of an aged politician's aneurysm—was elected to the United States Senate by a roomful of twenty-four friends.

Unanimously. That was important, and pounded out beforehand. Randolph almost wept. He was respected but distrusted. For months, his wife and children feared his coming home. Something must be found for him. Something plum. It was not easy.

So he was nominated to the court of appeals. Randolph remade his reputation with his opinion on *Pennsylvania Railroad v. Pennsylvania*, read even outside of legal circles. He could make true decisions there in court, not beholden to the whims of the Senate's eighty-nine Glorious Seraphim—as he called them.

Judge Randolph said to the Company's board of directors, "You watch. When we pull out of this Cuba business, we'll see a depression in orders."

Judge Randolph was wrong and, for once, glad to be. The land kept giving. Demand was strong. His fears turned to the unions, to the ministrations of labor policy. He studied the Pullman affair. The anarchy of Haymarket. The travesty of the Anthracite Strike. Insurrection could come from their very own camps! Blackpine, Randolph had to admit, was an ideal setting for such. There's always a copperhead in the woodpile—the war had taught him that. Few took his warnings seriously. He was humored.

They tore sweetness out of that rough unlikely place. They wrestled it down and made it give. Blessed by it again, and again, and again. By Theodore Roosevelt's second term, the timber logged out of West Virginia could reach the moon and back twice over. Cheat River Paper & Pulp had not even tapped their lands in Augusta or Nicholas. The timber outfits counted raw board feet by the billion, measured honest by the Doyle Rule, every inch cut by men's hands grown callused as boot leather from the double-bitted ax and the crosscut saw.

But for small interruptions, the boom would hold for years. Small interruptions no one would recall.

WHERE JUDGES WALK

FOR YEARS, Cur lived on the Cheat River, where three soldiers once linked arms around a ghostly tree. They were the distant gods of his smallish world. This was in the high timber camp called Blackpine.

Once, in the fall of 1904, he killed a blue heron that was hunting the Cheat River shallows, while the other loggers, the timber wolves, silently cheered him on. The heron held its bill like a spear for the sun-flash of fish. High-stepping the waters. An eye too sharp to overlook him or any threat. Any second it would fly. Cur reached down without looking and tested the heft of what his hand found there, a hatchet-shaped chunk of stone. When the heron paused and, in a barely perceptible motion, braced its muscles to fly, Cur lobbed overhand—saw the stone peak in the sun and, tumbling, fall—and the great bird folded in on itself. Cur splashed out, and cool river water leapt from his legs. The other timber wolves counted off forty paces, hooted admiration. No one minded getting wet, not for this. Scaly legs rasped against Cur's palms, which lifted a body the length of a child's. He put his other hand under the neck's slender stem. The heron's chest was gashed. It had a yellow cat's eye and a crown of two black feathers pinned back from the brow. They marveled. You could try a thousand times and not do it again. How could a sly heron be killed like that?

Cur, the wolves answered themselves. Another man could hardly take one with a bored rifle. Cur was lucky, and maybe always would be. They loved him for it. Duckweed pooled richly about their legs.

"You going to eat that pullet?" asked McBride, the teamster, in that storm-cloud hat. Where they stood in the river wasn't far from the railroad siding. The wolves of Camp Five began to assemble in their hundreds, waiting to be carried into the town the absentees had built for them. McBride gestured at the heron, then shook his head, like a man biting down into a drumstick.

"Maybe," said Cur. "You got the seasoning?"

"She might taste a wee froggy."

The rail ran flush to the river, in the same sinuous curves. Cur dropped the bird in weeds and eelgrass. All animals seem smaller when they're dead. Its coiled neck was lank and obscene.

Cur receded into silence, as they knew he would now and then, slipping back into himself from his easy, joking ways. He seemed to know something they didn't, and they hungered for his attention, his high opinion. Cur was a native, like most of the wolves, near cousins, why, nearly blood.

While the others talked of birds, Cur felt a hot needle of shame. He hadn't meant to hit the heron. Flinging the stone was just a caprice. He wasn't a violent man—an odd thing, considering what he and his partners planned on doing in the world. This evening, he was being sent to purchase weaponry and other tools of revolution.

He chose to believe what Vance Church told him, that these implements were for the defense of the striking logger: not for the firebombing of office buildings, not for Helena Bridge, not for any needless act. Now others, like Amos Church, said that senators and governors must die. Topple the steeples. Amos had lived in Chicago and other angry red cities. The old doubts rose in Cur.

There was no reason for what he'd done to the heron, except to sling a rock in sun, show he could, glean the praise of others. Cur hadn't killed an animal in an awfully long time. He had never killed a man. That's what really changed you. Animals only change you a little. He might have to change, and soon.

All heads turned to the piping of a distant train. An unsteady black pillar rose in the sky. Cur cast one backward glance at the heron. He could still feel the weight of its body in his hands.

Now he was joking, talking of other birds. "A pet crow. He took it off her head like he was born to."

"A pet crow?"

How it stole the shining ribbon from his stepmother's pretty head as she tended the garden. A rush of wind, a jerk on the scalp, the ribbon gone. It knew how to untie a knot.

"He says, 'Good morning, good morning.' 'Hello, hello.' Sitting in a tree, fat and proud as a deacon."

Then it took a slip of paper from Cur's brother's hand. It had been taught to steal paper money, a pickpocket's crow.

The others wondered if this was possible. Is a plain crow that smart? It didn't matter. They piled on their talk, eager to please, ginning up memories of country boyhood. Lantern-eyed owls that seem more catlike than anything, that preen themselves and hunch in the snow. If you nail a dead one to your fence post, it will protect your crop from hail, fire, and torrents.

A heron swallows seven trout a day if he can get them. And he will. He can see better than anything.

Not like a owl. Owls can see good day or night. He flies at night cause he *wants* to.

They turned to Cur.

"What do you think?"

"Of what?"

"Does heron see best?"

"Oh, I don't know," said Cur with a laugh.

The wolves drifted over to the arriving train. Cur peered through the gathering payday crowd, looking for Amos Church, his rival, who'd hated him from first sight with a burning, religious fervor. He didn't see Amos—was Amos hiding from him?

You put an owl's heart on a sleeping man, another said, and when he wakes, he will tell his secret—treachery, backbiting, anything. This was new to everyone.

Sparks flew down the rail, and the train screamed to a quivering stop. No one would miss camp—they didn't look back.

A HUNDRED MEN, there had to be, in Cur's railroad car. With a steaming sigh, the engine came to life. The block was raised. Rods and gudgeons and spindles pumped with a guttural cadence. Rich with sweat, the timber wolves had packed themselves in, smelling of salty flannel and hair restorer, heads slick and iridescent, their cheeks and hands still tacky with smut. The engine—a forty-ton Shay—jostled their smiles as it bounced the cars. Endless racking sounds, like billiards. The Shay, everyone's engine of choice and praised so dear, dropped through the cut at Big Lime with a silver keen. The young ones plugged their ears. The old didn't bother.

Like sunflowers, the wolves dished their faces to the sky. Light was a luxury the forest denied them. They clenched their eyes shut and savored the warmth, showing off the white undersides of their chins. They flexed hands to chase away the aches, the ones that made every knuckle joint sing. Teamsters and sawyers, filers and bulls, tallymen and grade crews, buckers and trimmermen with pitch on their hands. It was an open car, a cattle car really, which in their pride they tried to ignore. Hiss of steam, rack of pistons—it sounded like the metal would wrench itself apart. They squeezed their mouths tight against wheeling cinders, moustaches gathering bits of ash. Letters to post, women to find. Laudanum, too. Pay stubs!—now that would soothe an ache. Dizzy with motion, and rest.

September 30, 1904. Payday, and two thousand had money to spend.

Packed among the bodies, Cur tried to stand apart as best he could. He needed to find Amos Church—they were in the union together, and despised one another, but that is the nature of associations. Cur had been chosen for this errand of weapons, chosen over Amos by Amos's own father. Vance Church had taken a shine to Cur. The book in Cur's coat pocket beat on his ribs. Cur felt a thrill of joy and dread. That's right, Amos, he thought. Serves you right. Your own dad don't trust you.

Both were Camp Five. Amos must be onboard. Somewhere. Cur wanted to see Amos before Amos saw him, but the heron nagged at him, pure distraction, the thought of its frivolous end. When Cur was a boy, they shot every fish-eater they saw: eagle, osprey, otter, whatever stole a mouthful off your table. But Cur was a fisherman no more, nor plowman, nor hunter.

He overheard McBride, his cousin and friend, warning the young of the barber in town. "If you go to the barber," McBride said, "go early in the morning. He gets wobbly drinking green hair tonic through the day—come noon he can't cut your sideburns even, he'll nip your ear, say, 'Look! You moved on me! Look what you made me do!'"

Cur felt the wind blow through him, and he shivered a little in his wet clothes, a premonition of the winter to come, when even the rocks groan with cold. Amos was nineteen years old, a slippery age, new here and just young enough to frustrate Cur, who was twenty-seven in this long year, still wiry and strong, not old and not young either, because the Blackpine camps put hours on your life. But every season has its comforts and afflictions. Cur's father used to lay bets with friends on what morning they'd see frost on the pumpkin.

Switchback after jolting switchback. When they cut the grade, McBride claimed to anyone who'd listen, the lazy engineers followed a rattlesnake up the hollow. Cur chewed his thumbnail, then spat, cringing. Bite of pine pitch on his tongue.

Cur passed through the swaying bodies. When he finally spotted

Amos, he jumped a little in his skin. Easing behind, Cur felt a crazy nervousness, like a bachelor knocking on a widow's door. Amos had eyes a bottle-glass blue, a smart and mean cut of mouth. Perhaps Amos was the kind Cur ought to be. Or could not be. A bomb-thrower. An unsmiling man. These stories had followed Amos from Youngstown, Ohio. Cur wished he could ask if they were true. Had he bombed the industrialist's parlor? Killed the family inside? Amos once broke his own father's jaw—everyone knew it for a fact.

Amos realized Cur was watching him. For fun, he drifted out of Cur's sight line, to make him scramble and fret. Amos knew why his father had chosen Cur: a local man, not an outsider. Amos could work here twenty years and never be one of them. His own voice set people on edge—too midwestern, too clean, and theirs that warbling mountain twang. Still he despised the man. You could bend Cur like a reed in water. He thinks he can be everyone's friend, Amos thought. To be everyone's friend is to be no one's friend. Cur had that glad-handing smile, his good looks, but not too good, a handsome man knocked askew: a slouch to his right shoulder, the missing eyeteeth that made a tall void in his smile. A fellow like that could bite off puppy heads and the world would forgive him. So make him fret. Amos kept on moving down the car. He slipped a hand in his pocket, polishing the nickel-plated derringer with his thumb. His father's book of names gave his jacket a welcome heft, balancing the pistol. A five-dollar sort of gun that could reasonably be expected to blow up in your hand, taking every digit in a silver cloud.

Amos couldn't joke and didn't smile—the West Virginians could forgive much, but never that. He couldn't tell you a story.

The Number Four Shay shuddered north, hiccupping gouts of steam. Sooty green and Chinese red, what a vision, dragging a comet's tail of sparks and cinders. Couplings gnashed. Hot grease and ozone. Pummeling rods. The Shay stitched itself back and forth across the river and shook the trestles. The rails thrummed up through the legs. The wolves praised the engineer—he never pulled that whistle, not even on the blindest turn. He was a bellowsome man, telling how he'd whistle once for a cow on the tracks, twice for a woman, three times for God himself. Workers and wildlife ought to know better than to loll about a Cheat River line. He wore a Sons of Temperance pin, and it was said he'd like nothing more than to dice a sleeping drunkard, just to prove a point. "Got to check a weld," he laughed. "See how stout that cowcatcher really is."

The segmented cars cracked like a toy snake. Here, a flickering landscape of creosoted ties, deadfalls, and piles of greenbrier deep enough to swallow a country chapel. Here, a rowdy hand of crows laughing in a railside cedar. The tree had been overlooked somehow, not a single ax-bite upon it. A sawyer pitched a worn-out boot from the train. It left a quivering hole in the branches, and the tree shivered. The crows broke upward like they'd been called back to heaven.

"Caw, caw, caw!" a man cried after.

Amos clutched a slat for balance, and his hand stung, still tender from days of learning the ax. September was a slight chill pleasing his neck, the board bread-warm to the cheek. So much finer than the mills of Youngstown, where the smelter dried your skin to parchment, even singed the hair from your arms. Here, wind smelled of fermenting sawdust, salamanders, the faintly metallic bite of river water soon it would be cold enough to bleed hogs. Amos felt his hatband burning. Twenty-five dollars were tucked into the brim. Another twenty-eight were due him at the railroad office. He had plans for his month's pay, down to the last dime. He wasn't like the others, who had little but frolic in mind. They told that you'd get into the Eagleback by knocking three times and chanting, "Seven dogs pissing on a wall." If you went to the Winners Lounge, you shouted through the keyhole, "I want to lick the gravy off the platter!"

He didn't know that the older ones were having a little fun with him.

A few waggled themselves through the slats and pissed out the side. Amos cut his eyes away so no one would think him funny.

Cur was watching him. Amos nodded. Caught, Cur blushed and pardoned himself as he stepped through the bodies. He put on a showy smile and shook his head, saying, "What's the word?"

Amos regarded him coolly.

"Waiting on you to come over and pal up to me. Just do what I'm told, no matter how foolish."

"Hush now."

Hunkering down in an unclaimed corner, they made a show of rolling cigarettes, though neither particularly wanted to smoke.

Amos said in a low, guttural tone, "You're getting blasting caps off that funny lady."

"I'm getting guns."

"No, you're getting caps. Don't argue with me. You know where you're going?"

"I know her."

Amos smiled. "Sounds like everybody knows her," he said.

Cur wouldn't rise to that. Now Amos began to curse. This was his best trick: the sudden fury of a wasp. "By rights I ought to keep this money to myself. Do this right. I'm supposed to be in on this. I'd've stayed in Youngstown. This is a notch down. Hell, ass end. I should leave..."

Cur thought, Please do.

"I don't like you going round my back," Amos said, fairly hissing.

Others began to notice. Cur spoke in measured tones. "Nobody's going round your back. You're tetchy. This is between you and your dad. I don't stand in the middle."

"Yeah, it would be, but you go talking into ears and they go talking to Dad. You and Neversummer. I know how it goes. I should be running this."

Cur lifted the cigarette and licked the paper. "Ain't like that," he said. "I never said word one against you. Ask anybody." But everyone knew what he thought of this fire-eater, this devil. One time, in front of too many people, he called Amos a needledick. Backbiters seemed to run to Amos as quick as their gleeful legs could carry, to tell what they'd heard. Cur finished by saying, "I just do what I'm told." He hadn't meant to mimic the boy's earlier words. It came out as a slight, just the same.

Amos asked, "You think I do what I'm told?"

The train made it hard to kneel. Cur lit a match off a ragged thumbnail and brought it to his mouth. He puffed and watched the other men.

"You look sick," Amos told him.

Cur shook his head to cut the wave of nausea. It wasn't the motion of the train.

Amos settled. He had made his point. He reached in his jacket and worked a thick envelope out of his father's book. He placed it flat on the boards, then slid it to Cur. Needlessly said, "Don't count it here."

Cur eased another book from his person, cut the envelope into the pages, and returned it to the inner lining of his coat. The light from the slats played on his face. Amos frowned.

"That a Bible?"

"Naw. A cowboy book, by Colonel Gantry. Like Frank and Jesse James? They're a fine read." Cur felt he was babbling—Amos gave him nerves. "It's a two-in-one. No back cover. That's a good deal, right?"

Amos's face said nothing, not even in the lines of his eyes. Cur waited for a fleeting grin. It didn't come, and he felt stupid. He swabbed out his cigarette on the board. "Look," he said, "you be surprised how much I agree with you. No need bumping heads."

"People got a problem with me, they ought to lay it on the table. I'm straightforward. I say what I feel. I don't dance around it," Amos said.

"I'm not dancing. Everybody knows about Youngstown. It weren't your finest hour."

"They weren't even there! They couldn't even find it on a map!"

"I'm not the boss," Cur told him. "You got to talk to your dad."

"You're unreliable. I don't know how anybody could be dumb enough to trust you." Amos sucked at a tooth. "You know what I did in Youngstown? Some might not admit it, but I had a dozen begging me to do it and ten dozen thanking me after. Yes, it was a fine hour. You believe it. They know it's time to drain the swamp. People are tired of waiting."

"You blowed up a man's house. With his family in it."

"That's right. Could you do that?"

Cur didn't answer.

"That's right," Amos said, rising off his haunches. "You don't know what to say, do you? You don't know what to say unless five people tell you. What's worse is you don't even know what to think." With that, Amos walked to the other end of the car.

Red-faced, Cur unbuckled his belt and eased up to the slats. He was too rattled to go at first. The Shay gathered speed. He calmed and took a long piss, which fell in shimmering streamers upon the grade. He had the sickening feeling that Amos was right. How could someone just look at you like that, drill down into your mind, and hold out your thoughts in front of you? He dreamt of leaving the camps for his stepmother's farm, turning away from their cause. Amos was right—Cur was afraid of what they could accomplish in the world. Living in failure was easy. You could always blame someone else. The union had two months. Cur passed the days like stones.

He recalled an awful night meeting in the caves, just weeks ago. Before that, he had thought Amos liked him or was, at worst, indifferent. The union headmen had not finished saying their piece about a planned strike when Amos cut in, addressing Cur in front of the Woodworkers Brotherhood, a couple dozen strong. Amos said, "You're too close to Captain Ketch. Why's he always calling you into his office? You've been in there three times this week. He's a Company man." When Cur explained the captain was just a good feller and liked to talk hunting, Amos asked how many hours two men can talk hunting, and Cur said that if he had to ask, he's clearly no hunter. Several laughed shyly, digging in the cave mud with the toes of their boots. Amos kept on. "I heard you discussing rifles with him. Krag rifles. Why would you bring up the make, caliber, and vintage of rifles we're using?"

Cur felt like he'd been bitten on the face. "The captain's country people. Like us. You wouldn't understand."

"I understand perfectly," Amos said. "You have a particular friendship. You have to be giving that information to him purposely."

At this, Vance Church cut in and made Amos stop, but he also chastised Cur: "It ain't nothing against you. Quit talking to the captain. We got to hold everybody to a high standard." It bothered Cur. Why hadn't Vance jumped in earlier? Maybe he wanted to hear what Cur would say. Maybe Vance had planned this scene.

And now Cur was assigned to work with the one who hated him most. To keep an eye, perhaps. Near the long cut, mile marker 88, the Shay erupted in powdery bursts of orange and black. The engineer couldn't hear the soft thunks but reached out a handkerchief and swabbed the brilliant filth off the metal. He held the cloth to his face and studied it like a bill of sale. The train was slashing through a shivering cloud of monarch butterflies. Arms laced through the slats, the timber wolves felt smacking on their hands, like the raps of nuns and schoolteachers. A veteran of the Spanish War jumped back, thinking a bullet had nipped him. Cur caught one on the wrist. He pulled his arm into the car and wiped it brightly on a breast pocket. Between thumb and forefinger, he clutched a sheared wing that glittered with spots. Butterflies and halves of butterflies clung to hats and vests, dressing the men gaudy as dancing girls. One lifted a dusty finger to his tongue and made a sour face. To chase off the taste, the fellow—a worn-out sawyer with a caved jaw—worked a plug of tobacco into the good side of his face.

The sight of the butterflies distracted the engineer. He gave a little cry and wrenched at the brake. The train heaved itself around a bend, and everyone caught themselves with one rippling motion.

The sawyer choked on his tobacco and pitched forward, touching off a yawing wave of bodies. Amos took an elbow so sharp he thought he'd been stabbed. He found himself eye to eye with Vaughn McBride, the teamster with a mixed reputation, and a cousin of Cur's. McBride wore an epic and feathered hat, one you never forgot. Mended here and there with gut, it was decorated with what looked like silvery religious medallions pinched along the band. Closer examination revealed them to be worthless scrip from company towns. McBride had taken care to scour the coins of rust, taking the very words off them, even though his own neglected arms were stained from years on the reins.

Amos checked his pistol. The chamber was light by three .22 short rounds, but you could fill it in town for a dime apiece. A shopkeep kept them rolling loose in a candy dish.

"Why you keep your hand in your pocket? Can you not wait?" McBride asked, miming a jacking motion with his hand. "You can buy you a good old girl in Hell-town. Can't spin without hitting one. You know how to give her the copper penny test?" McBride didn't wait for an answer. "Take you a penny, rub it good on your fingers. When you reach down there, she burns your fingertips, you know she got a bad hole. Don't want a bad hole, do you?"

Amos shook his head, embarrassed. Calm now, Cur stepped up just in time to enjoy Amos's writhing.

"Or this will happen to you!" McBride held up a hand. It was missing the ring finger above the first knuckle. Everyone laughed, especially Cur. McBride stuck out his hand and demanded, "Shake! Shake my hand!" Having no choice, Amos took the battered claw. McBride's grin was a cracked jug. "Aw, don't sull up. No girl took my finger. Was a trash horse done that. The old stump-puller was sweet as could be; I shoulda known. That Belgian, I must tucked a ring bit in his mouth fifty times over without a hitch. One morning, *snap!* Him cocked like a rattlesnake to do it. Had a calm look in his eye all the while. I'm so startled I just look at him. Froze there, the both of us. Know how a horse bites? Once they clamp down, their teeths got to meet! I hear *click*, and I know my finger's lost and swallowed. Blue Ruin comes in and says, 'You look sick, Vaughn.' I says, 'Get me straw and sheep tallow before I bleed to death.'"

So smart, so evil, that horse! McBride admired it. An elder here, he wasn't sure of his own age but looked a hard fifty. He loved talking sex and horses. The only thing he hated on this earth was a horse merchant. He didn't believe horseflesh should be bought and sold, but why fight it? He once caught a merchant screwing a plug of gingerroot into the ass of a busted Percheron to make it lift its tail and step lively. McBride reached in, pulled out the plug, and told the merchant he was going to shove that gingerroot up *his* ass. But rather than feaguing the man to death, McBride simply kicked him. After that, the Company had McBride broker all their draft horses. He wasn't a union man. He would've laughed at the notion of a strike, even to Cur. He lacked that hard vein of anger the union men had. All the teamsters did, haughty craftsmen, unwilling to rely on any other man. McBride said wistfully of the demon horse, "He could've taken my whole hand if he wanted to." He looked Amos full in the face and said, "You ever see a Friday turn to Saturday in Helena?" McBride whistled through a gap in his teeth, big enough to take a ten-aught chisel. "Nothing like it used to be. Back in 1900, I come into a little money, and I'd keep four bottles of whiskey in four hotel rooms and treat the night like day and the day like night."

"I've lived in the city," Amos said. "A naked woman doesn't turn my head."

McBride leaned in close. "So you're learned in the sacred arts?" In a hoarse whisper, he said, "They got a woman at the Winners Lounge'll spurt water at you out of her thing." McBride's high, shivering laugh jumped men for twenty feet, even over the shriek of the gudgeons. "They call her the porpoise. She can snuff a candle. From five paces, she can."

Amos grinned in spite of himself. McBride liked that. He admitted, "There's no woman here like that. She's in the state capital, they say, where there's more call for amusements."

They passed acres of slash, stumps wide enough for men to sleep upon. The Shay slowed and snuffled, taking the grade. Sunning rattlesnakes felt itchy vibrations and eased from the rails. The scent of sodden sawdust rode the wind.

McBride pretended to notice Cur for the first time, though he'd been standing there all along. "Well, it's the birdslayer! Lock up your daughters and your cows! Sound the church bells in warning!

Yes, they wanted to hang him for unnatural carnal acts with domestic stock whilst standing atop a stolen bucket, but he bribed the jury, all of them kissing cousins, the J. P. was fit to kill..." McBride liked to sing his friends, could call you sister-fucker and make it sound like high praise. "Yes, I seen him drunk on hair oil and bent double with the walking clap, but we think a lot of ole Cur." He praised Cur above all others.

Several called Cur's name, slapping his shoulders, offering him sly, accusing looks.

Cur said to Amos, "I see you fell in with questionable stock. I hope you got money. My cousin here will make you spend it." Winking, Cur suggested a haircut, and started McBride cussing the barber again.

At the thought of money, Cur felt a flutter of panic. The envelope. He clutched his side like a wounded man and found it. Amos glared. It was a look that shriveled you.

They smelled the tannery, rank as a broken abscess. They had come to the limits of town.

HELENA WAS WEDGED into a godforsaken notch, hacked from the northern mountains of West Virginia. A place caught in perpetual storm, wind scraped, sun teased, beaten by hail, flooded with snow. This was in Tuscarora County, near the hinge of western Maryland, where three states met in a snarl of rivers and survey lines. A rough place people never quite took to, or that never quite took to people. The winter-bitten grass greened only in patches. A town of faded clothes. The natives—Seneca, Shawnee—had been wise enough to treat this as vague hunting ground, not a place to plant yourself. White people had lived in this particular high spot since the Irish arrived, fleeing there from a famine, only to find the gentler parts of the county settled. The Irish managed a few mud-daub cabins and a church until smallpox found them. There remained small-holding farmers in the country around, mostly of German stock, who regarded the Irish sidelong and were neither pleased nor displeased when they died off, if secretly proud to have outlasted this latest generation of settlers. Only the old ones remembered when elk grazed the balds and panthers lazed on chimney rocks. They knew the routes and springs, memorized them like a prayer book. Names like Seldomridge and Hamrick, Cogar and Mercer, Campbell and Moore. Then Helena was incorporated, the streets laid out in as much of a grid as the land allowed. Now it was a place of transients. A dozen came and worked the day through, a dozen left the next—ever since the rails had come for timber and coal. The land dabbed itself with stores, taverns, and brothels, like an immodest girl trying out makeup.

It was named for Senator Eugene Helena, of course. Rattling over the river, Amos Church knew that someday it would bear another name. Pull down the signs. Purge the maps.

McBride was pointing out the sights like a hired guide, as if Amos had not been here before.

Helena the town was nine years old. Before the absentees built it, perhaps two hundred had lived on that spit of land some called Corinth after a local church. But state census revealed how it grew under the absentees' care. Three thousand one year. Six thousand the next. Teetering now at seven thousand, counting the two thousand loggers of Blackpine who swelled it once a month. Helena had exhausted the level ground and spilled downhill, the houses propped on stilts and outcrops of graphite-colored limestone. Outside the mill, red piles of woodchips aspired to the blue mountains in the distance. The rows of white clapboards clutched slopes like billy goats, slaty trills of smoke curling from stovepipes. Men worked lumber with hand planes and whipsaws to build even more. The absentees had constructed empty echoing mansions on Rose Street terrace, the official places of residence they represented in legislatures, cabinets, and law courts. Their absence held sway. Everyone felt it. The town of Helena had become so successful it was rumored that cobblestones would be bought to staunch the shit-brown streets. McBride told Amos it would begin any day now.

Alone among the absentees, Judge Randolph spent a few precious nights here. Amos Church wanted to know those nights. Had to. Because he was here to kill Judge Randolph. No one knew that but him.

This was truly Randolph's town—the West Bank anyhow, Helena proper, where families lived alongside high-dollar merchants, the white school, two banks, three churches, and the tailor, a Romanian Jew; tended grass, children; clerks, bookkeepers, a well-known craftsman of splitcane flyrods; a lame gunsmith; flags and a bandstand. Nearby, the logging outfit: rossing mill, planing mill, stacks of pulpwood, shifting dunes of sawdust oxidizing in the light, oak and chestnut and spruce logs bobbing in the dead waters of the catchment pond, waiting to be fashioned into barrel staves and two-by-eights, ax handles and veneer. The algae-stained mill wheel turned, the grinding wheel of commerce that never stops, never stops. Not a single baked brick in all of downtown, Randolph claimed. "Nothing handy to bash a man's skull but your own fist, if you must. Perhaps this prevents violence," he once said to Eugene Helena. All was fresh timber.

When they saw East Bank, the timber wolves began to cheer. The muddy thoroughfare was crosshatched with wagon ruts full of standing water, which filled with jerking mosquito larvae come spring. East Bank was cinder bottom: Commercial Street, Division, Fishamble. Six years before the Mann Act was signed into law, a decade before the Harrison Narcotics Act. East Bank was where the poor lived. Who would choose the floodplain, that ditch of mosquitoes, if they had a choice? A strip hoarded the boarding-houses, midwives, pig's ears, blind tigers, brothels, hell-frolics, theaters, Little Italy, and the Gulley, where the few blacks lived. Only the crucifix of a small stone church, Corinth Methodist Episcopal, set it apart; sometimes the drunkest pounded its doors. All the preachers—except for Luke Seldomridge, a thinking man—threatened of the entire bankside slouching into the Cheat, dark and deep, when the first rough beast rises with ten horns whipping in its black mane of stars. The slum was a handy, bludgeoning symbol—the savior of many a dull sermon.

Mountainsides going gunmetal blue in the failing light. Town limits, mail flag billowing. A brakeman swung the lantern red. Clattering into the depot, the Shay dragged heat shimmer all around and made it look like a thumb-smudged photograph. As he did twelve times a year, a brave clerk stepped out and unlatched the car. Once, it had earned him a busted lip. Now, the clerk was engulfed in a lapping wash of flannel, corduroy, and merry blasphemies. Amos was dragged up sandstone steps and into a street of mud that never dried till July, perhaps. Strange hands on his arms. He hoped they didn't touch the gun, hard like an ingot on his side. He clutched his hat. McBride and Cur bobbed behind.

The other camps had beaten them to town and infested that strip of frolic, lifting schooners to another month down. You could hear their racket over on Commercial Street. Always, the timber wolves returned to the Blackpine camps on Sunday morning, blearily sucking the paws of their gloom, far from anything at all. Fifteen-hour shifts. Rain. Runny sores. Above all, the boredom. But tonight they shot dice and sniffed cocaine until they almost couldn't think of that place. Almost couldn't think. Logs in the catchment pond tolled like wooden bells.

The timber wolves assembled in rowdy, cheery lines at the railroad office. Nervy clerks, pink hands, freckles of ink. Pants fixed with galluses. Pencils scritching legal pads, names checked, envelopes passed from mesh cages: sums of twenty dollars or twenty-eight or thirty-two, depending. Office closes at seven, and this is your chance. This time in town was the anchor of your life. Some sent this money to wives and children squirreled away in mountain burgs.

"You ready for the Winners?" asked Cur.

Amos removed his bowler, piled the longish hair on top of his head, and pulled the hat down over it. "I'd prefer a hot shave and a cut," he said.

"Aw hell," McBride said. "We're showing you the town! Spit out the tit!"

McBride had decided there was a time to be had tonight, and that Amos, this fish, this virgin, should get a good hunk of it.

Cur told Amos, "Your cook up camp burns his hair off with a candle."

"I don't study after that cook."

"Damn it," McBride cried out, "I said all you boys get your hair cut of a morning! The barber drinks hair tonic! You'll come out of there looking like Tom of Bedlam!"

"Now there's some fast company," a voice cried.

They turned to see Vance Church and Asa Neversummer, the union headmen, stepping forward, stuffing pay into their wallets. Neversummer and Cur shook hands with grips of iron, being partners on the mountain, sharing ends of the misery whip. Indeed, the two of them were the captain's favorites for how hard they worked, for their easy manner. Amos felt the old jealousy seethe in his brain. Asa, Cur, his father Vance: these three fools. And Amos outside.

"We're thinking steaks," Vance said to his son. "Want to come along?"

McBride said, "No no no no no, we're taking the boy to dip his wick."

Amos looked away. His father laughed. "That's how you blow her in. See you at the New Northern Hotel, eh?" Vance said this for McBride's benefit. They weren't meeting at the New Northern. McBride would never be one of them.

"Ten o'clock," Amos said.

"Sure you're not hungry?"

Amos offered an unsmiling look to his father. "I'll live."

"I'll watch out for him," called McBride. "Vouch for him and everything."

The older men watched them go. Absently, Neversummer began to open and close a jackknife on the heel of his hand, a nervous habit. Vance made him quit.

"I'm glad he's taking to them better."

Neversummer didn't answer. The only way for him to remain civil on the topic of Amos Church was not to utter a word at all.

The last car was unlatched. Men hopped down and danced jigs on the gravel. Neversummer and Vance hung back, admiring their vigor and salt. No reason to hurry. The Choirboy wasn't expecting them till later on.

A cook went truckling past with four chickens to a hand, their yellow feet bound in twine. They made soft disturbed sounds in their throats. "Fryers," the cook said, wiping his forehead on a shoulder. He trailed a wake of feathers down Commercial. The two headmen followed the flap of wings and ate the greasy birds not an hour later.

WALKING TO EAST BANK, Cur was quiet while McBride and Amos snapped, jibed, and argued with each other like brigands. They couldn't agree on a thing. Some called this fun.

In a lit alley, a luna moth settled on the wall, worked its wings, and stilled. It was the clean color of absinthe, with a fletching of purple.

"Big one," said Cur.

McBride nodded, said something about the coolish night, and put out his cigarette on the moth. With a slight hiss, the swatch of green crumpled and fell. Cur cringed. What a waste. His dad would have beaten him for that. Amos looked at Cur and then away. Cur felt weak under those gauging eyes. He had never wanted a rival. Plain as it was, he wanted friends.

Their boots crunched on broken glass. How ugly town was, trash on the ground and signs on the wall the same flashing colors. When Cur was young, his father had apologized before taking them to town, he found it so distasteful. This baffled everyone, because Cornelius Greathouse, "Old Neil," apologized for nothing. Cur smiled, feeling a trill of affection. His father once caught a neighbor in a lie when they walked boundary lines together. "Come along," Old Neil had said to Cur. "If you know how to write your own name and remember our lines, I'll call myself a roaring success as a father and a man. And, hell, I'll negotiate on you knowing your name, you can always sign *X*, can't you?" The neighbor, jealous of Old Neil's land, had shown up with deed in hand and his best boots on. They first walked easy borders, then ventured on to the disputed line, for it cut through a wedge of good chestnut. The deed said "to big Cherry above old Wallow." The neighbor found a cherry, its purple bark bear-gouged and flushed like a wound, and made a precise speech as to why this was the proper corner. With each sentence, Old Neil's mouth turned up a bit more at the corners. Old Neil let the man finish, then pointed downhill. "Survey drove a railroad spike in." Indeed they found the spike's head, a scaly patch of rust, barely visible. The flummoxed neighbor had tried to gain three acres of good chestnuts, but Old Neil gave him five. "I am a law-abider," Old Neil said. They never spoke again. Old Neil loved to ferret out beastliness in ones the world called respectable. Now, walking Commercial Street, Cur realized that Amos was like Cur's own father: quick to take the measure of a man, then never deviating from that measure. It was a cruel but accurate method.

"Here we are," said McBride.

So this was East Bank, where McBride said in the old days they didn't let the goddamned preachers across the goddamned bridge. They turned a corner onto a street alive with jostling people, more Europe than America. The roadway strewn with cinders, too many bodies to let an oxcart through. Feet stepped upon. Offers whispered. Heaving a five-pound sledge, a tavern keeper knocked bungs from a line of kegs; toward pissing amber streams, men dove with cupped hands, glasses, and open mouths.

"I think that's what you're looking for." Amos pointed to a tavern full of skinny whores spilling into the street.

"Naw. Commercial Street's trashy, and they put meal in your minced meat."

They cut down an empty narrow lane that reeked of spoiled vegetables, the ground black and tan with rotten corks the taverns dumped. It opened onto another street, less rowdy. The wolves here tended to be a decade older. A crowd milled about the porch of an unmarked blind pig that seemed smaller than its two stories. Hands leprous with rosin, a fiddler scraped out something like a song, and a daft boy danced with cymbals tied to his heels. Men drunkenly pitched pennies at a hat. Now the boy walked on his hands.

Amos said, "I could stand a plate of food."

"Aw, we'll fatten on chits," said McBride. "Fatten on chits and tiger spit. Got to get on early. You play table games?"

They stepped out of the way as a logger led a plain woman up a set of outside stairs by the hand, like she was a child. The back of her dress was misbuttoned. The stairs led to rows of doors on the second and third levels. Cur followed.

"Where are you going?" Amos asked.

"He's going to get his apple polished," said McBride.

"With them?"

Laughing, McBride steered Amos into the tavern. The sun was going down.

On the second-story landing, Cur paused to look at the blunted ridge of the Alleghenies. For a moment it was punched out of glowing copper. He rolled down his sleeves to cut the chill. He lit a cigarette and put his hands on the rail, then threw the cigarette away half smoked. He couldn't wait. He walked to the other end of the landing, the planks creaking underfoot. He drummed on an apartment door. It rattled on its hinges. Zala Kovač, the Slovenian widow, called him in.

Beside an unlit lamp, a tallow candle stood on the table, the flame waltzing on the doorframe's chill. Zala didn't rise from the blankets. Cur didn't mind, not too much. He shut the door and sat on the one ladder-back chair. He unlaced his Cutters and shucked them, so the calks wouldn't scratch the floor. So cold through his socks. He tried not to look at her. It had been a month, and he tried to be calm.

"Lamplighting time," Cur began.

Zala snuffled and rolled to look at him. "Have you brought the kerosene?" Her schoolbook English: that's how you knew she was foreign.

"Brung something better. Ain't like Sally to lay a-bed."

"I am sorry. I have a touch of the cold."

When she flung off the covers, she was fully dressed. He said, "Here, Sally," but she walked on past. She unlocked the bureau with a key around her neck and took out a pillowcase. It was sagging and angular with its contents.

Zala was Sally Cove now—the name became her, as one says a dress becomes a woman. Zala had taken it on years ago for office work, knowing that the other clerks would laughingly mangle her given name, and she had never removed it or felt the urge. She preferred Sally Cove, wanted to be American, a native speaker, seeing no loss in giving up her smallish, weak land without its own borders, without its own army, without even the veneer of respectability. It couldn't keep its own people, except for the layabout, the bedraggled, the fawning. Her land was a Habsburg clerk, serving others. She felt haughty toward it and held her head high.

She said, "You just missed the man. Did you see him?"

"Nope."

Cur noticed her footprint on the lone window above the bed. Or someone's footprint. It was ringed in a silver hush.

When someone called her Sally, it took Zala a moment to register her new name. So she seemed lost in a dream, and was considered a little touched, a little light-headed. The other clerks didn't know she was married already and had been for years, and wondered who would marry a woman like her. "Sally, come here"—a male clerk would be holding his papers in the air. She'd get up. He could have easily stood and walked it over, but she knew the spiteful ways of men in offices, the pettiness of all bureaucrats. Their pale, blue-john skins. Their dollops of power. She would see them burn in hell. Zala was a natural at hating. If you went to her for sympathy, why, she would set you straight. You would not make that mistake twice. She was here because of her husband, who was no clerk and far from dead. Victor Kovač, the radical—and a friend to Amos Church. She had not seen her husband in four years.

Playfully holding the pillowcase behind her back, Zala held out the other hand. Cur gave her the envelope. Smiling, she counted out the money. There were other feelings. She did feel a kind of love for this boy.

"That man told me to keep back twenty," she said. The money was to pay off her friend, the owner of this room, and others the union knew. She was to mail it to a certain post office box in Wheeling, West Virginia.

"Between you and him."

"He treated me poorly. He thought I was common! I should tell him what I think of it."

"Don't you be doing that. He'll come over here and carve his name into you." Cur couldn't see her face but saw her body stiffen.

"He is that mean?"

"Maybe. Asa says."

"As if I would take money from you."

The fellow she spoke of was a union man named Caspani, one from the dynamite crew. She didn't know Caspani's name and wasn't meant to know. She believed in the Woodworkers' cause—at least, she believed in her husband, and their cause was his—but they kept her on the edge. She knew they were taking advantage of her sorrow; they praised Victor to her, but in the vaguest terms. After rent, food, and clothes, she gave all her wages to the union. This nameless Italian had reminded her of Victor. An angry immigrant, a murderous man, just like her husband. It had radiated from him in waves. She admired that. In the Carinthian Alps, Victor had slipped across the border in wretched shoes come apart at the stitches, to escape conscription in an emperor's army. Zala's brother was with him. The boys were sallow and young, sixteen, seventeen, and a few years later, they mailed her passage from a place called Helena, a name lovely on her tongue, where the Slovenians knit railroad trestles across river chasms. She never recovered from the voyage: the orange reek of vomit; the steamship *Le Havre* flying the flag of the Third Republic and its dour blessing by a French priest; a shared washbasin full of seasick; the Philadelphia doctor who pulled down her eyelid with a buttonhook to check for trachoma, in that room smelling of floor wax and bactericide. The address was pinned to her clothes. Her brother, she learned on arrival, had died in a sanatorium. Helena seemed the very end of the earth, and she married Victor Kovač out of fright. Victor had hands like shovels and an unruly moustache. When the visiting priest gave the wedding sacrament, Victor wore in his buttonhole a rhododendron blossom. It lolled like a puppet's head and left a sticky splotch on her communion dress when he crushed her in his arms. Even then, even now, she had fidelity to his vision.

"It is good he is our friend," Zala said with a touch of caution. "Turn your head."

Cur looked at the window while she feigned hiding the money in her bureau. She took care to make the hinge yawn and squeal.

Leaning over the bed, he scratched a few lines across the silver footprint with his fingernails. Yes, a man's print, too large. He swabbed it away. Cur felt a tang in his mouth, like a bad tooth. Whose footprint? Zala borrowed this room from another foreign woman, a prostitute. Here the comings and goings of strange men would not be noticed, or the clamor of foreign tongues. Beyond her own language, she spoke good English and Italian, the steamship German of stevedores, and other baffling tongues. She was valuable, and knew that, even if the world told her otherwise. She slipped the money into a black stocking and tossed it silently into an empty coal bucket. "Finished," she said and handed him the pillowcase when he turned.

He reached inside. The tin of blasting caps fit snugly in his palm, as if machined to be held. The cover was embossed with a rearing lion, the label scraped off. He held it up to a candle's spastic light. CALIFORNIA CAP CO. SAN FC'O. NUMBER 6. He unscrewed the lid with a grainy skirling sound, glanced inside, and nodded. In the pillowcase, he counted ten such tins. Half were Hercules caps, which weren't as trusty. Neversummer would throw a fit. Cur rummaged and found two crimpers, one new and matte black, the other with a busted tooth and a loose handle. It would do. Where was the rest? Zala watched his face darken.

"This all? I don't know why they went to all that trouble. There ought to be a roll of wire. Jesus Christ."

"Do not blaspheme." She slapped his hand—she could be religious, despite all. "What's his name? The gunpowder man?"

Cur drawled, "Well, he's Eye-talian..."

"I *know* that. Maybe you are 'Eye-talian.'"

"You'd like that."

She gave up. Cur popped a kiss on her mouth. "I appreciate

you," she said. She tucked her hand between his shirt and his ribs and laughed. She did care for him, she told herself. Neither of them had precisely the person they wanted, but still they had something. You don't get who you want, she told herself. The sooner you accept that, the better.

Zala lifted her dress over her head. She wore nothing beneath. It was unheard of to have a steady woman in town. Cur kicked rags under the door. His weight settled upon the bed. Through the bubbled window, the moon was a brash smear of white. Her friend was lucky to have a window. In this part of Helena, it was a thing to cherish. The panes brought light on cool mornings but still kept out the wasps that brained themselves endlessly, ticking against the dusty glass. Zala turned her belly to the wall. She lifted her head slightly, and he laced an arm under her neck. Her ass was round against him, like a Spanish guitar. His fingers left a smudge on the cord of her neck.

"I ain't too dirty?"

"It is passable. You should shave."

"I'll curry you like McBride's horses," he said and ground his stubble on her bare back.

She slapped his thigh and said, "I would rather touch McBride's horses than their owner." Laughing, she braced against the wall and tried to push him out of bed. She'd grown fat. Last year he saw the hard riggings of her ribs. He couldn't see them now, but he poked where they should be and she buckled up, shrieking. She read the Catholic Bible and prayed to beads, but here she was, pale and naked beside him. Widowed women go a little wobbly like that, Cur knew. Or maybe because she's from a place she never mentioned to Cur, though it was like this one: jade water, leaping trout, punishing winters.

Outside, a drunk fell into the road with a thump and set Zala laughing. He could feel her laughter through his chest, his ribs. Another man had been there before him, Cur felt it inside her. Maybe. It brought excitement rather than disgust—a surprising feeling that made him a stranger to himself. He gripped the flare of her pelvic bone. To slow himself, Cur willed his mind to wander.

His hangnail burning. Sally had fucked the man who brought the dynamite rig, he thought. She fucked Leo Caspani. Cur knew it! Caspani was a good-looking man—sharp, a talker, a fence—he knew where to find guns, rent safe houses, all the answers. They were both from Far Europe. Any woman would choose Caspani over him. Had to've been.

No. It was his imagination.

Zala felt his month without, his desperation pounding away at her. It usually didn't take long, a few moments. She didn't know Caspani, but Cur's intuition was correct in a sense—she didn't feel for Cur what she might have. She could have other men, as many as she wished.

Such a place, this was. The first time he'd heard of Blackpine, Cur was kicking around Jephtha, the county seat, forty miles southeast to the surveyor's eye. It was circuit day, when people griped and bribed their way onto exciting juries for hanging trials. He flattened a broadside on a saddler's window and read. It promised cash wages, opportunity for advancement: young stout-bodied men, no prior experience. The hawker rattled off addendum: "Taking spike-drivers and gandy-dancers in full matched crews!" The locals flew from their farms like thistledown on the wind. City papers—*Baltimore Sun, Wheeling Intelligencer*—brought the rest. "Bring nothing but good boots!" Of course, men brought what men bring: Bibles and fiddles, suture scars and dental plates, bone dice and discharge papers, histories of violence, faith, and fear.

Zala made a soft little yelp. She made him feel good enough to die—what else could he look forward to? She tucked a hand under his knee, and it finished him off. Cur put on his clothes in the reverse order he'd taken them off, except now he was conscious of the smell. He'd prefer to stuff them in a potbellied stove. He had been coming here eight or nine months, and still there was a remoteness to her. She never asked about his life, and she deflected his questions with jokes, with turns of phrase—she didn't understand the mountain. He had thought the distance would close with time. Perhaps he was asking too much. He felt for his Cutters.

Zala watched him lace his boots. He was a wonderful man, he

was. His skin had smelled of kerosene, which they used to ward off ticks and lice. When he looked away, she sniffed her hand. At least he lacked the red coronas of ringworm. Crazily, she thought of wiping him down with a rag and using it to light the lamp. She went naked to a chair and smiled and brushed her hair with harsh strokes, snapping her wrist. The ladder-back left an angry horizontal pattern on her skin. These unruly men. Her smile dissolved. She wished Cur would go so she could read the peddler's letter for the tenth time—a letter that had arrived that morning and still was fresh as a bleeding wound. It said her husband, gone four years now, had been seen getting a haircut in Monongahela, Pennsylvania. Or someone like him. A laughing ghost in a barber's cape. Many times this day, she held that terrible letter to the light, ink so cheap and brown it seemed to evaporate in front of her. *Victor is living and well, by all accounts. I shall share the address when I return to your part of the earth.* Written in an arch, slanting script. When would the peddler arrive? She reached for a stocking. It was good to have something real in hand. She wanted her lover to go, to die, to leave her alone. There was nothing worse than imagining someone else on top of you. If Cur died, well, she could begin again. Guilty now, she reached across and touched his arm, so he wouldn't leave so soon.

IN THE WINNERS LOUNGE, McBride abandoned Amos downstairs as quickly as he could. A girl led McBride to a room smelling of mold and small as a corncrib. She had short legs and a quail's darting looks.

A piano played a roll for "My Mother's Tennessee Waltz" with all the heart and soul of an adding machine. Amos was bored and infuriated, not knowing where Cur had gone with all that money. He couldn't stand being idle. He gazed at the bleary glass of the bottle in his hand. He'd asked for a porter, hoping it would fill his belly. This was Youngstown all over again: billiards, wasted hours, deranged women, braying on all sides. Imagine what workingmen could accomplish if there were no drink. The Temperance Movement wasn't such a bad idea. A bullet-headed riverman turned to

Amos, said "Watch this," and mule-kicked the piano. It jumped scrolls, keys a-jumble, and cast a hysterical calliope of notes. Wringing hands on a towel, the tavern keeper came cussing. He asked where the screwdriver had gotten to. On scabby tables, men played for double eagles, a handful of dollars, even punched scrip from the mines till someone shouted them off the table. Sawdust had been tracked in everywhere. It pooled in corners.

"Hey buddy!"

Amos turned to find another new fish—a fresh boy—from Camp Five. Though the face was familiar, Amos for the life of him couldn't recall his name. He wore a bandanna round his neck, had a crooked mouth and a crest of hair, red and unwashed. He and Amos had once sat side by side at a cookhouse table.

The fish swayed and babbled on without sense. "You like cards? Look at that money. That's a awful pile of trees. Lose your money?"

"I don't gamble."

"Lost your money! I knew it! You got a whole day and night left in this town. How you gone eat? Where you gone sleep? You can't go doing this, Amos. You'll have to suckle on mares and steal corn from shit. This ain't Chicago City."

Joe Goddard? Yes, Amos remembered now. Amos glared and crossed the tavern to lean on a wall. Goddard merely followed. They stood in silence and watched the room. Amos grew restless, picking at his pitch-lined nails. His stomach churned. Forget McBride.

"I'm going outside," Amos said.

Goddard followed him.

On the board sidewalk, Goddard rattled out a story about losing money at a game of five knives. Amos didn't contradict him. Neither one noticed the vigilante in the alley who had followed Amos and Cur all the way from the station. It was what Amos should've expected, because he usually expected the worst. They had followed him in Cleveland, so why not here?

Amos said, "I got to meet somebody. Be seeing you," and walked away.

Stunned at this piece of rudeness, Goddard decided to peep in at another tavern down the block. The vigilante sharked up behind him and, in an ill-lit street, put a gun to the place where Goddard's spine attached to his skull. The vigilante had mistaken the boy for Cur. When this stranger crooned *Hey there, Cur,* Goddard was too friendly not to stop and begin to turn his grinning face.

The Company had hired the vigilantes grudgingly, on Judge Randolph's recommendation, from a national firm. Not all were of quality. Carnegie and Frick had used them—this was much discussed. "Don't fret," Randolph had told the Board. "I'll oversee it. I don't care. I won't involve another soul." This was thought prudent. He knew the town of Helena. He was there four times a year.

Two blocks east of the Winners Lounge, Amos bought hard-boiled eggs off a vendor and sat in the square's patchy grass, peeling shells and throwing them on the ground. After swallowing the last, he rolled up a pant leg, to rub at a blue welt. It was the tip of a fish knife a playmate had broken off in his knee twelve years earlier, on Lake Michigan's steel shore, as they watched ore boats trundle back from Duluth.

He heard a gunshot back toward the place from which he'd come. Maybe a drunk shooting at the moon. He shuffled his own pistol from vest to jacket. In the distance they were lighting the gaslights. He watched them flare one by one, soft blue cats' claws on the fabric of night, then passed the bridge to West Bank and the Rose Street mansions. If Amos had known Judge Randolph was in town, he'd have taken his pistol, or a length of hog wire, or simply pried a loose brick from a wall and lay in wait for the man. He believed in the swift, staccato act. He was disappointed in Vance as only a son can be. Vance forever telling him to wait. But you could miss your moment. Amos wanted to fill the drowsing world with fear, to make the newspapers ripple. To move to the center from the edge.

He decided to wander around the railroad offices. He had been lucky before, and it wasn't far. Bolted back doors led to those offices, where clerks and telegraph operators and accountants worked out their cotillion of profit and graft. Soft men, spiteful and womanish. Amos skirted piles of horseshit full of oats, listening for everything and nothing.

For a long while, nothing happened. But, like a good fisherman, Amos had faith.

From where Amos stood in a cramped alley behind the offices, he heard a musical voice that spoke too quickly. A window at the first-floor level had been propped open with a stick of kindling. Amos leaned against the boards, flattening himself. The voice went silent, and began again. Caspani. That lilt. Caspani, the union man. It took Amos a moment to believe it truly was him.

What he was doing there, Amos knew and didn't know. The woodgrain pressed on Amos's cheek. He heard his father's name mentioned. Vance Connolly Church. Amos took a risk and peeped inside.

Fanning himself with a handbill, Caspani was speaking with three other men. One stood, and the others sat around a table, a blown-glass pitcher and stubby glasses strewn between them. A rick of ax handles leaned in a corner.

Only one regular policeman was among the hired vigilantes— Constable Green, a raucous local who wasn't above sharing a drink with a logger, who had seemed sympathetic. Caspani drew a paper from his sleeve and smoothed it on the table. A vigilante began to read haltingly, nodding the while. His neck and cheeks red with razor burn.

The three men had badges pinned to their shirts: shield-shaped, not the stars of sheriff's deputies. No one outside the police knew the vigilantes had come to Helena to prevent insurrection—no one but Judge Randolph and Amos, now, two kindreds. An oil lamp burnished the metal, and the man on the left kept running fingers through his hair till they glistened with brilliantine.

Caspani recited a few more names; Neversummer was one.

Amos was relieved and infuriated not to be mentioned. But then they said his name, and all was well. Now to tell his father. He backed away and brushed on something.

The heavy window fell with a shot. Amos had bumped the stick of kindling. He never looked back.

Chairs scraping. The pitcher fell, and the vigilantes broke past Caspani. Amos was halfway down the alley when they hit the door.

A woman stepped into the alley and sleepily raised her head at the sight.

Amos slid through horseshit but kept his footing. He glanced at the woman, and they bowled him over into a stack of crates and grabbed at his legs. He kicked one in the knee and sent him reeling and clutching himself. Constable Green held Amos's arm and tried to hush him.

Caspani beat Amos across the nose. They stood him up and tried to march him back down the alley, but he kicked and twisted and muttered blood, eel-wild in their hands.

The woman kept scavenging bottles, a burlap sack scuffing the ground behind her.

Amos cried, "Help me! Please!"

Opening her mouth, she gave out a sound between a laugh and a whimper. The vigilantes couldn't help but grin. They saw her every day and knew she was daft. Amos spat on Caspani's belly and they slapped him again. They found the gun. Amos cursed Caspani; Caspani pretended not to know him. Amos was in the mud again, the corners going out of his vision. His shirt gave with a long, muffled tear. He lost his hat, and one of the men grabbed a fistful of long hair, twining it.

ZALA WAS AWOKEN by noise from a sweet half-dream of her husband. She could pretend the spine she was tracing with a finger was not Cur's.

A pistol shot battered off the building's outer wall. Cur kicked out of bed. Outside, a woman choked on screams.

Cur grabbed at the pillowcase and flung open the door. Zala shyly crept up, covering her breasts with her arm, and shut it behind him.

Zala edged up to the window to see if the screaming woman had been shot. She peered through it for a long moment before realizing Cur had kicked out the glass. "Oh no. Oh no," she said. Cur's boots pounded down the flights of steps into silence.

On the way, he bumped a potted plant off the rail, and it shattered with a jagged sound. Two shovel-headed cats squalled out of the alley. Now he stood in Fishamble Street, eyes a fury of dust, the sack of blasting caps slung over his shoulder.

Loggers and their women watched from the porch. McBride hollered, "When I have daughters, they won't be the sort to come and stare at a fresh-killed dead man in the road!"

No one moved.

Cur found him kneeling over Amos. He thought McBride had pulled on another man's pants in the brothel, but they were just slick and coffee-colored with road mud.

"I don't know what happened. Upon my honor, Coleman. They come inside and tell me, 'Your buddy's laying in the road.' I says, 'What buddy?'"

"I told you to watch him!"

"I'm no nursemaid, damn it."

McBride's mouth quivered. He was about to cry. He'd said *Coleman.* McBride was one of the few that called Cur by his Christian name. They were shirttail cousins, McBride claimed, braided together by thin strands of blood.

It looked like the boy had been killed with a dull hatchet, not a gun. The jaw had come unhinged, and the skin was a canvas white, as though he'd been boiled. The lower half of his body lay in muddy water. They rolled the boy over, turning him belly-up to the stars. The right eye was nowhere.

"I don't know what I'll tell his dad." Cur dropped the boy's hand. But again he picked it up. The palm was blotchy with fresh blisters. The captain had set the other new fish bumping knots with a pole-ax, a low wrist-cracking job, but Vance finagled his son a plum job on a felling crew. Cur dragged the body a few inches into the light. This dead boy's hair was red.

Cur sat in the mud, so happy he felt tears building in his face. He'd been waiting for everything to go wrong, crazed with fear. Expectant. Amos is fine. Relief was a cool flood, and Cur began to laugh like a madman with a dead boy's hand in his. McBride was aghast. Neversummer had warned Cur that they were being watched, as in other towns, but no, this was just a plain Helena killing. Show your money roll and take a bullet in the eye. Flash a gold watch, and the whore's husband comes out of the closet and kills you for it. The other union men were too touchy, forever construing the worst. Cur had been infected by it.

"It ain't him. Thank God. It ain't Amos. It's Joe Goddard. Remember him? He's Camp Five."

McBride had a wild look on his face. "I'm no nursemaid," he said again.

"No, listen. This is Goddard. A new fish. Some yegg."

McBride glanced at the broken face. "I don't see how you'd tell. Awful. If somebody told you he laid down to sleep on the train track, you'd believe it. Poor fellow."

"His name's Goddard," Cur said again, senselessly.

Is, was. McBride picked the hat off the ground and turned it in his hands. With a quick gesture, he laid it over the dead man's face.

Cur's smile leaked away. It was sinful to give thanks for a boon like this. A moment ago this body meant the world to him. Now it meant nothing, no more than corn husk. Poor boy. Above them, the moon looked wrong, as if God had hung it too low in the sky. Ragged clouds. A smattering of fish-scale stars.

"Where's Amos?"

McBride said, "Went off a-shambling, I guess. Probably up to his oysters in somebody."

A few women walked off the porch to get a closer look at the dead man. They stepped and feinted, shy and curious as cats at play. Cur dunked his handkerchief in a rain barrel and tried to clean the coal dust from his eyes. That afternoon, he had kneaded his face to chase fatigue. Now he felt bright and jangly. The dead man lay in front of the alley where Cur had stowed his blasting caps in an empty crate. It took his damnedest not to glance. There'd be a swarm of police, no doubt. Taking the handkerchief, Cur swabbed so hard it looked like he was trying to clean the eyes from his head. Neversummer told him never talk to police.

From the porch, the tavern keeper called, "Who's that?"

McBride said, "Camp Five. A knotter, looks like."

The man gave an exaggerated nod and back-scuttled through the door.

"We best find the police."

"Shit…"

"I know."

"I hate to get sewn up in this," McBride said.

"Well, here he comes. Which is it?"

Bone-hard heels rang on the raw sidewalk. The good boots of a policeman.

"Tuttle. No, it's Green."

"Damn." Cur asked, "Should we pay him?"

"Hell no. It'll look bad. Not unless he asks for it."

Green, the constable, shook his head. He plucked a .32 out of the mud. Cur hadn't noticed the pistol. Green unloaded it by tapping it like a pipe and pocketed the shells. He went through the dead man's pockets. McBride knew Green well—he was known to requisition the finest horses for manhunts. He goosed them to a dangerous lather and left the owners in a sputtering rage. He loved to ride. He had hurried over after a vigilante told him what had been done.

"Got his wallet. Bet he was flashing his pay. That's like casting a bass-plug into the waters, every mouth takes note. I prefer towns run on scrip, myself." Green's face had a rich uneven surface, like marly limestone. Smiling, he kept a hand on his belt, holding up a slight paunch. He wiped the mud away and held the pistol to the gaslight's glow. He had the air of the man who knows everyone's gossip. "This fellow got a name?"

"He's Camp Five. Joe Goddard."

Green said, "Goddards, well, common as sparrows. He's no face to speak of." Forgetting the gun in his hand, he waved at the Winners Lounge with the empty pistol, and a woman dove to the ground. He laughed and walked to the porch, asking if anyone knew the man. At his approach, they drifted into the tavern. Helena justice. A drunken child smiled and curtsied, though, flashing her bright teeth. Green stepped inside. McBride whistled a tune, feeling relaxed. It would be suspicious to go. Ten minutes later, Green came back.

"Dumb."

"Nothing?" asked McBride.

"You want me to holler, 'Which one of you big men shot him in the face?' Shit, I got family."

"I didn't mean that."

"Ah, I'll go the railroad office Monday, study who don't show up to work. Tells you all you need to know. Girl says he was knee-walking drunk. She was out of plumb herself."

It didn't have to be said that if Goddard had people, it would be weeks before they knew.

Green absently tapped his badge. "Had my way, I'd ban a gun in Helena. Pistols, I mean. Pistol's trouble. Right *there* all the time."

The others offered no opinion. Cur's mind was on the wire that hadn't appeared in the pillowcase at Sally Cove's. He should find Caspani.

"You—Cur, they call you?"

Cur nearly flinched. He nodded and tried to reckon if Green, asquint, was memorizing his face.

"Thought that was you. We drunk together. That house out the Gulley."

"That's right. Woman was feeding you cherries out of a jar."

Green laughed in a wild way, friendly on the verge of violence. He cried, "You *was* there! I seen you with Fiddlin' Ed Hammons. We about burned the place down. Them jigs thought I was crazy. Been some babies thowed out the window there for sure."

"Wait."

Cur bent over to retch. The smell of raw blood had caught up with him. Nothing came out. McBride looked worried. Green only tittered. He let Cur compose himself before making the pitch. He said, "I need to get the death certificate signed and inquest him."

"I'll sign it," McBride said, standing now. "He's dead as…dead."

"No, I need a doctor. You help me carry him to the doctor's, I'll stand you a drink."

"Can't you get a wagon?"

"Road's muddy. Pissed rain all day. Did it piss rain on the mountain? I'll make it worth your while. State funds. Come now. Got to treat a body Christian."

Dusting off his hat, McBride said, "Poor son of a bitch. Be any one of us. Robbed and kilt."

"No. You're too smart." Then Green gaped at McBride. "That's quite a hat."

"Thank you," said McBride, who always construed the best.

They wrapped the boy in a bedsheet a woman from the tavern supplied. McBride hoped it wasn't a sheet men had rolled in but thought better of asking. When he leaned in to grab the dead man's belt and galluses, Cur smelled liquor off McBride's breath. Again he moved off to retch and this time succeeded. He cleaned his mouth with a bandanna and threw it on the ground.

With a groan, they hoisted the dead man. Cur glanced back at the alley and was pleased to see that no one was in it but cats.

Not much later, on his porch, the sleepy doctor untwisted the sheet. He signed the death certificate with a minor flourish and melted sealing wax upon it. "Leave him here," the doctor said. "I can have him buried if no one claims him. The state pays me for brokering it."

Green asked, "Can I get in on that?"

"Not in this lifetime."

"That's all right. I'm above plucking quarters off the eyes of the dead."

"Quit your devilment," the doctor said.

"Need us to carry him down to the cellar?"

"I've hired a colored boy for that." The doctor also served as the town undertaker, which made men grumble—he made money whether he did a good job of patching you or not. He turned the bolt behind them.

"Never liked him," Green said, pointing at his own stomach. "I had a rupture last year, and that doctor did his best to kill me. Told my wife I'd die. I lived, and he's never forgive me."

Walking away, the men cast final looks at the body. They felt reluctant, but there was nothing left to do. Green insisted on standing them drinks. He wanted to keep an eye.

"I got to find Amos," Cur said. "Lose track of him, his dad'll pull my ears off."

Green chuckled. It made Cur bite his lip. Speaking Amos's name to a policeman. Jesus. Cur seemed to be making nothing but mistakes this night. Neversummer said never truck with police. Vance drew pay under the name of a dead brakeman named Harris—Cur wasn't sure about Amos.

McBride said, "Let's go find the lost little lamb." He began to make a bleating sound, crying, "Here, Amos! Here, Amos! Church, Church, Church!"

Cur could've vomited again. For his part, Green was enjoying this to the hilt. Let the vigilantes worry. Tonight he will frolic with these men; tomorrow he might jail them. Putting two fingers to his temples, like the budding horns of a young ram, he chased McBride down the lane, in the direction of a tavern called the Eagleback.

McBride said, "Hell, I need a drink, chore like that. I earned it far as I'm concerned." He shook his head. He'd seen all manner of sights over the years. Few teamsters lasted three seasons, but he knew it was best to suckle the skinny company tit down to the dregs. He liked to say, "I'm thirty years old and I lived every one." McBride was actually forty-four, but no living person could set his days right. As they walked, he tried to kick feathers off his boots. The mud was pasted with them. This was the trail to the bird market.

Gaslights quivered in cages of glass. Beside, the Cheat ran roiling north to couple with the Monongahela, and bats sliced for mayflies above it. Voices echoed off the water. Just glancing at it could make you shiver. On the corner, a drunken veteran called out to remember the infamy of it all. "Two hundred and sixty-six American dead! Remember the *Maine*, to hell with Spain!"

"Hey feller, you a sawyer?"

A beggar tugged at Cur's sleeve. His lank white hair had gone yellow as horse teeth with age. One eye jogged crazily, drawn upward to the lantern-bright moon. Green and McBride kept walking, but Cur couldn't resist the man. Even in a crowd of hundreds, the touched or addled or righteous would always find him. Helena had more than its share. They knew Cur as a listener—it was his eyes. He couldn't look away.

"Hard living," the beggar promised. "I chopped two years run-ning till last week. Look what my partner done up Seneca. Ax slipped." Under the gaslight, he pulled a sleeve above his forearm and showed the ghastly underside to Cur. His skin was the color of leaf tobacco, but the wound was shiny with age. Healed wens and suture scars, the entire ligament gone.

"Last week, you say? That ain't right of them."

"They turned me out like a dirty shirt."

Cur fished out a promiscuous handful of small coins. "Get a doctor to take a look-see at that cut," he said with a wink. "You might lose it to the 'grene."

The beggar stared at the ground; Seneca Creek had been logged out years ago. Cur felt his ears redden. He shouldn't play with a desperate man. McBride dragged him off.

THE BEGGAR HURRIED ALONG, a late evening service to attend.

On his way to the same place, Luke Seldomridge, the Methodist pastor, happened across half his congregation sprawled in front of the post office on Sandusky Avenue. His feeble-minded, nursing their cracked heels in the dusk. Out of the old guilt, he cared for them.

Here, other parishioners gave them jars of half runners, the odd cut of meat, the clothes of their dead. Canny, the beggars took what came their way. Not that they didn't aspire to commerce—even those lacking fingers and legs had wares to offer. A deaf-mute sold hand-painted postcards for twenty cents: Abraham facing down the tangled ram, Salome demanding the Baptist. For a dollar, he sold flip-books of women cupping their breasts. Another carried a dented tin of woodchips: pieces of Noah's Ark. Seldomridge couldn't cure this addiction to relics, which he thought worse than the burlesque. Here, a halt woman sold twisted fetlocks from Rob-ert E. Lee's horse, Traveler, mummified and dry as braids of hemp.

As Seldomridge approached, the woman lifted her head. The pastor was tall, his bearing slightly martial. The woman smiled, cooing like a dove to see that wreck of a face. He turned, and his pockmarks made an alphabet of shadow. He greeted the beggars with a trembling smile.

"Time for Friday services. Strictly optional."

"Got you the good talk for us?"

"I do hope so."

Seldomridge had read all books, they said. The books came by U.S. mail, wrapped in brown paper. He told them there lived no evil in the world, only self-regard that ate a man bone by bone. That Herod was no worse than a postman, Salome no worse than a washerwoman.

Those who could rose to follow him. A blind man chased the tapping compass of his canes, the twittering bats. Only a few remained behind: a thatch-haired boy on a roller, a man with a broken foot that wept like a rotten yam.

WHEN SELDOMRIDGE FIRST READ the Bible straight through, he never quite recovered from the strange tales he found. He would shut the book and open it, shut the book and open it again. Lazarus is raised, but not Abel. Abraham's Isaac is spared, but not Jephthah's nameless daughter. Hagar and Ishmael, wandering on bloody feet. The women seemed to suffer most. Tonight, he decided to parse the story of Lot's daughters, one that had been troubling his dreams.

Seldomridge mounted the pulpit—*pulpit,* a word he'd never liked—and looked around.

Candles and a pair of lamps lit the sanctuary. The cool, wet limestone had been quarried with the most primitive of tools, hewn by the first Irish who came to this place. A spare oak cross rose against a wall stained blackly by hunters' fires, from when the church was abandoned, the Catholics dead. The sanctuary had little ornamentation but adze-marks on stone, hickory benches, and, outside, a screech owl no bigger than a girl's head that liked to perch on the roof.

It was not like old times, now. He looked at the disaster of his congregation, less than fifty strong. The mad and the lame on the far right—a granny woman who counted the strands of her long yellow hair, parting it with her fingers. The dregs of his old church were scattered through the sanctuary: respectable families, railroad clerks, petty merchants. On payday, they craved talk, the din of fellowship, phonographs, and gospel sings in parlors. The silent mill was unsettling. No squeal of metal, no shunting cars. But if they stayed home, they would hear the shouts, the slurs, the bottles crisply losing their heads in the street. A mild clerk sat with three daughters, a wife, and son. His name was Dronsfield or Mercer or Murphy. Even through the war years bitter as lye, Seldomridge had been famous for knowing thousands of names. No more.

Already he was embarrassed by the coins he would ask them for.

The pages were slick in the pastor's fingers, the cover cracked and dry as old snakeskin. He worried it with his thumb, and began.

"The tale of Lot is a caution to our comprehension. Lot, a holy man, sheltered visiting angels from the crowd. The men bellowed they wanted to treat the angels like women. Batter them. Shame them. Make no mistake, these men wanted to rape and defile the angels of God, and Lot offered up his two virgin daughters instead." His voice cast echoes, as though he were singing into a well. He had a fine tone, despite all. His accent had kept its edge: harsh, guttural. Burnished with the Germany he never saw. "Can you imagine the faith it takes to do that? This is more stunning than Abraham's offering of Isaac, because Isaac would fly to heaven, but Lot's daughters would have to live in their shame, be spat on in the streets, stoned or sold as harlots, not to speak of their agony. It is faith militant. It is a terrifying thing."

Someone coughed into a sleeve.

"But it did not happen. The way God tested Abraham—the way He tested Jephthah and Jephthah burnt his cherished daughter— He came for Lot with something to prove—"

A beggar muttered, "Jesus, Jesus, Jesus." The parishioners cringed. Who could make sense of this? It was like watching a crow and dog at play. The last years had been grueling. Their pastor used to cut to the heart of the matter: so clever, so uncommon spoke. A candidate for bishophood. Now he tangled himself in unsavory riddles. He had been like this since the railroad came, announcing itself with rude shots of dynamite. He was born in one place and woke in another.

To wake them, he cracked the pulpit. "So what of Lot? With only his daughters he is sent into the wasteland. He has no wife, no sons. A dead line. For his fidelity, he seems rewarded with nothing. Lot comes to live in a cave. A cold gash in the belly of the earth. They live there, if you can call that living. One night, the youngest daughter says to the eldest, 'Let us lay with Lot and conceive children with him. We are alone, there are no men in this country. Let us get him drunk with wine.' What put this notion into her mind? What pinned it there like a fang?"

A voice called out, "Ain't you paid to know that?"

People looked down at their hands, reading them like pamphlets. Mothers covered their daughters' ears, and boys elbowed one another, and Dronsfield or Mercer or Murphy began to cough again. Seldomridge heard the rustling of a paper sack. Was someone drinking in here? He felt a feathery tickle in his belly, his life tipping like an overloaded wagon off the mountain. He knocked over his glass. Water spilled down the lectern, but no one seemed to notice.

"Does the eldest daughter refuse? No. She lays with her father the first night and tells her sister, 'Do the same as I did. Get him drunk, take off your clothes, slip in his tent.' On one page, the daughters gain all our sympathy; on the next, they horrify. A man can love and kill with the same hand, he can stroke a child's head or smash it on a hearthstone." That paper sound again. And sighs. "The Book says nothing. There is no aftermath to Lot's story. Why is there no lesson at the end of this tale?"

The parishioners' faces were upturned, expectant. This was the pivot, the message of hope—the tone of his voice told them so—as unlikely as it was. Seldomridge had grown strange, but he had the beaming suffering face of a man with a story to tell the nations, who knows the night approaches when no man can work. They were ready for the answer. Seldomridge's mouth opened like a hinge.

He shouted, "I am asking you a question!"

In response he heard laughter and a girlish squeal.

A pale animal kited by the pastor's ear, then another. Children shrieked. Clutching hats to heads, women ran to the doors, flinging themselves outside with smiling faces. Seldomridge swatted the air with his hands.

The clerk's boy had let loose flying squirrels from a grocery sack. They glided to the highest rafters and the animals hunched there quivering, liquid eyes as black as onyx. Men stumbled over one another to help rid the place of vermin, secretly smiling, so happy for a chore. A ladder and broom were fetched from the cemetery shed. No one bothered with the pretense of spanking the boy. A winking man slipped him a dime. Beggars took nips on a flask going around. They were laughing.

SELDOMRIDGE STOOD ALONE at the moody pulpit. Shutting the Book, he felt numb, dazed, as one who has lost blood by the pint. He could hear his lost congregation milling outside. Their laughter chilled his bones. Lot and his daughters couldn't tell these people about their lives, but this habit of discourse and harangue was near impossible to break. Did they think him a show-off? He'd seen it in more educated men, but he wasn't like that. Or, he thought not. Seldomridge knew that parishioners want evidence of superficial frailties, not true ones. It was impossible to imagine them accepting, say, a repentant adulterer in the pulpit, or even a secret drinker.

He startled. Someone stood in the doorway. It took him a blurry moment to recognize his closest friend: Lis Grayab, a Syrian peddler who drifted by the church to pass the time now and again. Grayab turned a homburg in his hands. He was a small man. His skin was heathen-swarthy, hair so black it ran blue in lamplight. You're almost a priest, he once told Seldomridge, almost as good. Meaning, you drag your faith through the world like a chain.

"I didn't mean to scare you," said Grayab.

"I was daydreaming. Were you here for the service?"

"You didn't see me?"

"No."

"Truly? I was right by the door."

"Ready to run, were you?" Seldomridge had had no chance to say benediction before the congregation fled the church. It vexed him. Had forgotten to pass the collection plate, and doomed himself to a week of thin meals. His jacket was just as scanty, elbows worn through with washing and the habit of prayer he could not break. Soon, the cold would find every crack, every bone. He asked Grayab where he had gotten himself to.

"I only now returned. Oliver. Uniontown, Piedmont—twice!—it was good to me."

"Did you like them?" Seldomridge asked lazily.

Grayab laughed a dismissive laugh. "A town's a town. A city's a city."

They sat down in companionable silence. Grayab had made money in the north, and he was bringing word to Sally Cove of her no-count, bigamist husband. This Victor was just out of jail in Pittsburgh after a sit-down strike or some such mischief. Why are these men allergic to work? Days before, Grayab had written Sally Cove a letter, hinting at her husband's indiscretions, wanting to soften the blow, but now he regretted that, realizing such a letter could only doom one to sleepless nights of hideous agony, a lonely woman waiting on the hammer to fall. Grayab comforted himself with the bitter knowledge that no man is perfect. Look here at his friend. Once, Pastor Seldomridge had been the pride of this county. People had mentioned him to Grayab as far away as Baltimore.

Am I so strange? Grayab asked himself. He was the only one who had paid the sermon any mind, who even liked it, a bit. Any other preacher would use Lot to work himself into a stupid sputtering rage—cities of the plain, wife-to-salt—but Seldomridge didn't mention that, a weird elision. Grayab had heard such a canned sermon on two continents. He assumed the pastor was a lonely man, and once asked as much. Astonished at the question,

Seldomridge replied, "No, I've never been lonely a day in my life. God has spoken to me."

Grayab looked at Seldomridge now, sickened, though his last few visits had shown him this ongoing slide to the bottom depths. He reckoned the change was gradual to the regular congregants, if no less startling. Grayab's route kept him away months at a time—he would disappear into the coal counties, even Kentucky and the panhandle of Old Virginia. He was no fresh immigrant. Grayab couldn't quite recall how he first made the seven hundred miles from port to the Glen Elk warehouse, or how he wrestled rude army French into passable English, but the first time he met Seldomridge blazed in memory. Young, sitting on a knoll, the new wicker pack unbuckled and splayed on the ground. Below, a pastor spoke to a crowd of hundreds: "Behold, the dreamer comes." His voice parted the air like a set of shears. "Let us slay him and throw him into the pit, and see what becomes of his dreams." Grayab studied the shape of the mouth, picking apart the sentences, murmuring the words softly to learn this tongue. The country people on whose doors Grayab knocked were kind in the isolation of their homes, offering buttermilk or a chunk of ham, but when he crossed men away from their wives, they spoke words he didn't know: vile obscenities from rucked mouths. When Grayab heard the pastor's volume double, he thought the man was cursing too. Then saw the soft smile that followed each phrase. He squinted. The pastor was talking to him! The crowd shifted, regarded the dusky peddler who sat on his heels. Told to stand and come down. And Grayab did come down. Yes, the food was bland, but when he left Corinth three days later, he had a full belly, brand new hobnailed brogans, maps, dozens of handshakes and even the holy kiss, flints for the fire, three ways to build a compass, a King James, much profit, a knowledge of healing plants, and five times the number of English words he'd arrived with. Lis Grayab: a rich man. When drunken strangers called him a bluegum nigger, in his mind he sang, *Mais j'ai tant d'amis.*

Grayab said, "I brought you some books. I want to give them to you before I hike to Blackpine. It is walk enough."

Seldomridge made a vague gesture. Even this could not cheer him.

"What? You do not want them? You are tired of books?" When Seldomridge answered with abashed silence, Grayab said, "When I was learning to read English, I would try anything. Outside a Carnegie library, on the curb, I found a useful book, *Anomalies and Curiosities of Medicine*. It said, 'Rhodius observed a Benedictine monk who had a pair of horns and who was addicted to rumination.' Horns! Five verified cases reported. Luke, you have been warned." Grayab shook his finger.

Seldomridge smiled. In the shadow of his failure, he had one friend. Not all were so wealthy. Now Grayab asked a simple question. He asked what was wrong.

"Nothing."

"Come now."

After some cajoling, Seldomridge began. "You know, a few years ago, a man appeared. I was in the middle of shaving, and I asked him to wait outside. He said that was fine. A respectful young man. He offered me sixty dollars an acre for my homeplace. I couldn't believe it. I signed. I didn't care at first, but in the months to come, I went to see it. A muddy field of stumps and the cabin knocked over and a few listing stones where my family was buried. But you know, I had money! I no longer had to rely on the plate; I could say what I wanted here in the church, not that I ever flinched much from hard truths. But the money trickled away, and the people are gone, and what do I have to show for it? I made the decision in seconds. Do you deserve land you don't work? I asked myself that question."

He didn't tell Grayab the other things. How he no longer had to gaze at the rough, rushed stones that marked the graves of sisters, a relief. How, walking the riverbank one last time, he found a piece of broken antler. Considering this modest thing, he felt moved to pray—not just to pray, but to call on God. He knelt down and clasped his hands. No answer came. In the coming years, Seldomridge was unsure why God quit speaking: because He wasn't meant to be questioned; because He had said all that needed saying; or perhaps Seldomridge had chosen a frivolous question and disappointed Him. The silence was so full it seemed to roar. He had dared ask God why this place had to change.

"It's hard to know if you've done right," Seldomridge said.

"This is why we have churches," Grayab said, gesturing at the walls. "Why you have your vocation." This gave Seldomridge no comfort.

Even Grayab, an outlander, knew the change of which Seldomridge spoke. Grayab traveled more than most. He saw dying trout that wheeled in the shallows like rags. "Ain't it a shame?" the fishermen said when he tried to sell them hooks. When he touched the water at their insistence, he found it alarmingly warm for May. The gravel redds of trout, like small snuffed volcanoes, pooled with silt. Miles of oaks cut off on Kennison Mountain in one swoop. That winter, he found dozens of fawns dead in the woods, bony as greyhounds, so slight he could lift the rib cages and rattle them like gourds. A summer disease called bluetongue came for the rest. Crazed deer threw themselves into rivers, sloughs, uncovered wells. As soon as they drank a bellyful, they died in the water. Grayab sold oilskins to a farmer who'd dragged thirty-seven from a springhole, making his son wade naked into the river to hook them with chains. He made a pile and sent them up with kerosene, spewing black smoke into the sky. The gray taste clung to the palate.

Grayab shifted in the pew. The vision troubled him. "Let us take the night airs, Luke. It will do us some good." A small man, the peddler seemed skittish without the wicker pack lashed to his shoulders. He stood stiffly, hunched from years of wearing it. "Turn down the lamps." Beside him, Seldomridge's posture was poker straight, as if a healthy man lived in his body.

They stepped outside and saw the congregation had moved on. Without the bootprints, you would never have known anyone was there.

"THIS A SHORTCUT?" Cur asked.

They had been drinking as they walked. Constable Green

snickered and tipped the bottle he had produced from his coat. He was trying to salvage this walk. The wolves had told him nothing of interest, no incriminating thing.

Their legs and shoulders felt good, the weight of the dead Goddard behind them. McBride belted a song. Green swore this was the best route to the Eagleback, and Cur thought it could be a trick. He pictured a small, windowless room, full of policemen.

Crossing a boggy stretch, McBride pointed out a stagnant salt lick, where deer gathered while growing their velvet crowns, where center of town used to be—Salt Creek, Corinth. But the mill must cling to the river, harness its ballast. McBride waved at the stone church.

"We slept here of a winter, whilst running the traps. Called it the Foxhunters."

Green was already drunk, following something unseen overhead that seemed to batter in his sight like a moth. "You're going to hell," he said. "It's where you're meant to be, McBride."

"No more than them Catholics are. They're in bed with the Pope of Rome. Now listen. One March it come a cold snap, got to be thirty fellows inside. We slept piled like dogs. The air'd freeze your tears and it hurt you to breathe it. We fotched logs through the door. Lit a fire. Hot as a kiln and pretty soon we stripped near naked. I hear a groaning outside. Kyle says, 'What is *that*?' I says it's ice breaking on the river. A fellow says, 'Naw, bears.' 'Bears?' Poke my head out the door and see it's true. Four bears leaning against that church for heat, mean skinny ones out the den. Them just gawking at me. I was glad to have me a gun."

Green said, "I can't believe that."

"You believe what you want, I'm just telling you what I seen."

A pair of men stood about the church doors, conversing. The pastor everyone knew, and the Syrian peddler was recognized, a glowworm of a lit cigarette cupped in his hand. Lis Grayab took a drag and held the cigarette far from his body, as if it would sting him.

"I thought you was a pipe smoker!" Cur said to Grayab.

"I broke my pipe. You know me. I do not know you."

Cur said, "I bought a cowboy book off you once."

"Yes, up in the camps. Was it worth your time?"

"The start and the ending was. Middle kind of drug on me."

"That's the trouble," Grayab said. "They should cut out the middle and sell the end pieces. Give you what you need. Do you need any more *romans*? Eh?"

"Throw out the middle." Green flung the bottle into the weeds. "Throw it out like a peach pit. Or a corncob. Make you a good riddle: how's a book like a peach pit or a corncob?"

Cur's mind was back in that alley, with the hidden explosives— would someone find them? He ought to go.

"Hello, preacher," said McBride.

Seldomridge nodded hello. He knew all of them slightly, for he made a point of going to the siding and speaking to the wolves. Strangely enough, he never invited them to services. Time and again, a few came of their own accord—which was the point.

Grayab said, "You sell your books back to me, I'll sell them again. You're called after a dog, yeah? The Cur? That's you, I know you."

McBride snuffled out a laugh.

Grayab said to Cur, "You should play the numbers. I was told how the big tree fell and only knocked off your hat." It had crushed a pair of workers bumping limbs with hatchets. Somehow the fork of the crown was a hole that found Cur's body and did the trick of leaving him alive. Grayab shuffled his hands, and the cinder winked out. Then he reached between the buttons of his shirt, as if he'd been shot. He pulled out a quivering pup.

"Good Lord," said Seldomridge. "You had that dog all through the service?"

"He was sleeping."

Grayab slid the pup from one arm to the other like a sack of meal. The pup licked at its own black gums. A brown heart on its chest. Grayab held it out, and McBride cradled it in his arms. The pup curled its old man's face into his bare arm.

Grayab brought out a wizened apple. He took delicate bites

around the wormholes. "Think a man would buy him?" he asked, gesturing at the pup with his apple. "Half treeing walker and half something else. His mother ran straight coon."

Green muttered bullshit. Seldomridge laughed.

Then McBride lifted the pup into the air, like a child being baptized. "When the cook got in a fistfight Wednesday, this is how hungry I got waiting on supper." He lowered the pup toward his chomping mouth.

Grayab smiled. "I have been that hungry." He took back the pup.

"Hey, preacher, was your church a foxhunters' shanty once upon a time?"

McBride reddened and tried to hush Green. Seldomridge smiled. The light caught every mark on his lunar face with shadow. "Yes," he said with relish, "when I found it, the place was a wreck. Stock barns are cleaner. Little more than walls, really, that good river stone. A year later, I had a church full of parishioners."

"God wanted it," said McBride, "and it will always be thus."

While everyone else humored Seldomridge, Cur turned the full beam of his attention upon the pastor. He said, "That building, hard to tell what she'll be. Might be a church. Might be a barn again. Probably be nothing. There won't be churches in a hundred year."

"You blasphemer," groaned McBride. "Old Cur's gonna get churched for it."

"Times change," Cur said.

"It will always be a church," Seldomridge said with bitterness. "It was before me and will be after. What would you have it be? A cathouse?" But he felt nauseated just the same. What would come of this place once he died?

Cur answered only with a small, slack smile. Seldomridge registered a pang of disbelief—not in God, but in himself. Some thought Seldomridge was that wretched kind, a faithless preacher. It wasn't true. He believed deeply in God, and in God's disappointment in him. If God could feel let down, He was like us, Seldomridge once told his congregation. We are made in the image of a great disenchantment.

Seldomridge cried, "We rent nothing. This world was given to us. We don't haggle over it like eggs at the market!"

Nervous now, McBride kept buttoning and unbuttoning his shirt pocket. He asked, "You washing them souls clean, preacher?" Superstition had given him a healthy respect for clergy.

Seldomridge made a vague gesture with his hands. "Someone let flying squirrels loose in the church."

"What?"

A cry scattered the men. *High, high, high.* Up from blackness.

Grayab laughed. "That's the pastor's pet owl, he won't let anyone shoot it."

When Seldomridge explained it was harmless unless you're Mister Field Mouse, Green said to him, "My mother told me owls was in with the devil."

"Your mother was talking out of her neck," Seldomridge told him.

"My mother was a good Christian woman!"

"Once they're in the ground, every mother was a good Christian woman."

"What a thing to say! And you a pastor!"

The others couldn't quit laughing. McBride said, "You done got his blood up!"

Odd that Seldomridge lashed out at the constable, rather than Cur, the one who rankled him.

Grayab leaned in to shelter his friend, as he had again and again. "Our pastor," he said, "is the most thoughtful theologian in all of northern West Virginia."

Seldomridge winced. This talk was a black arrow in his side. He untwisted this arrow, gazed at it: "I may be a theologian, perhaps, but no pastor. I've lost that title."

Green said, "I don't like this place. Let's go drinking with sound people."

The three men left the pastor and the peddler without so much as a wave good-bye. Once out of earshot, McBride said, "That preacher's got flies on the brain."

As the revelers walked away, the pup began howling in Grayab's arms, hound after all. Grayab teased it with a scrap of salt pork he drew from his pocket.

"Here," Grayab said, holding the pup out to Seldomridge. "Take him or I must toss him in the river."

"Don't do that!"

Grayab laughed at Seldomridge. "Just for tonight. I need a room and a bath. The boardinghouse won't allow it. He's old enough to take meat. Stretch it with meal if you must."

Seldomridge cradled the pup, feeling its warmth through his jacket. "What's his name?"

"Name? I found him in a ditch."

The wind began to thresh and pennywhistle off the ridge. Like a mountaineer, the pup tried to climb Seldomridge's chest on toy claws. A smile tightened the ruts of Seldomridge's face. He made cooing noises. It was good to see him joyful, but Grayab couldn't bring himself to keep looking at that trampled face. Long ago, his own father, Elias, brought a rumpled Druze to their home. The children lined up, male to female, eldest to youngest. The Druze took the lid off a stone jar, reached inside, and brought up a soapy white flake on his thumb. Grayab watched his older brother take the thumb, guide it to his face, and snort the flake—his brother crinkled his nose and wiped at it. "Magic," Elias said. The Druze hooted. Grayab took the Druze's thumb in hand and studied the flake, which had the desiccated look of sea salt. He took it into his body and it made his eyes water. The Druze left with a number of coins. Besides tax collectors and census takers, it was the one time anyone other than a Christian crossed the threshold. After the threat of accidental death had passed, Elias explained they had snorted the dried scabs of smallpox chiseled from a survivor's body. "Magic," Elias had said. "Science is the magic of the modern man." Even now the thought of it made Grayab ill.

Seldomridge said, "My sermon edified no one. Not even me."

"No. It was of interest."

"Awful and interesting?"

"Eh? Yes, awe-fully interesting," Grayab said, pronouncing every syllable in a singsong. "I liked it rather much. Perhaps I am mad. Why do you not preach on Jesus?"

"That's what that McClatchy woman says." Seldomridge worked his face into a cockeyed leer. "'Preach them red words,' she says. 'Them are the good ones! Them are the only ones worth knowing!'"

Grayab laughed. "She is right. Nothing without Jesus. Otherwise we would be Jews."

The mountain a black rip in the sky. The leathery flutter of wings. Grayab and Seldomridge followed the sound with their gaze as if they could see it. The pup yawned.

"There were Jews in Damascus," Grayab continued. "One on Commercial Street, too. Lazar Graur. They wear hats like they are nailed to their heads. Well, I am walking downtown. I bar the door, keep my money in my socks. I come tomorrow for my hound. Sleep well, pastor. We have had enough high German mysticism for one night, no?"

Grayab made for the bird market, where the mud was scrimshawed with pinfeathers and shit, the wares gurgling and clucking in baskets hooded for tomorrow's sales. Waiting on the hatchet. Seldomridge watched him go, then carried the pup to the parsonage, stroking its ear as a merchant would judge the quality of silk.

SO MANY YEARS BEFORE, Seldomridge had killed his sisters in this place where he was born. He had wrecked his family, stopped his line. He hoped to see them in the sweet hereafter, and decided he would be a good man, a pastor. But what would he say to them? He couldn't recall their voices.

The sin ruined his face. He wore the plague brand now, pitted with crescents and pockmarks, his flesh tinged with purple and red. It was hard to shave over the scars. This was only skin, but girls wondered why he didn't grow a beard to cover it. A beard would be handsome. He had nice hair the color of gunmetal. He might have been able to snare himself a wife. A wife to tend the benches with linseed oil and clean the parsonage, rank and close as a boar's nest.

The first wave of smallpox didn't take any of young Luke Seldomridge's people, but it scoured the Irish off the mountain. Their cabins crumbled, leaving abandoned wells and cellars like the sockets of pulled molars. The Seldomridges had to clean and bury the last Irishwoman, handkerchiefs tied about their mouths. She'd survived six children and a husband, but why bother living in such a world with none but the sun and the moon for company? Five years old, Luke watched his mother clip the Irishwoman's nails. He was the son of a German family on the mountain; his grandfather was a Hessian mercenary who'd deserted for the promise of fifty acres, rocky but free. Plain people, plain as the dirt in a dog's eye.

Ten years later, in 1855, a different age, the sickness found the right road to him. The same year a voice crackled in Luke's ear like a phonograph: *Break the doors.* Luke was fifteen at the time, walking the road with a Plott hound. Luke stopped beside that church. *Break the doors.* Luke had never heard the voice of God before. Through a thatch of honeysuckle, tall oak doors came into view. The grass was waist-high, and he roused fawns that does had bedded there. A lashy pair rose on wobbly legs, trembling. A doe snorted and flared uphill, flying her white flag. Luke tried to step forward, but the Plott leered and paced and popped its teeth. Luke took it by the collar. The hound would not give. He waited for the voice to direct him.

No answer but the hot metallic shimmer of cicadas.

So Luke chose the whims of a balking hound over God's wish. Fever overtook him on the way home. His skin itched and teased, like blood quill feathers beginning to break. Luke fell in the road. His sisters, Ellen and Therese, found him a mile from home.

The girls' shoulders broke with boils also, but they died on the quick, the vanity of their lovely faces intact so they could go to heaven with heads held high. For refusing to enter that barren church, God struck him and struck his sisters harder.

After weeks in bed, his sores dried into hard, callused ridgelines.

His mother was amazed her darling boy was spared because, in her experience, death was as disinterested as the sharpest scythe. "You give your life to God now," she told him each day she sat beside him.

From his pallet, Luke prayed, Let me live and I'll go back. His mother, who could not read, had neglected to teach him the Gospel, but she told him now what she knew, a skeleton saga: Cain and Abel, Abraham and Isaac, the father and the prodigal. The people came in pairs, triangulated against God. Then this wild talk: the last shall be first and the first shall be last. This was good for people whose very hands are mattocks and plows.

In time, Luke was allowed to leave the cabin for light chores. First, he said a clumsy prayer over his sisters' graves. He had been too ill to attend the burying. When Luke made it to the church, he could hardly swing the scythe. The building was longer and narrower than he remembered, resembling not so much a church as a foundered ship, mud up to its waterline, bearded with moss so green it looked edible. Coughing, he hacked at weeds, where copperheads wallowed, smelling of cabbage, and cleared a path and broke the doors with a hammer. The leather hinges had rotted away, but the doors were rain swollen and the bulging held them in the threshold. With one more blow, they opened. Swallows stitched themselves in and out of the rafters, the floor and benches splattered with fossil layers of feathers and limy shit. Dirty sun spilled from a hole in the roof.

God spoke again: *These are your four corners.*

Luke would patch the roof with his own two hands. He returned with a ladder, and the swallows greeted him with eccentric, slashing flight. He went to work ill, teenaged, thin as a mantis. Luke crushed their mudnests with a wrecking bar, carrying the delicate fledglings to the tall grass, where they would be soft meals for foxes—it couldn't be helped. He scrubbed every surface with lye, hands raw and flaming as a fishmonger's. A week later, Luke preached to no one but his father and mother, but they were baptized in the Cheat just the same and proudly told. Word traveled: the boy had the Pentecost. He saved so many souls they spilled out his pockets; he couldn't help the way he looked. "Fey," the old ones said knowingly—marked by death, his face licked by eternity's sharp tongue. The Gospel told men to be kind to the German boy with the basilisk face, because he preached a good sermon, and it helped that he wasn't above jumping in to help Buddy Green winch a dead horse out the ditch with a block and tackle. Boy with the scars? You mean Luke. Yeah. Boy with the scars. If he hadn't preached, his face would have earned him a nickname.

Only the Methodists responded to the letters he posted. Their ways appealed to him, and they demanded no formal education. In return, Luke asked one thing—that this particular church be his charge until death. The bishop, upon meeting this odd, sickly boy, thought he couldn't live more than another year, and they might as well comfort him. Luke became Pastor Seldomridge and would live another seventy, outliving that bishop, in fact, and another, another, even the one that eventually defrocked him. In this lonely place, an incredible four hundred would appear on the Sabbath. A settlement gathered about the church at Salt Creek, with a smith and hostler. Just before the war, on the upswell of faith, Seldomridge convinced the people to call the settlement Corinth. When the Methodist Episcopal Church split like a melon on a rock, he clung to the northern half, of course, the abolitionists. Lean years. He was surprised when his father let him leave the land easily, with the other children dead, but life had broken his parents' will. By war's end, consumption took them both. When he inherited their acres, he let them go fallow and briary but continued to pay the property tax.

Seldomridge heard God's voice less and less, but this was fine, he had done well. The 1870s, 1880s, glad years. He took God's silence as approval. For a while.

LATER, WHEN THEY CAME KNOCKING, Seldomridge didn't know where he was. His sleep had been a deep one, the lakebed of dreams.

The pup yelped when he rolled on it. Frightened, Seldomridge lifted it up, and its legs seemed to dangle at all the proper angles.

The quilt sloughed to the floor. Planks creaked under boots out-side. He felt for his trousers and touched the walls for guidance. On the dusty boards of the parsonage, he'd padded a shiny path branching into the kitchen, the bedroom, the study.

A huge dobsonfly clung to the screen door with iron mandibles. He perceived a small group of men, their leader holding a hissing pine knot. It drew insects off the river, stoneflies and fluttering things. Weak blue flames ran the gullies of sap and threw a jerking cone of light. Seldomridge pushed open the door. He counted five of them in much-handled hats. Their skin looked as if it had been brushed with soot. They wore a brimstone tang like extra jackets. These men were fluent in dynamite: the tunnel builders. Panting, harried, foreign—they blew holes in strange mountains.

"Evening," said Seldomridge.

"Good night, father," the man with the pine knot said in a quiet, halting accent. "We hate it to bother you." The man wore a metal tab pinned to his collar, the kind used by the company to mark Italians. He shifted the pine knot, spitting sparks, from one hand to the other. Light caught the numbered tabs on each man and made them dance like hooked minnows.

Seldomridge asked, "Do the others have English?"

"None."

They parted, stepping out of the seam of light, and dropped a parcel on his porch. It was a body, wrapped in a cocoon of muslin.

Seldomridge turned to the leader. "My God. Who is this?"

"He's my brother," the man said, the sentence catching in his throat. "His rites I come for. This, my brother Nicola."

"What's your name?"

The question seemed to prick the man. "Leo," he said.

Leo Caspani. Who the vigilantes knew could be discreet. Who could speak fine English.

"Leo," Seldomridge said, trying out the name. "Why didn't you go to the priest?"

Caspani studied the toe of his boot, the desiccated leather. Once a month, a priest from Elkins rode the train into Helena to lay hands on the Italians and Polish that dug tunnels for the C&O.

Once, Seldomridge saw the priest marking these people on Ash Wednesday, dipping his hand in a bucket of water, then dipping it in a second bucket and bringing it up gray. The locals would point at them. The pup scratched at the door, and Seldomridge shushed it. He asked, "What did the father say? Come now. Tell me."

Caspani wouldn't look up. "I cannot ask the father," he said. "It is a sin."

"I don't follow you." Seldomridge hungered for a cigarette, something he only allowed himself behind the parsonage, by the ash pit. Only Grayab knew, bringing him unmarked sacks of tobacco. "What's the matter?" he asked them all.

The Italians stood there, completely still, waiting for Seldomridge to understand. They had incredible patience for abuse, for delay, sniffing out dud explosives and shooting dynamite into boulders with nothing more than a hand drill and a sledge, for waiting endlessly in any government office. Seldomridge stooped as far as his joints would allow and touched the body. Warm through the shroud. He unwrapped the cloth, and the men crossed themselves, looking away. Caspani crouched beside him. The pine knot cast a spastic glare.

The boy's eyes were haloed in black. Burst veins in his face like pinpricks. Seldomridge pushed the tongue back into the boy's mouth and closed it, his palm cradling the jaw. Caspani's brother was young, hardly voting age if he had been a citizen. Black blood in his teeth. Seldomridge felt the boy's neck. A tie? No, a noose made of hemp, a strawberry burn.

"Why'd they string him up?"

"Himself," Caspani said, pulling at his own collar.

"Who?"

Caspani stole the light away. "Him. Nicola."

"Ah. He did this to himself. Mercy on him, poor boy."

Caspani said nothing. A man in a gray vest turned and spat off the porch.

"Why did you come here?"

For a moment, Seldomridge thought the owl had begun to cry again. It was one of the Italians sobbing, the cry of one who's fallen on an iron spike. Something wasn't right. Why are these men so afraid? Seldomridge found their fear—even their grief—extravagant in this moment. The sobbing man shared his cries like one splashing chips on a poker table.

"No let him go to hell," the man pleaded. "Not go to hell. Please."

Seldomridge began to say, "There is no hell. We're redeemed..."

Caspani spoke to the sobbing man in his own language. He quit.

Stop your hairsplitting, Seldomridge told himself. He was being difficult. He asked the Italians, "How did you hear of me?"

Caspani winced. "Please," he said. "They say go to you."

Seldomridge tried to gauge the others' faces. Perhaps this Leo had been told the soft-hearted fool would allow anyone burial in his cemetery: infanticides and killers, loan sharks and whores. It had been the first fissure between Seldomridge and his flock. It was one thing to promise the poor the kingdom of heaven, quite another to parcel out the church's scant four acres, crowded with bone, to the unloved dead. The old limestone markers melted into the earth under the stinging rain, and gravediggers kept turning up shards of Irish children they hadn't known were there, or even entire caskets, because the chestnut boards so resisted damp. Where would the congregation bury their dead? It stung them. If Seldomridge had his way, virgin aunts would be supplanted by three-dollar women who'd been thrashed to death with fists and fireplace pokers. "Let the dead bury the dead," he'd dared joke from the pulpit. No one laughed.

He glanced now at the face's torn lip. The violence of it.

"Lift him up," said the pastor.

FINALLY, CUR MANAGED to peel himself from the others. He found the narrow lane between a tobacconist and a tiger frequented by blacks only, less rowdy than most. The blasting caps were exactly where he had left them.

In the street, someone sang, "Tell the preacher, tell the pulpit, I don't wear no greasy coat."

Cur waited for Amos behind the New Northern Hotel. He waited for Amos under Sandusky Bridge. He looked in poolrooms and stuck his head into unmarked doors in brothels, where the women cussed him. He returned to Sandusky. Amos did not come.

Near midnight Cur saw a man coming. He jumped and called, "Hey there, Amos!"

"You make a old man feel good," Vance said. "I must be looking jaunty."

Neversummer came walking too. Cur held out the sack of blasting caps. Neversummer rubbed his friend's shoulder and said, "You done good, pal."

Vance asked him, "Where's Amos?"

They waited awhile. They walked in circles, discussing. Finally they had to go. The Choirboy was waiting on them.

SELDOMRIDGE DOUSED HIS LANTERN and let his eyes adjust. The wind carried a promise of ice. Winter came early and stayed long, breaking into the world with its egg tooth of frost. *From whose womb did the ice come forth, and who has given birth to the hoarfrost of heaven? The waters become hard as stone, and the face of the deep is frozen.* A favorite verse. He held the sleeping pup to his chest, clutching himself like a cripple. *Do you observe the calving of the deer?* Clouds drifted across the moon, blurring its light like gauze thrown over a lamp. Last year, he took supper with Bishop McClung in Elkins. When he quoted verse to plumb the mystery, the bishop smiled the soft grin of a fire newt and said, "My son, be admonished, of making many books there is no end and much study is a weariness of the flesh." Then the broken-down bore wiped his mouth on a napkin, to cover his mirth. The bishop had longstanding concerns. Even the *Helena Vox* reported Seldomridge's strange sayings, such as an instance when he allegedly claimed all men should kneel and kiss the hem of Judas's gown. Since their supper, the bishop had sent Seldomridge many a letter. Seldomridge did not open them. Did not even hold them to the light.

The cemetery gate gave with a cast-iron wince. In the back

corner, lights shivered in the wind. Seldomridge picked his way through the stones.

The Italians had fixed tallow candles in a hoary apple tree that stooped over the grave. They seemed grateful to have tools in hand, and their shovels bit into the earth, bringing up the vinegar-wine smell of the rotten fruit. It reminded Seldomridge of his sisters' breath, when they had shared the same bed as children. The pup, warm on his skin, was indeed the first living thing to sleep against him since Ellen and Therese died, young and forgotten, like this one. You're not yourself, Seldomridge knew, till you pass half a century on this earth. Look at the dead boy there: his body rumpled as a scarecrow's. Mountain people hang their own effigies on the pole. They used Christ that way, something to drive crows off the corn, evil eye from the door, nothing more. A bellyful of straw, borrowed clothes, nails that drew no blood.

The Italians worked in a silence broken only by the clang of metal when their rhythm failed and shovel heads kissed. When that happens, Luke's father had told him, it means you will meet again someday, doing the same chore. Caspani and Seldomridge watched over the body, and Caspani offered Seldomridge a cigarette. Seldomridge paused, then took it. These Italians—they had a taste for gilt and for ceremony, incense and the swinging censer. They left their wives abroad, and then the letter came, saying she'd died in childbirth or found another man.

"Why would the boy do such a thing?"

"He did not like this place," Caspani said.

The answer chastened the pastor. It hurts to die in a foreign place. The boy had no coffin—no money, no time—so twisted cloth, worn like a robe, would have to do. They cut the noose, and Seldomridge plucked the metal tab off the collar like a hateful, blood-fat tick and tossed it aside, so the boy could go to the judgment his own man. Seldomridge said the Lord's Prayer and blessed him. Two Italians waded into the grave up to their shoulders, and the others lowered this Nicola into waiting arms. The pup began to whimper. Seldomridge told it to hush. The men looked askance. Bringing a dog to a burying. The low Protestant murk of America.

They climbed from the ground smelling of roots and clay.

Caspani tried pressing coin dollars into the pastor's hand, but of course Seldomridge wouldn't take them. Instead, Seldomridge traded the man his own extinguished lantern—Caspani's face was troubled with gratitude and suspicion, for this was the country where he'd learned that nothing comes from men without a price—and took one of the candles from the tree. Seldomridge walked back through the graveyard. Blades of grass sparkled with young frost. When he died, he desired his body burned to ash, to leave this life as he entered, traceless. Now he chased the candle's wanderings. In one flame, all flame: his mother's stove, Elijah's chariot, the sword of Eden, Moloch's furnace, the Pentecost on his own youthful tongue. It hurt to die in a foreign place.

It was a strange thought for a man with no home in the world. In the last three years, he had tried too hard to prick God's interest, make Him speak again. One Sunday, Seldomridge led a train of Helena's feeble-minded into the church. At first, the congregation was willing to absorb them, but cold months drove in incredible numbers. Their fits disturbed the services. A blind man stopped hymns with his keening. The beggars palmed money from the collection plate and walked out with hymnals, who knew what for. His church grew strange—and it cored the congregation like an apple.

Halfway to the parsonage, Seldomridge stumbled over a crooked stone. The pup yelped, and Seldomridge accidentally snuffed the candle. No trouble, though, the moon was bright enough to fish by. He let the pup roam loose on the ground. It lifted its leg to a stone. Seldomridge didn't mind. All waters run to the sea.

He leant down and, like a trick, the pup leapt into his arms. The feeling nagged him: something wrong in this night, a bad stitch. He should ask the peddler—a good gossip—about this Leo, this Nicola. It took another night and morning to realize what vexed him: that the dead boy and Leo Caspani, these brothers, bore no resemblance to one another. Even through the clots of blood, the dead boy's hair was blond as a Finn's.

ZALA KOVAČ LISTENED TO THE MUSIC of her own piss singing into the chamber pot. She had to leave this room. It had been better than an hour, but her hands were shaking still, part fear, part natural tremor. She clasped them together. What to say about the window? Fuck. She cleaned herself, stood, and pulled her stockings to the tops of her thighs. She lay across the bed and sadly fingered the narrow streak of gray that spilled down the side of her head, plucking at the one perceived flaw in her otherwise black hair that was thrilling enough to stop men in the street. But she was wrong. It was that streak of gray that caught a man's eye: its contrast to her chaste and somber dress, each button fastened, her patent leather shoes polished like volcano glass.

She hoped the knock at the door was Cur—she didn't want to be alone. She felt calm with him. Instead, she found Lis Grayab blowing into his hands like a shabby man. It made her jump.

"How did you know I would be in this apartment?"

Grayab chased the question away with a fluttering of his fingers. He rubbed his moustache, raspy as a bottlebrush. She shut the door behind him.

"Why, Sally, your window is broken!"

"Yes, I know."

He didn't know what to say to that.

"You could have hand-delivered your letter," Zala told him.

"Eh?"

"I received it yesterday."

"Ah, the U.S. mail. I posted it near Pittsburgh. In Imperial."

"It was bent and folded."

Without asking permission, he sat in one chair, and Zala drifted down into the other. He said, "Likely it was read. Do not look mortified. They open the mail at this post office. It is run on Company contract. Why would they not? There are things to be learned." Grayab flipped open a calfskin booklet—the one luxury he allowed himself—and said, "Victor Kovač. Works at J&L

Steel. A scarfer in a slabbing mill. Lives at 316 Barnard Street in Monongahela. Would you like to write this down? Yes, born in Kranj, Austria. Came here in 1891. Has been employed by said works steadily for fifteen months. He is your husband, doubtless. Here. Write this down. You are paying for it."

She gave a low crooning answer he could not understand. Pittsburgh is not so far away.

He gave her a soft look. "May I speak freely?" he asked, and she waved him on.

"He is living in a home registered to a woman named Dorothea Moore. There are children. This is a matter of public record. I learned all these things from the state marriage and birth records. In the courthouse."

"Mr. Kovač and myself never divorced."

"You could have him prosecuted for bigamy. But I am no barrister, understand. This is, I would venture, a thing you expected, eh?" Tentatively, Grayab asked, "Do you know the name Mayak? As in, the month of May?"

"Méjak. It is my family's name."

Grayab scratched the bridge of his nose, a tic which had left a pink patch there. "Your husband has used that name as well. Several times." He thought about listing a few reasons this might be—a blacklist, criminality, simple playfulness—but saw her face. She looked dizzy, like a patient bled with leeches. So Grayab spoke blandly of his travels through Pittsburgh, the new zoo to be seen there, not to be missed! Animals wondrous, the amorous plants so tall. The city rippled with gossip of U.S. Steel.

Zala felt easy in Grayab's company, his voice more music now than information. Her pulse began to settle. For his part, he knew she should not be alone. Yes, he was attracted to her, but in a harmless way that manifested itself in kind words, in easy gestures. Now he took pains to catch her attention.

"I need to tell you something else. They left the following week, he and Dorothea. The neighbors knew nothing. I passed by the place. The door was open. There was no furniture inside."

For some reason, this vision in particular startled her again.

Zala stood—she couldn't help but move—and though she didn't mean it that way, Grayab took it as a signal to go.

He rose out of the chair and, before he left, said to Zala, "You know there is a man next door tracking your comings and goings?"

The vigilante was outside watching. A good suit like his was rare in Helena.

"Yes," she lied.

THE MISERY WHIP

BY THE HARD TIME OF 1904, that moment of sedition and botched rebellion, Cur Greathouse had worked four years in the Blackpine camps of Helena, West Virginia. Some called them seasons, but the wolves worked year-round, through hail and flood, illness and mood. His cradle was seventy miles to the south, a place called the Three Forks of the Cheat, a headwater braid of blue on maps. The family's land was lost in a snarl of mountains, the fountainhead of seven strong rivers. Because of a botched survey, his father, Old Neil, thought they lived in northern Augusta County, and would die thinking that, but his land was actually an obscure jog of Tuscarora, nearly on top of the county line.

They had lived in the backcountry of Virginia so long it had outlasted their memory of any other place. Not even the dimmest notions of cities, seaports, or other ways of living.

Cur's mother called him Coleman after her maiden name. His twin brother, older by a hundred breaths, was called Jesse, though they weren't the kind to make the naming courthouse official. The frontispiece of the family King James, with its struck-through dates and inventive spellings, was the only documentation that held truck. It wouldn't have mattered anyhow. The flood of 1884 turned every birth, death, marriage, and land deal in the county courthouse to foursquare stacks of mold.

Coleman Greathouse remembered little of his mother but a wan smiling face, pale as a banjo head, and her singing of ballads of tedious length, fifteen or twenty verses, recalled with the precision of memory only the truly illiterate can master. Old Neil bothered her to death, it was said. Finally, a rattling surrey took her to a sanatorium in Anthem. The wheels tore brown plumes of dust from the road. She waved a handkerchief colored like a battle flag. A week later, she shed this world and left Old Neil with two boys at an age when they could be reasonably expected to fetch water without pitching headlong into the mossy oblivion of a well, or crack a pail of walnuts without mashing their fingers too badly. Addled by a dead wife and slim harvest, Old Neil let the boys raise themselves. And they did, learning to pry open cupboards, one standing on the back of another. Once, in his drunkenness, Old Neil considered aloud cutting thin slices into their cheeks, so when they cried, the salt of their own tears would sting them silent—a practice falsely ascribed to the Delawares. His friends laughed nervously. How could anyone be so kind to his friends and treat his blood so rough? Cur would never understand. Old Neil never struck them, comforted them, or raised his voice. When they cried for food, he said, "Go to find it. You got hands."

Their hands grew callused and sandblasted like those of bricklayers, and they lived in the mountain's blue shade, the clouds casting a moody play of light and shadow on the crags. In the day's last tatter of sun, Old Neil pointed out a granite gash on the

green mountain, a jagged fissure of rock where bears lived. A talus
of sandstone boulders gleamed phosphor-white, tossed there by
a frivolous hand. Wind roared and birds kited in place as though
hung with wire. Mountains argued the skyline, extremes of earth
and sky notched from the land by God's own hatchet, which had
laid it open for the shallow presence of man. It was not strange;
it was all they knew. They breathed in the smell of clean rot from·
the world.

At age nine, Coleman and Jesse could snap the head off a
chicken with a swift staccato crack, the scrawny bodies dancing
from their hands. They ran traps, mended their clothes, and loaded
the sixteen-gauge to keep foxes out of the yard.

Old Neil's beard grew forked and shaggy. Fieldwork whittled
him to the quick. Nothing comforted but hours at the plow and
a night of talk. The cabin gathered all rakehells and bad husbands, the place to shuffle and cut. If they couldn't find alcohol
at Ray Hooper's or the head of Laurel Run, they hunkered in
the willow-shade at Old Neil's till someone dug a bottle out of
the ground or fished it from under the porch with a hoe to avoid
copperheads.

While Old Neil's friends sat about swapping knives and carving at boot-soles, they watched the twins roll in the dirt with a
pack of Plotts. All of them tussled for a bone-hard cob. Dusty and
dark as wet buckskin, the boys were hard to tell from the brindled
hounds, except Coleman's and Jesse's hides lacked the slaty-blue
swirls of the German-true Plott lineage. It was noted that them
two was being raised no better than common curs.

"Two curs!" Old Neil said. "Will they tree a bear? Will they
bay?"

His brother Basil said, "I bet neither of them could piss their
Christian names in the snow. It's a awful thing. Where do they
sleep? In a pile? In the crib?"

Old Neil laughed on it, but then grew sullen. The thought
threw chills of hilarity up his spine. He turned to the dusky boys
and said, "It's best you learn to cipher."

They ignored him. He chewed the lining of his cheek. Since

his wife's death he'd spent much time drunk, even while coaxing corn and pumpkins from the earth. Among friends, he was free with hand tools and tobacco. Men loved Old Neil for his salt, and his three sisters-in-law hated him with the fury that is like love. Pushing for temperance, they named him as an example. Children felt drawn to him, though he liked to play at stealing the ears and noses off their heads.

While the thoughts of men and women meant little to Old Neil, he feared the judgment of a wrathful God who demanded certain things of fathers.

"You need to get married," said brother Basil. "You being a landowner and all. Them children are so far gone you need a hard-shell woman to fix them."

Another man shrieked and rolled off the porch, crying, "You got to get harnessed, Old Neil! Let her crack that whip. *Ker-pop! Ker-pop!*"

Old Neil said, "A hard-shell woman, she'd put me on the cooling board."

"Got to be careful with boys. They cut your neck, drink your heart's blood like wine."

"I don't even know where to find a right wife. I tripped over the last one."

Basil said, "The meetinghouse."

"Oh Lord."

"Marriage is a good thing," a friend named Jim Boggs said, putting away his knife, which he'd been using delicately to tease at a bad tooth. "A covenant. I got a cousin if you're interested. Rimfire's girl. She's of age."

"Rimfire? That sot?"

"Mean your future daddy?"

"I am five years older than him!"

Jim Boggs shrugged. "I've only so many cousins, Cornelius."

Nodding, the men rested on their haunches, drawing fire from clay pipes, the molten coals of tobacco crackling in their bowls. Then a bluetick nipped Jesse's ear with an audible click. The boy socked it on the muzzle. The hound yelped horribly and plowed under Old Neil's ladder-back chair, tipping him onto the porch. Six hounds rushed to the porch, kicking up husbands and cinders, a whirlwind of skittering nails. Everyone evacuated. Jesse wrestled a hound, and Old Neil pulled him back by the scruff of his neck. He made Jesse open his mouth and found a quarter-sized piece of hound's ear inside, like a bloody piece of felt. He turned to Jim Boggs, who said, "I'll lend you a suit."

THE SUIT HAD TO BE LET OUT in the shoulders, and Boggs's cousin Sarah turned out to be in a little trouble, which helped broker an easy deal. Old Neil's newly shaven cheeks were flat, dough-colored, and abashed from years without sun, but beard-growth covered them back soon enough. The Boggs men carried her trunk full of belongings to the meager cabin—nothing more than rough-cut chestnut chinked with mud, flax growing from the soft rotten places in the wood. They fled the place as soon as they could, before the shock wore off and she began to cry. The daughter was born a scant five months after Sarah set eyes on the shaven and funeral-suited Old Neil Greathouse for the very first time.

The newborn child, Ivy, tugged at his beard and cooed and made it all right. "There's miracles happen every day," Old Neil said, cutting back and forth to see if anyone would challenge him with a clever, accusing grin. "Read up on your Isaac and Rebecca."

"You mean Abraham and Sarah."

"Miracles is miracles," said Old Neil.

He was thirty-eight, Sarah fifteen. She was striking, with delicate songbird bones and hair like lampblack. Her laughter rattled the dusty house, riled dogs, and made the boys secretly love her. So they made a show of hating her, unnerved by the tintype gaze of their dead mother on the mantel. Sarah was five years older than the two curs she tried to cure with a belt, chunks of soap, and the dog-eared King James that doubled as their schoolbook. They fought her fist and skull until Jesse was dragged off by the Elk River. Jesse liked to wade out far, way up to his bellybutton, and cast his crawdad to the rocky shores and the big bass sulking there. Far away, the family watched the sandbar evaporate beneath him.

They went thrashing through the water, shouting for Jesse to drop the pole and swim. The bobbing head vanished in a riot of foam. Coleman felt his father pulling him ashore by the belt.

Sarah had to sit on Coleman to keep him from jumping in the water, black and deep, to follow his brother down. He quit struggling but wailed in a horrible way, as though they were carving off the soles of his feet with a bright knife. Sarah clutched him until he quit. Coleman broke the blood vessels in his face with weeping. For the rest of her life, Sarah nursed a terrible guilt because she had secretly despised wild Jesse and wished a humbling on him, the bite of a horse or a copperhead. "We'll find your brother," she said, kissing Coleman. "We'll find him."

And when they did, they buried him.

THERE WERE NO LONGER CURS, only Cur. He lost heart. He took to wearing shoes and scratching his alphabet and verses forward and backward in the dirt with a pointed stick. He would inherit the farm with no squabbling, become a landowner. To Old Neil's bitter relief.

In the county seat, people assumed Cur and Sarah were brother and sister, especially when they held hands to balance while crossing the long planks that forded mud streets. Cur and Sarah would blush but never had the nerve to straighten matters out. Old Neil would laugh and laugh, loving to make other men color by pulling the handsome girl onto his lap. He traded calves and bought her bolts of cloth, as well as a box of pumpkin-ball slugs and a keg of salt for himself. In a good mood, he'd buy his daughter an ice cream and dab at the nape of her neck with a cold drop on his thumb. She squealed and wormed.

Sarah gave Old Neil four offspring in six years, and his land fed them, one hundred and five acres of corn and pasture, uncut woods and patchwork crops. A mild bull was bought for stud. Late nights the family had in lambing season, easing quivering bundles into this world. Marked with swallow-cut notches in the right ear, hogs roamed promiscuously about the balds until it was time to hang them bleeding over pans, stoke cauldrons, singe the hair. Cur penned the dogs to keep them off the meat. After, they sat in a circle, eating salty brains and eggs off tin plates. While forking hay into the mow, Old Neil danced off a falling ladder and snapped his ankle. A hard year. He drank in bed, refusing to let his body heal. After he passed out and soiled himself, Cur had to strip him of his clothes and clean him.

Cur could have hated Sarah's children, but he didn't. The family grew close, and Cur grew up. He began to touch Sarah's arm or her back while easing around her. There were worse lives to be had. In the life of their marriage, Sarah and Old Neil lost only three children before adulthood, in an age when measles brought blindness, and whooping cough played its cruel parlor trick of drowning you in your own lung. When Old Neil grabbed young Daphne's foot in play and found mumps blooming on the sole, he knew. He went to his shop and chiseled the name into a chock of feldspar granite a week before she died. He did it late at night. Cur listened to metal strike rock and knew what the tapping was.

One year the corn failed and showed them how tenuous their lives really were. It was a marginal living on poor ground and couldn't have gone on forever. They hurried buckwheat into the field and grew sick of it before winter was out. All Cur's life, the taste of it would give him nausea. Even its pollen made him cough. Water would run from his eyes. It would be regular fare in camp.

Cur could have it all, the land shaped like a hatchet head, bordering a good trout stream and a ragged crosshatch of hogbacks to the north. His half brothers would scatter to the iron furnaces and brickyards, saltworks and tanneries; lose fingers and wives; unionize themselves, only to be shot and beaten by the National Guard; join the National Guard; turn silly chartreuse and indigo with vat dyes; be laughed out of courtrooms; end their days staggering jake-legged on buckled floors. Their history would be read nowhere but on the police blotter, the census, the walls of donegans. Never to own a handful of earth.

Cur noticed Sarah watching him as he sat on the porch rail, sharpening his knife on an oiled stone. Sleek, grating sounds. She smiled. The knife slipped, and a band of red encircled his thumb. Startled, Sarah walked over and lifted the thumb to her mouth. She sucked the wound clean, and Cur felt no pain. He was seventeen. She gave back his thumb and walked inside. Light-headed, he fixed his gaze to the east, to a hawk listlessly riding the thermals. He began to bleed again.

OLD NEIL WAS IN THE BARN looking for the posthole digger— had he lent it out to someone? He'd given it to half the county, it seemed. The tools always came back rustier, nicked and dull as any kitchen blade. He wished he had more German in him; they wouldn't lend out a pin. He looked to the ceiling, at the sound of mice scuttling in the mow, as if glancing up would help him listen. Then a thump. Irregular seams of sunlight shone through the boards.

This time Sarah had her hand over Cur's mouth. It was absurd they were never caught. It made it seem these lives were meant to be. Her other hand found the tuck behind his knee. A funny part of the body he would never again ignore.

Children poured into the barn, laughing and dancing about Old Neil. Now everyone looked for the tool—Old Neil made it a game, promising a penny. Cur was surprised to feel Sarah smiling into his shoulder. The tool was found. The barn emptied. The falls of Old Neil's heavy boots led them away. Sarah touched Cur's neck to catch the wild pulse, to cup it like a beating moth. She pressed her eyes shut. With that motion and a laugh, she stitched herself into his being.

THEY FOUND PLACES TO GO: the orchard's soft grass, a depres-sion by the river. This time, a scallop of earth where a tree had fallen, uprooting itself, roots clutching stone and secret earth. It had filled in with a bed of leaves as soft as silt. She said she could lie here forever. She wished she had a cool drink of water. That would make it a perfect day. Sarah had never thought she would live this way again—the sweet affair that had produced Ivy was with a traveling farrier, who left the unborn child a puckish nose that Sarah could remember him by.

Cur gathered her hair in one fat twist, then spread it like sheaves. She listened to Cur tell stories of sly Jesse, of Old Neil before she knew the man, the habits of animals in the woods and the river, weeklong hunting trips. He had never talked so much before. He gave his opinions on the world and the family, while she absently traced his bones, his veins. He went on until hoarse in the throat. He wasn't used to it. Indeed he had the reputation of being bashful. Most couldn't, if pressed, recall the sound of his voice. He could talk like this away from his father, unspooling sentence after sentence—but when he was around Old Neil, he was struck dumb, living in that warm shadow. Old Neil had no money, no airs, no special ability with gun or fiddle or dancing legs, but everyone listened to him, gathered at his feet. Cur and Sarah were just like anyone else to him. They were prisoners together. Cur longed to assert himself. He put her hair back together again. They ought be going.

"I forgot the blanket," she said and went running back when they were done, bounding off like a girl. "I'll bring it next time."

They took care not to return to the cabin at the same time. Nor did they talk there—did anyone notice? Leaning on his crutch, still nursing that black ankle, Old Neil never asked where Cur had been. He was of the mind that people should wander and be left to their wanderings unquestioned. Especially the young. Later he would change his mind and be jealous of everyone's presence, a seething sun.

Cur picked up a thread of sound—a child weeping. He ran. The others held Ivy, trying to calm her, the children talking all at once. The stove door hung open, coals blazing. Old Neil was trying to pry open Ivy's fingers when Cur and Sarah stepped in. Old Neil cried, "My God, girl, what were you doing?" He took Ivy on his lap and held her tight—it seemed he would suffocate her. Ivy had burned her fat little hand. It looked worse than it was, but it looked awful. Tears gathered in Old Neil's eyes. No one had ever seen that before. The children slunk away. Sarah began to shout at Ivy. Old Neil looked at Sarah blankly. He finally asked, "Would you kindly shut up?" and took Ivy away. He made the girl drive her hand into lard and wrapped it in felt.

In their hearts, Sarah and Cur blamed the girl for being stupid—that's how far gone they were, cruel in a way that frightened Cur when he thought back on those years.

The world wasn't real. They only moved through it, drugged, no consequence to word or action—was the afterlife like this? Tooth marks broke on Cur's skin, red sickles, purple dips. He studied them when he was alone. He slept well. The earth was holy. Even the hammer was light in his hand, found the sweet spot on every nail. But they spoke of other worlds. Would they ever have met in Anthem on a crowded market day? Would God—like all sinners they spoke often of God—have crossed their paths? In harsh moments alone, Cur wondered if Sarah would have chosen his brother instead. Yes, he told himself, I'm jealous of a drowned child. Even happy that I'm here and not him. When Cur told Sarah this, she answered with a shocked silence. Then said, "Don't ever say it again."

When Old Neil mentioned that Jesse had had the stronger character of the two brothers, Sarah lit up with a fury that shocked him. And later it did not.

Curled naked together, Cur and Sarah spoke in ways neither had before. Perhaps no one had ever spoken this way. They were that isolated, that unknowing. They could read the Song of Songs, but that was the Bible, not real people. As far as they were concerned, their lives had no parallel. She asked, "What will I do if he's about finding out?"

It troubled Cur that she didn't say *we*. He told her so. She had no answer.

They couldn't bring themselves to say his name; Old Neil was the sun, shining over all their lands. They didn't hate him, they loved him fiercely, laughed at his jokes, and felt dizzy when Sarah asked, if something happened to Old Neil someday, could they move to a place where no one knew their names? What could be done about the children?

A voice called Cur from the field. He cussed blue words. Before he left, Sarah plucked a stray dead leaf from his hair, smoothed his shirt, paying him a care he did not know.

MARCH CAME, WHEN DOES' BELLIES are slung low with unborn fawns. In this season, Old Neil caught Sarah and the boy tangled up in the back field. Her way of the last year, so cool to the touch, made sense in the cruelest way. Old Neil left in silence. It took him a while, still nursing his leg, still on the crutch. Cur pulled away from Sarah and dressed. He walked toward home, he didn't know why. Sarah didn't try to stop him. She sat there, the dress bunched in her lap, her breasts bare. Through it all, none of them spoke.

Not ten yards from the cabin, Cur saw his father hobbling out the front door, a crutch in one hand and the shotgun in the other. Old Neil leveled over the rail.

Cur buckled and fell. He heard nothing. While his father fumbled a fresh shell into the breech, he managed to get to the woods. He didn't remember standing back up.

Four miles. The crutch had skewed Old Neil's aim and saved his son. In short order, two pellets of buckshot turned Cur's entire arm grisly yellow-jacket colors. If he held the limb just so, he found he could trot. The last mile was delirium. He sweated by the pint. Cur's aunt on Arches Fork made him drink liquor, scalded a knitting needle, and shoved it into the blue-red smirk of a wound, twisting it like a corkscrew. He bit through the hickory branch. A double aught pellet of lead jumped out. Knees shaking, he pissed down his leg.

Frowning, Uncle Basil said, "Hold on, she ain't got to number two yet."

"You know what the Book says. Sow ice, reap wind," said tearful Aunt Harmony.

They knew. They had suspected it all, of course—this shamed him. "You awful bitch!" he cried. His aunt laughed nervously and bored again into his arm. She gave up. It was buried too deep. So relieved it hadn't touched bone, she cleansed the wound, patched it with terry cloth, and told him to tend it with alcohol when he could. That's when he understood they didn't mean to shelter him. He began to cry.

"Not drinking it, I mean," his uncle told him. "Rub it in there. Like a snakebite. Plug it with whiskey and clean mud if you got nothing else. Spiderwebs." Uncle Basil babbled on, as he did when crying. He slipped three dollars folding money and a note into Cur's jacket pocket, saying, "I'd do you better, but I can't. Now get. He'll be here next."

The flesh mended with time, capped with a pair of pinched white stars where the hair would never grow. The uncle's dollars were faded, thin, worried with age.

Old Neil blacked Cur's name out of the family Bible and beat the name out of his wife. No land was Cur's. The other sons walked boundary lines, savoring.

Near the end of her life, Sarah would walk to the pasture, lean against a lone tree, and stand there for hours, saying nothing.

YEARS IN CUMBERLAND, MARYLAND, ninety miles up the road. He worked every way, for every devil and liar. He swept streets of filth; he lit gaslights; he coughed in the foul tannery till they fired him for the purpose of denying him a month's wage. He resorted to larceny.

A letter from Aunt Harmony finally got him on with her cousin, a house-framer. If a middling carpenter, Cur showed up on time each day—till the morning a dice game brought on a fight and he cut an off-duty policeman. He grabbed his toolbox and ran.

So Cur walked rails into the Helena depot, having lacked the means to buy a ticket. At the siding, he found a lone man who sat on an upturned barrel and sipped openly from a square pint, nursing a swollen eye that bulged like a plum. The fellow stood, stamped his boots of mud, and sat back down. This in the June cool of 1900. The appearance of a new century had excited the people of Cumberland all out of proportion, but it was still odd seeing those fat ominous numbers. Some had prophesized doom or Jesus or both, then slunk off in disappointment.

"Hidy," the fellow said. "What you toting there?"

Cur shifted the toolbox under his arm. "I'm a journeyman."

"You come to the wrong place, hammerswinger. Corporation thowed up everything to a blueprint, not a bolt one out of place." He drank.

"I never gone hurting for work."

"Every crew has a carpenter and he makes two fifty a day and you'd have to kill him to get it. Rest of us get two dollars unless you're jackass silly or unskilled, one."

"You're talking about the timber outfits. Boards and pulp."

"You're outlandish."

Cur said, "Oh, I was born near here."

The fellow cut the air with his hand. "None born here. This is new country, clean as a dime." The man stuck his tongue down the neck of the bottle and pulled it out. He blew across its mouth, making it hoot. "Got to learn it all over. Nothing like it. You a good learner? Probably not."

"Buddy, you best set that bottle down."

He pointed at Cur with the bottle, asking lustily, "You my buddy? Well now. You note the spruce left up there?" A purple smudge of forest near the ridge of a mountain, swathed in deadfalls, and ringed again in greenbrier like pus around a wound. "Month time, he'll be more paper than you could read in a life if you're a reading man. They say the cities of Baltimore and Washington reads a hundred acres of poplar every morning over breakfast. You believe that?"

"I don't know."

"Don't know neither. How'd you like to slide rule all that?"

"I would not!"

The fellow grinned. "Me neither. Want a smoke?"

"Sure. You hack them down?"

"No. Teamster. I'm Blue Ruin, out of Camp Five. That's right, choice Camp Five."

"Roon?"

"Ru-in. Ruin."

The loggers called him this not only for his outrageousness, but because he drank the worst sort of gutbucket without flinch, even hair oil. Harsh drink had seared the tastebuds off his tongue. He never wanted food.

Cur set his toolbox down and took the tin of Brother Tobacco that was offered him. He asked, "You miss a train or something?"

"Woke up wrapped in a curtain in the town jail. You know what happened?"

"No."

"Me neither."

"I don't like the way you go about things," Cur said. "You talk in circles."

"How'd you like to slide rule all that?"

"Aw, quit deviling me."

They shared a match. Blue Ruin called it a lucifer, as all wolves did. He burnt his fingertips and cussed. "Where you coming from?" he asked when the cussing was done.

When Cur told him Maryland, Blue Ruin perked up. He asked, "By the sea?"

"No."

"My cousin Josie lives in Maryland. Know her? No? Hallelu. I thought everybody like you knowed Josie."

Cur shrugged it off. Blue Ruin smiled and nodded across the street, which shimmered in a bronze fog of dust kicked up by passing wagons. "Railroad office," he said. "That's what you're wanting. They're hurting for any man knows his ass from a ax handle. You won't have a problem, you speak the King's English. They'll probably make you a fucking foreman. They been hiring niggers and guineas and half-guinea niggers that can't hardly string three plain words together. Friday night, they fight like yard dogs with one another."

"Is it good work?"

"Nothing to it, long as you don't drop a tree down on you. Or hang a widowmaker. The others will smother you with a pillow, I seen them do it! Some trees ten foot across. A dozen fair and tender ladies could dance on the stump and nod and bow. Man forgot to yell hey and I seen one roll over four dagos. Wasn't enough left of them to scrape off the ground and fill a bucket. They buried them dagos in the same box and the nefarious tree is now a thousand newspapers. Fine gentlemens read it over their morning coffees and wipe their bungs with it and pitch it down the privy. Them people don't got a clue and wouldn't want one. They would not!"

Cur should've gotten to know Blue Ruin. He should've learned the man who, on a frozen mountainside, years ahead, would change his life. Instead, Cur peeled the cigarette from his lip, pitched it at the railbed, and asked directions to a store, where he would receive six dollars for the implements of a carpenter's trade. The shopkeeper held the handsaw up to a window, sighting down the teeth as you would a rifle. The little wheel on the chalk line was cranked, the drawknife thumbed. A nothing price, but to Cur, the math stood comfortable. He didn't prize his experience so much. In the railroad office, he signed his contract and carbon work papers. A ride to the mountain was arranged for him—it was nice to be taken care of.

On the train car, he slept on sacks of Mother's Oats and coffee, drowsy from the smells. Somber Italians roused him so they could carry provisions to the cookhouse. With hand signs, they made him help unload the week's supplies: hundreds of pounds of bacon, bag upon bag of meal. Not twelve years of age, the cook's helpers barreled out of the kitchen, carrying steaming crockery in rags to keep from burning their hands. Cur hung his hat on a nail and helped set a dozen meetinghouse tables. The cook wore a woman's calico dress. Amazed, Cur looked to the other men. They didn't pay it any mind. The cook cleaned his glasses on the hem. He had a flat nose that seemed to have been crushed many times.

That table was a sight to one of Cur's origin: platters heaped with catheads, buckwheat cakes, sorghum molasses, sourwood honey, boats of clotted gravy, pats of butter, angel food, pitchers of springwater, urns of coffee, haunches of beef one man couldn't lift, cauldrons of neckbones and beans. He wiped his face with a napkin. Seeing him idle a second, the lobby-hog scurried over and made him chop a boxful of kindling. On the porch, Cur worked the hatchet from a chopping block. He lapsed into an easy, staccato rhythm. The tool felt right in his hand. Soon he heard tack jangling and the clop of hooves. Teamsters led horses to the stable. The timber wolves followed minutes behind. They wore Cutter boots mended with baling twine, canvas pants thick as sailcloth, chambray workshirts, Big Dad suspenders, and scarred felt hats. Woodchips clung in hair and the folds of clothes. Cur found them oddly complected for workingmen till he saw sawdust gathered like the grit of gold and ivory in the lines of their faces. One covered a nostril with a finger, leaned over the rail, and cleared his nose with a blast of snot and pitch. Cur flicked a cigarette into the yard. A man with a neck-beard scowled and told him to stamp it out. Inside, someone had thrown Cur's hat on the floor. He colored to see that. He beat out the dust and put it back on his head.

Men shucked jackets and held battered hands flush to the pot-bellied stove. On each side of the tables, a dozen pulled out the bench and sat down in concert. Cur found a place as a wattle-throated man walked through the door, holding a vast mushroom and bragging upon it: scalloped and sulfur colored, perhaps ten pounds. The cook said he'd make a stew of it.

Cur felt himself unbuckle. These people spoke his English. No one reached for platters or pitchers. Would they say a prayer? He wasn't sure.

Benches tipped and bodies scattered. Hot gravy flew past. A fight had broken out. Cur sat on the floor and was promptly kicked in the mouth. Like men dancing quadrilles, the two fighters slid through the grease and hooked one another's suspenders, falling with a thump. A platter wobbled out a funny song as it spun to a stop on the puncheon floor. One fighter named Young Thomas held out his arms as if to block the sun. The other, McBride, sat on him and brought down cocked fists like he planned on doing it all day long. Then with a crack McBride tipped over. Just as the cook's boys came out to watch, Young Thomas had come up with a luck shot. McBride groaned on the floor.

When Cur sat upright in the gravy, the cook kicked him in the kidney. "I weren't the one fighting!" he cried, and the cook simpered, kicking at others. Cur tugged at a loose eyetooth. A shard fell out in his hand. "Shit fire…"

Captain Ketch walked through the door, and the cook explained that men had slipped in the mess.

"A man slipped?"

No, men slipped. A helper cleaned the gravy with a flat shovel and tossed it out the door. Men tilted up benches with one-two-threes and began to eat.

McBride was handed a rag to stanch his bleeding nose. Snuffling, he went out to the water dipper and came back with strips of cloth shoved up his nostrils. He wiped bloody fingers on his pants and sat down beside Cur, who could do nothing but hand McBride the springwater. Cur locked eyes with this maniac, who had both hands on the other side of the pitcher, with that ghastly cloth stuffed up his nose. They froze there, kilned clay sending shared waves of chill through their skins.

A fellow told them to hurry up, pour and pass, he had the Sahara lodged in his throat.

"That was slop," McBride said finally, whistling through a broken nose.

"What now?"

"Thought about biting your ear. Rip it off like a leaf."

"I weren't the one fighting you!"

"I hate slop."

The others tittered. McBride was still in a daze, unhinged. To Cur's horror, no one defended him. The broken tooth sent bright jolts into the side of his face.

From his angle, Cur couldn't watch McBride like he wanted to.

The room was silent but for forks and knives on crockery. In earnest, they stretched bellies and bladders like hides to hold it all. Once they chased down their daily bread and made it surrender, they daintily poured coffee and tore hunks of angel food. For many raised in want, the meals were what kept them there. They still had nightmares of hunger.

"Don't pick at your food," McBride drowsily told Cur.

Afterward, everyone moved out to the porch. Pain branching through his jaw, Cur couldn't eat much or drink water, but he could listen. The sun expired in a pink welter.

"They give us Election Day?"

"Don't matter. Old Cleve'll get his term as governor," one said, nodding.

Cur asked, "Who's Cleve?"

The others smirked. The talk turned, as it did, to the New Yorkers: Helena, Baxter, Randolph. The way cripples cling to God, they spoke of the absentees with the intimacy of ones who knew them least. The wolves called them Old Shelby, Old Eugene, Old Cleveland—distant powers that fire the furnace. They make money, and money is law. When the wolves left the camps, they would name their sons and hounds after the New Yorkers, clutching at the dream. In turn, the absentees thought of these men only in the abstract. Four thousand sets of hands; four thousand questions of loyalty. A column in a ledger.

"She's pretty," McBride said and nodded to the sky. A tawny moon lifted in the west, yellow with pollen the saws had kicked up in the day. McBride offered Cur a pinch of tobacco. Cur didn't know what the smoke would do to his mouth—soothe or inflame—so he refused it. McBride shrugged. "What's your name?" he asked. "Tell me or I'll hate you."

When Cur told him, McBride looked up as if he'd been poked. He asked, "Are you from Augusta County?" Cur didn't want to say, but McBride kept prodding, so he admitted he was from the Three Forks of the Cheat. McBride said, "Hell, I think I know your mother! I'd lay money on us being related."

So Sarah Greathouse crossed Cur's path this day—did the same happen to her? He hoped so. He needed it to be true.

On the spot, McBride decided they were cousins, if by a thread of blood, a belief he adhered to until the day he died. But Cur clutched his past like stolen money. He drew the talk back to his busted tooth and by association, to dental oddities he'd observed in the motley faces of workingmen. McBride passed his new cousin a numbing draught of laudanum. With hand gestures, he explained its magical properties. Cur asked why he'd gotten in a scrap. McBride said a thing had galled him the day long: at lunch the teamsters shared a jar of coffee. Young Thomas, who'd been sour all week, said he preferred oxen over horses. McBride gave him a look. He said he didn't mean nothing by it, just if oxen spooked, they stood stock-still in the traces, never jumped over the hill like a horse will, and never got notions to bite a man. Young Thomas cited McBride's lost finger as example. McBride allowed you must watch horses but they have a spirit and a loyalty no ox can muster—great skill and great pridefulness go hand in hand, no way around it, that's why the brightest angel got flung down. McBride reckoned horses aren't meant for draft at all, much too proud, the fact it can be done says something about what man can accomplish. To harness the ballast of so much unruly flesh. A true marvel. Young Thomas spat and said, "I don't see it that way." Then McBride realized something about Young Thomas. He wasn't complaining about horses. He was complaining about McBride.

Others stepped onto the porch; McBride drew them. They shared their tales. Cur did too. The laudanum made him feel so fine. In a way, it was like talking to Sarah.

"Dogs caved a bear in Hesh Mountain. So us boys crawled in with the musket. Wrong cave! Uncle Basil shined the light. Had to be a hundred rattlesnakes balled up if they was a one. 'Deed I seen nothing like it. We went back and blowed it up with a half stick of dynamite somebody stole off a mining rig. Didn't know enough to stand back. Rained rattlesnakes and we was covered in blood and bits of skin. They come down like a ticker tape parade…"

McBride goaded Cur on, asking, "What happened to the bear?"

"What bear? Oh. Nothing."

Under starlight the listeners slapped the walls and merrily called him a liar. Cur held court. Discussed: hellbenders and house coal, floods and fires, and the sheep-fuckers of Mineral County, where boys were known to pick up hoof-and-mouth from their dates. Between silences and stories, he divvied out only the slivers of his life he wanted to. It was a way to avoid talking about himself, to keep the world at arm's length. He would never have to speak of Sarah. Cur took this bitter comfort like a drink of gin. They were men. They would not pry.

To them Cur seemed measured and balanced, like a good

watch. It was the way he carried himself. In the first months, he wasn't grievously abused as new men were.

Soft laughter spread. McBride asked, "You know the Yankee Marcum wrestled a ape at the Spring Fair? No, he didn't do it for money, he did it for love!"

McBride yawned. It began to catch. Cur found an empty bunk in the corner. Thankfully no one fought him for it. Underneath bunks they kept shaving kits, mirror glass, yellowed chunks of lye. He owned nothing but his walking shoes and stowed them there. He listened to the tackhammer of the lobby-hog, who mended a chair broken in a disagreement.

They went to bed on the rim of the world and slept fitfully, like men in ships.

In and out of this sleep, memories came like dreams. She taught him how to read, to talk. Asked him to unbutton the back of her dress. So nervous he snapped a mussel-shell button, and she slapped his arm. Not in a loving way. She put the button on his tongue and told him to swallow. When he did, her eyes grew wide. "I was just funning you," she said.

MORNING CAME UNDER STARLIGHT. They woke to a tin bell and tromped out with pinched faces. Breakfast was identical to dinner, and would be every day. Teamsters left early, harnessing horses and walking them to the slides. The Shay huffed up the grade. If the wolves hurried, they'd catch a ride. They guzzled coffee and made for the siding, tucking in shirttails. Half carried flapping briar saws. Cur needed to marry, as was said. They scurried onto cradle cars, clung precariously, and tucked chins to chests like owls to cut the cold. The Shay passed through last year's cuttings—its yellow eye lit the scene. No one looked. The sun began, washing them in thin light. To the west, nude mountains. The train pulled past broken lands into fog and mist. Rains had slashed the ground into spastic runnels. A sow black bear scrawny with summer loped up the hillside and dove into the brush. They marked the spot for Captain Ketch, who was quite a hunter. The hollow closed, hemming them in with outcrops of barn-sized boulders dressed in lichen and a few clutching windswept pines, bare and stunted on the side facing the wind. When the mist gave way, they were among trees. The steam brake hissed, and the timber wolves clambered down. Not knowing where to go, Cur trailed them into forest bathed in permanent twilight. Not beautiful, but frightening. Woodpeckers hammered their skulls against the wood.

A man with drooping lids and a big jaw told Cur to follow him. He seemed to know the way, but once they were out of sight of the railcut, Cur trembled like a compass needle. The others fanned out into unseen places. The earth smelled of rain and ferns. Riggings of grapevines hung and animals skittered over the branches. Hemlocks and red spruce strained above him and vanished into a green oblivion. Sunless dark and the odd javelin of light. The forest was old here. He heard the bite and sigh of crosscut saws and, further on, the staccato cadence of men notching tree boles with ax and sledge.

Here a wild cherry. Young Shelby Randolph had leaned against it decades ago and felt the scalloped bark through his Federal blues. A bear had raked it in the night, red gashes through the purple rhytidome. But Neversummer led Cur past it, to an even bigger tree, a spruce.

How to knock one down without killing yourself was the puzzle. Cur whistled. "I didn't know God made them that big."

The man spat on his hands. Cur didn't see how that could help at all. He took a moment to consider this new partner: over six feet, with an unsightly Habsburg jaw and auburn hair cut too short, to Cur's eye. Not a scar on him besides, no lost fingers or any of the typical wounds.

A felling notch had been cut into the tree's base, tall enough for a child to stand in, crescents of wood littered about. Cur ran his fingers over the raspy grain. The man motioned him around to the lee side and Cur took the other end of the briar. This man took famous care of his saw. When Cur touched the blade, his fingertips left glowing wormtrails in the verdigris.

"I'm Neversummer."

"Is that one word or two?"

"Asa is my Christian name."

Neversummer scrabbled tobacco into his mouth and said, "Try and keep up, is all I can tell you. I'm the cuttingest on this crew, not afraid to say it, drove my last partner right off the mountain. He's in the infirmary, and they'll kick him out if he don't mend, I'm sorry to say."

Cur drew the seven-foot saw. Neversummer murmured, "Don't fight me now. Simplest thing. If you don't got rhythm, you're the poorest man. Can't make chicken salad out of chickenshit, can you? There you go. It's like fucking. Don't think too much about it."

The handle warmed Cur's hand and drew blisters within the hour. The man said hurry up. Dust was spitting all over. It hung in their noses, brows, and hair. Cur tried to wrap a bandanna about the handle, but sweat and pitch made it hard to hold—it tried to jump from his hand. He cussed and finally stuffed the bandanna into his pocket. Occasionally they dribbled kerosene on the blade. Wolves called the crosscut saw the misery whip, a name understood by anyone who's ever used one. Finally, Neversummer said quit, for if they cut anymore the tree would fall of its own choosing and that's the last circumstance you want. When Cur let go of the saw, its rhythm hummed in every finger.

"Get on my bond side," Neversummer said. Shoulders straining, he swung the ax, hollered a Jericho shout, and gave it nine licks. When it began to wince, he flushed out of there and cried gamely, "You ought'er run."

With a metallic groan, the tree twisted and fell—so fast, so slow, the drizzling molasses, as they all do. It parted the forest like a blade, the world shook and blurred with its percussion. Branches snapping, birds flaring. Like a courthouse coming down.

In a moment, the forest was as still as the day it was born. The spruce had torn a hole in the canopy and let down the light. Tons of timber, a tree that took 212 years to grow and kept rain off generations of deer. Its absence was more powerful than its existence.

Cur heard echoes, or thought so, then realized other trees were falling, five, six, ten, with the distant sounds of a battery. His hands shook. He stuck them in his pockets so the fellow wouldn't see. Cur glanced sidelong, such as you gaze at the solar eclipse—he couldn't quite look directly at Neversummer. This is the one I want to live like, he thought—Cur's immediate attraction to the man was almost sexual. He couldn't explain it, but he felt that small knowledge tucked in his brain, a thrill, a recognition. Neversummer radiated confidence, patience, proportion. What Cur felt was love. Cur had not felt this way since Sarah. He'd come to cherish McBride also. Cur would be nothing without them.

For his part, Neversummer, the unknowable man, was admiring the saw's black sheen, the spangled kerosene. Then he put out a scaly hand to shake. Cur had no choice but to offer his trembling fingers. Neversummer knew better than to smirk and shook anyway.

"You did all right. Proud to work with you," he said. "You get used to it. You can get used to anything. Captain Ketch asked me to break you in." Neversummer slung tobacco from his mouth with a finger. "You ain't broke yet. Let's get on to number two."

They cut fifteen by time Venus rose, a fat green drake off the river of night. They walked to camp in a soft blue drizzle, in silence. Cur's hands wanted to fall off.

ASA NEVERSUMMER, Vance and Amos Church. Luke Seldomridge. From Zeltenreich, seldom rich. Seldomridge The hurls and edges had worn from their names, in the way stone is eaten away by water. Especially the German names: Zyrkle becomes Circle. Schaefer, Shaver. Origin as rumor. Zala becomes Sally Cove on paper. Victor Kovač becomes Imre Mayak and buys a gun.

A cloud of names. Cur entered it here. His life filled with them. Where the mountains pierce clouds and open lobes of rain. He could smell the water on the wind.

THAT FIRST SUMMER, learning the work, teething the bit, Cur felt his old life slough off him. He would hew out a place here with nothing but his two hands, tough and brown as saddle leather. A baby copperhead bit his palm and teethed and didn't break skin.

Blue Ruin ate a live hellgrammite on a two-dollar bet. "Chew it up afore he can pinch you," Cur advised. Blue Ruin would eat anything or nothing, he didn't care.

McBride sang, "Staving Chain was a man like this, couldn't get no woman, he'd fuck his fist." They masturbated continually, and no one went blind, though McBride warned of it.

Up in the mountains they saw ridges and valleys sprawled below, laid out like a map on a table. Even the illiterate could read off features—Elkhorn Creek and Buffalo Trace, Red Indian and Pigeon Valley—named for things settlers had peeled from the earth.

"This," McBride said, "is the highest town east of the Mississip. Can ye believe it?"

It was said they might even earn themselves a post office.

Western flank of Small Bear Mountain, highland pine and a hem of hardwoods. Teamsters rigged fallen spruce with gang hooks and J-grabs, horses snuffling and tossing heads like schoolgirls, fetlocks and bellies draggy with dried mud. Just ahead, young men chopped small branches off the trunks with hatchets, the worst, a low wrist-cracking job that paid little—paysheets called them knotbumpers. They scurried like mink and cussed every branch. Awful days. Blisters of sap burst and made their pants stiff with amber. They never worked fast enough for the teamsters. Even the horses seemed to despise them. Teamsters hollered with blade-sharp voices used to driving stock. McBride encouraged playful abuse.

A boy muttered, "Squawk, squawk, squawk! Just like old mother turkey," and McBride told him, "Do your job, and I won't have to do no squawking. Hurry up and wait's all I do."

Captain Ketch shouted, "Hey! I'll give the orders. Boy, hurry your ass up. All you."

McBride stooped to uncoil a chain and noticed Cur working a tree downhill. "How you keeping up, cousin?"

Cur had to catch his breath. "Getting there."

"Getting there? You're a better man than me. I don't even know where 'there' is."

Neversummer, reluctant to grin, bent to gather shims.

McBride itched a particular bone in his hand. His horses' ears toggled, their sweaty coats a satin sheen. "Asa there works like he's getting paid on commission. He's a tree-chopping fool. What you got against trees?"

"They all want to kill you till you get them on the ground."

"True enough. Hey, watch that poison ivy! Stuff jumps on me. I bawl like a calf."

Cur said, "It don't bother me. I can eat it like salad. Bet you a day's wage."

"It's on there," said Neversummer.

Cur plucked an oily trefoil leaf, folded it into his mouth, and chewed it down and swallowed. He opened his mouth to show them the evidence: empty.

They had to stare. There were times when Cur seemed to skate outside the edges of his personality, these wild little trills that surprised them. Killing a heron. Teasing a preacher. Any small contest he seemed to win.

In the grim decades, these would be the sweetest days to recall.

"Did he have the leaves of three?" McBride asked, laughing all the while. Neversummer had to admit it was so, and McBride told him, "If the young boy don't bloat and die on you, you pay up now. Some'll do anything for money!"

"Let's go make it then." Neversummer measured the next tree, a tilting hickory, against his ax handle. "Good one," he said, snickering and looking about. "Wide as Ketch's wife's ass."

"I won't gainsay you that." McBride paused to chew a splinter out of his dirty thumb and made a sour face. He urged his team onto the skid road with the gentlest words, snaking a log to the slide. The chains groaned as they tightened. Underbrush crackled. McBride sang. He liked bawdy songs with animals, how the preacher met the bear, how the farmer's wife met the long-necked goose. Singing, he left Cur and Neversummer to their work and far flickers of light in the distance.

Weather was their god: hail the size of toads, furnace blasts of heat, feathery snow in July, August that drove dogs mad, snow that foundered trains. The loggers gossiped of weather, because they perceived storms as they perceived women: familiar but unpredictable. McBride once saw heat lightning flash on one side of the ridge, hail slam the other, and wind lift the roof off the Camp One cookhouse and set it down on a train car like a stylish hat.

Around noon, black reefs of cloud formed to the west. Neversummer wouldn't acknowledge the threatening sky.

Cur could taste the bite of static on his tongue. He said, "Company rain! If it come a-morning, Captain Ketch would give you an extra hour or two abed."

"You store too much by Ketch. He's not your daddy. He's the Company man."

Lightning danced in silence and now and again tethered a ridge. The proximity to weather up there made their joints ache. Craggy thunderheads formed a second line over a hunching backbone of quartzite, a place called Seneca Rocks. It looked like a complex mirage: two ridges—one earth, one sky. Perhaps a third, heaven above. Seneca shone bride white against a smudge-pot sky. Cur reckoned the storm ten miles away, but it was hard to judge.

"Where's that foolish ax at?" said Neversummer. Cur tried to hand it over, but Neversummer told him, "Show me what you've learned, scholar."

A red spruce, two feet across. Cur lifted the ax and set his body like a jaw-trap, quivering with power held at bay. When he swung, the head glanced sideways off the bole. He dropped the ax. Nettles bloomed in his hands.

"You made me nervy."

"Ha. Marty Ketch calls me the Schoolteacher." Neversummer bounced the keen ax twice to get its weight and showed Cur how to sway gently and twist from the waist. He said, "Put your ass into it." His right hand slid down the handle with the stroke. The blade bit. With a quick jerk, he worked it free. He made the second cut higher, throwing a big crescent of wood. Four, five. Sap drooled. He handed the ax to Cur. "Just like a natural," he murmured, as you would to a touchy horse. "No, you're ringing too far. See how you want her to fall? Otherwise you're in a world of shit. Good notcher aim it like a rifle. There you go. You're a killer now."

Cur found his rhythm, chips flying. Metal touched heartwood. The birds were silent.

A clap and its mumbling, a low stump-grinding sound that rolled like the gray ocean neither of them would ever see. The first raindrops fell hard as tenpenny nails. Seneca Rocks had been engulfed in cloud and roaring curtains of rain. They ran with the saw flopping its funny music and hid in a hollow den tree. The sycamore was large enough to stand inside or even light a fire in, a living cave that smelled of damp and spiders. The wind threw dervishing funnels of pine needles and tore them back down. They had to shout over the rain.

Cur had dropped the saw thirty paces back to bait the lightning. He asked, "You scared?" Neversummer's fear was touching to Cur, and bracing. The man had seemed perfect until then. Yet the flaw improved him.

Neversummer's eyes rolled at the thunder. He worried over his gold tooth. He took off his hat and raked his fingers through his hair, black as a tar brush with sweat. At times, Neversummer caught Cur staring at his off-kilter jaw. They spent so many hours together and yet, Neversummer realized, Cur knew nothing much about him. Sometimes he would feel a twinge of guilt at this imbalance. But not now. He was looking at the sky.

Cur told him, "Don't you worry. You don't see the one that kills you."

"I could gut you like a fish," Neversummer said, but his spirit wasn't in it. He fidgeted with a pocketknife, opening it and closing it against the heel of his hand. "Lightning kilt Jack Earnshaw. Grabbed his ax. You could smell it for a mile. They never found his shoes."

The forest leapt up in jagged light. It was as if God had leaned down to tap them once, twice, and cracked the mountain like a hen's egg. For a moment, the flash blinded them. Blue sparks rode the split pine up and down its length in a crackling helix, chasing sap. A scorched, astringent smell curled in their noses. It was the same spruce they'd been working over. The crown had fallen, peeling the tree in two through its center like a split hair. Needles crackled.

"You okay? Asa?"

Neversummer didn't answer. A dead jay dropped from the tree, wings splayed. Smoke began drifting in rills and rattails. A narrow tongue of flame animated a dead bush.

Cur said, "If it gets any bigger than that, we're running."

"Big now."

A flag of fire. Trees creaked like ships in the wind. The men watched the rain fight the flames, till the wind changed and the storm snuffed it out.

The clouds rolled on. The ground had been scored in jagged black. They ran their hands over secret splintered heartwood, the cooked sap. Neversummer lifted the squares of charcoal with his knife. A woman could paint her eyes with it, he said. He smeared some on the back of his hand, rubbing it in a circle. "Supposed to be good luck," Neversummer said—so Cur did the same, working it into his skin. It had been grazed by the sky, the mystery. "We need it out here."

"This log is ruint. Cut her right in half."

"Might get a few boards out the crown. Tedrow can tell. He's got the rule."

Shyly, birds began to call. The ground steamed, and the men moved to the next tree, knocking another blue hole in the canopy. Occasionally, one fell with a wincing cry and thresh of leaves. A calm, calm sky. The light glared down.

Cur said, "Hold on, I need to tie my boot." He sat on a fresh stump.

Neversummer said, "That's a awful goddamned lot of work to make yourself a chair."

FOR FOUR YEARS, Cur would work alongside Neversummer. A rare happy marriage among men, who often quit one outfit and went to work another at any slight, real or perceived. The two of them were the hardest workers, craft-proud and haughty, the closest Blackpine had to an aristocracy. If you could work tirelessly or make others laugh, that was fine. If you could do both, why, nothing better. What did Neversummer see in Cur? Well, someone like himself, who had little to live for. Neversummer was near fifty. He knew the empty decades ahead, behind. His past was nothing but labor camps and tedium and the odd broken bone. He didn't think it worth speaking of. Neversummer had cut trees for seven years, but he never considered himself a logger.

COME NIGHTFALL, WIND RAKED the roof. It was a year into Cur's tenure on the mountain. He slept near a man who'd been struck by a falling snag that morning. The hurt man groaned now and again, sides heaving like a set of bellows. He had managed to keep working through the day. Now the blow caught up to him. Every few minutes, he leaned over the edge of his bunk to spit. His mouth gave out a gentle sound: *suss, suss.*

Come morning, the man was stiff and blue. The cook's helpers carried him to the Shay. Over breakfast, no one spoke of the dead man. It seemed to embarrass them.

Neversummer whispered, "Do you see what I mean?" And if Cur, in years to come, had ever been asked what finally radicalized him, not that anyone asked, he would point to this vision. He was trusted now. Over the saw, Neversummer murmured De Leonism, trade unionism, pure communism, the shades between. Land redistribution! Dying for a cause was a blessing on men such as themselves—a ghost to quicken the wooden floor. If Neversummer believed in anything, it was this. Cur was drunk on it, intoxicated by ideas. They all were. They had come of age in famine. Childhood had the odd Bible, the stale sermons, the moldy primer, a page ripped from a catalog and read just before you wiped your ass. It cheered Cur to think of men across the waters thinking this way too. They spoke of them as friends, as prophets. "Our present modes of trading," Neversummer said to Cur, "are a delusion to the worthy, active members of society, while continually enriching the vagabonds." Neversummer could recite passages with such precision that many thought he was speaking extemporaneously. "Civilization will soon come to nothing, and government end in chaos, if labor is ignored. The power lies in the hands of the producers. Will we help ourselves? The ballot is but a secondary consideration." This from one of those foxed pamphlets, cranked out by some shadowy press in Olathe, Kansas, in 1894. Cur thought Neversummer had made it up himself and was embarrassed to later learn otherwise, trying hard not to let on. Dreamier than their rivals, and sentimental, they would fight up-current against this tendency and finally drown.

ONE AFTERNOON CUR LEFT to piss. When he returned, Neversummer was on his haunches, rolling cigarettes with a smiley fellow. They were the same age, though the new fellow's hair was gray and bristly. He'd been used hard. It had to be Vance Church, a Camp One luminary. Everyone else seemed to know him. As is common with disquieting strangers, Cur felt a vague hostility toward the man, then immediately liked him once they met.

"Now young Cur is quite the ax-man," his patron said, "and you know I don't go saying that about nobody. Good West Virginia boy he is. You're meeting family."

"You a real timber beast, are you? And West Virginia too?"

"That's right," said Cur, bashful now. "From south of here. Round Jephtha."

Vance had an accent from here and from somewhere else, hard to reckon. He cried, "Old Jeff-town! County seat of Two Brides County. Know it well. The double-cunted county!"

Cur didn't have the heart to tell him he was thinking of the wrong place, but he forgave the man in his mind. Neversummer told him, "Vance worked the Great Northern Rail for years on years. Hell of a mechanic. Shay broke at Big Lime, and the crew can't do a thing. Vance marches over and digs into the pistons up to the shoulder. Had it running in an hour."

"Why'd you give it up?"

Vance tapped ash. He got run off the job. Something had to be done, and was. Pure wildness: swing shifts and slashing of pay by 28 percent, buildings burned, rails shut down, him in a cell, all Chicago held at bay. But the workers held the line and cracked open that jail and set him loose. The government lost track of Vance Church in Ohio. Cur asked if none had tried striking here.

"You could say that if you'd a mind to be generous. A guinea name of Victor Kovač tried to get a thing up here once. Bridge crew captain. Couldn't find his ass with two hands."

On a payday, Vance and Neversummer would visit Sally Cove and receive information she stole from the Company, including the names and pay scales of every man the Company employed. Sally Cove considered her estranged husband a wonderful and heroic figure, and when speaking with her, they bit their tongues. They knew Victor through their contacts in Ohio—indeed Amos Church, soon to appear in West Virginia, knew Victor well in Youngstown—and they feigned deathless friendship. Sally would give them the keys to the railroad office and the safe—Vance knew she would come around.

"Let's not speak ill of the dead," Neversummer warned him.

"Let's not speak ill of the truth. He was a fool-headed man. They stomped him out like a grass fire. Cur, he set this place back ten years. A real mess."

Vance said farewell. Cur and Neversummer went back to their work. Nothing was said till they left walking under the first stars. A possum scuttled past, awesomely ugly.

Cur said, "That guy's a real hell-raiser. He'd pull it up by the roots and dump kerosene on the flames."

"He's a serious man," was all Neversummer was willing to say.

That night, Cur lay in his cot, studying nickel scraps of moonlight through a shoddy roof. The crickets were ceaseless in the wall. Cur felt his foot being shaken. Quiet as could be, he felt for his boots and rose on stocking feet. He husked over the boards. None stirred, but as he passed through the bunk, he saw, in a rhombus of light, Blue Ruin's black eyes watching him. Cur lifted a finger to his lips, then realized it was unnecessary: Blue Ruin slept with eyes wide open, like a fish. Cur slipped to the porch.

He and Neversummer skirted the railroad bed's crunching gravel, striking for a trail tamped with pine needles, a trough of silence. Clutching one another's suspenders, they forded a creek full of mossy boulders. Neversummer held an unlit torch high overhead, taking care to keep it dry. On the far bank, they changed into fresh socks and jerked on boots. Cur had trouble judging distance at night, but he thought it three miles or so before they spoke.

"Kindly hard to see."

"Pay it mind on your way back through."

The Cheat was louder at night, as all rivers are. The late shift had come on: the tree frogs, the foxes and voles working out their sagas. At the boulder field called Devil's Marbleyard, Neversummer took out flint and tinderbox. He struck it to the torch, which had been soaked in hog fat, the type of mountain torch you use to jab at a hornet's nest. It enveloped them in heat and illuminated a globe of mountainside: bone-colored boulders, krummholz, bleached wood. The ground became rockier, quartzite and tripping roots. They heard the sluice of water and bats piping like bone flutes. Cur's free hand scraped rock, and Neversummer told him stoop down low. They entered the caves, passing through a cool curtain of air. Now the rock was wet to the touch. The karstlands of West Virginia. The air was rich with soapstone and dripping sounds of water, as if they roamed a distillery.

The big room was lit with torches and pine knots, candles and coal-oil lanterns. Each man held his own ration of light, and the smoke ushered itself out through a fire-stained crack in the ceiling. Near thirty sat on upturned crates or leaned on ancient wooden equipment Cur didn't know the story of. These were oak-and-cucumber-wood hoppers that had been pegged to the walls and preserved by the cave—they'd been used to harvest gunpowder during the war, leaching saltpeter from bat shit. At one point, this place supplied over half the Confederacy's gunpowder. It belonged to Old Virginia until their kind was driven from Tuscarora County—the absentee New Yorkers themselves routing the copperheads, their great small victory—and a different set of hunched old men and haggard boys, Federal loyalists, took over. Four years toiling with pails full of nitrogen-rich shit, their arms chalked with lime and blacked with charcoal, their eyes ruined for the sun.

All the Woodworkers Brotherhood looked Cur over. Besides Vance, there were some he'd met in passing on Helena payday, a couple fellows named Blizzard and Mullenex, always spoken of in a pair. A bald fellow with jug ears he couldn't remember the name of but liked very much, an ace at billiards, fluent in angle and velocity, and known, when drunk, to make fancy trick shots to impress the ladies, who politely feigned interest. Stanton was his name. Knots of men resumed their conversations. He recognized sawyers from Camp Four, as well as a few Italians, one holding a miner's Davy lamp. Cur would have been disturbed at how much they knew about him.

One Italian stuck out a hand. "I know you."

"This is Leo Caspani," Neversummer said to Cur. "He blows tunnels, gives it no more thought than you or me putting on pants."

Cur shook with the man, whose deft swarthy hands were curiously unmangled, unsinged, for a man who worked with explosives. Pronouncing each syllable with care, Caspani said, "Good evening, sir. I hear you are going to help us make history." Caspani spoke in excellent if mannered English, which made him sound just as foreign here as those with the thickest accents.

Cave rock drooped from the ceiling, and water dripped after relinquishing its burden of calcium. Some hangs were toothy, but others rippled like sheets of bacon in a smokehouse, looking more liquid than stone. Cinnamon bats had tucked themselves here and there. One broke like an icicle and flew overhead. "Least we can rile the bats," a man said, and everyone laughed.

Cur was introduced by Neversummer as a friend of theirs. Cur grinned shyly, looking from man to man like a debutante being paraded about for the first time. They saw his missing teeth. A bare majority vote had invited him here. Vance had voted nay, but Cur won him over in time, and Amos was a long time from coming to Blackpine and whispering in his father's ear.

The Woodworkers came forward each by each with names of possible commitments for a general strike. Some read from lists; others recited from memory, and halfway through Cur realized they couldn't read or write. Vance scribbled in a book black and plain as a hymnal. When Caspani recited a litany of musical names—D'Andrea, Salvastore, Caluso—a few turned their faces to the ground in order not to smirk. Proud Caspani ignored it. He folded his paper into a neat square and drew it back into his sleeve. Next Neversummer spoke. From Camp Five, he named Proxmire, Tracy Sixx, Bull Aberegg, John William, and Dale Keough, who you don't dare mix up with Levi Keough the paregoric drinker. Cur was surprised to hear Bull Aberegg named. Neversummer had poked fun at Aberegg's harelip more than once.

Cur asked, "What about McBride?"

All turned to his voice. Vance gave him a look. It wasn't Cur's place.

"He's a mule skinner," Vance said.

"So?"

Neversummer patted Cur on the shoulder. "We'll talk it out. We're just in the beginnings here. This has to be thought with care." Then a man from Camp Eight read off his list. Neversummer took it when he was done. "Don't sound like much, do it? Papers said there was a hundred thousand workers in Illinois, and I'm convinced it was twice that. Vance told me it started out three guys in a Pullman shack drinking rye, bitching around a table so tiny one of them had to stand in the door. Ain't that right, Vance?"

Vance said it was true.

Then the arguing. Its ferocity startled Cur. No goodwill. No cheer. Caspani saying, "In this country, you are naïve. By taking a moderate stance, Asa, you welcome those who would crush you, yes you do. You have not lived in Europe, you have not seen how the liberal parties are the worst because they forever stand in the way, they propose half measures, they give voice to the loudest outcry—still they want their horses and townhouses and maids and dining sets. You know nothing of them. If there exist any liberals in this room, they should be placed against the wall and shot. It will save us from having to do it six months from now."

Neversummer told him, "You don't understand Americans. It don't work that way."

"I understand men. That is enough."

"This ain't some ghetto."

"Calling me a Jew is not going to win you your argument."

Only here could they shout their endless spiraling derision. Cur could tell more about what was meant by their faces than by their words. They might as well have been clutching knives. Caspani was calm, his voice lilting, but Neversummer's voice grew raspy and scouring. Caspani would claim vast knowledge of the intricacies of statecraft and dare you to question him. Always had an answer. But Neversummer had answers too, and Vance would hang back, hoarding his words, waiting to pronounce judgment, somewhere between them, or sometimes even more radical, surprising all. The others organized themselves loosely around the one they agreed with most, slapping hats on thighs, jeering and hissing. There were sunflowers seeds and peanut shells stomped into the floor, a granular muck. Cur watched Neversummer—so calm, so sure of himself. Others would say that he lacked passion. But Cur had seen what passion does to lives.

DYING HORSES. UNMENDED BONES. Rain, drudgery, bleeding hands. They wanted a doctor to visit the camps once a week, not once a month. Twenty-five cents an hour, not two dollars a day. A hot lunch. A ten-hour shift, not one without end. Collective bargaining, glory, power, recognition, revenge, a right to jury trial for strikers, the contracts shredded and thrown away for good. Neversummer pulled the right ones aside whenever he could. They listened in twos and threes. In Camp One, they crowded around Vance, then his angry son.

Their small union solidified—radicals, true believers, and wayward souls like Cur. Vance praised them as men whose time had come. You got to get the public behind you, he explained. Roosevelt was softening, had brokered a compromise for wage and hours after the Anthracite Strike. The time is now. The nation is tilting. He wasn't afraid to tell them what could happen: the National Guard firing down, corrupt trials like at Haymarket, prison terms, unlucky ones shot and hung as agitators, corpses defaced,

genitalia knifed out. "Don't die with a whimper in your bunk."
Vance made them promise they would not.

EACH YEAR, CHEAT RIVER PAPER & PULP commissioned a
new map of its holdings, and many times, cartographers dragged
the logging outpost of Blackpine miles up the Cheat, as a chill
climbs a person's spine. They blew the pages to dry the ink and
dusted the paper with sand. Wolves uprooted the satellite camps,
stacked bunkhouses and blacksmith shops on railcars, and chased
the forest upriver—the wolves called Blackpine the Wandering
Jew. When roving musicians walked the tracks, they lamented the
jaunt seemed longer each season.

Blackpine was encircled with sagging piles of branches in di-
verse states of rot and twigs and bark husks crunching underfoot,
crossed by slides and corduroy roads, rough paths like boardwalks
for the horses to travel on, made by laying split logs in the mud.
By firelight, the wolves played backgammon and a few hands of
five knives, cards tacky with pine pitch and a little blood. Fatigue
dulled their brains. Few could read, but some kept Bibles or
penny dreadfuls. Tom Blankenship had a much-handled postcard
he'd share for a nickel, the heavy woman spreading legs under a
drugged smile and a pile of hair. A quarter set of encyclopedias
propped up the jake-legged bunks and could be browsed if no one
was napping. Some papered the walls with garish advertisements
torn from catalogs until the Company made them quit. In hot
months, the rancid straw tick would drive them onto the porch or
to walk their saws to the filer.

In 1902, Cheat River Paper & Pulp cut 175 million board feet of
timber; in 1903, 186 million; and in 1904, it would peak—but not
end—at 191 million. Blackpine ate a caterpillar's trail into the steep
eastern flank of Mozark Mountain, even the dry rain shadow. Men
came and went, some to other outfits, others mashed or dead on
the Shay. They buried no one in this moving place. Unlucky Tracy
Webb lost an eye to a thorn, then gave a thumb and forefinger
to a slipped J-grab and went away. McClatchy died of alcohol
poisoning. Some lived like sleepwalkers, kept up the night long

by red bites rising on their flesh, the farting and the snoring. The stench was enough, they said, to drive off bats. Cur didn't know if the winter cold would deaden the smell or the potbellied stove would cook it up. The straw tick was rife. Men had different cures for fleas and lice. Some slathered their limbs, hair, and crotches with coal oil. Italians in Camp Three would tear off their clothes and turn them inside out to wear, jumping back into bed before the parasites were the wiser. In his private room, Captain Ketch sunk the legs of his cot into buckets of applesauce and kerosene to keep vermin from crawling up them. It almost worked.

The long lyric of their days. Neversummer turned fifty-one years old and let it go without a word. He was aloof, patrician. He had other concerns. He watched Cur grow, learned his character and mood; he read three newspapers a week; he wrote and received letters in obscure code, bribing the postmaster to leave them be, memorizing names and faces. In the woods, the two of them burned pamphlets and kicked leaves over the ash. Cur adored him. March of 1903 and the river breaking.

THESE ARE THE DAYS Cur chose to remember, the easy early ones, cutting the trees, doing the work, learning the mountain with Neversummer and McBride. When tools were sweet in his hands. The days he would go back to if he could. Everyone had a kind word to say. Those other matters and faces would fall away in the great elision to come.

The Woodworkers chose November 25. They sped toward it like a planet in 1904, the whiplash year. They would take over the railroad office and drive the clerks outside, lock the mill and block every rail into town, dress Helena Bridge and the Rose Street mansions in dynamite. Vance would announce their demands. He knew the rest of the camps would join in. There were workers in near counties, at Parsons Timber, Leivasy Paper, and dozens of smaller outfits. Vance said they would rise.

Someday, Sarah Greathouse would hear of Cur on the tongues of other men, on market day in Jephtha or some other town. The thought filled Cur's heart with polleny light.

LIFELONG TERMS

On the night he died, Amos Church planted his shit-smeared boots on the doorframe, and the vigilantes punched him back into that small room in the railroad office, hammering his back with fists and gun butts. He was an animal, ear torn, blood in his teeth. The vigilante with razor burn hobbled after them, tears standing in the corners of his eyes. Amos had kicked him hard in the knee. Caspani scooped up a coil of hemp rope off a barrel and stepped inside, turning the bolt behind them. Amos fell to the floor and cracked his own jaw.

"You're trash," he said to Caspani when he could speak again. "You're trash." They beat him with an ax handle, and when he began to cry, Caspani slapped him. The book Amos carried held

names, diagrams, musings, addresses, passwords, towns, compa-
nies. It belonged to his father, Vance. When they tried to shove
a newspaper down Amos's throat, Caspani found this book that
clapped against his side. On Fishamble Street, Neversummer and
Vance leisurely twisted chicken legs from fryers, and Seldomridge
spoke his sermon of Lot. On his knees now, Amos spat a bib of
blood down his shirtfront.

With a gleeful look, a vigilante leafed through the pages of the
book. Another stepped outside and plunked the nickel derringer
into a rain barrel. It bored right to the bottom.

Everyone was looking at Caspani. He said, "This is the one you
want."

Amos said nothing when they asked his name. The others ex-
changed furtive looks. They wondered who the other boy was—
the dead boy. Their sudden good luck stunned them.

"You ruined someone's night," said Constable Green, and they
sent him to see who it was.

They sat Amos in a chair and asked their questions. He didn't
speak, even when they tore at him with pliers and put out cigarettes on his neck. He spoke only once more. When Caspani said,
"I'll make you fuck your sister," Amos replied, "I don't have any
sisters."

The vigilantes laughed nervously and blushed. Caspani untied
Amos, only to tie the rope again, in a new way.

"There's nothing else," Caspani said. Almost as if saying it to
himself. He fashioned the knot soundly. A vigilante told him to
hurry, but Caspani saw no rush. Caspani tossed one end of the
rope over the rafter like a man raised by acrobats.

Amos felt a cauterizing pain in his chest. He wished it would
end. They prodded him, made him stand on a chair. It was difficult. His eyes were swollen. He could not see.

Amos drifted from his body into nothingness. In that moment
he knew again there was no God.

Here it ends. But not for the vigilantes. It took them longer to
arrange this death than they would have liked.

Caspani left them and returned with D'Andrea. They had

four of their countrymen in tow, men so fresh they didn't know a word of English besides "work please" and "good, healthy" and "need food, need water." They had the stunned, bewildered look of newcomers.

Entering the office, Caspani was relieved to find the vigilantes gone. The fresh Sicilians doffed hats and crossed themselves. The legs of the hanged had quit their awful shivering. They cut the body down, and it fell into waiting arms. His pants were soaked with piss. Before they wrapped him in a sheet, Amos Church was christened Nicola Caspani, tab #307. Caspani pinched the metal onto the dead man's collar. Amos's eye sockets were already greening with death. They carried him off to the Methodist minister known to be a fool.

HOURS LATER, WITH AMOS IN THE GROUND not a mile away, Cur walked a hollow—down into the Gulley, the black section of Helena—that doglegged where Leatherbark Run met the river. He joined Vance and Neversummer in the trail, with a black man beside them—the Choirboy. Cur had been here once before, in the drunkest night when he followed the Choirboy to a dice game where he was, except for an albino with palms the color of crawdads, the only white man.

The Choirboy carried a weak lantorn. "It's the old coal train," he said to Cur. How did he know Cur's real name was Coleman? Probably from McBride. "Always on time. Always."

The Choirboy led them through the shantytown, tarpaper shacks crafted from scavenged crates. A dog approached. Instead of snapping, she rolled on her back, offering a view of flapping dugs. The Choirboy leaned down and gave her a rub, plucked a swollen tick and tossed it at the creek. A woman in a bright apron tended an oily cookfire with a spade, raking embers under the kettle. Her man had three catfish nailed through the nose to a tree, and with pliers he peeled the skin with care, as if removing a lady's stocking. Other black men stood around drum fires, staring. Cur had never felt like such a stranger. There were no donegans, and the people washed clothes in a creek that turned rank as a gut wound in summer's swelter. A man burned planks to sift nails from the ashes. Another carried a phonograph in his arms from one house to another.

The shack was a three-room shotgun. At a table with a jug of wine sat Caspani and a girl with slack olive skin and combs in her hair. There were oak leaves in the corner, the floor buckled and out of plumb. Like any carpenter would, Cur noted a four-inch rise from one corner of the ceiling to the other. He shook his head. "You better beware the next sound wind."

"Ain't much," Vance said, "but we don't want much or need it."

The Choirboy asked if they could pay him now. Caspani made the girl go to the back room, and Neversummer pulled out a roll of bills. "This is for two months," he said, high-handed. "Should cover four damn years. This ain't much of a place."

"You're paying for a shut mouth, and I'm darning mine," the Choirboy said. "Just like a dragonfly done it."

"Thank you, Mance. I knew you'd understand."

"Mance?" Cur had to ask. He couldn't help himself.

The Choirboy tucked the money under his hat. "Emancipation. Dad was in bond to John Riggs. Ohio River, port of St. Marys. Had Dad running the ferryboat across, one of them old cable types. The army come and throwed John Riggs in jail. They turned Dad loose. He asked the army to give him the ferryboat, but no, they kept it themselves. When John Riggs got out, he cussed emancipation, and Dad said he like to name me a thing worth cussing."

There was no mirth in the telling, but Caspani laughed, never looking away from the jug on the table. He asked, "Is this hospitable, Mr. Church?"

"Oh yeah. Quite. You done good."

Caspani looked over at Cur and said, "This is where we are going to make history."

Cur thought about the Choirboy. They knew one another slightly—that is, not at all. The Choirboy's younger sister ran the colored school and had married the year before, shucking the name they held in common. She paid the Choirboy an allowance to stay away from the house. Some counted grievous sins against him, but he was little more than a confidence man, a fallen gospel singer, a somewhat reliable fence. In Southern towns they would have hung him by now.

The Choirboy could find you lots of things for money. He could find you a safe house even if he didn't think much of you. A white man would turn on you like an injured dog—when you pay it kindness, that's when it goes for your throat. But their money was substantial: a pleasant surprise. The Choirboy was glad to leave this place. It all gave him the willies. He had promised to watch it for them through the month, while they worked on the mountain. He never promised to go inside.

As the Choirboy walked off into the Gulley, the others took seats at the knife-scored table. Neversummer said, "Ought to get three houses for what we're paying."

Caspani smiled and said, "Asa and his math." Caspani rubbed a water stain on the wood with his thumb. His hands were stained with mud, and his shoes had left clots of it on the floor.

Vance kept checking his watch. A chill fear working him. It spread to the others.

"Amos'll be here," said Neversummer. "Probably just found himself a little honeysuckle."

"We have an hour. He may come. Boys of that age are distract ible," Caspani said.

"Amos was never like that. Not even as a child."

"I was only trying to comfort," said Caspani. He didn't understand these men. They found lying so hard, even harmless lies that oil society and let it wheel. He didn't hate them. He'd only been mistaken in leaving for this country. For three years he regretted it every day. It wasn't his family, or even the town of San Cataldo, that drew him. He had never liked the place: the ugly shops, the cramped parlors, the sniping *assessori*. But he wanted his own pinched reality, not Helena's. This country would never be right. Here he had no name, no history. He felt the scolding looks of clerks at the railroad office, how men looked through him on the street. He saw the fear in their women's eyes, heard the things they said. They didn't bother to whisper, never believing him wise enough to speak English. He'd been taken for money at stores before he knew better. He saw a nativist rally in Oakland, Maryland, where people burned a man-sized doll that turned out to be the pope—straw and a butcher-paper face, and green stockings for arms. It shook him, though he had always regarded the church as a joke, a pageant for children and old women, as any sensible person does. And even his countrymen here seemed the very dregs of their villages. He had to give the simplest directions time and again. Hated being yoked to anyone else. He was not them. He only wanted to be Caspani. He felt the bit in his mouth. His bleeding gums. It was too nasty a place to change, but it could change you. He needed passage back, and money. Milan or Rome was meant for him.

D'Andrea and another countryman inched through the door, carrying a wooden crate. Vance thanked them at length, and Caspani interpreted. D'Andrea nodded, pulling at a cigarette, noncommittal.

Neversummer stooped and lifted the lid. The sticks of dynamite were waxy in their bloom of glycerin. They seemed to sweat next to the banded coils of wire.

They scooted the table. Neversummer snaked out a jackknife and pried up floorboards in the middle of the room. Underneath, a pit had been dug by Bull Aberegg, the big saw-filer, and it was fresh enough that roots poked through whitely and the room smelled of earthworms and loam. There sat on the bare earth an iron strongbox painted green, cans of ammunition, and .30–40 Krag rifles wrapped in waxed canvas—for a bribe of fifty dollars, and a good price for each one, the rifles had been diverted from the Spanish War by a canny railroad agent. Beside them, a sack bulged with books and red pamphlets. They lowered the crate. Cur reached into his jacket and gently tossed the sack of blasting caps inside.

Vance tacked his gaze to the door. This was a small place, meant only for a dozen. The rest came at the hour, grumbling to pass by dusky women and wretched tomato vines, and children calling,

"White man coming!" They thought night would cover them, but it was Saturday and people wandered from shack to shack, conversing. Conversing about them. It was bad, but not so bad: the black residents of Helena had nothing to do with the police. Their gossip would remain in the Gulley like a low fog.

Salvastore Caluso and Nick Olivette appeared. Nick swung a fresh jug onto the table, smiling at one and all, especially Caspani, as was natural. Everyone showed but Amos, Aberegg, and Clark Posthlewait, who'd taken sick with shaking fever. Even without, they leaned or sat on every surface.

Finally, Neversummer said, "Here on out we meet in town. Once you're in here, it's all business. This ain't no blind pig dollar-at-the-door bullshit."

Vance nearly crawled out of his skin when the door opened. It was Aberegg, sheepishly apologizing and swearing he'd buy a new watch. His show of locking fingers in a prayer of supplication and mercy was met with quiet laughter.

Neversummer looked at the door. "Damn me, have you seen Amos?"

"A boy got shot," Mullenex told him.

"What? What?"

Cur said, "No, that wasn't Amos. Me and McBride was there. It was a boy from camp. Listen to me! It was a Goddard. That had nothing to do with us."

"Amos and teamsters never got along," said Mullenex.

Cur could have killed Mullenex right then.

Caspani said, "When are we going to talk about striking?"

"Right this minute."

After, most left for the taverns. Aberegg stayed behind—to prove he was serious—and told Vance to go talk to the police and ask for Amos. "Tell them you're a friend named Haslett or something." But Vance said he couldn't, he'd done things they wanted answers to, he had an alias for payroll but the police had his picture. His voice was low, banked like a fire. Cur said maybe he could get a woman he knew to ask the police. No one answered.

Neversummer wasn't listening. He rested his chin on a fist. He wanted to call it all off, wait for spring. Double or triple their numbers. Others would refuse. Caspani would never go in for it. A swampy smell of greens and baby shit came through the window. A dog began to croon.

"Strike still on?" Proxmire asked them.

Caspani said yes, Neversummer said no, and Vance didn't answer. He was socking a fist into a hand in dumb, monotonous rhythm. Cur didn't feel it was his place to offer an opinion.

Neversummer glanced at him and felt a dart of disgust, reckoning if Cur would always cling to him, if he would ever make a decision on his own. Cur had stumbled into this life, taking hold of a particular saw on the mountain, rather than five hundred others, and only in fraught moments, it showed. But the moment passed, the feeling of any great man toward a devotee.

The Woodworkers had little to do but return to the Blackpine camps come Monday. For another long drudge.

Caspani slipped out of the safehouse. He followed a red lane that had been walked smooth as soap by a thousand bare feet, the roots hacked out with sang hoes long ago. He tried to ignore the dumb vigilante who stood in the window of a nearby shack. Obvious as a falling star.

THE WOODWORKERS SLEPT all day and some didn't rise till Sunday supper. They would live at night and prepare. They had trained their bodies to sleep whenever they could. They had two months, now.

That evening, downtown, the streets began to fill. On the margins of Helena, a railroad bridge arced over the Cheat. In deep shadow beneath the bridge, Cur stood with Neversummer and watched bodies move in the trusswork above. Clever as spiders, they were learning to climb the span in darkness and know the metal and stitch dynamite to its sides. Grease on their skin, spiked boots. Tackhammer and wax. A pair of pliers fell, and the river swallowed them in silence. This was practice. Cur watched them swing and climb and tease at the metal. He winced as a man let out a faint little yelp. But no one fell. What would it be like teetering there, the river ripping below? Would your knees burn? Would you be afraid or giddy with height? The men grew faint against the black span.

With splashes you couldn't hear over the milldam's churn, bodies dropped into the shallows. Shivering, soaked to the waists with river water. Cur handed them dry sets of clothes. He felt a prickle on his neck: Vance and Neversummer needed some of them to be killed—to earn the sympathy of the public, the press, the country they called their own. Loud garish deaths were called for. He thought of Sarah and Old Neil—surely they were still alive, farming those acres as they always had. But he couldn't go back. He would die here in Helena. That very first night in the caves, he'd made the decision to be willing, to welcome the chance like an old friend, such as his betters hoped he would. Cur had no family, no people, no child to orphan. There would be no regret, no final temptation to bargain or give up. He would lean against the wall and let his body catch those bullets. Let them print the limestone with his blood: the wheel of history catching. He was young and sound looking, except for his teeth, and a local man, liked and respected by most, not an undesirable Jew or Italian, or an agitator like Amos, and along with Neversummer, he was the hardest worker in Camp Five, according to Captain Ketch, so eager to please. He remembered then Amos in the caves, frenzied: "The Supreme Court is the hand of an invisible Tsar! They have lifelong appointments! This nation is a dictatorship with a rotating head so the people do not suspect it. It's ingenious." Where was Amos? Now that he'd disappeared, Cur craved his brash bracing presence. Amos shouted, Amos made you feel alive—that's all you could ask for in this life. Memories of their rivalry fell away. Cur forgave Amos that spectacle in the caves, if only he turned up, if only everything could be set right. It isn't hard to forgive the dead—a sentiment Cur didn't yet realize. He watched the men dress beside the river.

No, Cur wouldn't be the one to die. It was his fate to live.

Pleased with this practice, the union men left for their various lives; they had to rent rooms and were light-headed with hunger and, for the first time, dizzy with confidence. This was not talk. Everyone was sick of talk.

THE LEDGERS WERE TIGHT on the shelves, one solid mass, even before the spring damp swelled pages and buckled the binding. In a fashion not befitting a man his age or stature, Judge Randolph, the absentee, grabbed hold with both hands to wrench one free. It gave with a crack. The violence made Randolph's head swim, but he had the taste of brandy on his tongue and in such a state, he liked to read. The ledger weighed as much as a child. He thumped it on the table and smoothed his mussed hair, which his wife thought a fine patrician gray. He unlocked the clasp, stooping over it, as if under leadership's burden. For safekeeping and sentimentality, Randolph kept the Company's filled ledgers in his Helena residence, on Rose Street. The clerks delivered a new one each month, with a certain ceremony. Senator Helena and Senator Baxter didn't care; they rarely left the capital. He couldn't blame them, but he liked to come to Helena now and again to check their creation. He was a rare man, that way, among absentees. Cheat River Paper & Pulp was one of nine great corporations—smaller only than Blackwater Timber, Davis & Elkins, and Parsons's outfit—not to speak of a hundred lesser moons that wildcatted with woodsplitters and coffeepot mills when the economy was bullish. The Company's mill never quit. Randolph believed it cheaper to cut at a loss than to cease operation, so the band saw ripped eleven hours a day, even if the stacks rotted in the stockyard, fringed with milkweed and sedge, for reasons of supply and demand—let them sit until the market improves. Stacks of oak, older than Columbus or the Gutenberg press, turned to mush.

The housekeeper peered into Randolph's office. She retreated when he acknowledged her with a little wave of his fingers. Only that morning the stout woman set out with a claw hammer to open the windows, pulling nails with a squeal. The rooms had grown musty in Randolph's absence, sour with oxblood leather and dust. One curtain was sweet and sickening with mold. She swore you can't keep a room of books clean.

Bound in calfskin, the ledgers logged tasks worthy of the generations: board feet, wages paid, track laid, pulp ordered and paid for, staves crafted, lifespan of band saws and locomotives, minutiae of hand tools, softwood versus hardwood, the red and black of commissary record, worker deaths, entire catalogs of railroad lore. Randolph flipped the pages. The paper was cool to the touch. For months the Company had known of radicals in the camps, and because others had failed to move with alacrity, the situation had bellied out, extended. Whatever the outcome, it must end. Let it boil over and they'll take it off as a barman slices the foam off a head of beer. He didn't want to think of all this. Shouldn't have to. Maybe they should go ahead and offer a raise to the rank and file. Why, a few more cents an hour, it wouldn't make much difference either way. No, he reckoned. That would be a sign of weakness. He tried to sip from his glass and found it empty. He called for the housekeeper, but she was in another wing.

They had done it themselves, Randolph thought miserably. By inviting rails into this place, they'd trucked in unrest. Infected it. But if there existed another way to move timber at such volume, he didn't know it. Before the boom, two-thirds of the state had been covered in virgin timber. Now it was 20 percent and dwindling. If the workers wanted syndicalism, they ought hurry while there was something left to syndicate. In five years, he'd as soon give them the mill. He'd hand over the key himself. A moderate, Randolph loved republican government and election of the wise, hated internationalism, was suspicious of Jews though he considered Cardozo a good acquaintance. He gave openhandedly and endowed professorships at his middle son's alma mater, the University of Chicago, though he had been sullen for the months when the boy chose it over Yale, the first of many disappointments his sons would inflict upon him—gambling debts, an unhealthy love of horseflesh, attempted suicide. He was faithful and loving to his wife. He believed government should provide a pension for aged war widows and that democratic capitalism was the most efficient and just way of organizing society, in line with Christian principle, and this was important to him, though he was a rare attendee at service. He was known to give the odd hardworking boy of obscure family a hand up. His daughter's wedding had five thousand Wellfleet oysters delivered on special refrigerated cars, and he loved her more than life itself. He thought communists, socialists, and anarchists should be tried for treason and, if convicted in a fair trial, be subject to capital punishment. Trade unionists were, for the most part, merely misled and suffering the typical human temptation of laziness. When Louis Lingg cried, "I hate your state, kill me for it," Randolph wished he could have been judge on that bench. He would have said, "All right." So droll. He loved telling this at parties. Randolph was a stranger to doubt. Many mistook his simplicity for wisdom.

Yet he would have been stunned to learn that any particular man wanted to kill him. Stunned, unbelieving, then proud. Any threat, real or imagined, made his pride flare like a coal.

Small-town lawyers harried him now and again. In the *Gazette*'s first issue, one wrote of the absentees, "A poacher who kills a hundred trout is sent to the county jail to sweat out his sins; a man who kills trout for a hundred miles downstream is praised as an entrepreneur." Judge Randolph had the man disbarred.

A vigilante with a badge and a head full of brilliantine knocked on the door. He hobbled in on a bad knee, his clothes spattered with mud, and said good evening.

Randolph dropped a page, which shone through with whiskey-colored light, and set his glass on a tag of linen. It took him a moment to recall the man: one they'd hired, from a respected agency—respected if overpriced. The agency that thus far had failed to move with sufficient alacrity. Randolph had come to use this phrase often.

"You wear that badge," he said. "You don't work for the state."

"We try to keep things official."

"You mean *officious*. Ah, that's a joke. You don't get it. Isn't that badge obtrusive? I should think it would interfere with your work."

"I'll take it off when I go. And tell the others."

"Good."

The vigilante began to tell Randolph that they had attained a list of no fewer than ninety-two names. It made Randolph jump in his chair.

He cried, "You don't cozy up to it. If I learned anything in the war, I learned that. My God, I am shocked at that number and that your agency has let this happen. What are you gawking at? They killed the president, they offered their left hand and shot him with the right—you look at me as if I'm speaking in tongues." Randolph paused, to let the line take effect. "Am I mad? Do you understand English? Should I slow down? Should I enunciate slowly as if speaking to a dumb wop in the market district? Should I speak in declarative sentences? In short commands? Can you answer any of these questions? Am I wasting breath? Yes? No? You are nodding, what does it mean?"

Silverfish were tunneling through ledgers, wreaking the small havoc of their jaws.

"Just complete your job," Randolph said. "That's all I ask of you. I'm tired of seeing your face."

Indeed, Judge Randolph did look tired. The vigilante left the library shaken. He'd expected praise, of course, and inflated his numbers in hopes of this. The housekeeper let him out onto Rose Street.

Randolph was upset, but not as upset as he made himself out to be. He ran a forefinger down the quality paper. The ledgers were printed on the very pulp whose destruction they recorded. It would last not forever but for a good time, generations beyond him, he knew. His name would be remembered. He would endow this new city; he would be its Carnegie. In time, statues and universities would be raised to him, but that, well, that was out of his hands. Tonight, the binding crackled under his touch. His finger whispered on parchment till he saw a fast animal slither under the pages. He reached out and crunched it with his glass, leaving a mashed body and a ring of amber on the pages. Silverfish, quick as hell-bent mercury. Ink blurred and ran, and he tossed his glass across the room. It didn't break. It fell solid to the floor. I'm not angry, he told himself. I'm not angry, I'm disappointed.

Why doesn't jurisprudence satisfy him? Why do his partners answer only one letter in three? Why don't his sons measure up? Don't they understand the world doesn't owe you a pin?

WALKING BY THE METHODIST PARSONAGE at night, passersby saw Luke Seldomridge was book rich. How does a man acquire so much paper? In the light of oil lamps, in high windows, shelves gleamed with promise. Volumes spanned wall to wall. Some behind glass, like treasures, bound in the skins of various animals. Even when the people of Helena thought him addled, they accorded him a certain respect—not just as a minister of God's word, but as a learned man, with access to other worlds, if he had a mind to reach up and pull them off the wall. But he had grown tired of books and the fossil lives contained inside them.

He was having a dialogue with the dead boy he had buried the night before. That rope around your neck. Ripped ear. Bloated tongue. The black slivers of blood between teeth and gums. Your longish blond hair. You look nothing like your brother. Bothered as he was, Seldomridge didn't even hear the revel of the loggers outside, their second night in town. He recalled the hangings of old, when the sheriff stepped aside and let the mob have their way. He had buried more than a few in his plot of earth.

At least the peddler's dog was here to roll on the hooked rug and keep company. Outside, wind thrashed the thorny apple tree as if to punish it. The cold was too needling for September. Seldomridge hadn't bought cord one of wood. The sight of the books on the wall made him sick.

It was fun, ripping the pages. It made a stale cloud of dust, and first he fed the fire concordances and Emerson's lectures. The leather leaked a green smoke he would taste on the roof of his mouth for days to come. Next, the collected sermons of fools, hot-burning pamphlets, and Russian novels thick enough to stop bullets. A distillation. He craved empty shelves, clean of dust and sour pages. Perhaps this was the next turn. He thought of the land, the earth's old rucked skin. His church would be shaken off like a mite, if he didn't take care, and maybe even if he did. Time had come for him, exposing all with its grinding slow annihilations. The onionskin pages he tore out by the fistful. Erudition comes from books, but knowledge is harder won. Mustn't a preacher expand his conception of time, as well as his flock's, and think of his future and beyond that, beyond these brittle buildings? Toward a geologic sense of what's to come—he once read Sir Lyell's *Principles* and found much to admire there. He had wallowed too much in the thin muck of his immediate past, like a hellbender in its slime, where his killed sisters lived, where he walked a hayfield that he sold.

I failed you, he told the dead man. I failed you. The dead man touched the rope with his fingers and said, Yes, you did. Who am I?

Sometimes at night, Seldomridge walked the railroad track, stepping aside only when the eye of the electric light was a white and shivering wall. The brakeman saw him. The red lantern quit swinging in his hand. The brakeman knew it was the headless ghost that haunted the place—for eternity he toted his glowing head in his arms. If you speak to him, he talks back from his open neck. There is a spill of blood down his shirt. Everyone the brakeman told believed.

The dog, raking its claws on the rug, looked up. Without knocking, the peddler Lis Grayab entered the parsonage as Seldomridge used a ragged shirt to open the potbelly stove. He tossed *Quo Vadis* and a stack of Bibles into the fire.

Grayab leapt forward and plucked them out bare-handed and slapped the books against his chest. The cinders died but left singed places on the edge. He cried, "You in this country are spoiled. I knew no one who had books in the home."

"There is no magic there. A little glue. A little hide."

"Listen, I will sell them. I leave tomorrow. I will give you a percentage."

"Well, that's fine. All I ask is that you don't sell them to plain fools."

"You do not choose your customers. A man in your trade knows this."

But you do.

Grayab took out a slight pair of scissors and excised the burned places. The same pair he used to trim nails and hair. The dog, ignored, milled about his boots.

"I bury bodies and speak to empty heads. That's no respectable trade."

Grayab didn't understand. Seldomridge told him of the night before, and the Italians bringing a body to him with a rope about the neck. Was it his place to bury the man? Should he have spoken to a priest? Waited for the light of day? Consulted the police?

"You do not care about that," said Grayab. "There is something else."

"I'm not sure he is who they say."

"Ah." Now Grayab understood. Party to a crime, real or imagined. Grayab said he would find out what he could, but he said it without vigor. He didn't look forward to the task.

"I would appreciate your help. I've not had a stranger night."

A weird thing, Grayab agreed. He noticed a tremor in the preacher's hand. He said, "Perhaps it is best to leave it alone."

"I can't imagine that to be the case."

"Fine. I tried."

"I'll pay you for your troubles," said Seldomridge.

Grayab waved that off, but of course he'd take the dollars. He had paid off his passage debt, but it had addicted him to the ways of commerce. He'd do anything. And when Seldomridge had a mind to know something, you couldn't shake him. He was stubborn as a vise.

"Perhaps I should ask the congregation what to do."

Grayab cringed. He thought, Oh Lord, do not do that. So he said as much.

They sat awhile. Seldomridge toyed with the dog. Grayab trimmed the blackened pages. He couldn't have imagined this life a decade ago, when he looked west across endless ocean swells and thought of tossing himself overboard. Grayab hated about his own church that it denied a suicide a Christian burial, though he understood the sound theology behind it. Grayab had forgotten that long-ago feeling of wanting to embrace nothingness—he had felt it before. He could admit such to Seldomridge, but this was not the proper time. It would mean shattering this calm with an ax.

Grayab could not know of the hateful silence God had inflicted upon his friend. Especially when enjoying a silence such as this one, so loving and benign.

Even the most pleasing time must end—a person often craves it. The dog was scratching at the door.

Grayab offered to take it, but Seldomridge waved him off and stepped outside. Now Grayab weighed the books in hand, figuring if they'd be too burdensome to carry up to Blackpine. Books were hard to figure. They sold immediately or not at all. He'd left many to rot in the woods. He went out on the porch and slumped in the rocker, but not before placing tobacco on the rail as an offering, as Seldomridge so loved the rich smoke. Grayab's talk of narghile pipes at the Souk al-Hamidiyeh, spread by the dozen upon worn rugs, could make the pastor giddy. Grayab dreamt of bringing one to his friend. His family had a witless young neighbor, Michael Shaheen, who returned from Upper America—the only one ever to come back. Shaheen just didn't like that place. He had pined for the air's dry bite, the mulberry rows, arrow true. Then a regiment of Asakir-i Mansure-i Muhammediye appeared and called the people outside. The soldiers staked Michael down and marched over his back for an hour—he had left their land to escape conscription and was daft enough to return. The Ottoman Army needed troops to put down a Druze uprising in some far place. "Let the blackies fight," Grayab's father said as his mother wept. "Or the French." So in 1891, Grayab boarded the wretched Greek steamship. He'd never thought of the ocean before, merely assuming its existence in the abstract, as one thinks of hell. He tried to perceive the slight curve to the earth's blue horizon and honestly could not. He put a leg over the rail. A sailor shrieked and dragged him back and locked him in the captain's room.

Seldomridge returned from the old salt lick, where the animal had crouched to shit. The pup kept teething at his shirt, so he popped a thumb into its mouth and ran it along the pink roof. It made the dog sneeze. Seldomridge grinned at the tobacco on the rail—that secret habit kept from his parishioners—and Grayab stood to take the pup in his arms, crying out, "My, Luke! He's better fed than you." Grayab made funny faces at it, and the dog whipped its tail against him.

Seldomridge opened the parsonage door and tossed the tobacco in. His face was as harsh as a woodcut in this light. "It may be time to leave the ministry. The bishop, God knows, wants me to."

Grayab was about to nod in agreement but remembered his friend's face made him look decades older than he actually was. "You are too young for that." But living alone aged you so.

"Oh, not so young. I've preached the Gospel four decades now. That is a long time for any man. Too long. They need a new voice. In the humane old days, they burned you alive or threw you to the lions. You were ended at your peak. You never faced the loss of your powers."

"It is hateful to hear you speak of yourself in such a way."

Seldomridge's wan smile fell. "I joke…"

"No. It is beyond heinous."

"Forgive me. I've only lived one way. It's hard to imagine another."

For a fleeting moment, Grayab thought of shedding his peddler's pack, asking Seldomridge to partner in a store. This was silly, but for a moment he was in thrall to his desires. He had a plan written on butcher paper, a sort of charm. 1908—OPEN STORE (OR BUY INTO ONE), 1910—WRITE HOME FOR HER, 1911—MARRY WIFE, 1912—FIRST BORN, 1913—SECOND BORN.

"Here," Seldomridge told him. "Follow me."

The pup trailing at their heels, Grayab was surprised to be led out to the tiny barn where Seldomridge kept his lacquered surrey. Seldomridge had long offered to sell him the unused rig that was growing weeds about its wheels—yes, someday Grayab would rise and ride and grow himself a paunch. Under a thin coat of dust, the surrey still was a handsome cart, the black body trimmed with hunter-green wheels, the springs kept immaculate with grease. Too fine for a peddler's rig, but Grayab pined for it just the same—the wheels so balanced, so smooth of spoke. Compared with the genteel squalor of the parsonage, it was a miracle. They had concluded that fifty-five dollars was a fair price, paid in lump. Then there was the matter of horses.

"I don't have the money." Grayab had twenty-nine dollars and twenty cents laid away. There was a long winter ahead to walk.

"Take it."

"Eh?"

"I don't want it. Where do I go?"

"I have no horse," said Grayab.

"When you have horses, it's yours. Why not buy them cheap from the Company? Sometimes McBride sells off draft. Most are broken, but if you have an eye for flesh, you can find sound ones on occasion, enough to pull a small cart, if nothing else. Do you know horses?"

"No," Grayab cried with joy, "I know nothing!" Untrue. He knew Seldomridge needed any scrap of money to survive. The surrey was his last possession of any material value.

"We'll go together. If you can scrape together some dollars, per-haps you can buy a pair. Even if they're old, the division of labor will make the burden light upon them. I was a farmer. I suspect horses, unlike all else, haven't changed so much."

Before he left, Grayab beamed and poured his praise. Which Seldomridge ignored.

"Farewell. I will find out about that boy for you. I will learn who he was." Grayab turned to go.

"It isn't about that." But of course it was. Seldomridge still knew the human heart.

THE CLERKS WORKED THROUGH A SUNDAY on payday week-ends, even if it was a sin. Mr. Colum, boss of the office pool, im-plied there was a choice, but there wasn't. Especially for Zala. A toad of a man, Mr. Colum watched her closely. Some said Sally Cove was a female doctor, an abortionist. She had been seen on the East Bank—it was never said by whom.

But even Mr. Colum had to slip out of the railroad office to take his lunch. His room was left unlocked. Zala brought the ledger to her desk, obscured it as best she could with loose papers and an adding machine, and tried to copy a thousand names for the Woodworkers.

> NILE C. POSTHLEWAIT, $2/DAY, CAMP 2
> (MRH. 1896–JN. 1900) CAMP 7 (JN. 1900–), SAWYER.
> LAVEN TETER, $1.35/DAY, CAMP 3 (FEB. 1902–),
> KNOTBUMPER, DISSOLUTE.
> SALVASTORE CALUSO, $1.25/DAY, DYNAMITE CREW.
> ITALIAN TAG #97. HAS ENGLISH. HURT BADLY.
> JUNE 1900, SEVEN WEEKS ABED, OWES $~~40~~ DOC FEE.
> $~~32.~~ $~~27.~~ $~~6.~~ $2.50.

Every few moments, she clacked out doggerel on the adding machine. She noted who had been cheated, who had been scorned.

Any moment Mr. Colum wasn't there was a happy one for Zala. Five years she had worked here. The day she appeared at her desk, the clerks, all men, thought it was a joke—Mr. Colum had a dry streak. After a matter of hours, they realized she was an actual employee. Then, the following Friday, several in concert made observations about a smell in the office. Finally she realized they were accusing her of not keeping her menstrual rags clean. It was not time, and her periods, when they came, brought piercing headaches, dizziness, and a curiously small amount of blood. She lived through the humiliation of explaining this to Mr. Colum behind closed doors. His cheeks took on a sudden, allergic blotchiness. He stuttered. He said matters would be "set right" and shooed her out. She assumed he was too mild to do anything, a stickman, a neat moustache. In the afternoon, Mr. Colum came in roaring drunk and raked the clerks, while managing never to actually speak of what was going on. He made reference to "certain rumors" and modernization and kicked a wastebasket. It left a dent, an emblem, in the metal for all time. Resigned, the clerks set about ignoring Zala. She ate alone at her desk. She was too attractive. Either they looked through her or casually insulted her as too bony in the face or too heavy round the midsection. Fat men who couldn't push a wheelbarrow up a hill if you offered them a thousand dollars said this. Mr. Colum wanted to promote her but did not.

She felt for them a carbolic burn of pity and disgust. They were pale, frightened, and lamentable when they cast lots to see who'd stand duty in wire cages and distribute pay to the wolves, weather their insults and promises of buggery. The clerks winced to be chosen. They begged for the mesh to be installed. Magnanimously, they assured her she would not have to interact with such roughs. In these moments she laughed in their faces, taking her revenge.

But she was realizing how her beauty allowed her to get away with things: her impacted bitterness, her smirking, her general silence. She was forgiven much, now, but this would change as her hair thinned and grayed and her skin grew coarse. Her obscure bosses would let her go on the smallest of pretexts. Her eccentricities would not be forgiven.

"Who has the paysheets?" a clerk asked, peeping about. "Miss Cove?"

This one always called her *Miss Cove* with acid precision. Zala unearthed the ledger and walked it over. He nodded at the corner of his desk, and she left it there. She felt faint. She focused on a dated calendar on the wall. This copying was for her husband's friend. He had first appeared at her door a year after Victor left for good. He said his name was Neversummer. She wept, and he tried to pat her hand, which set her scowling. "Your name is ridiculous!" she cried. "So you know it's got to be true," he said, and had her there. He called her Zala, not Sally Cove, until she made him stop. He hinted that she would see Victor again and was quietly pleased when Zala said she desired no such thing—though of course it's all she wanted. She stopped crying. She would never cry, never again. She would live in the black rind of her life. He took to bringing friends around, and they drank wine: Italians she didn't know, and Cur-named-for-a-dog, the one she slept with. These men made her happy, from time to time. But they asked much. She didn't want to hurt the soft clerks. She didn't want to give up the key to the office. The strikers wanted to slip in through the back door and make a spectacle. She could not sleep. Three days awake, then four. She couldn't allow what the union wanted. They were the thin chain to her husband. For reasons only Victor could know, he never wanted to see his first wife again. "She just don't get it," Vance would lament to Neversummer. Neversummer didn't much care.

Yawn of clerks. The ceiling smoky from their cigarettes, a yellow haze.

Scribbling, Zala had managed to copy 218 names and their accompanying information and conditions before he called out. She imagined every other clerk was watching her, though they were not. Her hands throbbed something fierce, and she tried to knead the ache out of them.

That night, a fluid-filled cyst ballooned on the underside of her wrist. It looked wretched but didn't hurt. Shaken, she showed it to her walleyed landlady.

"You got you a Bible bump."

"*What?*"

"Not a problem, missy. Lay your arm on the table."

It was the size of a fat acorn. The landlady lifted the Bible— Zala thought the woman was going to pray over the swell—and cracked her wrist. Hard.

Tears stood in the corners of Zala's eyes, but the swelling went down right away. She felt nauseated.

"Got to show it who's boss," the landlady said. "Can't be dainty!"

Zala cringed. The fact that the fluid drained without leaving her body disturbed her.

She crossed town to her friend's room. Wind whistled through the broken window. She lay on the bed. She didn't even take off her shoes. She woke to find two men standing over her. One covered her mouth when she went to shout. But it was gentle, somehow. They smelled of the wood, of brush fires. When Neversummer pulled his hand away, she was smiling.

Vance said, "You got to lock your door, honey. You got to take care."

She was embarrassed, but Vance had brought her a jug of wine and, in a moment, they were joking softly. They got drunk and laughed over some of the funny names. She showed off her blue-black wrist with pride. She handed over the list. They thanked her and even tried to press a little money on her, which of course she would not accept. This was the men's last errand before going back to the camps.

Before they left, Vance gave her a parcel and asked her to open it later. She ripped it open the second the door was closed. She found a slender book of verse with cream pages, bound in blue cloth, embossed in gilt. By Simon Gregorčič. Printed in Ljubljana. She counted the wrinkled dollars that had been smoothed out, soft as felt, and placed among the pages. No note, no dedication, only the money inside, $110: an exact replacement for the money Victor took to Chicago so many years ago. The book was pristine but for a torn flyleaf. Her heart leapt like a trout.

Vance had sensed her uneasiness and made Victor Kovač trickle out this gift to her.

Americans called Victor a Grainer. They mangled it out of his home city, Kranj, and, well, he could never quite master their language. It made her angry to think of—why couldn't he just speak it? So lazy. Any free man can learn a new tongue. And now she knew it had been her own foolishness that gave him the notion to leave. A month into her time at the office, Zala told him pay records showed his bridge crew—foreigners all—made less than the American crew. Far less. He slammed their door off the hinges. He wanted a trade union. Victor's father had been a guildsman, a foundry worker, but her own family was country people, so she knew nothing of politics. She had been so young. She listened when Victor blamed her infertility on the moon, the seasons, the anti-procreative effects of a woman working with ink. Actually this is why he left, she supposed—the other thing was good pretext. In Helena he grew agitated. "You're being robbed!" he shouted at passersby. "Not from your pockets! From your souls!" The Americans chuckled at Victor's street-corner exhortations; the ones who agreed feared deportation. Victor would get drunk, and she'd carry him up the steps: a black time like a lesion on the brain. She never comforted him; she didn't seem to know how. Captain Ketch hinted to him that he would soon be fired—maybe he ought to look elsewhere for work. Victor appeared at Zala's late one night from the camps—they only lived together when he returned for payday. This is the chance, he said. They would assume him dead. She told him to slow down. He explained the fortunate wreck of a little sidewinder train, mangled and blackened with fire. He would leave for Chicago. He'd made a botch of things, yes; he must try again. He would reapply for a position under an assumed name, and Zala would doctor the papers. Victor would return in a year with other agitators. She thrilled. She asked how they would get to Chicago.

"You are not going, dear one," he said. She must mourn, keep up appearances. A widow in name at twenty years old.

Victor took all their money. Every week, she received postcards unsigned. Then once a month. A year passed, and their anniversary. Nothing more. Not a word of greeting, love, or homage.

Still she knew he was a great man.

Zala began to read from this book. *Julian March, The Snared Bird's Lament*—banal, undistinguished verse that could move only a pure native of that land. When she turned page nineteen, a green paper fell. Written upon. 6017 LAUSCHE AVENUE, CLEVELAND, OHIO. DOROTHEA MOORE. It was a laundry slip. For the woman with whom her husband lived.

6017 Lausche. You could find it on any municipal map. Did Victor want her to find him now? He was a laughing ghost. She couldn't believe the laundry slip was just a mistake.

COME MONDAY MORNING, the train would return the timber wolves to the Blackpine camps—that way, the Company didn't have to pay for Sunday supper. With this night, September gave way to October. Sunday evenings held a stillness infused with religious sentiment and the regrets of men who had blown through so much pay. The town looked tattered and so did its people.

A few hours after Zala received the book of verse, Cur arrived at her borrowed room tired, on edge, a red scrim to his eye. She welcomed him without speaking and stepped into the back. A clean tablecloth printed with cornflowers. A pitcher of water, radiating cold. She'd made an effort to clean up, even if she could only hang a bolt of linen over the broken window. Cur wished he had brought her a gift. It was a strange thought, but he couldn't decide why.

Her collar was askew, and he took it in both hands to right it. Afterward, he smoothed her shoulders. "There," he said. "Pretty as a bookplate."

She rolled her eyes, an exotic gesture. He expected her to ask what had happened Friday evening—the gunshots, his running away—after all, she was one of them now. She would put the key in his hand.

Instead, Zala insisted he look over a book a cousin—she'd never mentioned a cousin before—mailed her from Cleveland, saying *Cleveland* as if it were the enchanted kingdom. The book was gibberish, the type misaligned on cheap pages. The glue would never stand up to spring. At first he mistook the diacritical marks for flyspecks—the *strešica*, the little roof.

Zala kept averting her eyes. When Cur tried to touch her, she circled the table. She busied herself making tea. A grating silence: spoon rattling in china.

"What in the hell is the matter with you?"

Zala didn't answer, and Cur took hold of her arm. He saw fear in her eyes and softened.

"I cannot do that," she said.

"What in the hell?"

The key to the office. She would not give it over.

"Well, why not?"

"You will hurt them. The clerks. I know you will. I cannot give it to you."

"We promise humane treatment," he said—trying out a new word. "We won't hurt nobody. We'll let them out. We just want the building. That's all. That's all we want."

"I do not believe you. You do not speak for them all. They will do worse. I know how they will. I can tell by looking at them."

"Listen, Sally."

Cur's eye began to twitch as he tried to impress on her the importance of what she must do, the justice of it. Zala thought, *Only a child believes in a just world. Does he not know that?* It made her seethe. In one another, they had sought replacements for those they truly desired; they lived a cause they thought they believed in, though the path had been gouged by others, and they traveled blindly down. At least, Zala told herself, I am aware of it. She wanted to say, *I have a husband, a living husband, and I cannot divorce and I will not be common and I will not break the laws of the country that harbors me, I will not be deported, I will cease speaking in other tongues forever, I will hold my oath of citizenship, I can only pray my husband dies (I will kill him if I have to) and frees me to find a widower and mother his children*—in her heart she still was Catholic, divorce was beyond her ken—*there are a hundred such men in every town. I do not care to change this earth, I want a meaningless life, I am not cold enough to be radical and neither are you, my friend, no matter what you think, what they tell you, even if you kill a thousand men. This is not your part. These men have stitched you to another's shadow.*

Instead, she told him to leave, and to leave her alone.

"You ought to think of your husband," Cur said. "You're doing this in his memory, and you're letting a good man down. You're failing every good man on that mountainside."

She began to scream. "You do not tell me about him! You know nothing! You know nothing at all!"

"Be quiet." He glanced at the broken window and the cool breeze stirring the linen.

"I will not!"

Cur flung her book against the wall. It splayed like a bat and fell.

"We don't need you," he said. "Sally, we don't need you. We'll get in there one way or another."

"Then leave me be!"

She laughed at him. This made it worse. He was no clerk. His voice rose.

"We won't treat you no different than the others." He could feel the hole open beneath him. "Keep your damned keys. If you tell anyone about this, I'll kill you. I'll kill you, and I won't feel a thing."

He was doing this on his own. He was moving outside himself. He turned and left her.

Stunned, she watched him go. Had she heard him, or had she imagined that? For a moment, she thought he had hit her—she could barely convince herself he had not. Her body tensed, her stomach cramped. She sat on the clean floor and began to retch. Her neighbors heard it all. This would be the talk of the street. She was a common woman, screeching at a man.

Outside, Cur had to pause. He put both hands against a wall, as if rehearsing for his role.

The vigilantes knew all of their secrets except this one: that Zala had a key. She wasn't supposed to have one—Mr. Colum had given it to her out of pity and convenience. The union had this one small advantage.

The next day, Zala pushed her key through the grate of a blazing stove.   .

HOUNDS WHIRLING ABOUT HIS FEET, Captain Ketch of Camp Five watched black men dig holes and strain to upright the creosoted poles—such trash work was reserved for them. More trudged behind, unspooling telegraph wire and crowning it on these false trees, teetering on homemade ladders. This would change things. For better or worse, he did not know. This Monday morning, bringing his workers back to him where they belonged, the train snuffled as it took the 9-percent hairpin at Big Lime, then screamed on down. Heat blur and the dark engine shimmering satin in its molten eye. The black men jumped clear of the cowcatcher at the last possible second, the engineer piping and shaking his fist. McBride cheered them for their salt.

The captain's head count came up light. Vance and Amos Church were not aboard.

For the first time in Cur's recollection, Neversummer slacked off. He barely nocked his saw, let it grow dull, cut listlessly. By afternoon, they'd downed only four of the pines the natives call Canaan fir.

Cur said, "Stop. Just stop. You're worse than worthless."

"I'll have to take over. See it coming on. He's done for."

"What?"

"Vance didn't come back. He stayed in town. They'll fire him. Company won't stand for that."

Cur didn't know what to say.

Vance Church was walking Helena, sticking his head in every door, asking after his son. Hotels, funeral parlors, jail cells. He had one weakness. The world had found it.

"Nobody knows yet. I'll need you to help me smooth it over. He might be gone for good. We got to plan for that. Plan for the worst could be."

Cur said, "He can still be in on this."

"Won't be the same. I bet he cuts out if he don't find Amos."

"You think?"

"I don't know. Let's talk to Caspani. Soon as we can, let's talk to him."

"He's over on Sand Mountain. That's a bastardy walk."

"We'll slip on over."

"You're the boss…"

"Don't call me that."

Cur tried to keep his voice calm and coaxing. "Hell, I think you'd run it better."

"Well, I thank you."

"Needed saying."

But Cur could only think of the bad moment when the others learned Vance was gone, had given up on them in favor of blood. They would be cowering in the caves in nervous meeting. Everyone looking at Neversummer, yawning and dabbing eyes with their palms. Neversummer wasn't the talker Vance was. He was a good man, fair minded, but he couldn't hide his true feelings. The others would pick up on his despair. The falling apart would begin there. The union men would leave the warmish air of the cave and cinch their scarves against the flesh-stripping wind. The boulder field would sparkle with frost. Cur dreaded it: the laying of bad news at the feet of your friends, as a dog delivers the prize rooster it's killed.

He missed Amos again. Cur, who would dither, told himself that Amos had to define himself in opposition to another. It just happened to be Cur. All was forgiven.

Neversummer picked up his saw, feeling the teeth with his thumb. "I really let this son-of-a-bitch go," he said. "Couldn't cut paper. Couldn't cut dog shit."

"I need to tell you about Sally."

"Godamighty. What now?"

Cur told him they would have no key to the offices. Neversummer thought awhile. They had rifles. The key wasn't necessary, but it bothered him just the same. He said, "Is it funny to you all this went to drizzling shit soon as Amos cleared out? I can't get past it. I really can't."

CLUTCHING HANDKERCHIEFS OVER their noses, the vigilantes poured cartons of quicklime on Vance's body.

SOME PLACES THRIVE ON TEXTILES, money-lending, or coal; Blackpine's true economy was rumor. Some said Vance hopped a freight to Youngstown, or the Mesabi Iron Range, or the mines of McDowell. His son lucked into a gambling score, and they left town, fearing for their lives. Or it was over a woman, or women. Most said Vance and Amos had stolen money from the union— that was easy enough to believe. More knew about the union than anyone realized: a man had nothing to do here but talk, and some were flummoxed as to why they hadn't been asked to join in this, whether willing or not. Pride kept them from asking. Regardless, Vance was gone.

As soon as they could manage to, Cur and Neversummer stashed saw and wedges in a hollow sycamore and walked the grade, casting wary looks behind. They passed mile marker 112, where the rails made a loop and the track beyond was yet to be hammered into existence. Unlined ties shimmered with fresh creosote, and incautious bottle flies stuck there like twitching sapphires. Mount Sand hunched in the distance. It had gray chimney-tops of rock. The forest intact. It was good to see a fresh mountain, even if it meant months of labor to turn it brown. But first, Italians had to punch a tunnel through and run a new line of rails. Figures climbed about the base, about three hundred yards off.

"Fierce looking peak," Neversummer said.

"'Deed it is. Be there before you know it." That mountain, claimed Cur, would grieve mothers.

Hand over his eyes, one of the Italians peered down the track at them and waved with a raw stick of dynamite. Neversummer waved back, not realizing the man was trying to warn them. Cur tossed himself into a stand of rhododendrons.

The mountain shrugged and shed rock in galloping dusty waves. Handfuls of grit and sand pelted Neversummer's face. He dropped to one knee. A stone the size of a crock wheeled overhead, and shock waves ripped through.

When all was still, Neversummer touched his brow and brought back a splotch of blood like enamel paint. It broke and lined his hands in a red cross-hatching. The bright hymn of tinnitus hummed in his ears.

"Motherfuck," said Cur.

A sliver of rock had only notched Neversummer's brow, but it was enough to rattle him. He went to the branch and laved water into his eyes, which had gone a violent color.

Italians rose from under horse blankets, their hair and arms dusty. Two more approached alongside Caspani. Knees winked through cloth. They wore suspenders and riveted waist overalls but went shirtless underneath. They carried the neutral smell of ash.

Cur nodded over to Neversummer splashing in the branch. "Now you done it," he said. "That's all it took. He's going to be wound tight. Just like a bird dog."

Rueful, Caspani wagged a finger in the air. "Good to be jumpy. Good!"

"You could have warned me," called Neversummer.

"I tried."

Caspani tossed him a shine jar of lard and honey. Neversummer unscrewed the two-piece lid. He took a finger of the stuff and staunched his brow.

Caspani said he had a surprise for them, and Neversummer smiled, despite his cut.

Cur looked at the other Italians. One he recognized from the meetinghouse, Salvastore Caluso. The Americans called him Sally, which he hated, and McBride in particular had named him Yellow Sally, after a stonefly that hatches off the Cheat. He hated that even more.

Another Italian here was D'Andrea, one of the union's betrayers. He never said much. At some point, D'Andrea had gone without oxygen in the mines. His skin was tarnished a strange bluish cast, like a skink's tail. He'd mined coal in Canaan Valley, and in three years' time, having taken the money he earned informing on the union, he would return to that way of life and die at Monongah, killed when the pocket of firedamp sparked. The operators' official dead list tallied 362. In fact, 900 workers were killed.

The syncopated ring of hammers returned, driving hand drills into the rock.

"This is man's work, ain't it?" Cur was tired of trees.

A few squirrels were barking at the explosion. Neversummer drew a book from his jacket, one he'd bummed off Cur—a Jesse James novel with a torn cover—and handed it over. Cur hated to see it go, remembering a character he liked. Caspani cut the book, quietly showed the dollars inside to D'Andrea, and clapped it shut. It was money owed for the safehouse. D'Andrea smiled, showing off a roan tooth.

Caspani said, "I have more fixings for you."

He meant explosives, and Neversummer was pleased to hear that: good news, finally. He asked, "When do I get them?"

"Next time we go to town."

Neversummer casually whittled a branch. He called Cur over. In the sand, he diagrammed fuses, detonator caps, the workings of the cartridge, the ingredients for cordite, and wire that burned at how many minutes per how many yards. He made Cur repeat each fact back to him three times before moving on. The pamphlets had been burned. Caspani watched, admiring, murmuring yes now and again. A swallowtail flew past in jerks.

After this lesson was over, Caspani said, "That is exactly how it is done. Perhaps you should be working here."

Finally, Neversummer said to Caspani, "I would tell you that Vance is gone off, but I bet you know it. You always seem to know things."

Caspani was grim and mock-indignant. But yes, he knew.

"Well," Neversummer asked him, "what do you think?"

"I cannot see him just up and leaving. Perhaps he was arrested. What of it? You look surprised. We must consider the possibility."

"I don't see it that way. People don't just get took in and you don't hear of it…"

"What about Amos? Did he fly away on the wild goose? We have all been followed. Who knows? Perhaps the Churches have been killed—it would explain much. For us, they will be martyrs. Every movement needs such. We should strike the very next time we're in town. Why wait till November? I do not see how that helps our cause. We should rip off the bandage. Let the scales fall from everyone's eyes."

Neversummer grew agitated. "Maybe you should run this damned thing."

"No," said Caspani, "I am not an American. I cannot lead them as you can."

"I know you was close to Vance. I hope you stick with us through this thing. Tell your people that. I don't care what you hear, we respect you all. A blind man could see that. We appreciate you." Neversummer was trying to tease something out of Caspani. It flummoxed him that the man—so radical, so proud—hadn't made a play for power. Was this so sour no man would want it? "If I wasn't around," said Neversummer, "they'd fall in behind you."

Caspani demurred. He took Neversummer's hand. "Do not worry, Asa. We are going to succeed. This we can agree upon. We cannot waste our time. I urge you to move with speed." When Caspani tried to look serious, eyes pursed, skull flat, he had the look of a predatory bird. He was a better-looking man when he didn't try.

Caspani would return to where he was from, the journey he began months ago. His mother's hair gone so gray and brittle it broke off in fistfuls. The blue aching sky. The mud cracking with heat. The Laurel Parade. The laughing girls and brown ankles in the surf. Smallish dogs and ugly shops.

Neversummer and Cur walked away, not so sure, not so confident. Neversummer didn't go in much for that popish martyr bullshit. He said, "I'd rather keep my own hide."

"Do you really think somebody killed Vance?"

"Hell no. Caspani's gone a mite crazy."

"Stranger's happened."

"I don't know about that."

THESE DAYS—THESE WEEKS—had a weird weather to them. McBride noted Cur was changing: sullen, slow with a joke. On the cuttings, Cur saw the same in Neversummer. Hard, mercenary, level. That stern morality. His brain crackled like a hornet's nest. Cur felt pulled between the two older men. For McBride, life was easy and gay, a time to brawl and joke, eat and fuck until the earth shucked you out. Sitting at the table, filling his belly, Cur realized that if he took his own father and split him like a rock along his planes, you would come up with McBride and Neversummer. Even here, he couldn't escape Old Neil.

He lay in his bunk, waiting to be arrested. For what? Who knows? They always come up with something. One time, at a house party, Constable Green told him, "We never get you for the worst thing you done. We get you on the piddling stuff."

At least the air held a pleasing chill. September had been sweat and yellowjackets, but October was a cool breath off the Alleghenies. It dried the coats of horses to salty waves. But back in hateful September, Captain Ketch had made boys clear deadfalls off the grade for two hundred feet on either side, fearing stray cinders from passing engines. New policy, he had announced at supper. Fire like that could put us all on the corner. Send up ten thousand acres in a wink, no doubt. Captain Ketch felt guilty, slightly. But quota was all. He hazed them on. The sight of a man who had worked his hands to bleed satisfied the captain. So the boys wrapped bandannas around their mouths to strain dust, pollen, flying ants. A cruel month. Three lads nearly died of heatstroke. One twisted an ankle ink-blue, another lost his finger to a rattlesnake. Captain Ketch felt so bad he gave the boys a quarter out of the coffers for every dozen rattlers and copperheads. Camp Eight held the record, more than seven hundred killed off Spruce Knob. Dale Keough swallowed a fresh-killed rattlesnake's heart, claiming it would make him brave. Keough, a new convert, whispered he was ready to have a rifle in hand, and Cur shushed him. Cur had come to like Keough but worried over what people claimed: he was like a catfish, all mouth, no brains. Silence was hard to teach to laughing men. Especially when the cool made them feel so talkative and good. There were fewer snakes. Captain Ketch gave out no coins, but no one cared.

In the fat middle of October, they received two days of rain. At day's end, Cur held his hand up to the wind, welcoming the change. He could feel it in his muscle, a cool medicine throb in the welted star where his aunt had pried out buckshot. If there still had been aspen trees on the ridge, wind and light would have played their leaves like silver coins.

McBride was watching Cur, who held up his arm like a man hailing a train. McBride peered down the grade. "Who you waving at?"

Cur kept his hand upraised. "The wind," he said.

"This place has turned you woods-queer. I expect I'll suffer the same."

Laughing, Cur dropped his arm. He didn't spend as much time with McBride as he used to and savored these moments. Cur said, "You got to get into town now and again. I had a aunt go woods-queer. Lived on the head of Shaver's Fork, where you don't see the sun for days of winter. Tried to cut the tails off her pigs with a carving knife."

"Did she think tails was a sign of the devil? Heard Hessians bob a pig's tail."

"I don't know." Cur fished a bootlace out of his pocket and held it up so McBride could see. It had seventeen knots in it. He ticked off a few, as you would the beads on an abacus.

"Too long to payday," Cur said. "Got us some time yet. Wednesday it is."

"Bah! No use counting. They'll tell us when to quit."

There were serious timber wolves who didn't keep track of their days, as rich men let gold dollars roll loose in any old drawer. Cur couldn't understand it. He tucked the bootlace away in his pocket. It reminded McBride of the way a midwife he knew had murmured the five decades, the mysteries, though his own mother said a person needed no other device but two clasped hands and a little humility for God to hear you. McBride reckoned either way fine—that is, hopeless.

"There's something the matter with you," said McBride. "Has been for weeks."

Cur panicked a little until McBride told him, "Your poor circulation has put you in the distemper. You got to give it priority. Watch me now." McBride jumped up, did a handstand to get his blood moving. His hat fell off. Cur laughed.

But McBride did know. There was agitation in the air. A tic in his blood told him the disturbance was coming. In his years here he had not felt a season like this. He wouldn't mind a break from the horses for whatever reason, but after a day or two of strike, he knew he'd miss them, as after a payday. It would take a day or two, then it would end. As such enterprises do in this country. He felt badly for his friends. He reckoned everyone gets to fail in their own particular way.

Then a voice calling one, calling all. They had stayed close to Camp Five that day.

"You hear the captain," said McBride, falling out of his handstand. "Time for pitchers."

A photographer from *Harper's Weekly* magazine had followed them a few days' time, to record images for a human-interest story on Senator Helena's achievements as a businessman. Captain Ketch gruffly advised everyone to ignore the bastard the best they could, so of course they obsessed over the photographer's whereabouts. They promised him the biggest trees and feats of strength and slipped him twists of candy and helped him set up his box.

First, the photographer worked with McBride; hands on the bit, the stolid teamsters in suspenders and handlebar moustaches lined up and stood by Belgian Shires and Percherons that gleamed in the sun like oiled gunmetal. McBride, their doyen, stood in front. All Camp Five was to appear. It took some strategizing. Now the photographer posed the cook's helpers in a huge felling notch that grinned out of a grandfather like a trap. For weeks, secretly thrilled, Captain Ketch had been saving back the hulking spruce, calling it the President Roosevelt.

"Oh yes, this will give us perspective," the photographer said of the tree, which rose alone from the slash. "We might feature it on the cover. This will give us perspective!"

The cook's helpers sat in the notch with honest smiles, legs dangling, straightening one another's clothes. The tree was seven feet across, even this far above the level ground.

Captain Ketch told him to hurry, saying, "This thing looks to give with the next sound wind." He sidled up to the President Roosevelt, slapping it with his hand to test the give. Now Captain Ketch wanted his favorites in a prominent place, shooing Cur and Neversummer ahead like nervous hens. They were made to lean rakishly against the trunk with felling axes. The rest of the sawyers formed up in rows, crosscuts bent whapping over their shoulders in silver arcs. They had scrubbed faces red with lye and built neckties from a flayed pair of pants, as McBride had taught them the tricky four-in-hand knot with a rabbit that runs round the tree. Early pignuts fell in a way that alarmed the photographer. He made a blushing John Whitehill hold an umbrella over the camera box. The photographer bent above his machine, tweaking the men into existence. The sawyers had seen old-time cameras that flashed like flintlock rifles and were quietly astonished at how this machine worked in silence, gestating its magic.

The photograph took fourteen minutes. Cur flinched, knocking his eyes slightly out of plumb. He was a handsome man, with a strong honest face women liked, despite his teeth, and it was a shame the one picture taken during his good-looking years didn't do him justice.

The photographer considered jotting down their names but ultimately didn't bother.

When he said they could move, Cur's neck prickled with feeling—it's hard to stand still, he discovered, having never been posed before. He rolled his neck. And began to fret. What if someone in Cumberland, Maryland, held a subscription? As he hadn't in years, he thought of the policeman, who wore the bloody knife like a carnation. It was so long ago.

Would Sarah Greathouse see a copy? A silly thought he couldn't resist.

Working the kink from his shoulders, Neversummer regretted the picture for other reasons as soon as it was taken—the curious world had him preserved in its amber. The lapse would haunt him for years, even into the mines of Logan County. When Cur told him, later, it had been a mistake, Neversummer grew angry and said he had nothing to hide. "I'm tired of crawling around in the maggoty dark," he said. "I want to do something."

When the platinotype was developed—paper slipping into a cold bath of ferric chemicals and potassium chlorate—the cook's helpers and the teamsters, Neversummer and the sawyers rose up in the liquid true to life, but a smudge of morning light made Cur a silver ghost. The photographer lamented that, because the big spruce looked fabulous with its felling notch. The cook's helpers seemed in true danger. By the time it smiled through the solution, the President Roosevelt had been diced into thousands of barrel staves. Due to the flaw, the image would never make the magazine and lived among the photographer's files for thirty-two years— not that it mattered much, because *Harper's Weekly* canceled the story about Senator Helena, needing space to feature the opening of the New York subway and the aftermath of the Russo-Japanese War. When the photographer died, his nephew shoveled the files into a dustbin.

THE OLD FOREST was being ground down with increasing speed, as if trees could outrun the Company. Even the timber wolves commented on it, bashful now. Someday they must run out of land. Their labor, they reckoned, was maybe a shame. Yet they worked harder, and Captain Ketch never let up. As the wolves hung their own laundry like washerwomen, they saw themselves implicated in each clothespin. The wood clean of grain and smooth in hand. They were satisfying desire writ large. They hurried on wash day, slapping clothes on the rocks of the Cheat as if to kill them. They were not ignorant men, no matter what the world thought of them, if it thought of them at all.

GRAYAB HAD BEEN LOST a day now, a ridge farther than he ought to be. Every mean plant hummed with threat. He rubbed a Saint Sophia medal for luck. His hound made roving loops, sometimes ahead of him, sometimes behind. It had grown so much in the month or so since he took it back from Seldomridge. It could even run off and tree a coon. This skill rendered the hound more valuable, but Grayab was growing dangerously attached to it— dangerous because he still meant to sell it. He couldn't allow himself to be this sentimental.

Though he made money in the camps, Grayab still hated going there, to suffer the abuse of the captains. Worse, in the eyes of some wolves, he saw them wondering how much money he had in his pockets.

This was a forgotten trace, cut by deer and buffalo. An old place, where the sound of metal still was strange. The world was an unearthly green. The trail braided with a branch of Mare Creek, where trout turned knife-bright in the current. When Grayab first came to the Glen Elk warehouse—his only words of English being *Good day* and *Would you like to buy something?* and the narrow jargon of dollars and cents—his cousin Thomas said if he ever found himself lost in the mountains, go downhill and find a road or a river that led to a road. Yet this trail angled up, away from water. Going downhill meant wading through a slick laurel hell. Grayab stayed on the trail, stooping under a wicker pack crammed with bedsheets and candles, silverware and china, scissors and thread. He had lashed a yellow oilskin over it and could hear the chattering wares. Another handful of dollars, he'd have his team. Grayab kissed the medal and slipped it away. His mouth was dry and puckered, as if he'd tried to swallow a handful of salt. All he'd eaten today was a salad of young fiddlehead ferns. Deer tracks chopped the ground around a chain of puddles in the trail. The water shimmered, holding a poor reflection of the forest around. Tadpoles darted, tails whipping, clouds of them. He stopped at the first pool that looked reasonably clear and leaned his pack against a tree—his jacket was glossy where the straps of the harness had rubbed. He soaked a bandanna and sucked water from the cloth. A centipede slithered in a cup of leaves, its body shiny and purple-black like a busted eye. Grayab shivered. At least snakes wore faces. He pissed on the centipede and made it go wild. Satisfied, he shouldered the pack and waded in ferns up to his thighs. No one had walked the trail this year, and he had to crush weeds with his boots, sending up an acrid smell. The ground steamed, and within an hour he was soaked to the skin. Pants sodden, cuffs slapping a miserable cadence against his boots. The air nettled him more than anything: a second skin of grease. His boyhood had been drum tight and dry with heat, the sky wide, a violent blue etched with date palms. Entering the gates of this country, a doctor had checked his gums and, seeing they were pink, waved him on. The last document he ever signed was on that stone island, where he was recorded a subject of the Sultan of Turkey, whatever that meant now. A square of paper had burned in his pocket: RAHALL, MILLER STREET, CONNELLSVILLE, PENNSYLVANIA. Syrians had taken to riding the spine of the mountains down to the very tip of the tail if they had to, where trade suited them, ranging fifty or one hundred miles. Rhododendrons brushed his face, the blooms rotten and liquor sweet. Spiderwebs shone and sagged with dew. He cleared them with his walking stick and passed a place where a bear had rolled in a stand of bushes, its shit full of berry seeds and studded with flies. Finally he made the ridge.

A train whistled. Grayab caught his hound, tethered it to a tree with a strip of leather, and eased downhill, taking each step with care. He didn't want the camp dogs to attack it.

There, the C&O filled its boiler from a wooden water tower, and three crewmen slung themselves out and pissed in a row. Once the train rounded the bend, Grayab stepped onto the grade. In either direction, there'd be a tin mile marker to show him the way. The sun came out and made Grayab's shadow its dial. He walked upriver, picking over the ties with his stick.

His ear caught an angry sound, like ten hornets in a wine bottle. The rattlesnake was a coil of greater darkness in the shadow of a tie, its black head nocked like an arrow. Grayab stabbed, and the snake whipped about the walking stick and shuddered. With all his weight, Grayab screwed the stick until it split the skull, found gravel below. The body went slack. He lifted it to the light. Green-checked skin drained into a dusky black near the tail. He draped it over a dime-bright tie, and the body squirmed with the suggestion of life. He counted: five and a half years old. Grayab flicked out his penknife—the bone gave with a snip—and took the rattle. He shook it with his hand, testing the paper-thin contraption tagged to the tail like God's own afterthought. His third that spring: the last one, thick as a bicep, had a rattle six inches long. They loved to curl on sunny metal. He left its body there, a bleeding rope, so the train could dice it again, and tucked the rattle into his shirt, where it lined his breast pocket with blood.

Minutes later, McBride noted that the figure in the distance favored his right leg. Captain Ketch's dogs rushed to meet the peddler.

Grayab cried out. He tagged one on the flank with his walking stick. It returned hobbling and cowered under the porch, trying to shake the pain out of itself.

The cook's helpers collared hounds and popped them on the

skull. A dozen men came out to greet the Syrian like a flock of chickens will. Their off-Sunday in camp.

"Yes, I sharpen knives. Yes, Square and Navy Snuff, I think I have a bag of Drum. Playing cards? I have some with ladies on them."

Now this was excitement. Some called him Chief, assuming him an Indian. Grayab eased his wicker pack onto the porch. He pulled back the oilskin and unlatched the cover, revealing his wares, which were wedged meticulously together like a jigsaw puzzle. Without the pack, his body filled with a floating sensation. Grayab nursed his shoulder.

McBride said, "Upon my honor, you had to carry two hundred pound easy."

"And I am feeling each one of them."

"That's near two hods of brick! You're a wiry little fucker, ain't you?"

McBride handed him a dollar, and Grayab passed back a twisted bundle of cloth. Grayab's tongue darted into his cheek. "I saved that special for you," he said.

"Appreciate that."

"What's that?" Cur asked.

McBride untied the bundle and showed Cur and Bull Aberegg. Five tasseled roots, each one shaped like a little man—arms, legs, head. "Ginseng," McBride said. "Chinamen use it to make themselves right with Chinawomen."

"It shall make you stiff as a wrecking bar," Grayab said, making a lurid motion with his hand. "It could get painful." The Syrian talked like this in the camps.

"I'm a old man," McBride said. "Takes more than a fat ass to put the get into me."

"That's our Vaughn!" Aberegg cried. "He'd fuck a alligator if you hold its mouth shut."

Laughter and others swarming out the bunkhouses. Out of the corner of an eye Grayab regarded Cur, recalling him from that September night in front of the Methodist parsonage.

"You got any more of that, Chief?" someone called. He meant the ginseng.

Grayab said, "Two dollars, two dollars."

"How come it's two dollar for me?"

Without taking his eyes off Cur, Grayab asked if Caspani was around. No, he was told, the Italians were still on Sand Mountain. That was a shame, Grayab said: he had dealings with Caspani. Not true, but he suspected Caspani could tell him of midnight buryings. He knew Caspani was a snake. Ah well. He had others he could ask.

Cur shouldered forward, picking through a stack of old books—spines broken, cloth covers turning his fingertips green and blue. Novels and a muddy Mennonite hymnal, a book of abbreviated Greek myths, Aesop's fables. He lifted an illustrated Bible. The cover was bound in twine to keep it from falling off.

Grayab said to Cur, "You are a book reader, no?"

"A mite."

"I am not surprised! You are a friend of that Methodist, no? He has a grove of books, a collection to be much admired. Indeed these are some of his."

"Who?"

"The pastor. At the old stone church, in Helena. Where we spoke the other night."

"You couldn't call him a friend. I just run into him now and again. Everybody does."

Grayab said mildly, "You should see him the next time you're in Helena. He gets lonesome." Grayab winced—he'd said too much. "I mean, you ought to talk to him."

Cur's eyes lost their frivolity. McBride had been listening in and now was laughing. He asked, "You been a bad boy? Your mame hear you was a-whoring up the town? Oh no, she's set a preacher on your trail! It's nigh easier to shake a hound!"

Grayab said, "I meant no such thing. He is not that sort of preacher besides."

"How much?" Cur asked, holding a book aloft to change the subject.

Grayab was making change out of his vest for others; even

while speaking to Cur, he didn't lose the thread of his sales. "One dollar," Grayab said. Cur clucked with his tongue and began to wedge it back. "Seventy-five cents," Grayab said. The books were too heavy. He should have left them behind. He lifted his pants by the belt and cinched it up another inch. His belt was made out of last fall's blacksnake. "The best I can do. It has pictures."

Grayab expected Cur to nod yes, or speak again of the pastor, but was asked: "Do you stop at the Greathouses? Near Three Forks. Down near Tuscarora."

"I don't think. No."

"Ah well…"

"Around there I stop at Nedermeyers," Grayab said. "I stop at John Sole. I stop at Jim Boggs. I stop at Jim Bohrer."

"I know them!" Cur took Grayab by the lapel, saying, "Jim Boggs. He was a uncle to me. Like a uncle, I mean. You got word from them?"

"Well…no. Not to you. Should I?"

All around the wolves were shouting for Grayab's attention and money-changing. They didn't know Cur to be so demonstrative but, in their fever of acquisition, didn't notice. Grayab had no time to answer him.

"Look at her going to town!" Joe Rexrode had found the hatbox full of dirty postcards. He held up the picture like an auction card. It was grainy, and McBride had to squint to see: one woman burying her face between the legs of another.

"Goddamn," said McBride.

Grayab's eyes went flat. "Put that down," he said. "Put that down! Five dollars."

Mullenex handed over most of a week's pay for it. He'd cut 189 trees in that time. They'd been high country spruce, and one was a Methuselah. Though usually not a thoughtful man, Mullenex had gotten down on his knees and counted the stump's rings, blade of his knife ticking over them: seasons of mast and drought, flood and fire. Then sawyers cut it to sixteen-foot lengths—eleven of them and a fag end. He held the picture close to his face, as you would a work contract. The woman's eyes were clenched in pleasure or agony, one.

By some caprice of the brain, the stag picture reminded Grayab of an errand, of having visited the bigamist's wife in town. What a fellow she'd shackled to. Sally Cove, like all wives, was willing to pay dear for awful news. Where do they find such fellows? In the doorways of poolrooms, hollering out like trash. Most women have the sense to keep walking, he knew. Not Sally. You must not pity the ones fool enough to stop. That's how you end up the bigamist's wife.

Someday, he would think of her as the assassin's wife. He had, like everyone else, misjudged the husband of Sally Cove.

Grayab counted greasy coins. Four dollars. Seven. A few more and he could quit hauling this load like a slave, buy draft horses, take Seldomridge's surrey.

"You think she likes that?" another asked. He grabbed at the postcards and the hatbox exploded, sending them fluttering into the mud.

Grayab cried out and slapped at the men. "Those are hard to come by."

"If he can't come by them," McBride said, "you ought to offer a refund!" He feigned jacking off, to the others' glee. In the confusion, Aberegg pinched tobacco from the Syrian's pack and began asking around for lend of a paper.

Captain Ketch stumbled out of the donegans, buckling his belt. "Get out of here!" he shouted. "You know better than that! No peddling! You do that stuff in town."

Grayab fought for the postcards. He fell down in a place where the dogs had pissed. He dropped coins and scrabbled for them. The scabs on his knees reopened, and he felt the warm blood. Mud slopped over the tops of his boots.

Captain Ketch kicked the pack, and the wicker gave with a sickening crack. "You know the rules. You don't get out of here, I'm going to throw it off the porch!" He kicked again. China broke obscenely.

Neversummer lunged in front of Captain Ketch, cutting him

off from the peddler. "Quit that, Marty!" Neversummer murmured, "You've no right."

He put his hands on the captain's shoulders, turning him away.
No one had ever touched the captain before. All flinched, expecting a blow would come. To call the captain by his given name
dared an intimacy. The captain looked aghast. Then glared. Then
made for his office. Halfway across the yard he stopped, looked
back, thought better of it and went on.

Now that they couldn't be seen, some were telling Captain
Ketch to leave the peddler be. Once inside his office, Captain Ketch slapped around logbooks, making a scene. Cur said
nothing—he didn't want to upset the captain—it made him feel
traitorous.

McBride cried, "Asa! He's gonna put the rails under you!"

"Aw, let him."

"You don't put your hands on a Company man," McBride said
needlessly.

Grayab lifted his head, hat askew. He closed the pack and lifted
it onto his shoulders. A few lost coins winked in the mud.

"You don't have to go," Neversummer told him.

Grayab shook his head and went off hobbling. The untied oilskin flapped like a broken wing. Soon, it was small as a feather,
then small as nothing at all. The railroad bend swallowed it up.
Cur watched him go, cradling two books against his belly—a
cloth Bible and a Francis Lynde novel. Others were milling, pock-
eting scattered pennies, passing the postcards.

From the office window, Captain Ketch hollered, "Get back to
what you were doing!"

"We weren't doing shit!"

"That's right. Not doing shit, that's when you're at your finest."

Cur ran his thumb against the grain of the pages, ruffling the
foxed leaves. Bile crackled in his stomach. He had stolen these
books. Did nothing to protect the man. Only thought of what he
could get. Quite the revolutionary, he thought acidly. What would
Amos have done?

That night, before turning to the cowboy book instead, he tried reading the Bible to cure his aching head, but he bogged down in *begat*s and geography. He found LUKE GREER SELDOMRIDGE penciled inside the cover. Cur didn't know what to feel about that.

"MCBRIDE TALKED HIM out of firing you," Cur told Neversummer.

"Well, I'm glad I'm not getting fired for doing right. That puts a man in danger."

"Come now..."

"Am I supposed to wallow in front of him? For the pleasure of running a saw? We won't have jobs in a month. We'll have the means of production." Even now, Neversummer could believe, at times, in free unthinking moments, that they would succeed.

"Captain ain't so bad."

"You say that now. He'd be the first one to line you up against a wall."

"I got trouble believing that."

"Well the world's got your best interests at heart, don't it? Wish I was you."

Neversummer was disgusted. When he reached into his pocket, Cur thought he was hunting a handkerchief to blow his nose but, solemnly, Neversummer took out a faded slip of butcher paper: a crude map. Cur read its legend: THOMAS A. HUNGERFORD FARM. BLUE STAR PIKE. LOGAN COUNTY.

Neversummer told him, "I got a place. Vance said if we ever have to pull out real sudden, Logan County's got people. They got a firm movement down there. By the thousand! They're moving along. Not like us, moving backward. Scrip down there and they pay by the ton, but at least you got a reason to bust your ass, not this two-dollar-a-day bullshit."

"What're you talking about?"

"It's coal mining."

"Mining? Where?"

"Logan County. It's down by Kentucky."

"You mean leave out of here?"

"Listen to me. We ain't dropping nothing. We're moving up. This is not about Helena. This is about the entire country. We talked about this. We can't think of just this here. Hell, we can go right now. I don't know why we been fooling here so long."

Cur said, "I don't give a shit about the entire country. I'm from here."

"Just go to the train yard. Jump a rattler and ride. Break down the guns and carry them down. Or hide them in the caves. Wrap them in oilskins. They'll keep."

"You never told me of this."

Neversummer gave him a stern look.

"Wish you'd told me a couple months back," said Cur. "I got plans here."

"Fuck all, what plans is that?"

Cur tasted copper in his mouth. He had chewed a thumbnail down to bleed. He would never see Sarah Greathouse or his father's land again. He said, "You been working on this for ten years, Asa. Leave it all on the ground to rot? I don't see that."

"Don't you hear me? They got thousands. And money."

"Ten more years, Asa. You got the patience for that?"

"I'm not going to give you no milk-and-honey talk. Can't live off angel food forever."

"Better grow you the colt's tooth."

"Don't be nasty."

"You'll regret it."

"I don't know if we can do this here without Vance..."

"This don't turn on one man. You said that. You want to leave all this behind?"

Neversummer paused, regarding his boots. "We can put it to a vote."

"That don't answer my question."

"Payday, we'll all meet at the house. I'll bring it up. Tell them what I know. We can talk it out and vote."

"No point in it, Asa. You say it, they'll vote yes. It'll all be over here. Just rolling over. You'll kill it here. Everything we worked for. Nothing ever will change."

"Damn it, this is not about Helena..."

"Don't you want to talk to Caspani about it?"

"No."

Cur asked him why not.

"I just don't want to." Neversummer stalked off to the bunk-house. He wouldn't speak to anyone for three or four days. On the other end of the saw, Cur withstood this hot silence.

ABOVE ALL, BLACKPINE WAS a place of forgetting. The rest of the world you kept at arm's length. It was ideal in this way. You could forget your own brother's face.

On the mountain, the timber wolves never thought of Helena, never thought of the lives there spooling out. Cur could forget how he had threatened Sally Cove. Almost. It jolted him in bed now and again.

If Helena was distant, it was even harder to imagine a scene such as this one, with Zala hanging around at Seldomridge's church, after a service, listening to a parishioner—one of her fellow clerks—publicly berate a preacher. She stood there, still among the benches, like stock in a paddock. She couldn't resist its delicious strangeness. She, a polite woman, stared.

The clerk was saying to the ugly pastor, "I'm never bringing my family here again. This place is not fit for decent people. I'm writing the bishop the minute I get home."

Seldomridge for his part knew better than to say anything until the clerk had finished his harangue. He seemed to have an aquifer of patience. He answered by saying, "I'm sorry I disappointed you."

Zala admired this non-apology, just as she admired the brusque fashion with which he opened his sermon by saying, "Over the years I've tried to prepare you for death. That is the preacher's only task. I will not equivocate. I am not here to comfort." Zala could not eat, could not sit still. The man she half-loved had wished death on her—and she longed for him as she never had. She blamed herself; she had goaded him into it. It was all, she told herself, a misunderstanding. But that wasn't true. They understood one another. In the days after Cur threatened her, she felt the tidal pull of religious feeling. She wandered among the few churches. None pleased her, exactly, though all were more or less acceptable.

Why wasn't there a priest? She was ready to confess all. Finally, she had settled into the pews of Seldomridge's church, in time to hear his own strange confession, his sermon-that-is-no-sermon.

"They came here in the night, asking me to perform an errand—the errand of burying a suicide. I did what I was asked. He lies there just yards from us, near the trees. As in accordance to the bounds of decency and popular sentiment, we buried this man under the cover of dark. That wasn't right. We should have done so by day, with full honor and spectacle. Don't suicides deserve special attention? We should show off this wrecked body to our children, not as threat, not as morality tale, but as evidence of the central truth of existence..."

Zala covered her mouth to calm herself—she had not even noticed her hands floating up. Any whisper of suicide did this to her.

In excruciating detail, Seldomridge explained the strange circumstance of that night. "I wonder, though, I wonder," he said at last. "Was he murdered? He lies there, asking me. The more I consider it, the surer I am. What should I have done? What should I do? I am asking you as my congregation. I am placing this burden upon your shoulders."

A clerk called out, "You ought to tell the police."

Zala cringed—Seldomridge actually laughed at the man. He said, "I think you trust the authorities overmuch. You are childlike in that way."

The clerk began to sputter, unable to find an answer to that. He couldn't bring himself to cuss in this place.

Zala was witnessing a man kill his own church. Seldomridge was relentless.

And now it was over, the public agony. She watched a few family men admonish him. These were the same clerks she had saved from Cur—they would never know.

Suddenly, she was alone with Seldomridge in that stone room. "What do you think of all this?" he asked her. "This is the first you've been here." Before she could answer, he dropped down in a bench and before long, she was consoling him—she, who had come to confess. Seldomridge wept openly. An electric shock ran

through her. She touched his arm and spoke soft words. Everything
will be all right. Everything. This is what men want of women:
consolation. It wasn't fair, but it was true. She knew that now.
If she had done this for Victor through his failures, she could've
kept him forever—same with Cur. They sensed this lack in her
like a missing limb. There must be a black kernel of bitterness
inside her, for she couldn't perform this simple task—an aberrant
woman—and, besides, no one had ever taken her hand and said
I understand your troubles, your fears, your hungers. There there,
no one said. Keep trying and you'll get over. She handed Seldomridge her handkerchief, and he lowered his head and wiped his
eyes. "Thank you," he said. "You're a good person." He didn't say
"good woman"—that pleased her. She wasn't lowering herself. She
wasn't. She would give them what they craved: soothing words
to go along with her soothing touch, which evidently was not
enough. When she saw Victor, she would apologize for denying
him this trick of solace—no, she'd simply offer it up. He would be
shocked. There was no shame in accepting your role. None.

THE LAST OF HIS PARISHIONERS, the holdouts, would cross town
to attend the services of Eustis Marks, a young Baptist. Privately
Seldomridge called him Useless. Seldomridge learned where the
parishioners had gone off to in dribs and drabs. He had to over-
hear it in the street from some old gossip. Why hadn't Grayab told
him? Damn his grace. Seldomridge knew that in the priestly class
there are an inordinate number of charlatans, certainly a majority,
if not a totality, but it was worse in the lean years just after the war,
when every carnival shill with enough money for a patched tent
and a mule was a Man of God. Was Eustis a charlatan? Well, yes.
Was Seldomridge? Well, maybe, he could admit, but he reasoned
that if he was worrying about it, then likely not. The preacher's job
is to prepare you for death. When Seldomridge told his congregation that, he was cracking open his bones and showing them the
black marrow. Don't give the people what they want. From time
to time, Eustis warned of the apocalypse, but it was halfhearted,
a pot metal bell. He could only prepare you for life. He was more

a friend to his congregants than a preacher, but that could be forgiven. Eustis was young and smiling and hadn't yet learned. Let one woman sidle up to him, let tongues wag, and no matter what Useless does with her, he will learn.

One still had to live through the evenings. Without his books, Seldomridge was at a loss. He sat on the porch, offering a wave to passersby. Now and again, a body might stop and pass the time—not so much as in old times, but oddly enough, a visitor would be kinder now, solicitous of the ruined man. No one came to him for comfort. He was, he knew, one of those old men that people feel sorry for. He had been a young man that people felt sorry for. In four decades he had traveled precisely nowhere.

On the porch, not three days after meeting Zala, he took up the dipper and drank water. Then put it down. Someone was approaching, but he couldn't quite tell who it was.

Constable Green lowered himself onto the bench opposite. "Hi there, Rev."

Seldomridge remembered the clever policeman, though he couldn't recall the name, even though he had watched him grow up in the fields and lanes of Corinth. Once, for several months, respectable farmers would wake to find their mules' hindquarters painted in whitewash as if they were fences—that was Green's doing. He left tin cans on the desk of a schoolmaster who had the chin hairs of a goat. At least he was creative.

"Do you remember me?" asked Green.

"Slightly."

"You know that colored lady used to do the cooking?"

"Nan?" Nan was fifteen years dead. She actually had been hired to clean the parsonage.

"Remember how her bloomers got hung on the hitching post?" Seldomridge blushed. "That was you?"

Green laughed. "She give me a popknot you wouldn't believe. Don't know who told her I done it. She reached out your window and whopped me with a ladle."

Seldomridge smiled. "She was fit to kill. You deserved it."

"Some would say I still do!"

They sat awhile, wrapped in the webbing of the past. "You know," Green said, almost apologetic, "when you go burying somebody, you need a doctor. You need him to inquest and sign the paper. That keeps it straight and narrow. The doctor can see what we don't. Like that McElleny fellow? Wife poisoned him. What if we'd just chocked him in the ground? She'd be walking free."

"I don't think that was a medical mystery. He wretched green bile for a day and a half."

"We could have you charged with interfering with public process."

Seldomridge was taken aback. He grew agitated.

"I'm not here to do that," Green said. "You think I want to charge you? Hell no. Excuse me. But you climb up and start talking how you violate civil law, well, I don't know what else you want. You put us in a hard spot. That's a shame about that boy. It really is. He come here to work and it weren't what he wanted and now he's dead. He should of just gone back where he come from. But he didn't and you're sewed up in it and you got it all wrong. Why you getting people all worked up? You filling up that collection plate?"

"Just go." Seldomridge's voice was a whisper.

"I ain't ready. I'm taking my ease."

"He wasn't Italian."

"So? He could be a Rhode Island Red. They don't divide them up at the gates of heaven."

Seldomridge paused. He was looking at Green, and Green could almost perceive the realization blooming in the preacher's eyes.

"You did this," Seldomridge told him. "I know you did." Seldomridge took his own chin in one hand and leaned back. He looked exhausted.

"And you're the crazy old feller emptied out his church like a wash pot."

"That isn't true," Seldomridge said, though he knew it was.

"Don't matter. That's what town thinks. You never let nobody help you, Luke. My dad said it thirty year ago. It's come and bit you on the ass-end. I hope you get your house in order. I really do. But don't go dragging us in this. I'm doing you a favor and you slap my hand. I like you. Always have. I'd wish you a good day, but I wouldn't mean it."

"You can't threaten me. I have nothing to be afraid of."

"Well then a bad day is the worst thing I can wish on you."

"You killed him."

"Nobody believes a thing you say. You like to talk, but you can't prove much."

"That changes nothing."

"Oh, but it does." Green stepped into the road.

COMMERCE WILL NOT RUN ITSELF FOREVER, no matter how much we desire it. There comes a time for decisions.

The absentees had decided to coalesce here in their Washington office, but as usual, Senator Helena was late, though he lived just three blocks away. At the table, Judge Randolph built a chapel of his fingers. Senator Baxter hung by the window but didn't bother peering out. The room smelled of linseed oil and strong solvents. Light caught the cherry table and ran its grain. They'd had to break down the doors to bring it in. A Last Supper table, Helena liked to call it. He'd gone to the mill and chosen the slab himself, then had it shipped to the capital. Thick enough to take a mortar round! Even the foreman noted the purity of the tree, no heart shakes nor spalting, not a single flaw. It was the one thing Helena ever did well on his own, Randolph said; Helena's father staked Cheat River's initial investment, so they named the depot Helena, and the depot became the town. The irony, Randolph liked to say, would have shamed lesser men.

Randolph loved and hated him in lavish measures. He liked it that Helena was a little afraid of him. And hurt by it just the same.

A handblown pitcher of ice water and crushed mint sweated on the sideboard. Baxter toyed with the shade. The slats ticked together, orchestrating a latticework of light. He wore a jacket from one suit and pants from another. Baxter was color-blind, and his wife was away. Normally she laid out his clothes. He removed his tie and rolled it into his pocket.

"Let's wait until Eugene arrives." Baxter pulled a single cigarette from a worn case and screwed it into his mouth. "I am not ready to discuss this, Shelby."

"I just want to note preliminaries."

"This courthouse issue has become an unhealthy preoccupation of yours."

"Oh, it is healthy. We're proposing to buy ninety thousand acres. The largest single tract is twelve hundred and twelve acres. The smallest, nine. Many transactions." One of Randolph's ledgers was open on the table.

"Where is he? He just *does not care*."

"A local candidate for tax assessor would be sympathetic," said Randolph.

Baxter pretended not to hear. He lifted the chimney from the oil lamp to light his cigarette off the mantel. Any closer and he'd singe his eyebrows. Baxter was allergic to controversy—his peers laughed at his record for missed votes, even party-line routines. Like a fretful widow on a pension, he preferred each day to be identical to the one that preceded it.

Randolph continued, "Without our taxes, this county would be a wasteland, without road one. I defy you to give me one good reason the courthouse should be in Jephtha."

"It's been standing for thirty years."

"A good reason, I said! The law supports us. Helena has thirty-five hundred year-round residents. Jephtha has seven hundred. By statute, the courthouse is to be within a day's ride of the majority of county residents."

"Who rides horses anymore?" Baxter asked languidly.

"The courthouse belongs in Helena. It's obvious to anyone with wits about them."

We can do what we want. Eminent domain. Condemnation. Forced transfer. The tax assessor will do what we say. The lawyers there are loyal.

Randolph said, "We'll offer to build it, free of charge. Neoclassical

Revival. Lovely Ames Limestone from Nicholas County. We'll offer to build a new courthouse and give the county free rent for fifteen years. The metropolis of Jephtha cannot afford that."

The absentees owned a 40 percent stake in the Nicholas County Quarry.

Baxter said, "If the commission votes for it, they can. They can raid county funds."

"Two of the five votes are sympathetic. Rush and Davis, versus Stowbridge and Staley."

"What about, who is it, Sproles? The young one."

"Don't worry about him." Sproles had already been slid the money.

Randolph had to spur the Company on. If only the others would apply themselves. He wanted to schedule expansion into Nicholas and Greenbrier counties, southern tablelands with oaks so grand the wolves had to dynamite them. Randolph had deeded that land himself, just as he'd acquired the Company's first twenty thousand acres. He had ridden there in a wallowing carriage, staying at foul boardinghouses so ill-lit the owners seemed to be rationing light itself. He walked ridges, survived a fistfight with a mean clubfoot in Drennen, hired the first land agents, drank branch water right off the ground, and straightened out botched surveys from the inaccurate spider-hair staff compasses and Gunter's chains from days of yore. It was Randolph who remembered that first tract they bought on Painter Run and the promissory note for $115,000 he held in a shaking hand. Remembered with love. He laughed at the time he passed bribes to the state secretary of agriculture, then belatedly realized it wasn't at all necessary. A week later the secretary sent him a letter, asking the name of Randolph's tailor— he wanted some of them good shirts. Everyone loved this story. Randolph had considered writing his memoirs. He embodied the Heroic Age of business.

Senator Helena stepped in. He cried, "Behold, a compaignye of sondry folk! The Summoner, the Merchant, the Man of Law!" He'd grown a moustache and muttonchop whiskers since Randolph last saw him. He whittled at his mouth with a toothpick.

"Gene."

Helena slid off an otterskin riding coat, one that repelled water and was sleek as the animal it had come from. "I've thought of this courthouse of ours," he said.

Ours, thought Randolph. He held himself together to ask, "Have you now?"

THE MONTH WAS ONE LONG drudge through trees. Percussion of the ax, endless sighing of the crosscut saw. Days grew shorter. Mountain winter coming on, as it would in October, long before they were ready. A union man snapped his ankle and wept in the sickhouse, unaware the injury would save his life. He swelled so much they had to cut him out of his boot.

Two paydays left in town. October 28, November 25. The Woodworkers were obsessed with time. What would happen if, when, the National Guard arrived? They didn't know what Neversummer was about to propose. Neversummer didn't have much to say these days. He reasoned there wasn't much *to* say.

The future, again, was out of Cur's hands. He let it be so. But wasn't letting go an act of choice? He had allowed himself always to be borne along in the wake of others. Well, he had labored in almost every other task the land had to offer, so perhaps he was suited for a miner's life. The Logan mines: a carbide lamp strapped to his skull. Leather and fire. Setting pillars as you lay on your side, twisting your spine like a braid of rope. Everyone had heard the awful things. The earth straining above as you worked. Silicosis. Slither of falling shale. Should he let go? He clutched at Blackpine. It was as close to his native ground as he ever could be. A strong horse could make it to Three Forks in two days or three.

He touched the bark of the trees he cut—he might miss them. A lassitude fell over him. He thought more of women, of Sarah Greathouse, Sally Cove, and others he'd known slightly or not at all. Sex was on his mind, and he would wander off in the woods to masturbate. He slept as much as he could. In his twenty-seventh year, a bit light-headed, he began to understand himself and what, for good or for ill, Neversummer perceived in him. He was one who would do what you asked of him. Maybe Sarah had reckoned this. Amos, too. Cur was a flame that guttered in stronger winds.

In camp, the stove was prime territory. Water would freeze tonight. Twenty degrees colder here on the mountain than down in the valley. At this elevation, they had to burn pine and paper birch that shed a foul smoking fire that barely gave any heat. They shook heads over the poor wood, feeding it to the stove.

Blue Ruin stepped inside and shook snow off his back: the year's first, to fall three days without cease. Cur glanced at him. Blue Ruin was the first timber wolf Cur had ever encountered, on that long-ago day on the siding, the very moment he stepped into Helena, but they had never become close, living sidling lives. Blue Ruin had the shining eyes of prophets and epileptics. It warned you off him. Even the working women shied away. He claimed not to remember the first time the two of them met.

"I dread that conniving winter," Blue Ruin said. "We're going down in the gullet of it."

McBride flipped through a calendar that told them it was later in the month than they thought it was. Courtesy of a bank in Elkins, it was printed with the crenellated cities of Europe. This month, St. Petersburg.

When a new fish asked as to the logger's craft of a winter, Cur told him, "Don't stand downhill of nothing," and another said, "Don't stand uphill neither."

"Hell, I'd rather work winter," McBride explained. "Muck freezes, and it's easier walking. Lot of vexation in the hot months. Rattlers and yellow jackets. Poison ivy, Cur boy's favorite vegetable…a feast of it. A feast!"

"Black-widder spiders."

"Copperheads."

"Deer ticks." Their drab bestiary. They praised the cold. They took pain, boredom, and desperation and called them mother's milk, sugarcane, honey in the rock. A mouse huddled in the corner, working its wiry paws in an attitude like prayer.

Blue Ruin pitched a boot at it. "Damn summer. You take it. Once we cut a oak and didn't see the dead place about fifteen foot up. You ought have seen the hornets gush! Nige there, his eyes welled shut for two days. Three, was it, Nigel? Guess you'd know better than I."

Hiss of snow on the roof. Clack of backgammon, slap of foxchase. Nailheads in the wall were freezing to the touch, and night was blue out the window, and wind was singing in the flue. Cook struck the tin bell for lights out. Rags were stuffed under the door. Before they crawled into the hard lumber of their beds, they pulled on woolens heavy as horse blankets. The old familiar smells: stale semen, boot leather. It would be remembered as the Cruel Black Winter.

At his usual four in the morning, McBride rose in the dark and tugged on boots. Stepping out, he greeted his last Blackpine winter. He told no one that, not even his Cur, but the cuttings seemed to know because they kept trying to kill him: hemlocks falling like scythes; otherwise sweet horses braiding leads on the steepest of grades; links popping on brand-new chains as though forged by drunkards. He'd never known such vexation. Or perhaps he was growing older, cherishing pain. The moon stood in its halo of ice. Four stars blazed in its white hoop, so he knew how many rough days of weather to expect. He walked to the barn. McBride snaked open the door-bolt and sent a lone deer crashing from its bed somewhere up on the ridge.

Young Thomas was already there. McBride grunted in approval. In the first stall, a colt was learning winter against its mother's side. Nostrils smoked like shotgun bores. The mare was near crippled with ringbone, and he'd shoot her after the colt weaned. McBride felt a twinge between his legs. Come spring, he planned to change his life. For a price, a woman might accept an offer of marriage, and they'd retire to a distant town where her reputation was not known, only guessed. To a cousin he wrote a postcard asking after the availability of work on the Kanawha River coal barges and rents in waterside tenements, little more than common rookeries, which he didn't know. When the arthritis bound his left hand in an aching hitch, he thought of that easy river trade: three weeks on, ten days off.

That's all you can hope for—a little easiness, a little time off. He wished Cur and the others could understand that.

Wordless, others appeared in the barn. They wore woolen underwear, brilliant green-and-red-checked Richie shirts, mittens with leather palms and knit backs, muffed caps and jackets.

McBride lit an oil lamp and broomed hay from under it with his boot. A fire here would be the end of them. Steam rose from places where horses pissed. They snorted and shuddered, chewing stall doors where the wood was bleached, rough-hewn boards worn smooth as silk by wandering teeth. They mouthed iron bars as well, seeking salt in everything the tongue could touch. McBride lifted collars from the wall and tucked a ring-bit under each arm to warm the metal. Horses stamped in the moment before dawn, working blood into their legs. McBride slipped a hoof-pick into his pocket. He saw wet harnesses lying in a heap and shouted, "Pick that up! They'll go to rot." Without comment, Young Thomas looped them over his arm. In winter, work doubled though their pay did not. Even so, McBride drove a team so hard you'd see your reflection in the hides. He liked matched Percherons from Jephtha, though Belgian-Shire crosses were normal fare in the camps. They beat two thousand pounds and seventeen hands high, but it didn't keep them from rolling in the snow if you let them. McBride was far famed with horses, known to fall asleep at day's end with his face pressed against their hides, ribs working against his face. *Be calm with your horses, boys, your horse is your buddy. You see fellows bawling them out, but the best gives a little flick of the reins and that talks louder than Gabriel's horn. Start off a slow good gait and let them know when to get ready. You surprise a horse, she shall come to hate you. I break horses easy, I'll show you in the spring when new flesh comes...*

And no one minded his sermons, because McBride was said to be a man whose team could pull the moon from the sky and stomp it ugly. Except for foul Blue Ruin, who often said he'd like to buy McBride for what he knows and sell him for what he *thinks* he knows, turn quite a goldpiece that way. They laughed but knew Blue Ruin was sour, likely the one who said McBride's a lunger.

The rumor of his sickness never took root. Blue Ruin would never be promoted.

Outside, sleepy cook's helpers handed out sandwiches. Snapping down breakfast, the teamsters walked to the corduroy roads. Hooves clopped on split logs with sounds of muffled handclaps. This roused other men in their bunks. Their own skin cold to the touch.

Cur woke from an unsatisfying sleep. As soon as he opened his eyes, his misfortunes returned. Amos. Vance. He worried at their absence like a missing tooth.

Crews ranged onto the choppings with briar saws and kerosene in hand. Before they left, Captain Ketch delivered poor news from the telegraph. Snow and ice had foundered the trains. They had Negroes clearing the tracks, but by his reckoning, it would be a week or two, at least.

"Might miss your payday," he admitted. "Now get you a breakfast and get at it."

The little meat they had was salted, jerked, or full of sinew. Ghastly leavings: knuckles, feet, the very dregs of the hog, chitterlings that resembled boiled tapeworms and were just as chewy. Cur struggled to choke them down, muttering, "My God." He had no appetite.

Leaving the cookhouse, most ignored the shivering helpers, who wore coats as thin and ragged as rat's hide. Smoking, Cur and Neversummer watched the boys split wood with a maul. What lives they had. Ten years old and illiterate to the bone.

Neversummer asked, "Know what I'm thinking?"

"I'm afraid so."

Neversummer kneaded his face. They might not even get to *town* on November 25. It was a small, bitter truth. Why had Vance Church pushed that day? A general strike in winter, even if it happened, would be plain disastrous. Men cold and desperate, shelterless. Only a fool would have designs on winter. Spring was better anyhow, when orders are high at the mill. The Company would tremble at any delay. Now Neversummer had to tell everyone, dozens of men, call it off. What would Caspani say?

Neversummer was succumbing to despair. Each depth gave way to a deeper one. He breathed in and out, sending silvery bursts of breath to heaven. He should have known. He had not paid the god of weather proper deference.

Oddly, and if for a moment, Cur was comforted. The Churches, Caspani, Neversummer—he had thought them infallible. No, they were as bad as him, and as good.

They felt themselves being pulled to the mines. At least they had another route. Not all were so lucky, Neversummer reminded himself to remind Cur. He wanted the boy along with him, though he didn't need him. Maybe Cur was dragging him down. Cur's argument against the mines was senseless, foolish, ill timed. Their cause had no room for sentimental geography. He reckoned Cur would give in.

Winter was when the loggers felt their smallest, like mites that live in the tuck of an owl's wing. They had obscure fantasies of Captain Ketch firing them all at once, society having no more call for their timber.

Cur asked, "What do we do?" He meant give up.

"Cut some trees, I guess."

Cur tossed the twanging saw over his shoulder, and they walked out, but not before taking bones from a pile out back and blackening themselves under the eyes with marrow, so the snow wouldn't strike them blind. They clenched their teeth against the wind. The dawn was a silver smear that moved like a slug across the sky.

Each deadfall was covered in inches of powder—the world seemed to have kindlier dimensions. Frost had formed, spreading ferns on any idle piece of metal, whether inside or out: wedges, saws, piles of chains frozen so solid they had to pour buckets of boiling water on them.

It took an hour to make the cuttings. Along with Cur and Neversummer, there were two knotbumpers, two buckers, and Henthorn—the bad feller who feather-edged his ax on the grindstone till it was near worthless. They crossed a swampy bottomland full of hooped briar. Spiked boots scritched along. The track of foxes and birds braided in the snow. In the distance, the mountains were ink-scratched a faint blue with pines. "Watch your step!" one called as they picked over loose rock they couldn't see. Beyond that lone call, no one spoke. Cur found a game balsam they called blister pine for its resin. He slapped it, trying to work blood into gloved fingers. They spread out burlap to sit on and nocked the saw and found a rhythm. It was so cold the resin didn't run. The knotbumpers scurried after, chopping branches, then went on. Cur pounded wedges into the notch, the clanging of metal on metal the only sound in the world. In the sump of winter, Cur discovered his mortality: wincing shoulder, knee-joint flaring like a tiny furnace. One toe complained against every step.

Red sawdust vibrant on the snow, the saw's lamentation, *Can't, lick, less.*

As it had not been for years, this was mere labor. Cur and Neversummer had nothing to live for here. No hidden spirit animated their days. Blackpine and Helena would not rise.

"I'm not going to Logan County with you," Cur told him. "I'm not going into them mines. I don't think I'm going."

"Well."

"That ain't a living for me, I don't think."

"You happy just running a saw all your life? That all you want?"

"Better than them mines."

"You ain't sure."

Which was true. In these sullen days, Cur had studied on the blackened fields, the rivers of mud. He began to suspect that this, the stripped mountain and its filth, was the true revolution. One hundred years from now, even two hundred, the people would live on in Blackpine's wake—not in the aftermath of an industrial dispute and the haggling over rights and dollars and his own meager life. He and those like him had ignored what was happening to the old forest—you expected the immigrants and the outlandish not to care, but Cur knew the place as it once was. The slash, the slag: all this to fuel great cities of the north none of them ever would see. No one would walk this ground and know it as Cur had with his father and brother. Cur had folded himself into the cause, as you fold a letter into an envelope. All else was forgotten, and while one thing absorbed his interest, another was happening. He saw that nothing here promised lasting life. When the Company pulled out, the wolves' corduroy roads would rot away and slough into mud; their towns would disappear from maps; even the absentees, their gods, would be forgotten, not to speak of this small dispute. No statues would rise to them. Only the weather would remain, distant, implacable. He looked at Asa across the saw. To be drawn forward in the wake of another is a hateful life. Those thoughts left Cur cold. He regretted nothing, and all. You had to fill your years some way, and he had. He was only a worker now, a pair of arms attached to the contraption of his body. He hated the faceless swarms that hived there in the cities he'd never been to. They took everything. They took his land and his life and his years.

WHEN THE MOUNTAINS HELD a snow line a third of the way up the sides, like women in skirts, Grayab was deep in his winter swing. On the back of Clendenin Knob, the hound trotted alongside, nose in the air. Grown fond of a traveling companion, Grayab had been halving his meals for it. As they walked, axes rang out. Grayab tried to give a wide berth, keeping to the standing forest. He feared Captain Ketch. But this was time to profit: mountain families, panicky under winter's jar, would pay top dollar, fearing they wouldn't see town for months. Wares reminded them they're alive.

Shrill cries, a clatter in the trees. A pillaging hawk ripped into a squirrel's drey of leaves. A yearling tried to escape, and the hawk corkscrewed around the limb: so nimble. Under vast wings, a parcel twitched with tail curling. What a way to wake! Flattening its ears, the hound bawled at the commotion and fell silent when it caught another scent on the wind.

Sailing downridge, the hawk lit on a dead limb raised like a falconer's arm. In the Souk al-Hamidiyeh, Grayab had seen the Saker falcons for sale. Twice a year his father, Elias, went to Damascus. At thirteen Grayab was allowed to come. The souk was rank with wood smoke and sweat, a banquet for young eyes: bolts of cloth, carved cedar, hooded falcons on their stands. Desert tribes used falcons to hunt gazelle. They would topple the running game, harry them, and rip sight from soft eyes with their talons. Tribesmen fell on the gazelles with knives, or turned out their saluki hounds. They bred saluki to have long feathery ears, which they grabbed and twisted to pull the dogs off the kill. One ear was always docked. Grayab didn't know why that was, but he never wanted to interrupt his father's reverie. As Elias spread his hands to explain the grace of the saluki, he caught a boy pickpocket in the act and slapped the Mohammedan till he bled from the nose. Now the hawk draped her wings over the dead squirrel, in the attitude called mantling. Its beak turned from yellow to red.

The hound sensed it before Grayab did and flattened. Now he felt the prickle on his own neck. He was being watched.

A lion cleared her throat. Grayab turned, looking to the tumbles of greenstone, the deadfall timber. Now the lion cried. A stand of beeches shivered in the sky, crowns bouncing under her weight. Grayab held his face in one hand and clutched the back of his neck with the other. The hound fretting and pissing in fear. He opened his eyes. She'd gone on. Grayab worked the buttons on his jacket like a rosary.

He found the tobacco he didn't know he'd dropped. Later, he would find a sickle-shaped alphabet the lion's claws had scrawled into a beech tree. He'd study it, a language he couldn't cipher but would like to know. He'd like to live in the country that spoke it. In a moment, he grew curiously lonesome. The claw marks wept a clear sap.

Grayab caught the lion walking proud and haughty across a skid road. A sleek silence. Her haunches yawing. She stopped midway to roll in the snow, kittenish, her long tail whipping and tipped in black as though dipped in an inkwell.

He guessed sixty yards. If he had a gun, would he have shot her? You could make money that way. The lion rolled. At this distance, he could appreciate beauty, grace. Who had the heart to shoot and unbuckle her body? The lion perked. She must've heard the imperceptible crackle of Grayab's pack. She threw herself wheeling, leaps of ten and twenty feet, kicking up powder. She vaulted a fallen treetop and the land closed around her.

You'd never outrun one, he told his hound. Never. He examined the ruffled snow where she'd rolled, a blue-black train of tracks. He touched a print with ungloved fingers. Four toes and the pad, claws and dewclaws invisible but no less real. Against his hand he memorized the print's dimensions. Finally the hound quit its whining.

On the mountain's saddle, out of the wind, Grayab watched the piling up of white. Calm now, he boiled snow for coffee stretched with chicory and watched his hound pogo in the snow. It found highways of scent and looped through the woods.

"Catch him!"

The white shimmer was a snowshoe hare, and the hound leapt over Grayab's pack.

Before Grayab saw the blue smudge of storm, he felt it coming in his lower back. He pulled out a rope and a piece of canvas, eyeing places to build. A trough of bruise-colored clouds poured into the ridgelands. They galloped. They carried black bellyfuls of snow.

WHEN NEVERSUMMER CRIED OUT, Cur glanced up to see a young hound come dancing over the snow. It high-stepped and crooned, tail wagging. Black and tan, but no certain breed, if a dash blooded. They dropped their tools to greet it. Cur reached out to rub its flanks and asked it, "Where you come from, foxy? Huh?"

"Long ways from home."

Cur grinned and said, "I know him!"

"Oh, you do not."

Cur scratched its skull. "Yes I do. He's the peddler's."

"You're right. Hound, your daddy about got me fired. What he been feeding you, fatback and gray? You're nigh grown, foxy."

The dog stopped, perked its ears. A two-note whistle, up in the cove.

"I'd call him a few rods off," said Neversummer. "He's the little lost boy."

The hound took off kicking snow. They watched it go.

"That peddler keep his tack on him? I'd like to beg a potato or something off him."

A lashing scream in the distance. It cut the air again. East. Cur started. "You hear that? That a woman?"

His friend went all smiles, a welcome sight. "No, son. It's a cat, and no barn cat neither."

"Pret far off."

"Not too far. Fat dog ought to move. That sounds like a lion."

When Cur scoffed, Neversummer claimed there were still some about. "Blue Ruin was a longline trapper, he killed them in his time. That's what they call a windfall. Know what kind of bounty you get? We bring in a grown painter, we'd get lawyer money. What I'd give for a gun." Neversummer seemed happy again. There were hard clouds like anvils in the sky.

Cur told him, "McBride has a gun. A pistol."

Neversummer didn't know that. Now that was interesting.

SHE LIVED IN THE WORLD like a rumor. The lion, a female of many winters, was at home in cold months most of all. Fewer men, and she roamed farther, edging up to fields to snatch the straggling farmers' sheep. In the warm, when men walked freely, they confined her to a dwindling archipelago of old-growth where she could hide in lushness. But the lion had not eaten flesh in awhile. Deer were few. She made do with voles and hares, bloodied her pads digging them from the ground. She grew lean and wild on long, elliptical walks for food. You could see haunches working under her skin. Not starving, but a week from it. The lion had not mated in three years' time. It didn't matter. She was too unhealthy to whelp.

The sweet smell of lathered horses, and the rank yellow sweat of men. Leather creaking in the cold. From the crown of a spruce, she watched the team. Her claws tensed on bark.

Skid roads frozen solid as pig iron, log slides glittering trails of ice. McBride encountered felled hemlocks sawn to sixteen-foot lengths. Nimbly choreographing the horses, he set about fastening six logs end-to-end with grab hooks and chains, as if he were re-constructing the tree itself. Most teamsters only went four, but this was McBride. He laid a grouse chain to slow their descent. The train constructed, he flicked the reins, cried "Back!," and the horses scuttled and crawfished up to the mass. He hooked them to the drag chain, relaxed the reins, telegraphed thought. A small shudder went through the team as they sensed weight attached to the traces. Connecting chains snapped tight, and legs slanted forward, hooves digging earth. They moved downhill with even strides, logs tearing snow down to black earth and muck of leaves. McBride followed.

"Good team," he hooted. He knew horses. He convinced them to work till they were hot as scarlet fever to the touch, and that, they said, is a different thing entire.

As McBride was daisy-chaining another train with grabs, the wind sang in a new pitch from the northwest, and he saw the rolling storm.

The team heard it too. By the time they were halfway to the landing, the air had grown heavy with charge. Tails and manes stood with static electricity. "Goddamn!" he cried. The tail had brushed and shocked him. He sucked his finger. "Goddamn."

McBride had to calm them, he couldn't badger them on. He stepped forward to coax Dulcie, the nearest one. She was Mc-Bride's freshest, white gone yellow, mane the color of sun-drenched wheat. She looked at him, blinking snow from her lashes. She was a sweet one, and he'd named her as he named only the best. Once a dog walked through her legs in a figure eight and Dulcie paid it no mind. That poise was rare, he knew. Six years old, in her prime. When he touched her neck, she tossed her head and feinted, so unlike her. Only a single sixteen-foot log was attached to the drag chains, and he managed to walk the team downhill a few steps, snaking it. Dulcie's eye rolled, and she stamped a hind leg, cocking it like a pistol's hammer.

McBride spoke soothing words and saw a blue shadow falling on—across—the snow.

The lion struck Dulcie's shoulder like a wrecking ball. It fastened on, raking red. The horse rolled on her side, lion clamping at her throat, digging for the vein deep in the neck. The other horses dragged her and logs and lion downhill, screaming, eyes rolling like billiards. McBride dropped the reins and pulled the pistol from his coat and cocked it with both thumbs. One side of the log caught a stump, turned sideways. Chains shot links. He held the pistol in shaking hands—finger docked, he needed both to steady a gun—and drifted the sight onto the lion's shoulder. He fired, and the lion went running. Again, again, he pulled the trigger.

The team pulled in three directions. When the log came tumbling forward, the butt end pinched McBride's belly all the way to the ground, and the log went derricking over the hill. A wheeling horse stepped on his knee. He didn't feel it crunch.

Dulcie wrapped the traces and spun the others, and a sliding cherry log pinned her against a stump. After a sickening moment, the stump sheared off her foot with a terse crack.

McBride tried to sit himself upright. He could not. Overheated, overwrought. Grime and sweat gathered in the creases of his skin. He tried to strip his jacket and unbutton his shirt, but his hands didn't seem to be working. Snow slapped on his shoulders. He couldn't yell for the other teamsters. Blue Ruin, Young Thomas— they were out there somewhere.

Dulcie tried standing on a peg of bone—she had lost her foot just above the coffin joint. The blood flowed from her throat in alarming quantity. The others dangled broken pieces of tack like jewelry and shied away, blinking fiercely. They turned their heads to McBride, waiting for a command. None would come. One dipped its head and nosed at him, to beg the words out. And smelled the lion on the wind. Tethered together, the horses could not run.

JUST AUDIBLE, THE TINHORN CALLED *come back, come back, danger's about.* Neversummer cried, "It's about time!" Flakes clung to his eyebrows and lashes.

Sparks crackled on metal—sawteeth, wedges. In the distance,

mute lightning branched and lit the snow, something neither had ever seen before. Foolishly they'd kept working, waiting on the horn while the others had left an hour before. In the wind, it was difficult to tell the precise moment when the screams of horses became the screams of a man, but the gunshots couldn't be mistaken. Three, in stuttering succession. Cur and Neversummer looked at one another. They threw away the saw and ran toward the sound.

"He shot that painter! I'll be damned I will. I bet you he shot it."

"Look." Ahead, a red medallion on the snow. Then snatched away by whiteness.

Lungs burning, they pulled one another over fallen hemlocks. On the crest of a bare hogback, they peered into the cove. The tan flag of a man's face.

McBride was alive, but his coin-hard eyes were for the next world. He pawed at the leaves with his right hand as if he'd dropped something precious there. The teamster Blue Ruin was on his knees beside McBride and called out, "I just found him!"

Cur kept saying, "Oh no, oh no, oh no…"

McBride had managed to sit himself against a log. He clutched his belly with his left hand and used his right to wipe his mouth. The hand came back covered in blood and spit. Flakes of snow fell in the warm froth and melted. He'd half worried himself out of his shirt.

"Seen my gun?" he asked them.

"Hush now."

"Gun? Stole it off a police, did."

Blue Ruin said, "It's a awful thing…"

A little blood trickled from the corners of McBride's mouth, as if he'd tried to swallow a spoonful of paint. Full of air bubbles. He tried to pull off his jacket and couldn't, and Cur made him stop. The flannel shirt was greasy. A horrible, septic tang in the air. The smell of gutshot, sharp with cold. McBride held out his arm. "Take," he said. It was a fistful of bills in large and small denominations.

"Stop it. Just stop."

"Want you have it. Have your fun. You my cousin."

"That's right," Cur said, running a hand over his own face. "I'm your cousin."

"Spend it!"

Cur wouldn't take it. McBride held it out to Neversummer. When no one took, McBride dropped the dollars on the snow. His breathing was wretched, swampy.

Away from them, the bleeding animal lay on her side and made sounds you don't expect from a horse. Smelling blood, the others bawled like newborns.

McBride said, "Ain't right. We shouldn't of laughed and drunk. After hauling that dead."

"Shh."

"We shouldn't of sung…"

Cur said, "We'll carry him in our coats."

"Three mile?" said Blue Ruin. "He'll jostle to death."

A sudden lucidity. Eyes flashing, McBride tried to speak. They couldn't quite hear.

"What, McBride?"

"Kill me. Just kill me…"

No answer but the snow hissing down. They saw an incomplete brace of horses jerking through the trees, and the snow was ruffled pink all around.

"Coleman? That you?" McBride managed to say.

"Yes."

"You was unioned up. Will arrest you. The law. You need to fly way."

Neversummer smirked. The world knew about them—time for Logan County, to hide in mines. Then the look dissolved. He asked, "Where's your gun, buddy?"

"Coleman. You need to fly."

Cur told him to hush. He slipped a bandanna out of his pocket. "McBride, where's your gun? Vaughn! Look at me!"

McBride opened his mouth but nothing escaped. They raked hands through the snow and went through the teamster's jacket.

McBride's famous hat was gone. Blue Ruin left to look for the pistol where the horses were.

"Naw," said McBride. The breath hissed out of him, a set of bellows with a hole in it. He shook his head from side to side in an exaggerated way. "Naw…" McBride couldn't tell him about the pistol wedged under a nearby log.

Cur and Neversummer didn't have to say a word. With shaking hands, Cur tied the bandanna around McBride's eyes. It was the same way teamsters wrap jackets around horses to blind them in spooky places, full of rock and rattlesnakes. McBride would have been proud. Neversummer took hold of McBride's shoulders to steady him, and with two hands, Cur covered McBride's mouth and nose. He had once heard a preacher say that life is a narrow but treacherous river dividing two rich countries, but Cur wasn't so sure. He thought those two countries might be barren white lands where no one speaks, no one makes decisions. McBride's skin was cold to the touch. His arm shot up like a fencer's, and Neversummer reached out to hold it still.

Cur pulled his hands away from McBride's face. The teamster wheezed and sucked air. He'd begun to cry. They could see it through the bandanna, dark pinpricks.

Neversummer murmured, "There ain't no other way."

"Let's carry him."

Neversummer began to shout. "God bless, can't you see he's hurting? Damn it! Give it here."

So Neversummer put hands to McBride's face. He held McBride's mouth from behind, and Cur held his arms. In the struggle the bandanna slipped off McBride's left eye, but no one bothered to fix it. Half a minute later, McBride's legs began to shudder. Cur leaned on them to keep him still, and McBride's eye gave one last flicker, barely tangible. The shadow of a moth. His head lolled, his leg kicked a final time. Cur sat in the snow. He began to smooth McBride's clothes, so the teamster wouldn't look like a madman in death. A long raucous sentence of forty-four years, ended with the period of that final anonymous day. Twigs and leaves stuck to

McBride's shirt. Cur plucked them off. His own back was covered in snow. Once Cur had picked off the larger pieces, he began to pry small burrs and preachercuss from the cloth with fingernails. He tucked in McBride's shirt. He broomed the loose bills into one pile.

Blue Ruin returned empty handed. When he saw McBride was gone, he shook his head.

"We got to make camp," he said finally. "Come on. Let's go. It's cold."

"All right. Pick him up."

Blue Ruin cried, "It's too far to carry him in this! We'll freeze first!"

It was hard to speak for the wind. You couldn't see the mountains for the snow.

"We can't walk into it," said Cur. "Let's find that peddler. He's right here."

"A peddler?"

"We seen his dog."

"A peddler, huh?" Blue Ruin said. "I thought I seen Jew-tracks in the snow. Hooves!"

"Wind's letting up a little. You could light a fire in this."

Blue Ruin sneered "If you say so."

"Camp's too far."

A snort. The horses were watching. Cur walked to them. Could he ride? No, they were spooky, wild. He didn't see what the lion had torn into the dying horse's neck.

The lion skulked on the ridge, licking her chops, waiting for them to go. Dull, throbbing hunger. Her mouth smeared with gore.

In a studied motion of afterthought, Blue Ruin scooped up the loose bills. "Come on back, Cur. We got to go. Them ain't riding horses. Let's get out of here. Let's leave him."

"We can't."

"This is beyond stupid. It's a good march past it."

"Are you helping or not?"

Shaking his head, Blue Ruin took hold of the legs—the easiest job. The others lifted McBride's body by the jacket. The weight made them stumble through the snow like drunken men. The horses watched them go.

The lion leapt from the tree and parted the storm, following the trail of McBride's team. Eating pink snow as she walked. The horses lay down.

MCBRIDE'S BODY WAS TOO MUCH, and they had to stop again. The storm foundered them—they tried to keep the granite gash of Storm Gap ahead, but it was no use. In a tree, there was an owl the color of smoke, then none at all.

Blue Ruin sat in the snow, uttering a singsong of blasphemies. He wouldn't acknowledge the dead man. McBride's face had quit melting the flakes that fell upon it.

Cur said, "We ought to've cut circles for the peddler."

"I'm so goddamn hungry I'd eat my own tongue. We should of left him. McBride had sense. Not like you two brains. He would of told you to leave him himself."

"That's enough," said Neversummer, curt enough to cut all talk.

Camp Eight territory, with its sloppy habits and ragged stumps, revealed them to be five and a half miles off their mark. They built a teetering monument of wet black sticks. Despite the kerosene they trickled on it, the fire would not light. The wind kept stealing Cur's match, no matter how solid the chapel he built with his hand. Three matches left.

"Give me your lucifer," Blue Ruin said. "Give a man a try."

"Hold on."

"Give it to me!"

By the time the scuffle ended, the pyre had been kicked over, the matches trampled. They were too tired to hurt each other.

"Hey!" Blue Ruin stopped.

Cur threw another wild blow.

"I said hey!"

"Why'd you quit?"

"There he be," Blue Ruin said.

An orange worm of fire among the trees. Lifting McBride, they went toward the glow. The snowdrifts ate their legs to the thigh.

When Grayab saw the dead man in their arms, he quit hailing them. He crossed himself, and the hound flattened its ears. Blue Ruin rudely dropped McBride's legs by the fire. The hound bristled at the body, rumbling in its throat. Grayab called it back. He ministered to the fire, and the first thing the timber wolves offered was to feed it the rest of their kerosene flask. Grayab nodded, patting his small dog on the flank. Fire flared in hissing blue antlers. The hound squalled at McBride's body, then tried climbing into the peddler's lap.

"Horses killed him," said Cur.

Grayab wanted to say, Every time I see you a bad thing happens. He held his tongue. Finally said, "I sold him roots. Vaughn. The joker."

"That's him."

"He would overpay me a dime or two." That meant much to Grayab. He dragged another log to the fire. They sat. When the hound nosed at McBride's body, Grayab kicked it back. For awhile, the others' lips were too cold to converse. There was an empty skillet turning a molten color in the fire. Blue Ruin asked where the peddler was going.

"A settlement. They call it Foxtree."

"How far is it to Foxtree? Can we make the walk?"

"Twelve miles as the crow flies," Grayab said, "but we are not crows."

"Sure enough," Blue Ruin said. "We found us a new jokester."

He and the peddler had taken an immediate dislike to one another. Now Grayab felt his life shudder, as a hawk turns on a pinion and teeters on a knife-edge of wind. If he was surprised to meet them in that place, it did not show. He cleaned snow from a few round stones and rolled them into the fire. He hadn't shared a camp in weeks. He wasn't sure how to act.

No one dared mention the embarrassment with Captain Ketch, the shame of the camps, Grayab squatting in piss and mud in his hunt for coins.

Grayab said, "If it gets colder, we can sleep with the stones. It feels good between your legs."

When the wind finally died, a lunar silence filled the land. Snowflakes clung to Grayab's moustache. He smoked, letting a finger of ash grow. Behind him, a lean-to had been crafted of dressed canvas and raw limbs. Dry heartwood popped like small-bore loads, a rimfire noise. They held hands to the fire, as if they were pleading with it. Grayab had woolen socks steaming on a stone. None of them looked at McBride.

Neversummer did not speak. So he would be quiet this night. Had all the world gone to shit? Cur thought of McBride, a man who owned little on this earth but a mouthful of teeth and a chestful of ribs, jealously guarding their questionable bond of blood, their cousinhood. Cur was too stunned to cry. His famous luck was swirling away into the sky. He would have the miner's life and rebel and take up arms when he was told. Let his father die. Let Sarah Greathouse fade into an old woman without a sepia photograph to her name. Let trees be slivered to clothespins, let his lungs receive the seeds of sickness. He was finished with this place.

Grayab wrapped a blanket about himself. A sudden gust tossed Blue Ruin's cap into the woods, and he had to run after it. They laughed at him, and he came back scowling. Blue Ruin was a famously ugly man, with a ropeburn-red face, creased as a dog's cunt. Blue Ruin, McBride had always claimed, was deadly jealous of his hat.

Grayab said, "It is cold out. You need to keep it on your Golgotha."

"Golly-what?"

Grayab pointed to his own crown. "The place of the skull."

Cur grinned, then felt guilty for it with a dead friend so near. Cold and fatigue were making him loopy, his mind darting here and there. Blue Ruin, too, seemed a little crazed. He danced a jig about the fire and sang. Happy to be alive, with the dog pirouetting wildly about him. He bowed to invisible partners and dared the snow to kill him graveyard dead. The fire was his best partner. Grayab's eyes narrowed to slits.

Neversummer, the one who ferried McBride from this world, was stony silence.

Blue Ruin said to Grayab, "You just range out like a wolf, don't you? Right at home."

"If you say so."

Blue Ruin reckoned in the peddler some gage of black or Indian blood. In firelight, Grayab's teeth showed the mark of a year or two spent without enough food.

Cur flinched when Grayab reached into the fire bare-handed. He pulled a small loaf from the fire, tapped the bread of its ash, and broke it into fourths. As if he'd willed bread from the fire. They began to eat hot fistfuls, which gave their palates a hint of pentecost.

Suddenly Grayab said, "Nothing is strange to me anymore."

Blue Ruin said, "Seeing a dead man druv you crazy."

"No."

"No?"

"Honestly, I am amazed there are not more of them in America."

Cur asked, "That how you see it?"

The wet wood seethed. "There," said Grayab, "we hated the Druze, they hated us. We fought, and they killed us by the cart-full, they burned our schools and our churches. A quarter in Damascus gone, and we would have done the same to them if we could have mustered. We hated the Mohammedans, the shayks, the pashas, the Ottomans, the Brits. We hated—eh, *la noblesse*, you know?— the keepers of good lands *en perpétuelle*. In America, you all hate someone and you do not know who it is. You are angrier than we."

Cur said, "I don't hate nobody."

"You should."

A cinder popped from the fire onto the dog's coat. It yelped and rolled its back in the snow. Blue Ruin chuckled at it. To Grayab, the man's laughter was the crackling of thorns.

"You're your own man," said Blue Ruin. "Ranging out here with everything you need. I know because I lived that way myself. You know how to live shank's mare."

Grayab didn't answer. He was bothered that Neversummer

wouldn't speak. The hound whined for a heel of bread, bored now with McBride's body. Grayab hushed it, saying tonight it could do without.

"Glad I ain't your dog!" cried Blue Ruin.

"Dogs are like children. A soft life is bad for them."

"Aye. That's sense."

Cur asked, "How long you been walking your route?"

"Ten and some years," Grayab said.

"Ten and some! Hmm," said Blue Ruin. "I was near on the traps that long. Surprised we never crossed. Yes, I was a trapper, running the long line. I was like you. Drop you out here with naught but a knife and sound boots, you'd make Helena."

"I am not making for Helena."

"Not many you could speak that of. Glad we found this peddler."

"Me too," said Cur.

Blue Ruin winked, which confused Cur. "My, that's luck," he said.

Grayab made no sign of hearing, but he heard all. He ate his ash bread. He'd planned to fry a couple potatoes and now cursed the men for showing up. He didn't have enough to share. Grayab said, "The guy I inherited this route from…" He paused to swallow.

"Yeah?"

"He died in a bear trap. No one found him for two seasons. Why, I am sure the trapper did, but he didn't say anything. The trap had been chained to a tree."

"That so?"

Grayab shrugged. "That is what they say. Could be a tale."

"Was it a Newhouse Number 5?" asked Blue Ruin.

The others gazed at him.

"The trap. It's writ on the pan. Was it a Newhouse?"

"I do not know."

Blue Ruin said, "Don't look at me like that! It weren't mine. Just asking a simple question."

"I was not casting aspersions."

"Good. You had a look on your face like a cat shitting glass." He pointed to the skillet in the ashes. "You got potatoes, onions? No? Damn. I got the worst kind of luck."

They told riddles to stay awake: "Crooked as a rainbow and teeth like a cat, guess all night and you can't guess that." After a while: "What's that?" "Come now, it's a greenbrier." Blue Ruin said, "Round as a ring and deep as a spring, and it's killed many a pretty little thing." "A rifle," said Cur. Then he admitted, "I heard that one before."

"You rascal! Least you're honest."

Cur could never help but tell the truth. Neversummer hated that about him. The years had roughened their notions of one another.

Grayab said, "The red, the yellow, the 'delible green, a man can guess it as quick as a queen, the Man in the Moon come tell me this soon, come tell me this riddle tomorrow at noon."

That one lasted them several big logs on the fire. Finally Neversummer said, "It's a rainbow." This the only sign he'd been listening.

"Don't sleep, Asa."

"I won't."

Grayab said, "This is the kind of night when one goes to sleep and does not wake up." But they were not men to lean to one another for warmth.

Snow gathered on McBride's face, and Cur bashfully leaned over to brush it off. It had drifted against the dead man's sides as well. Cur still did not cry. The wind cut once more, a knife through his clothes. The hound gnawed a stick of wood and cracked pieces in its jaws.

Blue Ruin asked him, "Got any riddles on you?"

Cur thought a minute. He said proudly, "Out of the eater came forth meat, out of the strong came something sweet."

A story his mother had read to him and to Jesse, one with defiled corpses, marauding armies, bloodshed enough to keep a boy's attention. Cur missed his mother, even if he hardly knew her.

Grayab smiled. "What is sweeter than honey? What is stronger than a lion?"

Blue Ruin said, "I don't follow you."

"The rent lion full of bees, the one he killed with his hands.

At the wedding feast, Samson asks the Philistines to answer his riddle. If they cannot, they owe him thirty garments. If they can, Samson must pay the same. When they can't guess, they go to Samson's wife and threaten to burn her father with fire. 'Did you invite us here to take what we have?' And she throws herself weeping at his feet, 'You love me not, you love me not,' and he says, 'Behold, I have not told it to my father nor my mother, and shall I tell it to thee?' But he relents. She tells the Philistines. Samson gives her away to another man and kills thirty men at a river crossing to make good on his debt. He strips the clothes off the dead. He lives a long life."

Blue Ruin snickered, like the spill of coins upon a floor. "You're some scholar," he said to Grayab. "A right grandstander." Then he told them of a bounty of kits he once made. His proudest. His best wage, thirty dollars paid out by a fretting town, and all the farmers stood him drinks. He kept them in a fitted box, and when he lifted the lid, people saw two kit mountain lions, curled head-to-heel like a set of dueling pistols. If you stroked them, their pads were rough as grit paper. Blue Ruin licked his lips to recall it.

Grayab waited patiently, then told them of the screaming that day. Blue Ruin perked his ears. And to know they still lived.

"We heard it too," said Cur. "You didn't see it?"

"But I did. Walking across the clear."

Blue Ruin said, "Had me a gun, I'd light out and track right now. I'm wise in the snow."

Then go, Grayab prayed. Go lose yourself. But he told of the one other lion he'd seen in the flesh. It was a buck panther splayed across the cowcatcher of a Shay locomotive. This ten years before. Pliers and tree saw in hand, the stoker and the engineer contrived to sell the eyeteeth for five dollars apiece and the claws for three. They're still passed around Garrett County to this day, rubbed to a yellow shine for luck. The pelt couldn't be saved.

After a time, Blue Ruin turned to Grayab. "Know any songs?"

"No."

Neversummer slept. He couldn't make good on his promise.

Twice they made sorties out to scavenge timber. It neared

midnight, and Cur tended the fire with grim resolve, mending its corners, as if he could will it to survive wind and wet and plain poor luck. The cold sapped him, and he succumbed to the wistfulness of pain. He would forget McBride for a moment, then remember. A painful cycle he would observe all his life—forget, remember—it ground on him like a millstone. Sarah and Sally Cove and the broken union and the bare, scraped, fire-scalded earth. He could never complete the act of forgetting. That was a trick he could not learn.

Finally, Cur pulled two dollars from his boot and offered it to Grayab. What he'd considered doing for the last hour.

Grayab quit rubbing the hound's back. "I will not take money for food."

Blue Ruin asked why not.

"It is against my faith."

"No," Cur said, with a shaky smile. "I owe it to you."

Grayab gave him the flat gaze that betrayed nothing. He was trying to triangulate this offer against his past, his future.

"I owe you money for a book. Captain run you off before I could get square with you."

Grayab swallowed the last heel of bread. Yes, he remembered the book. Of course he did; he knew his wares to the cent; without them, he had no life. He leaned across the fire. His hands, small but gnarled, looked like he could drive rivets with his bare palms. Blue Ruin was watching him. From Cur's fingers, Grayab plucked the bills like a leaf.

"Now your mind can rest easy," said Blue Ruin.

Grayab reached into his sheepskin jacket and married new money to old. He settled back onto his haunches. The men sat close enough to touch one another.

Cur had to get out of that grueling exchange. "I got to make water," he said, and walked a bit into the cuttings. He took his time. Biting his lip against the cold, he worked himself out, and it wasn't as searing against his raw skin as he thought it would be. Piss crackled in the snow—he couldn't see but it was dark, alarmingly yellow, almost orange. It was silent back at the fire except for the hound's low crooning. He heard footsteps breaking crust.

Cur hiked up his pants and returned to the fire. Grayab was trying to keep from nodding off, chin bobbing on his chest. Out of the shadows, Blue Ruin stood with a chock of greenstone, the size of a chopping block, and raised it overhead. Cur shouted. Grayab scrambled, but the stone caught his shoulder with a dull crack. He fell to his knees, and Blue Ruin tackled him, beating and gouging at the peddler's face. The two men rolled into the fire, Grayab horse-collared in the crook of Blue Ruin's arm. Grayab's head scraped sickeningly on the rock. Fire-logs clattering and a pant leg ripping in the hound's teeth.

Blue Ruin was trying to pull off the man's jacket. He wanted the money roll. Cur rushed forward as the peddler scooped a handful of coals and flung it at Blue Ruin's face.

Shakily Grayab stood, dripping strings of blood down his face. He'd lost his hat, and his pate was brown and hairless, smooth as a hickory nut. The blood began to pump out in gouts. Blue Ruin was slopping snow into his own eyes, shouting to get the bastard, get him quick.

Cur grabbed Blue Ruin by the jacket and dragged him through the snow. The hound was still attached to his leg. Cur couldn't hold him. Neversummer was awake—at first thinking this a dream he'd been ripped from—and blinking at them. He moved out of the way.

Grayab tried to pick up the stone, but it thunked to the ground. He winced, clutching his shoulder. The hound yelped. Blue Ruin had kicked it in the muzzle.

Blinking, Blue Ruin tried to pick up the skillet from the fire—the iron was a dull orange. He dropped it hissing in the snow and moaned wretchedly. Neversummer knocked him down.

Cur shouted at the peddler to run. Grayab trotted into the night. The hound followed.

Blue Ruin didn't seem to hear. He was crying, "Get the bastard! Get him! Poke his eyes!"

Grayab began to run but didn't make it far. He didn't have to. The other men wouldn't leave the fire. A mile off, he leaned against a fallen log that was dressed for skidding. Even had the brand of Cheat River P&P. The hound nuzzled against him. He'd lost his pack, his wares, his fire, but never mind, he kept his hound, his money roll, his life. Adrenaline canceled the pain. But not forever. Grayab's collarbone had been snapped. Soon every breath would tell him so.

CUR WAS TOO STUNNED to speak. He couldn't arrange his thoughts. Blue Ruin plunged a scorched hand into the snow. His back was black and ashy from rolling in the char.

Neversummer asked what in the world.

Blue Ruin was loud. "Goddamn you, he's just a peddler! You see that roll of his? It'd choke a horse." Getting all of McBride's money had made him want more.

Cur did not speak. As long as he did not speak, he was in control.

"Come on," coaxed Blue Ruin. "Fire don't kindle itself. Quick afore the coals die. Quit biting your thumb. That's dirty. You're always doing that."

They nursed the fire. Afterward, Blue Ruin watched his hand blister, turning it every which way. He said, "Quit looking at me like that. You wasn't there! He jumped me, I don't know what for. We had words. He cussed me! If you was there, you'd see it from my angle."

Cur shook his head. The lie's brazenness stopped him cold. "He got that money honest," Cur said—breaking his vow not to speak.

"'Honest' and 'peddler' is two words don't couple. Nothing honest about it."

Cur tried calling Grayab back to the fire. The peddler was out in that swallowing dark, and no one would walk there for him.

"I tell you what," said Blue Ruin, "you must of had a easier life than me. You must of had a easier life to let that kind of money walk away from you. You see a chance, you got to take it. Yes, you two had a soft living, the captain's pets."

Neversummer said, "You're a fucking caution."

"He'd of done the same to you!"

Cur laughed bitterly. "You think?"

In the storm's wake, the temperature fell. Blue Ruin began to untie the peddler's pack.

"Leave go of that."

"You want to freeze to death? No? You best get serious. I'm living. I plan on it."

In desperation, they went through Grayab's wares and his lean-to. A miniature Dutch oven, a bedroll, three mended pots. When he found the two potatoes, Blue Ruin hollered, "I knew he was keeping back from us! That little slick." Penknives and horsehair brushes, paperbacks, some dirty pictures, which Blue Ruin slipped into his pocket. They pulled on pairs of socks and wrapped scarves and shirts around their limbs till they looked like pudgy ragpickers. Cur wanted to sleep far away, but he had to cling to the fire. He called for Grayab again.

Blue Ruin snagged a shirttail with one of his penknives and dunked it in the small jar of lard he found. With that, he doctored his burned hand the best he could. Halfway through the night, Blue Ruin tossed the pack onto the flame, where it hissed and popped. He watched Cur sleep. It took a mighty effort not to take the skillet and mash Cur's head like a rotten pumpkin. Blue Ruin picked it up. He put it down again. He was being watched.

Neversummer wasn't sleeping now. He would stay up as long as he could, staring down the teamster. Daring Blue Ruin to do something. Neversummer scowled. And Blue Ruin was afraid of him. He could kill you. He could kill and wash his hands in the snow. Soon this life would give him a chance. In Logan County he would aim his rifle at soft, living men and pull the trigger.

The night buried yearling deer in the drifts. The lion plucked one bawling from the snow easy as a child pops the head off a dandelion. She gorged and vomited and gorged again. Sated, the lion moved. A low pelvic urge to find a mate.

Cur and Blue Ruin slept in fits. Neversummer listened to the susurrus of snow on snow.

Once in the night, Cur thought he saw men moving through fields of stumps, the black articulation of marching legs. A legion. Searching or running or walking. His lips too cold to call. He woke and saw only one man on the ground: McBride, half buried in snow. Half a dream.

At a certain time, Blue Ruin woke and rose. Still dark. He clutched his throbbing, blistered hand. Without warning, he walked from the fire. Neversummer had the insane thought he was going to fetch the peddler and apologize. But Blue Ruin was gone for good. Neversummer could feel it. Let the shitheel go. He was too weary to protest it. Now he slept.

The fire had been snuffed, but Cur could see the world clearly. The black logs, the scrim of snow. Light and no warmth. Light from above. Cur sat up.

The sky shifted colors and slid, like mercury on a glass. Over the ridge was fox-fire blue, sloshing green, and one pink tongue. Cur stood to see. There was nothing in his experience to compare. These thoughts he tried to piece together—shards of teaching, his mother's Bible—the chariot that carried Elijah up to the bosom of Abraham. He would be saved, assumed into heaven.

But no chariot came. It was only the aurora borealis, creeping south.

ACHY, CUR AND NEVERSUMMER rose as Captain Ketch's dogs gleefully spilled down the snowbank like runnels of ink. The air had warmed to nine degrees. They were alone with McBride's body, and their hands had cracked and bled in the cold, making them look like hog butchers. A pair of men in red hunting shirts appeared against the whiteness.

The rescuers were from Camp Five, a pair of northerners the cold couldn't touch: LeClair out of Halifax and Driggs from Greenville, Maine. They flopped on the dogs and collared them and handed Cur a warm brick out of a sack. Later, they said seven others had gone missing, and they found all but Blue Ruin and one Marylander, who turned up in spring, his bones nothing but stakes propping up a tattered tent of flannel. The Marylander had frozen not thirty yards from a dry, warm cave he never found.

Captain Ketch came hobbling on a walking stick. A metallic cough rattled out of him. Despite the cold, his sleeves were rolled above his elbows. Once he caught his breath, he blew on the tinhorn. It was met with a few scattered cries and hoorays. Then he saw the body.

"Oh, God bless."

Neversummer managed to call out, "It's Vaughn McBride. Killed by the horses. We tried bringing him back."

Captain Ketch began to weep in an unconvincing, luxuriant way. He told Cur and Neversummer that he thought of them like sons, a revelation that did not comfort. Cur's lips were too cold to explain it all. Driggs offered him coffee. It warmed his mouth, and soon he could speak proper. He just wasn't sure what to say. He managed, "Blue Ruin's gone."

"Let's get you a fire."

LeClair walked circles to cut sign for tracks. They had been covered in the night, but he did see McBride's dead horse, guts ripped and strewn, buzzards feasting with their gut-colored heads. He warned them back with a stone. LeClair knelt to see what had been, only to jump back. A young fox poked its head out of the belly's red cave. It had eaten its fill and grown drowsy in a warm bed of flesh. The fox licked its chops and retreated inside. LeClair noticed birds ferrying from one dead thing to another. In the distance, another kill was bright against the hillside. Grayab? Blue Ruin? LeClair made for it. At first he thought it a deer till he saw a long tail. Grayab's young hound, splayed open like a small goat on a spit. LeClair puzzled over this sight. The insulted birds had to wait him out. He didn't know the night's trials. Peddler and hound, banished from their own fire. The dog kept trying to climb into Grayab's lap. The pain made him nauseated. Grayab had a gage of laudanum in his coat pocket. He could hear Cur calling him, until the calling stopped. He'd been stupid to flash his money. Jagged pain in his shoulder, forking up every nerve. He pushed off the dog with his good arm. Grayab's boot was full of snow, but he feared he wouldn't be able to get it back on if he took it off. Thank God it wasn't in his left boot, where he kept his fat roll. What kind of peddler would keep real money in his jacket? He smiled. Elias Grayab, who'd walked the souk with the selfsame ease of the city dwellers, had taught him to keep it close. Grayab's hound wailed, and its master wished he had a match and a mirror, to know if his lips were purple or blue. The cold made him drowsy, too drowsy. He tried running circles to warm himself, but the broken bone was too much to bear, and the dog thought it a game. Grayab had to sit. Pain kept his shoulder warm—the wrong kind of warmth. He fingered the knife. Eyed the hound. He'd yet to name it, entertaining the illusion a coon hunter would spend big money, but he'd grown to love a traveling companion and less-lonely evenings. He wasn't sure he was strong enough to pin the hound, open the body like a trunk, and reach his frozen hands into the steaming guts. By feel he clutched his hound, tilted back its head, and dribbled the laudanum down its mouth, massaging the throat to make it swallow. Grayab hugged it to his chest, waiting for its sleep. He would miss the hound. He glanced into its eyes. It knew. It would die so he could live. That is the way of the world. In Grayab's shoulder, bone scraped on bone. He flicked open the knife. He remembered the one-eared saluki hounds, Bedouins dragging them off the kill.

LeClair decided to leave it be and not mention the slaughtered dog. A sight to haunt his dreams. They had enough madness as it was.

More searchers appeared. Captain Ketch wiped his eyes. Driggs, who Cur barely knew, cuffed him on the shoulder. "You caused us worry and woe," he said.

"Sorry, fellows. I hate to drag you out."

They laughed. "You ain't the weather-maker," one told Cur. "Let's fresh you a fire."

The dogs snuffled and plowed snow where Blue Ruin had tussled with Grayab and his hound. They began to whine. Driggs was told to go find McBride's horses and bring them back if they lived.

The others lifted McBride and mournfully shook their heads. They made for camp, giving up on Blue Ruin and the Marylander without a word.

Cur walked in quiet, head bowed, like a prisoner. It was strange. No one asked where he and Neversummer had gotten all their layers of clothes.

THE COOK'S HELPERS and a saw-filer took turns watching over McBride. The cold kept him through the night, his face gone the color of candles—the skin looked as if it would take a thumbprint. Cur slept for fifteen hours in his bunk. Come morning, the air warmed past freezing, and the Shay rumbled up on the grade, cattle cars dripping grimy clots of snow.

Everywhere the men were sick and hungry. The camps didn't have winter provisions, and the Company grudgingly decided to evacuate the high camps till the weather broke. This was a radical break with policy and much talked about by the wolves. The tracks were cleared just enough. In the valley, the snow and ice were almost gone.

For the first time, Cur and Neversummer rode up front in the Shay, the heat tight on their faces. The stoker shied from the dead man, staring at the furnace as if it spoke to him. His arms were gloved with soot. He went back to work. They listened to his shovel bite at the coal.

The two of them were returning to their lives. In a way, the white mountainside had been a shelter. They spoke freely. The stoker had no English.

"I'm calling it off," Neversummer said to Cur. "I don't know what Caspani'll say, but I tell you, I don't much give a good goddamn."

"Sure enough." In this moment Cur didn't care. He found himself counting off the ones who had shaped his life—his brother Jesse, Old Neil, Sarah, McBride, Sally Cove, Vance and Amos Church—and now Neversummer, most of all. Cur poured himself into the mold of stronger people. Whatever he had, he had gleaned from them, and all were lost but this one. He had done nothing on his own. The thought was searing, poison from a spider's bite—it spread through his body. Neversummer sat there, saying nothing. Cur had tried to make a father of the man. But Neversummer didn't want a son. He wanted a comrade. One as unflinching as himself. Amos had been perfect for him, if only he could have known. Cur would disappoint him before it was done. A matter of will. A matter of time. Cur looked out the window. In thirty miles, the only life was a lone hen turkey picking its way among the stumps, its head another black stick.

In Helena, the stoker helped them lift McBride and rest him on the siding. As soon as they did so, dozens rushed out of the cars. They wanted to be the ones to carry McBride to the burying ground; they argued in the way of country people trying to get onto juries. So Captain Ketch brokered a peace among the wolves—they insisted McBride receive full burial with all the trimmings, a rare thing, for most who died at Blackpine were simply buried by Negroes on the quick. No, McBride was different. The wolves would take turns carrying him to Seldomridge's church, passing him around so often that none grew weary. Now Captain Ketch had to go borrow a wheelbarrow full of chains from the machine shop, to lower the box. He held out a hatful of money, the blocked crown full of coins and sweat-wrinkled bills. They had taken a collection, and McBride's pal Cur ought to go negotiate with the coffinmaker, it was only right. Someone had bottles, and they began to drink and sing, toasting the body. The mud streets were thawing. This was turning into a rowdy vacation. Cur looked grim. He saw it coming on.

When Cur was walking off, Captain Ketch hollered at him.

"What you say?"

Captain Ketch told him, "I forgot—stop by the police and report the death. You was there, you'll have to tell them. Got to keep it on the books."

Cur tasted a little bile in his mouth.

Neversummer whispered, "I'll see you tonight at the house. With Caspani."

"You know where he is?"

"Not at all. You going to the police?"

"No."

"Good."

In the cluttered shop on Fishamble, Cur shook the coffin-maker's sharkskin hand. There was an ash box in the corner, tools scattered on the lid, waiting for a man to fill it. By the time Cur made it to the stone church, the men would have dug up a four-square hole and the sour smell of earth too long under snow. What would it be like to encounter Seldomridge again at the cemetery? Why had Grayab brought it up? Of course Cur wouldn't report the death—he couldn't go to the police, Neversummer would kill him. Never talk to the police was the union's first rule. Captain Ketch probably wouldn't even ask after it.

What if Lis Grayab was dead? Twice Cur had failed him.

In slush and mud the wagons moiled. Cur crossed the road on planks lain across the mess. There, joking with a market woman, was Constable Green.

In passing, they greeted one another with a tip of the hat, but Green didn't break off talking with the woman—he had a fancy for her. He didn't notice Cur's rough look.

Cur kept walking. Until some trick of the light convinced him to go back. It was a sudden, almost casual desire. Tell Green of McBride right quick, then run along to the burying.

"Well, you don't know whether you're coming or going!"

"Can I tell you something?"

Green bid the woman good-bye. He said sadly to Cur, "That was a play-pretty. I wouldn't break that off for nobody."

"I'm sorry."

"Just funning you. Here, let's go to the station. I need to sit. Got a crick in my leg."

Cur felt his stomach fall. It was too late to turn back. He owed this to McBride.

The clerk told them to go on back. Green sat at the sheriff's desk, which was speckled with ink from a thousand paysheets. Unconsciously, Cur removed his hat.

Green spread his arm grandly. "Sit yourself down. Make yourself at home in the seat of power."

When Cur began speaking of McBride's death, he couldn't stop. He spoke in one spew, of Blue Ruin and the peddler, of their fighting, of that awful night. Poor Grayab, still out there. It only took a minute or two, but by the end he was breathing hard, as if he'd recited for hours. He owed this to Grayab too.

Constable Green waved him off. He didn't write a thing. "Your peddler's fine. Seen him today. Well, not fine. He'll live. Made it here on his own anyhow. He's a tough little knot. Your mind should rest easy on that account."

"Oh, thank God. That takes a burden off my mind. You got no idea. That takes a burden off."

"You know this fellow's true name? Blue?"

"Naw. Well, he told me once, but I can't recall it. You can get it from the office. He's ugly as can be. Everyone knows him. Just say Blue Ruin, they'll know. I'll ask the captain."

"No point, really. I'd say this state will not see his likes again. Would you stay?"

Then Cur noticed Green's cloudy, traipsing eyes. He left the room for a few minutes, returning with two mugs of coffee. "Egg-shell coffee," he said, "like mother made." Green blew the surface, and a cloud of steam scudded along. "I'm hearing things from your camp on high. I'm telling you this cause you're a buddy to me. If you hear of anybody raising hell, you come to me. There's money in it for you. Some fellows are trying to shut down the mill. What do they call it? Wildcatting. Yes, I'm serious. Honestly I'm surprised it ain't happened before. What's stopping them? Me? It's coming on strong. They're greedy for money."

Cur felt a feeling like his soul drifting up from the body. The room's corners dissolved. He managed to say, "I ain't heard nothing like that. Sounds funny to me. Might be talk."

"Might be. But they's money in it for you, you know? If." Green smiled and wagged a finger. "'Where there's smoke,' they say."

NEVERSUMMER SEARCHED through the day and finally found Caspani on a side street off Sandusky Avenue. He was warming his hands over a drum fire with others of his kind. The two of them went walking side by side through slush in the streets.

Caspani said, "I will be there at the house. At nine? Yes. We must reconsider. Bring Cur. Bring as many as you can."

Neversummer began to tell him of the mines of Logan. Caspani said it was an excellent idea.

WIND CUT THE BEGGARS and everyone else on East Bank. In the few shacks that had them, windows rattled in their frames. Leaves skittered off. In the Gulley, a rude pair of hogs rooted in penned darkness for bread heels and rotten squash. Yet it was, for them who lived there, the black people of Helena, a cheerful time brought on by the cold. A favorite day would come soon, when they all gathered to gospel and slaughter hogs, the blood singing into pans. It would happen spontaneously the first Saturday the chill held through the frost, maybe tomorrow. You saw all your friends, your old playmates. But that was a life the white men and the Italians did not know. To them, this was the black Gulley in all its despair.

Cur and Neversummer walked the lanes of this place, talking in low, fevered tones. They were late. It had taken awhile for them to find one another, and it was well past nine.

Up ahead, they found the shotgun house the Choirboy had brokered for them. The windows were lit. They could see silhouettes moving inside, many men. Would they all come to Logan? Leave these lives so easily? Cur and Neversummer threaded their way among row houses and the clack of a tackhammer in the dark. Looking up, Cur waved lightly to a leatherpunch, who sat on a stoop working shoes with a peg and awl. The man was old enough for everyone to call him uncle. He lifted a hand and flashed.

Cur felt a hot wind push him back. The world stuttered, and the leatherpunch dissolved in a blinding curtain of light.

The safehouse grinned, opened. A body flung across the road. An explosion: that sound catching up to what had made it, thunderclap after thunderclap and a high muffled grinding and shattered

boards. Fiery bits of wood and glass falling. Shards of metal zing-
ing past. A stovepipe lay in the trail, its end split and curled.

Cur caught a board in the knee and sat down heavily in a hissing
shower of dust. His fingers bled. Ringing in his ears, deep beneath
a layer of deafness. Tarpaper swirled like blackbirds on fire. Rancid smoke stung the eyes and raked the throat. An overwhelming
smell of gunpowder and gelignite hung in the air. Men—no, a
man—stooped to pick him up. Neversummer. Cur put his hand
on the ground to push and came up with a loose shoe that wasn't
his. A low rushing murmur in his ears, like swimming underwater.
Fiery pierces fell hissing and steaming into the river.

Where's the house? Cur wondered. Where's the house?

Nothing remained but one corner and one wall. He turned and
looked each way—the blast had turned him around. It was over.
It didn't seem like it should be over. There was a scorched pit and
a dozen small fires. A sash of purple caught his eye. Cur saw the
shack next to theirs, the outer wall ripped open. He could see
right into what passed for a parlor. Cheap furniture and the roof
slouching into a void. Violet wallpaper. Toppled chairs. A crying
child and dead and dying people. Dogs began their tedious howling. Families were racing from their shacks, holding their ears,
looking for their people.

A fallen man clutched his belly, but there was nothing left to
hold. Salvastore Caluso. He rolled upward and showed his face,
a red smear. No one, Cur thought crazily, would call him Yellow
Sally again.

"My God," said Neversummer. "My God."

All around, they heard moaning in the dark and panicked
shouts. They rushed among fires, looking for union men. Cur
found a chair leg and two green pieces of the strongbox. The barrel of one of the Krag rifles had twisted itself around a scraggly
pear. He found a belt buckle, a glove. It was Bull Aberegg's hand,
still warm with life. They found Proxmire and the bald pool-shark
named Stanton dead and another Italian more or less whole, but
he gripped his own shoulder, and the life went out of him. A

handful of union men had shown up early to drink wine, and their lips were dark with it. Cur and Neversummer couldn't find a single living man. They would never know how many had been inside or fled in the night.

Women dizzily wandered the yards, looking for—what? Children? Their hearing? Someone rang a church bell, or maybe the one in the colored school. By now, the entire neighborhood had arrived. A hog gashed across the snout ran about screaming, sending gouts of blood each time it shook its head.

Cur took Neversummer's arm. "We got to run," he said, noticing a strange echo when he spoke. He couldn't tell if he was whispering or shouting.

"The stove touched it off. That stuff in the floor. It's my fault." Neversummer had the eyes of a cornered thing and seemed to be grinding his teeth.

"Asa, please. Come along. Police are coming."

"What?"

"The police done it. They knew. They done it."

Neversummer was coming back to his senses. "Yeah. You're right."

A girl, too stunned to talk or cry, held a shuck-doll to her mouth, watching them. The doll had no face and Cur would always think of that.

"You smell that?" Neversummer asked him

"What?"

"Gelignite. Gelignite and guncotton. We had none of that. We wanted it."

Cur said, "I don't know."

"No, that's none of ours…"

"Asa, please!"

They fled past men and women who hauled sloshing buckets from the creek. Water sizzled on fires. This wasn't the right side of town or even near the mill, so the water wagons took a long time coming, then had to be navigated up the meager, rooty trail. The town was coming, to save or to see.

It took Neversummer a full hour to remember that ten years of his pay had gone up with the house. Thousands of trees, thousands of hours. He couldn't recall a single one.

FAR AWAY, ON WEST BANK, the sound Zala heard was very different. Jerking her from sleep, the crack was sudden, muted, but she had time to savor the echoes off the mountains. They receded into an awful silence. The wind picked up. She sat in the dark, groggy and listening. Then fell back to sleep. She couldn't help it. She was so tired.

On the nude mountainside, above the fires, Caspani, D'Andrea, and two vigilantes sweated through briar-torn clothes. The climb had been awful, blind, scrabbling. One vigilante looked through a brass monocular for the blackened crater of the safehouse. Caspani raked spare blasting caps out of his pocket and pitched them into the brush.

One by one, the fires winked out as figures doused them.

"Can we go?" Caspani asked miserably.

The vigilante didn't seem to hear, so he asked again. "Yes. Of course," the vigilante said—he seemed embarrassed to have forgotten how badly the two Italians wanted to leave. Wordless, he handed over what was owed.

Caspani and D'Andrea pitched themselves up the trail. When they made the ridge, it seemed to Caspani he was riding the very shoulder of the earth. He could see in every direction.

D'Andrea pointed, saying, "There he." Just barely: the orange flare of a match meeting a cigarette in the valley. The engineer. A train car waited for them on the backside of the mountain.

After dividing the money, Caspani and D'Andrea traveled the night through, not saying a word. Just before sunrise, they leapt off at the Hendricks depot. They didn't shake hands or wave goodbye, but stood at opposite ends of the siding, in abashed tension. D'Andrea's train arrived first. His mouth was stale. He boarded it, setting out for the mines of Monongah, west of here. To Caspani's mind, that wasn't far enough. Not nearly. Caspani went east, sleeping in private cars, arriving in a harbor full of gulls. Bite of salt on his tongue. Pilings draped in seaweed and lost fishnets sweetly rotting. In West Virginia, you could forget about the ocean, and maybe he had. He looked for good shells waved and whole but found not one. He was in Baltimore harbor. His ship would first sail to Philadelphia—and then, on.

Sketching birds, he crossed the ocean to the island he'd come from. He would not die in a foreign place. San Cataldo. His bones would turn to grist there. Live a life, father children. A dozen people met him at the port—how long had they waited?—with tears of gratitude and cigars and a shiny pair of kidskin boots. "Why?" he asked his father, and his father said, "So you can throw those American boots into the sea." New boots were drawn on, but his father's heart would break. Caspani had Milan in his eyes. He wasn't long for this place.

SHOUTING ON THE RIVER, on both sides. The stone church just ahead. Neversummer tried to wipe the sweat from his eyes. "Somebody seen us on the bridge. They done this. They knew." Neversummer couldn't quit talking, like a man taken with fever. There was nowhere to go.

Cur said, "I know the pastor. He won't turn us in."

"With all these people? No, let's go. The train yard."

"The train don't come till morning. They'd find us."

"Who you think done it?"

"Told?"

"Amos did."

"No…"

Neversummer said, "That's how he got off from Youngstown. Amos killed people. Who goes loose after a thing like that? He acted mighty to keep us off it. Like a police would. Arguing with his dad like that. Saying, 'It ain't enough, ain't enough.'"

. "You think? He done that to his own dad?"

"His own dad weren't going to the electric chair. That's how they do in Ohio. Paid him too, I bet. Not nothing to them. Cheaper than what we want anyhow. Amos killed people."

"Maybe."

"You got to start thinking like they do." Neversummer slid his thumb along a chain, fishing out a tarnished watch. The hasp was broken, so he delicately pulled a one-penny nail out of the hinge and lifted off the cover. "I dread the morning."

"We're safe here." Cur gestured at the church.

"We got to go. The house is gone. The money's gone. Forty guns gone…"

An acrid smell. A beggar approached, crying, "Good evening, gents!"

Neversummer glanced up with eyes so hooded and dark they looked countersunk. He managed to say, "How are you, friend?"

"You ain't broke bread with us before."

Cur said, "I know the pastor."

"Cat minister," the beggar said, slapping a hand into the ham of another. "Cat minister."

"What?"

"Afraid of water. Methodist."

"Right."

"Not like a Baptist."

Neversummer said, "He said he got you. Now leave us alone."

At this, the beggar grew agitated. "No, damn it! I am allowed! I am allowed!"

"Settle down, damn you."

"The stone which the builders refused is become the head stone of the corner! This is Our Lord's doing! It is marvelous in our eyes!"

This is what happens, thought Neversummer, when you educate an idiot. The keening and blubbering seemed to break over him like a wave. He began to nod, exhausted. The long night on the mountain, shivering under the aurora, was eating at his body, his bones. Cur steered him up the steps and pushed through the doors. The beggar didn't follow.

Cool as a root cellar, the church was lit with candles of varying heights. The sickly sat on benches, whispering to one another or dozing bundled on the sunken flags. A popeyed woman handed out jars of broth. Tramps—consumptive, chilblained—thanked her, coughing into their sleeves. They warmed hands on the jars before freeing the steam and drinking. Seldomridge ministered to a wizened man who had a sort of ague or shaking fever. Yawning, Seldomridge stirred a bucket of water with a copper ladle.

"Hello," Cur called softly. "You remember me?"

"Yes!"

The other times Cur encountered Seldomridge, the pastor had seemed dour and troubled. Now he was jovial, weird. In a way, Seldomridge's meeting with Constable Green had brought him back to life. He had tasks at hand, he was manic, hadn't even paid the sound of the explosion any mind. He reckoned it one more train wreck. Ideas were spilling from his mind.

Cur said, "Can we stay? Be gone by light. Cheat River turned us out."

Neversummer said, "Yeah, we quit." He was poor at looking nonchalant. He only looked right when he was talking theory or swinging an ax. Cur felt the blood rush to his ear, his cheeks.

Smiling, Seldomridge asked, "Which is it? You quit or you were fired. You can't have them both."

"He's too proud to say," Cur told him. "He's a proud man. That's his way."

"You must have fallen asleep on the ax. I was under the impression it was easy work to get and to keep. Or were you a backtalker?"

"Said we was lazy." The lie was bitter in Cur's mouth. He bit his own thumb.

"Your friend is tetchy," Seldomridge observed. "You didn't commit a criminal act, did you? If you went and clapped a lady with a pair of tongs, I would encourage you to go face justice. No? You're not the head-clapping type?"

"We're just poor men."

"I've thought of you often."

"Come now?"

"Pardon," he begged of Neversummer and brought Cur to a lonely corner, where they could talk as equals. "I just mean when we spoke before, in September. You said a thing. About renting this place. Any place. That you can't hold onto the land. That nothing belongs to anyone."

"I don't—"

"It was profound. I know that now, because it stung me at first. But it makes sense. I thought I had been too radical. No, I wasn't radical enough! Like they say, 'The pulpit is the fearful preacher's stronghold.' I never thought they were referring to me."

"Look now, I was just talking out of my neck. I didn't mean nothing by it. Not the way you do. I'm just a woodcutter. You're putting something on me I'm not."

Finally Seldomridge recognized the fear in Cur, the frantic eyes. "I didn't mean to vex you. Just hear me out."

"I don't put words together like you do. I don't fuss with them. I mean what I say."

"Calm down."

"Wait!" Cur bent double, thinking he was going to vomit. The fear caught up to him. Those broken bodies: Blizzard, Mullenex, poor Stanton. And McBride before. His only friends. His belly was caustic, rolling. His life was over. Hell had come. He began to heave, but nothing came up. Before he knew it, Seldomridge was leading him outside, into the chill night, to a horsehead pump. He made Cur drink.

"I ain't drunk. Just sick at myself. Just sick."

"What's wrong?"

"Preacher..."

"Yes?"

Cur had to sit down on the wet slab. He wanted to talk. Telling Green about the peddler had put him in a confessing mood. He grew wistful. Now Seldomridge hunkered down, sitting on his heels, as the old people of that country do, and Cur began. The Woodworkers and his radicalization. Neversummer, Caspani. Amos Church. Mullenex and the others, that awful redness where Caluso's belly used to be, poor Stanton, that poet of the billiards table. Cur told of dynamite and railroad trestles and men's bodies disassembled like clocks. Why they'd do such. He told Seldomridge not to condemn this, don't you dare, he'd read the Bible and knew the holiness of war, of the rape of Dinah and men circumcised and slain. The time had come. The time had come and his side had lost.

"They been waiting on us. They was ready."

Seldomridge's heart beat in a dangerous way. He considered these who had tried to take the world in hand and shape it, like a hoop of iron. Seldomridge had been unwilling, sullen, plain. He was no visionary.

"Maybe you can't organize loggers," Cur admitted. "Too proud. Too lonely. Every man for himself, you know? Working out under the sun. Aw hell, I don't know." Cur looked at his hands: the scratches and the mud and russet patches of dried blood, all covered over in soot. What had they told him that first night in the cave? This is war. Only one's going to win, there ain't nobody allowed to stand off to the side. They stand off to the side, they're against us. Man, woman, or child. Amos had said that. But Amos betrayed them—Neversummer told him so. Yet he had the feeling that Amos should've led them, Amos who raced through life like a blinkered horse. Amos was cruel. Amos wouldn't have let them fail. He would've ripped them through the needle's eye with all the force of his will.

"All this happened tonight? Yes. I hear the bells. I hear them ringing for a fire." Seldomridge seemed himself again. The crazy light was gone from his eyes. He said gruffly, "Walk with me."

In the cemetery, Seldomridge took him to the apple tree. Here was the grave. "At first I thought it best to bury him by night. He was Italian—a Catholic—and I thought, his family is across the ocean and doesn't even know. It may be best, having died by his own hand. So I thought little of the marks. Their tale stood. Does this have something to do with you?"

"I don't know."

"His name was Nicola. His brother came to me. A dynamiter. I could smell the powder on them."

Cur felt ill again. "Caspani," he said. "Leo."

"Yes! You know him. I thought you would know of this."

"I know Leo Caspani. He don't got no brother."

"It was the night I saw you."

"Before or after you saw me?"

"Later. A matter of hours." Washed out, gray. "Was he a young feller?"

"No better than twenty," said Seldomridge.

"He was a friend of mine. Amos. One of us. He was American."

"Can you find him?"

"Why, he's dead."

"No! Caspani."

"I thought he was in the house. God, I—I don't know. I never seen him. He could be killed."

"He turned you in. He did this to you."

Cur felt a growing denseness in his chest as if his ribs were tightening. Caspani had been the proudest, the most radical. You could depend on him. You always knew where he stood. Cur was arguing this against the obvious truth.

Seldomridge spoke breathlessly. "Listen to me. I know you hate him now. But he's a petty thief. A common criminal. His transgressions are nothing, really, compared to what's happened. Look around us. The land is scraped clean. Who took it? Everyone and no one."

"To me of all people, you saying that. Me, and my friends dead." Cur's voice was shaky, though he knew what Seldomridge said was true. He felt oily sweat on his back. Enough talking. Enough. Seldomridge wasn't offering him comfort, and Cur felt a hysterical anger.

"Listen! Stop thinking of yourself." Seldomridge was smiling again, expansive, spreading his hands. "Yes, there are laws and statutes, but soon there will be no reason to enforce them. They've made their money. Soon they'll go. Do you understand? No one will want this. No one will make us leave. We can claim it. Just take the land over. It belongs to us truly."

"That's—no one'll let you."

"How do you know? It's ruined for a hundred years. Who else would want it? We will redistribute all the land. Remit debts. Men will be idle, ready to work. Hear my plans. I have sketches—" This was not specifically true. Seldomridge was breathing hard. All this had overtaken him in the days since speaking with Green. "This is possible," he said with finality.

"I don't know."

"To know," said Seldomridge, "is not to do. Have you read Tolstoy? The writer?"

"What?"

"Go back up there. To the camps. You have to. The time has come for people like you. Don't leave Helena."

"That's fine for you to say."

"I know that," Seldomridge told him. "I know it is. I'm being foolish. Here. Sleep. Talk to me come morning."

"I got to see my buddy."

"Then go."

"I aim to."

Seldomridge said, as Cur began to walk away to the church, "You've misunderstood me. Will you come see me in the morning?"

"Sure."

"You'll do it?"

"Yeah."

"I don't believe you," Seldomridge told him.

Cur stopped. "No, damn it, I'm not coming to see you. This ain't none of your goddamned business in the first place." He was frenzied now. "I want to get on. I want to get a hundred miles down the road and I want you to leave my ass alone. I don't got time for breakfast and tea at the preacher's house."

"You're making a mistake."

"Would you kindly shut up?"

"You're making the mistake of your life."

"You're not God," Cur told him. "You're not God. Now go back to your little house and sit there."

Cur turned and left. He thought Seldomridge would follow him back, but the old man just stood there shaking among the stones.

Inside the church, the candles had burned down, and nothing cast light but the stove lid's molten seams. Speaking softly, Cur tried to calm Neversummer, who seemed taken with a kind of fit, ready to run, ready to bite through that stone wall if he had to. He kept picking loose threads from his shirt. Hunger had come and gone.

"We got to move," said Neversummer.

"There's no point. We're good here as any place."

"I'd like to sleep, but I'm scared of what I'll wake to." Delirious with fatigue. Hands still aching from the saw. "Police might be waiting at the trains, see who's hopping on. I don't know. They might come here."

"May think we're dead," said Cur. He didn't have the heart to tell Neversummer of Caspani. Not yet.

"They shitting well might. I want sleep so bad. If but an hour..."

With that, Neversummer wandered into a corner, weaving around bodies like a drunken man. Amazed, Cur watched him go. Neversummer lay down and slept dreamless on the flags.

Wide awake, jittery, Cur went outside and sat on the stoop—a raw slab—and kept watch on the lane, waiting for someone, anyone. The moon plain as an earlobe above. Over the river, bats swiveled and drank on the wing, tipping to the waters. He noticed a smear of blood on his knee. He couldn't know if it was his or someone else's.

McBride once explained there's metal in the blood, and this exerts a magnetic pull: it is an excitable metal, and that's why sorrows pile upon sorrows and joys upon joys, so take care when you rile the blood. Then again, McBride claimed swallows winter on the far side of the moon and hummingbirds travel south riding on the backs of geese. Cur managed to laugh. He'd miss McBride so. He regretted he wouldn't be there to return McBride to the earth. And Cur would soon be digging his own—what more are coal mines than living graves? He had known only one miner, Rexrode, who lasted a vile year underground before coming to Blackpine. Near the town of Davis, Rexrode had stood on the dome of Mount Garynorris and gazed into the Valley of Canaan. It throbbed orange and black in the night, a thousand beehive coke ovens rendering coal down and seaming the earth. An evil pulsing sight, one he never forgot. Rexrode did nothing but cough, his spine aflame, and seemed to carry more coal in his lungs than in his bucket. Cur abandoned this for better thoughts. For a moment, he allowed himself to remember Three Forks. A young girl with a shy smile, teaching him the alphabet in an afternoon, putting her hand on his to guide the sharpened stick, etching language into the hen-pecked mud. Sarah Greathouse toed the letters away, and they began again. Long after he'd learned the letters—even mysterious *X* and *Q* and *Zed*—he failed on purpose, to feel the touch of her long fingers on his. She caught on and slapped his hands. Even so, he caught her smiling. The one who guided his hands.

In the morning, Cur woke among sleeping bodies and stretched his limbs as an archer will. An unrefreshing sleep. His brain felt raked.

A smudged rectangle of light in the church doors. He stepped outside. This was real. This was real. The sky was pale and veined above, the bright lining of a mussel shell: a shade of calm. He enjoyed it while he could. He was too stunned to feel hurt or betrayed by Caspani. That would come, like all things, in time. Neversummer stepped up beside him.

MARKET DAY. Fishamble street, thick with carts and bodies, the sun flash of pans. If you can't buy it here, you best go to Elkins. That's eighty miles. A girl not eleven drove ewes and rams in the roadway with a switch, gave no quarter, and passersby cheered her brass.

After the year's first storm, in this warm snap that implied a final week of good weather, everyone craved commerce. By noon, the temperature broke fifty. Country people appeared, muddy to the knees. They wanted to see unknown faces, handle wares, and get a brimming eyeful of town to remind themselves why they didn't live there. Clans of nine and thirteen children were led among the barkers, eldest clutching the hand of the youngest. They held crisp postures so none would think them mountain trash. The country people gave the timber wolves a wide berth and picked their way over mud bejeweled with green, green glass.

Just ahead, the manner of the crowd changed. A boy was passing out broadsides for a nickel each. He could not read, so he rattled out, "All the news that's fit to print or wrap your trout or wipe your shit!" This usually got him laughter and stray coins. Instead he felt scathing looks. He saw the dead men and was quiet, too.

In front of the police station, people filed past the bodies laid gape-mouthed like fish on cooling boards. Carl Blizzard. Peter Stanton. Salvastore Caluso and another foreigner. Keough, armless. Proxmire. Constables were asking passersby to identify the men by their blue rustled faces, especially the wop, though they knew full well who the dead men were. The private vigilantes had told them. Stanton was shirtless but for a sleeve of winter-dulled flies. Mullenex's leg was red meat, and the side of his face a black-and-pink char, hair singed off. Watching as if the dead men could up and run, Constable Green chewed a little cigar—"monkey dicks," he called them—to a wet nub. He'd liked shooting billiards with Stanton. Just goes to show. He leaned over to gently close the man's eyes. Stanton had splinters in his cheek and a torn ear. Sorry fucker.

That day, Green saw hundreds of faces—perturbed, enthralled— constellations of blinking eyes and chattering mouths. If this excites them, he thought, they ought to've seen the others. Then he noticed Seldomridge glaring. Not at the bodies, but at him.

Seldomridge. Green shivered. This was the one face to unsettle his guts. He turned to the other constables and said, "Give it a hour and haul them to the doctor. Get your affidavit, now."

"You said show them to the general public," a constable told him. "We got a ice-wagon coming."

When a girl began to retch, the crowd parted around her. A yellow sock of vomit hit the boards. Green noticed Caluso's leg was flung at an impossible angle. His shoes had been blown off. More eyes filed past. Seldomridge had moved on. "We been general enough," said Green.

In the crowd too, Zala worked her fingers as if saying a rosary, a nervous tic of the muscles. In her heart, she knew the effects she had held in her hands—no, delivered, not held—had killed these men, the blasting caps and the wire. Indeed she had taken them out of the bag and handled them when no one was around, feeling a thrill. The dead faces were drained the color of butcher paper, except for patches of heat-blister and soot. The bald one on the left she once saw grinning with Cur. A crescent-shaped wound on the temple. Green veins, red lips, as if he'd been kissed hard by a harridan. She prayed, and she pined for a rosary. The sloppiness of these deaths angered her. She had aligned herself with the weak of a strong country. They would forever be servants and laborers, spines bent, so many spent horses—just like the people in the land she'd fled. Her husband would never have allowed this to happen. But Victor Kovač had reduced her to just this, this servitude. She was alone. No. She focused on these others, incompetent enough to be victims. She wasn't like them. She looked for Cur and Neversummer among the bodies and did not find them. A photographer set up his machine on a wooden tripod. Afterward the dead men were lifted into galvanized tubs. One's body turned out to be too tender. Quickly they rolled him into his container, but not quick enough. The crowd groaned. The blue spill of intestines would haunt Zala for years. Ice was shored up to their chests. It took on a pink tinge.

Sudden, unmistakable, like flashes of heat lightning, she experienced stark thoughts of suicide—as she did now and again, ever since Victor left her. Zala saw her own body in ice. Her hands, her thighs. She remembered the whitewashed chapel named for a saint she couldn't recall. Nuns kissed the red punch marks of the Five Holy Wounds. Those clean slashes were nothing like this, this craven flesh. Even on ice, the split man smelled of offal. Is this what we accomplish—blowing ourselves up? It was enough to make you weep or laugh. Or had the police killed them? It did not matter, she decided. Stolen pages. Comings and goings. She wondered what could be traced to her.

It was a justification to go. She reached into her pocket, for the green laundry slip that gave her comfort. If you kill yourself, a Slovenian priest once told her, you shall wear those wounds for all eternity. They fester and never heal. You shall greet your Maker having blasphemed His craftsmanship. Wear a halo of flies. The priest said that women care more for vanity—that is why men hang themselves and women prefer to cut their wrists. So he was a fool.

But Zala wouldn't do it. Her husband was alive, had sent her a book. She still worked on his mind, and now she would find him. He had given her back the burden of hope. She rubbed the green paper with her thumb. Cur was leaving her mind. His memory wouldn't survive the years. She had given all her money to the Woodworkers, a bitter regret. She'd have to work another two weeks to buy a ticket, even third-class. She prayed there was no disruption.

A constable watched Zala work her hands like a madwoman around the laundry slip. She noticed and clasped them.

6017 Lausche Avenue, Cleveland, Ohio. On any municipal map.

A black woman had been hired to brush the few hardy flies off the dead men's faces with a funeral fan. The sight of such grim labor made a boy faint. He hit the ground with a slap. In the confusion, Zala slipped away. The train schedule tacked behind glass—she already knew it by heart, but through a trick of the brain, she didn't think of where she was going, but where she had been, as if a train could vault the sea. Grass so rich it looked blue. You almost wanted to bend over and grind it in your jaws. Sugar cliffs. The smell of karst. The limitless lake of Bled. Singeing the feathers off a gander with a tallow. Hanging it from a tree in her father's yard, the father who told her gruffly that she must go into service, if not here, then somewhere, a choice that was no choice. His word was law. She withered in the face of it.

As if she could will her destination to *be*. To be a child again, and a fool. As Zala departed, departed forever, Seldomridge drifted back. Like any other townsman, he couldn't resist the sight. He wore his good suit, neatly brushed, and a clean shave that revealed a pockmark on his cheek as big as a sabot round.

The union man Stanton was shirtless and bloody, and they shored fresh ice over his chest. A boy tried to steal Caluso's brogan, and a constable shouted him back.

A broadside was passed into Seldomridge's hands. The same one the vulgar boy was passing out. Typescript there, sloppy and bold.

> The Editor understands the nervousness of natives regarding these recent immigrants, yet cautions restraint from such heinous methods. Natives are urged to work twice as hard and to make themselves indispensable so that employers do not have to look elsewhere for efficient labor. John 'Bull' Aberegg, Will Proxmire, Peter Stanton, and Carl Blizzard, each of them according to local sources blustery and tempestuous sorts, were known to badmouth Italians. It is public record they had running fistfights with Italians on two separate occasions. Aberegg was known to be jealous of migrants taking jobs from the native born, as well as for consorting with American women. (The sad cases of Miss Foster and Miss Propst need not be reported again.) One of said women, in fact, had rebuffed the braggart Aberegg's advances. The sheriff believes Aberegg stole the dynamite from the Sand Mountain jobsite. Foremen had noted supplies gone missing in the last week.

Seldomridge felt his stomach roil. Four men, it said, tried to blow up a shack full of Italians in the Gulley, misjudged the charge, and destroyed themselves. Salvastore Caluso, Janaway Davia, and an Italian man known only as Nick were also found dead. Two others, Mr. Caspani and Mr. D'Andrea, had gone missing and were assumed dead. The sheriff had arrested two more Americans—Dane Shaughnessy and Will Hostutler—and they were being held for questioning.

But the other things Seldomridge did not know, would never know. The night before, a vigilante had woken the printer's devil from his cot. He handed the boy a story initialed by the editor and walked him over to the office of the *Helena Vox*, promising him extra dollars and a cup of coffee. The printer's devil—a foundling a year into apprenticeship—set the tale backward in type, each letter chosen with care. Wiping sleep from his eyes, the boy worked the press again and again, creating a Saturday broadside. One hundred copies, two hundred. He puffed up the page with advertisements for the New Northern Hotel and a nine-dollar special on suits by Lazar Graur. Pressed ink to paper and made the crime—bigotry, envy—official, inevitable, somehow personal. Laying Vance's book flat on the table, the vigilante took out pictures of Allegheny logging, which had been passed along to him by the *Harper's Weekly* photographer. He gazed through a jeweler's loupe at sawyers in rows. He turned to the book's list and began to match names to faces. Full moustache. Harelip. With care he circled heads with red ink. Short, tall. Sagging eye. Habsburg jaw. Asa Neversummer, right. When the printer's devil called five-hundred, the vigilante shut the book. He even liked the brash font the boy had used.

Seldomridge let the paper fall. Such lies. He tried to spit, but his mouth was dry and gritty as alkali. Maybe Cur was right about him. He should go sit in his little house.

AFTER ALL THIS, Seldomridge walked in the harsh light of a day that could not decide if it was winter or fall. In old times, on any market day, all the preachers came scrappily to the commons to earn a few souls or just to cajole the revelers out of drinking themselves to ruin. Seldomridge had done so for as long as he could remember. But today was different. He hadn't even brought his book.

On Drake Street, the Baptist Eustis Marks was speaking, the whites of his eyes bright with youth. The sermon seemed to be titled, "If they put you on trial for being a Christian, would you be found guilty?" He exhorted them with a fish's asshole of a mouth. "Are you ready to make the great decision?" Eustis bellowed as best he could. Seldomridge laughed his husky German laugh, like a stiff broom on a mortar floor. Was he a fool like this one? A walking featherbed. He couldn't believe Eustis was the one who stole his congregation. It was like having a blind man rifle your pantry. A few glanced over, uneasy at his chuckling. Eustis Marks cried, "There is no water in hell! It ain't the Chicago's World's Fair! It's something to take mind of!"

Seldomridge found another place, an empty patch of ground on the market's edge. That ringing voice, with a scrim of harshness. "Oh Lord, I'm hungry, does anyone have a bite to eat? Could you share with an old preacher? I'm light-headed. I might drop."

Passing families looked up in embarrassment. It wasn't a beggar but a man in a good suit, with an ugly smiling friendly face. In time, a greasy chicken's wing wrapped in newspaper was passed to him. Seldomridge ate with relish. He wasn't hungry. They stood about, watching him. What else could they do? He didn't even wipe the grease from his hands. They worried over his good necktie.

"Thank you! Thank you. This meal is so satisfying. Life is good. The earth is a feast. God laid the table. A feast. Of course, you cooked it, and you cooked it so well."

The woman colored at this, unaccustomed to praise. Seldomridge swallowed. He was gesturing with what was left of the fatty chicken's wing and spoke loudly to the shy knots of people beside him and those passing by.

"When I was young, I ate all the chicken. I even ate the feathers. Yes I did, by the bagful. I filled up on them. I was a walking featherbed. You know what that does to you?"

"What?"

"Turns you into a preacher. All stuffing, no substance." Laughter ripped through the tiny crowd. He had them. "Thank you for cooking this. To me it is a feast."

"You're welcome, preacher! You want some more?" The farmers liked seeing an old man eat. "You need some meat on you."

Seldomridge said, "Oh, I've had my fair share. When you come to the feast, you want your share. Would you allow the first man in line to pile all that chicken on his plate? You, you big fellow, would you take all the chicken you could?"

The grinning heavy farmer answered, "I always take all the chicken."

"I bet!"

The people looked at the farmer, who could laugh at himself. Seldomridge laughed too. They imagined heaping meat. More wandered up, thinking he was offering free food.

"Would you let the first fellow take it all? No, you'd make him come back and put it back on the platter. There are people who have robbed the feast." In my way, Seldomridge thought, I am one of them, I've hoarded too much. "It's time to call them back to the table. Put it back on the platter. Have you seen the good soil wash away with the rains? Where you used to hunt deer, is it there now? No, that's right, the grove is gone, the river is mud. It's worse than worthless."

Twenty people, then forty, with more of the curious slinking there from the gutscrape fiddlers. A cooling wind blew. Seldomridge thought nothing, his mind curiously empty in these moments. He could see pollen drift through the sun and settle on hats of men in the crowd. He had escaped the stone box. He was outside.

"They say business puts money in circulation. Money is in circulation, but what circulates? Did God care for money? No, He reached into a slimy fish's mouth and withdrew the temple tax, that's how much He cared for it. Does He care for it?"

"No, He don't," an old woman cried lustily.

"That's right. He only circulates fine things—the blood, the waters, the stars. It's easier to be poor in the country than it is in the city. So much of what you need is here. This is such a good place. Or, it *was* a good place. I don't need to explain what happened—you saw it yourself. You are intelligent people. It's just as much your fault. It's the fault of many, especially you, but you are the only ones to suffer it. There is broken glass in your food. Do you taste it working its way down?"

"Tell it!" Yes, they felt, they saw. Perceptive people, they named their world with flourishes of poetry, even the slight things, the scanty flowers—they named them trout lily and larkspur, Turk's-cap and jack-in-the-pulpit. They knew. "Tell it again," the fat farmer called. The crowd was clapping and crying out. This was the turn.

"The life we've made here cannot stand. We are the dog that eats its own tail, and it doesn't fatten the dog. Oh, we try. Look at your boys. The hoe handle doesn't fit their hands anymore, isn't that right? They want to work in the mills and earn hard dollars. They want flash. Of course they do. But in ten years' time, what'll your boys do? There'll be no mills. They'll go and take your daughters with them. Why stay? Nothing belongs to us. The land under our feet is divvied up in deedwork like the Christmas goose." Seldomridge finished the wing, giving them time to think this over, in these charged moments of silence, and threw the bones to a skinny starveling dog that ate as smackingly as the pastor had. A time ago, Grayab said to him, Come down. Yes, speak to them, of this world and their trials, their fears and precariousness. But they also wanted elevated talk. It was no ornamentation—they craved a heightened reality, they consumed it like bread. He asked them, "How much does one man need? Will you feed to bursting? And how much *land* does one man need?" The crowd was quiet now, fixed on that shining suffering face. "We have been warned. 'There is the noise of a multitude in the mountains like that of a great people, a tumultuous noise of the kingdoms of nations gathered together. They come from a far country, from the end of heaven...'" The crowd drew closer, dared intimacy. Even if he didn't trust in God's mercy, he trusted in language. Stories of betrayal and empty houses, black suns and lightless moons. "'Wild beasts of the desert shall lie there and their houses shall be full of doleful creatures and owls shall dwell there and satyrs shall dance there. And the wild beasts of the islands shall cry in their desolate houses and dragons in their pleasant palaces and her time is near to come and her days shall not be prolonged.' Isaiah speaks of us, or a people like us. All people like us. The liver torn out, the dross thrown aside. Would you be dross? Be the mess on someone else's hands? I'm asking you to consider another way." They'll get to suffer in new ways, he told himself, but that shall be their business.

WHEN SELDOMRIDGE PAUSED AGAIN, the crowd turned to march to the river. He was startled. They expected a washing after a sermon, though he asked for no such thing. The Methodists didn't even call for full water immersion. But he followed.

To the Cheat, sliding down the year's dull grass. Seldomridge unknotted his tie and slipped it over a branch. He removed his shoes and set his folded jacket atop them. The river's surface was covered with floating pieces of bark from the mill and the odd, bobbing bottle. From the foot of the knoll, the riverbank, you couldn't see much of town. No one owned the water. The people—seventy or eighty now, country people—let him pass through the crackling cattails. Seldomridge loved Christianity for its adoration of clean water. He waded into the Cheat, the cold river climbing his clothes. A sloppy wedge of ducks broke from the cattails. What had he called them to? Certainly not to fall on their faces and bare necks to God or man. You can incite them to uprising, or incite them to subjugation: perhaps no middle exists. He ached for the crowd. They had trust in their eyes. Most were women. He longed for a world ruled by them—he recalled Zala, comforting him. Was she here? Women are quicker to understand. They do not fear change as men do—rightly or wrongly, Seldomridge believed that.

The crowd divided itself into a line. They knew how this was done. Seldomridge could just make out his church, with green stains down its walls. He would never go back inside. Everything that came after—actions that would trouble the bishops further—began on this day.

"We need not wait for God to shape our lives. He shaped the land with water and that is enough."

"Thank you for doing this," a woman, third in line, said to him. "I ain't seen it done in some time." The people kept giving their thanks. For a moment, they could ignore the mill above, the fish kills, the broken glass on the shore, the putrid smell of sawdust in ferment. The water was cold and bracing, like the old life that was gone forever.

If only Grayab could be here. Under Seldomridge's touch, the bodies shivered. He was able to enjoy each smiling, gasping face. For the first time in ages, he felt he had done right. He knew they would come hear him again—he said he'd be here, when they'd asked. By the time he worked through twenty, he couldn't feel his legs. His skin was chill, bearing all his afflictions plainly, but he cracked a dinner-plate grin. His high feelings would hold through the day, until he saw Grayab in his infirmary bed and heard of the wretched night. But for now, Seldomridge drowned them lovingly one by one as they held their noses, trusted him. He felt their feet give way as he firmed his arm and pushed them down. He felt appreciated. Maybe that was all he ever had wanted.

NEVERSUMMER SAID, "Looks like somebody kicked over a damned anthill."

So many people in the street. Cur felt bile trickling up his throat. The crowd knew. They had found the exploded house, the shattered guns. Someone had gotten up a mob, and Cur would receive their treatment. Beat him ragged enough to care for nothing. Grab each arm and pull, the muscles shear with a fleshy stage whisper. In his Maryland days, he'd witnessed the lynching of a pederast; a deputy merely unlocked the cell and the crowd dragged the spindly man to the town's nearest oak. In a place like this, a hundred men is the law. That day in Cumberland, the gallows limb was rotten from heartwood out, and when they kicked the ladder from under him, half the tree gave way, delivering the body toward the earth gently as a babe. The pederast was torn to pieces before he ever hit the ground. A logger pointed at him and Neversummer. Cur felt faint.

A mule ran down the street with campaign posters and crepe stapled into its hide, oozing blood. Its cart bucked and threatened to topple. A bottle shattered, then another. Cur jumped at a gunshot. Neversummer began to laugh senselessly—Cur thought he had lost his mind.

What Cur mistook for pistol shots were children touching off Chinese fireworks that bloomed crazily and slapped against gutters and shop windows. A merchant beat out a fiery bale of hay with his hands. "We're fine," Neversummer told him. It was only market day. Cur felt stupid, then exultant. They slipped off to the depot and not a soul tried to detain them. An empty freight pulled out moments after they arrived. It was even heading south. They ducked into a car. Helena let them go easy.

Cur felt drunk with joy. He had found this place on the tracks, and so it made sense to leave this way. A bracket on his days. Laughing, the two of them rode and felt a pleasant jostling in their bones. Cur's throat was burnt and raw from the night before and his voice was husky.

"How do we get to Logan?"

"I'll show you," Neversummer told him.

In an hour they were at the Low Gap terminus, where the train made a long stop to take on pigs of smelted zinc. A half-hearted railroad bull checked the cars, but Cur and Neversummer merely sank into shadow. There was some confusion as to what wares were to be loaded. It seemed the train would never move.

Neversummer yawned. "That bull ain't coming back."

"You still tired, Asa?"

Neversummer nodded. Cur yawned too. Nights of fitful, feverish sleep had run him like hounds. He tipped his hat over his eyes and, in time, drifted off while listening to the rough grunts of men loading the cars and the gondolas. When the Shay backed up in reverse on the rails to shift to another track, he started a little, but didn't wake.

Neversummer did. Cur wasn't vicious enough, no way around it. He was water; he would fill whatever container you poured him into, and then you could freely pour him back out. It would happen at the worst possible moment. For the last few months, Neversummer hadn't been able to shake this feeling. Cur wasn't up to their cause. He wasn't up to Logan County. He can't kill. Can't be merciless. Neversummer sat on the edge of the open car, legs dangling over the tracks.

The train began to move, and he jumped. Neversummer would get to Logan County, yes, but by a different route. He would have a shocking life in that place. And Cur would be spared the shame and the endless disappointment that was this manner of living. Neversummer told himself it was because he cared for the man. He wasn't abandoning Cur; he was saving him.

There was a briar patch on the edge of the rails, a gulley where tramps bedded and cooked their grubby meals. Neversummer whispered hello to them—"I'm no bull," he said—and sat on his haunches. The Shay pulled off. He never saw Cur Greathouse again. He wanted no reminder of Blackpine.

HEADLESS GHOST

THE COUNTRY ROILED, but you'd never know it here. Charleston, West Virginia, was a world away from Blackpine—179 miles by train exactly, the quickest route if not the most fashionable. A fitting site for a backwater capital, an unlovely river town, squat and smoky. Judge Randolph's offices overlooked the rivers and their endless barges of coal, near the confluence of the Elk and the Kanawha. Brown water moved, just barely. He had an invitation in hand to a gathering of judges in Washington. He feared going and not going. Country Judge Randolph, some called him behind his back, pretending they didn't want him to hear. In public he liked to say, "I only have the truest of credentials, my own good sense and experience; in this nation, thank Providence, self worth and striving are all you need, not a bride's train of noble titles!" In his bedroom, to his wife, he lamented the fact he'd only read law rather than making a formal study of it at a university. If he were offered a higher office, he would take it; if not, he would honor and esteem his current one. And bear in mind, he had strengthened the nation with commerce in a way no public official ever could. He was no cloistered legal monk.

Saying such, his temples pounded.

He turned the invitation over and jotted stray thoughts on the back. At least, he told himself they were stray. They had been, in truth, elaborately rehearsed.

To be a public man means to expose oneself on all sides.

Randolph's name was being spoken in many quarters, said to be on the president's shortlist of Supreme Court candidates—a life-long appointment, a bulwark against chaos, against time—all he had ever wanted. His competition was a Third Circuit man. Perhaps he should take steps to better position himself, or sow doubts about his rival, a leonine man known to poke fun at unlettered judges. Only a fool respects the powerful, and every day Randolph was amazed anew at the storehouse of fools that was this world.

Every day, he wrote, *men mistake superstitions for virtues.*

Randolph did a startling thing. His jottings became a letter. He would write Eugene Helena for advice. Senator Helena was a popular man. Beloved Helena. Hated Helena.

Closing the office even to his clerks, Randolph wrote every after-noon, draft after draft, but didn't post the letter. The desired tone, perhaps humility, would not yield. On Tuesday, he let his clerks return—he didn't want to become the topic of fun. He tried at the letter one more time. Randolph bent to rummage in his drawer for a fresh bottle of ink. Frosted glass blocked out the world.

His hand shot to his neck. To cup a sting. A wasp in winter?

Glass doors fell in a shower. Randolph didn't see the flash, but he felt the pressure change in his ear. Smoke, splinters. His neck bleeding a bit. Now shoes crunching glass. The door was blown open. One of his clerks clutching his ears, as if to keep his head from coming unscrewed.

Another man sat on the ground, too still. His lap was red, and his arms seemed to vanish into the redness. Randolph couldn't understand the explanations others gave, and it took him the afternoon to realize he'd gone deaf in his right ear.

The doorkeeper had lost his hands opening the package. He was lauded as a hero, and Randolph a survivor, and the anarchist who did this the worst of all cowards. Mere inches and the debris would have slashed Randolph's throat. The papers called it a miracle. They gleefully noted the bomb crippled only a member of the working classes. Helena and Baxter wired well wishes and promised to travel from Washington when some political squabble ran its course. Randolph wouldn't have to post that hateful, fawning letter to Helena! All Randolph's children returned to Charleston, and he joked if he'd known it would bring such a reunion, he'd wish for a bomb every Tuesday. It made his youngest daughter cry. "Oh, Daddy," she said.

They went out for a nice meal at the Clipper, on the corner of Euclid and Jackson. His daughter made them take a circuitous route so as not to pass the court offices, which hived with journalists. Another table picked up the check. It could have been any number of men. With pride Randolph wore his garishly plastered neck. He was a tough old bird. His survival, it pleased him to know, would strengthen his reputation in certain circles.

The next day an unsigned letter arrived, postmarked from Lydia, a lonely terminus. *May God have mercy on you because we won't.* Randolph considered releasing it to the papers. The clerks convinced him not to. Attention, one said, emboldens the insane.

Fear didn't find him until he went home to lie sleepless, and so aware, in roaring silence.

Anxiety felt in silver jags. The clack of streetcars in the distance.

From then on, Randolph felt comfortable only in public. On flimsy pretexts, he called distant friends and acquaintances and asked them to dine. Each noonday, you could find him sitting across from an oil landscape at the Clipper. A poor reproduction of a poor painting by a so-called European master. The only person he had ever heard praise it was Baxter, colorblind! Randolph recalled privately mourning, as a young soldier, the fact that Baxter couldn't see the mountain's gaudy blooms—the flaming azaleas—in the full color God granted them. A matchless sight, Helena agreed. In fact, they had discussed their friend's lack many times over the years.

Randolph didn't speculate as to what lacks his friends had discovered in him.

They had been lucky when they linked arms together around that first towering tree. If they'd known the obstacles to success, Randolph reckoned, they would never have begun. Thank God for ignorance. Thank God for youth.

Two weeks after the bombing, Helena cabled his arrival at dinner hour. As he tore bread at the Clipper, Randolph studied Helena's face, which betrayed nothing. The saying *mean as a minority whip* was said to become popular during Helena's tenure. Still, Helena had the glib social grace of a fraternity president. Randolph himself was dour in comparison, too used to the medieval deference lawyers paid him in court.

The bombing, Helena saw, had elevated his partner to the realm of the unbearable.

They agreed the meal was passable ("Not bad for West Virginia," Helena said.) and were brought coffee without having to ask for it. Randolph smiled to the waiter, a scraping fellow who seemed to work every shift.

Finally, finally, Helena brought the president's greetings, shared his own perceptions, and said Randolph was one of four names circulating. A distant fourth, Helena felt no need to add. Why inflame the searing jealousies that dwelled in his partner? Helena avoided Randolph when he could. Even in casual conversation, Randolph startled the more sensible with his vehemence. He showed them what they truly believed.

"Four candidates?" Randolph asked. He'd be left wandering the small geography of his ambition—pinched in rat-hole Charleston forever. Vouch my name, he wanted to shout. I gave you your livelihood!

As he misremembered. He was nothing without his friend.

Helena said, "Who ever heard of a waiter with a hat?"

Randolph turned. It wasn't the usual man. The waiter, an immigrant named Victor Kovač, once employed and perhaps mistreated by the Company, approached the table. Time skewed, slowed. The waiter held the hat in his left hand, but used it to cover his right. In consequence, his bearing was almost formal. Randolph wiped his lips on the napkin and rose, pushing back his chair. It fell.

The waiter's neck was a little grimy. He pulled the hat away, and Randolph took a step into the man's path, because that was the route to the door.

It was not a gun. It was the bill. The waiter handed it to Randolph.

From a distance, it looked as if they were shaking hands, because no one had ever seen a person rise to make commerce with a waiter.

The waiter's wife, Zala, would open a Cleveland paper and read of this, and grow woozy in the street, where she would live out a sad and precarious life.

Face flushed, Randolph dug for his money clip, and a second waiter came sharking alongside. The gunshots began. Senator Helena was on the floor, dead instantly. The waiters fled out the door. They would be caught in Covington, Kentucky, placed on trial, and hanged from a scaffold at Fort Leavenworth.

Even in this, Randolph was to be outdone. He touched his chest. They hadn't wasted a single bullet upon him.

THE VALLEY AND RIDGE, country first knit together of the desperate, the religious outcast, the indentured fleeing their contracts. Hen-scratches of fields and half-wild stock. Corn was planted on hillsides canting greater than forty-five degrees, with rocks chocked under pumpkins growing between the rows to keep them from rolling down and snapping their vines. Cur passed a surveyor on the road sighting down his theodolite. He wore rimless octagonal glasses and a buckskin jacket. He raised an arm in greeting but never looked up.

Cur had put aside the Cutters for town shoes, and the soles

felt thin as frog skins lashed to his feet. He sucked a horehound drop, clicking it on his molars. Jacket flung over his shoulder, a sporty fugitive, he wore a shirt bought from a starched foursquare pile, his cheeks blue from a day-old shave. The road descended into a swale of limestone river valley with buxom sheep on shorn hillsides, where a few well-off farmers lived: Paxton, McJunkin, Stowbridge. Redbrick farmhouses rose like frigates on green swells, riding a gentle storm of geology. A pair of hawks flew uphollow, then a third. Spindly colts tumbled through fields like tossed handfuls of jacks.

When Cur had awoken at the Low Gap terminus, drowsy and confused, he reckoned Neversummer had wandered off to make water, but when the train picked up speed, he knew the man was gone. Cur jumped off the train, earning himself a little gravel rash. He walked past the jungle where Neversummer was sleeping. Cur knew where he was going. He didn't pause.

Now he made his way southeast through Jephtha, to the Three Forks of the Cheat River, his father's land. Eventually, the Company's logging would have taken him there, he reckoned, but that would be a sour homecoming, tearing at his own disinherited ground, as though in revenge. This was better. Why had he waited so long? Cur was glowing, full of light. Sarah would be there. It's where he belonged. Neversummer's abandonment, a blessing.

A rooster crowed. He hadn't heard one in awhile. He smiled. His father used to say, "That's old chanticleer. Doing what he does."

Cur had obscure fantasies that once he saw Sarah Greathouse, all would be as it once had been. His first thoughts were physical. A decade ago: bare shoulders, Sarah's deft hands, lazily moving his prick as they lay in tall grass that was soft after a cool night. Suddenly his whiteness on her belly, her hands. He would have a life again. Jephtha was halfway to that sliver of land where he'd come of age. His half brothers would remember him. A premonition told him Old Neil was dead.

It was night when he made the outskirts of Jephtha. With dark coming on he grew somber, savoring the cold, his blistered feet. A walking failure. Sitting in the caves, Cur had—like all the young, and the old—indulged in fantasies of matchless heroism, of Sarah and others hearing his name spoken on all good tongues and regretting the loss of him. The world was more vicious than that. He hadn't been willing to weather its indifference, be deft and patient and cruel. He feared a future. Neversummer had guessed his true and dithering nature. The road was wet and wrecked with hooves. The mud filled his boots. No one at Three Forks would welcome him. What you wanted most was the thing denied you. He had lived his life in backward order. It kept getting worse. The Greathouses would scowl and order him off the property. He wondered if Neversummer was thinking of him.

WHEN CUR SAW THEM, the meager lights of Jephtha were brighter than they ought to be. Did they have gaslights now? No. These were flames.

Bright as a harvest moon fallen to earth, the vision of fire drew him off the road. A crowd a hundred strong had gathered about the burning Tuscarora County Courthouse. Stones cracked and hissed with jubilant sounds. The false white moon of the courthouse clock turned orange, turned black. A man slapped him on the shoulder.

"How you doing, old buddy?"

Cur jumped. It was Constable Green.

"Well now, you're the jumping frog. You're outen your territory, my brother. What you doing in old Jeff-Town?"

"Just passing through," Cur managed to say, finally, when the shock of seeing the constable wore off. Helena was running him down. For a second he had to glance down the street, to make sure he wasn't back in that place.

Green winked. "All us too," he said. "Just happened to be here."

Cur glanced about. He recognized many from Helena, even some working timber wolves, no layabouts either. Had the Company given them time off? They had rifles, shotguns, and crude cudgels, but seemed happy, men at a bonfire, cussing merrily. The Jephtha militia—a dozen bewildered fellows, rubbing sleep from their eyes—could only watch. No one brought buckets from the

river, no church bells rang, no lacquered hose-wagon drawn by
horses that had been trained with torches not to shy from fire.

Green tossed a thumb over his shoulder. Dusty hundreds of
deed books had been piled under a stand of locust. "We rescued
them. Got a safe place to keep them too."

The high sheriff of Helena and the high sheriff of Jephtha were
arguing in the street, but they couldn't be heard over that sloshing roar. The clock tower tipped, and everyone jumped when it
fell into the flames, tossing slivers of rock like grapeshot. Helena
men hurrah'd. That night, the Jephtha militia's commander—a
banker by profession—would drink Paris Green out of shame and
lie down beside his wife, kissing her sleeping face one last time,
his favorite place on the ridge of her cheek, for she had a drop of
Indian blood. In a year's time, a new county courthouse would rise
in Helena, where it should have been in the first place, as Judge
Randolph told everyone: "Never was a fire so fortuitous." On the
West Bank, under flags and bunting, Randolph and Senator Baxter and Senator Helena's widow would sit, the men sweating, the
lady fanning herself, as the governor blessed this rock of justice,
quarried from Nicholas County stone.

"Ought to accompany us," said Green. "Get a few dollars for
your efforts."

So Cur hoisted his share—two deed books, heavy with transac-
tion—and carried them to the depot. It was almost like a hunting
party, a hundred men beating north. Green passed him a bottle,
and Cur took three good swallows to drink himself calm. In time,
the two of them began to horse around, swapping tales like old
times. Cur nearly felt better. At least, it kept him from throwing
himself into the Cheat. He tossed the empty bottle without a care.

Green turned to him and made a gesture like a man toting full
buckets in either hand. "You know what you call a farmer come up
to you with a sheep under both arms?"

Cur cracked a grin. He didn't know.

"A pimp!"

They fell poleaxed laughing into one another. Cur was beyond
mend. He said, "I thought you'd say a big, a big—"

"Bigamist?"

"Yeah. One of them."

At the Low Gap terminus, men slung deed books into the cars, and the sheriff begged them to be careful, but quick, can't be sugar-footing around. Some discharged guns at the moon for sport. In the window of a Climax engine, the engineer played a harpoon, a brassy muttering, as they waited for the switchman to snake open the track. A Shay idled on the opposite side, pointing southbound. It was attached to a dozen empty coal hoppers. There. Cur should jump it, go south or west or anywhere. He had the envelope of pay in his pocket. Go now to Logan County. Prove Neversummer wrong. He too could be cruel. Ask anyone. Ask Sally Cove. Chop coal and bring revolution down on the world. Cur was sweating alcohol.

Green hollered, "You coming?"

Cur told him to hold on, he had to go to the bushes and take himself a piss.

Go to Logan now, he thought.

Nodding, Green turned to his sheriff. "You know what you call a farmer comes up to you with a sheep under both arms?"

Cur rejoined the crowd. Green was his friend. The trip to Helena took but an hour. This was easier. Work. Accept your lot. Cur had been drawn back to what horrified him, as a dog circles and whines at its vomit or one of its dead in the road. Wobbly, his feet touched Helena proper. He let the other courthouse men carry him along. At the Eagleback Tavern the doors were chained. They said the proprietor, Cecil Braintree, had refused to pay the protection tax. Constables slaughtered three casks, over 11,000 bottles of beer, ninety bottles of fighting whiskey, cases of Mumm's Extra Dry, and put axes through the gaming tables. The crowd moved on to the first place you could find a drink, and Cur paid right out of his envelope of pay, years of money he'd planned on giving to Sarah. A procurer and two women joined him. The one on his left had the smallest ears Cur ever saw on a lady. Green took a seat. They changed from beer to whiskey. More entered, congratulating one another. The bar was named, merely, the Tavern, but jokers called it the Razor Strop.

Cur would find the preacher here in Helena—he shouldn't have cussed Seldomridge, he ought to make it right. Neversummer was lost to him, but Seldomridge was here. Didn't the preacher say they could do great things? They would talk. Make this new way of living. Be redeemed. Take back their land. It belonged to them and their fathers. Cur was misty-eyed, sentimental. Under the table, the small-eared woman scratched at his fly with a fingernail, making a noise on the corduroy like a tiny saw. He took the tortoiseshell comb from her hair and tried to twist it in his own. They were leaving for a private house or something. They stepped into the alley. Cur's pockets were hanging out, dead men's tongues.

Green's face floated in front of him like a balloon. Cur felt pressure on both of his arms. Was he having a stroke? Two deputies were pinning him against the wall.

"I didn't touch the man! I tried to help!" In his drunkenness Cur thought it was because of Blue Ruin and the peddler. He kept hearing a two-syllable word, like a curse.

Green was saying, "You set fire to the county courthouse in Jephtha, West Virginia, and destroyed it at great cost. We have many a witness, so feel free to begin your denials."

"Please..."

Cur finally realized the word they were saying was *arson*.

"I thought you was a friend," Green said. "Come along, now." He was shaking a bit. He'd thought up arresting Cur on the fly, and he was proud of himself for it. And he would be rewarded.

IN HIS FIRST YEAR in the Moundsville Penitentiary, way up in the northern panhandle, Cur bought paper and pen at the commissary. He tried writing Sarah. He tried writing Seldomridge. Tried Neversummer, Sally Cove, Grayab, Blue Ruin, Caspani, Captain Ketch. One desperate week, he tried his hand at a letter to the editor of the *Helena Vox*, pleading innocence, for burning a courthouse made no sense—he was no anarchist, he was a gentle sort, a stalwart Company logger, ask Captain Marty Ketch. He would pen a few sentences and find them insipid and stop. The paper grew dusty. In time, the ink evaporated from its tiny bottle, leaving a blackish ghost on the glass. He never bought a single stamp. He traded the paper to a murderous artist who drew the same stylized waterfall over and over. Near the end, Cur thought of Seldomridge more often. Of them all, only Seldomridge would understand.

It was a place of block and towers, built by Confederate prisoners. He learned to bow his head and walk the red line to the mess, left hand on the wall and your right on the shoulder of the prisoner in front of you, in shuffling elephant step, with rifles aimed from ports upon you. He served in the brickyard, then the carpentry shop—one time he built a gallows. He shared a five-by-seven cell with a twitchy boy who had killed his own sister. On the upper tier they sweltered together. More died of heat exhaustion than anything else, especially those afraid to wander the yard in a place where a dozen guards watched seven hundred men. Stone killers claimed the shade from the walls.

The warden made Cur a trusty in the carpentry shop, and he wore the white T on the back of his prison beige. He broke an arm in a scuffle when one of his charges attacked him.

Not a week after he was released from the infirmary, the first riot broke out. Guards and informers were taken hostage, including the trusty who sold tickets for public executions, which had a going rate of twelve dollars apiece even in those lean years. The guards were made to strip naked, wear chains round their necks, and belly crawl on cement; informers were tortured with knives; the warden turned off power and water for days. "Ain't he a trusty?" some asked of Cur. They went to his cell, and he suffered there in ways it's best not to recall, though they made his cell mate watch and the sight never quite left the boy. Finally the National Guard came firing. When light shone again, the trusties carried fifteen dead prisoners to the yard to bury. The yard was 352½ feet long and 82½ feet wide, and Cur knew every inch. His crew buried the men with crosshairs chasing them like horseflies, the rifles leaning out of gothic battlements. He buried the same men who abused him, and he wasn't above kicking a corpse.

Cur had trouble turning his neck anymore—his jerky motions

could scare a child. It would get worse with cold and the passing years.

IN PRISON, CUR MISSED MUCH and Cur missed nothing. The work changed and it didn't. No matter how good you are, the world can make do without you. Blackpine traveled on.

Captain Ketch was most impressed by the new steam donkeys for loading logs, barely had call for horses. "You would not believe," he wrote to old wolves with whom he kept correspondence, answering promptly in the florid penmanship of the semiliterate. "Ain't sure how we made do without them gadgets." Captain Ketch grew fatter and was the first to admit it. "Same old Cap," he wrote. "More of him."

In the kaleidoscope of faces, Captain Ketch only half remembered the fellows called Cur and Neversummer, and he met new boys: truculent Renner, happy Ben Truax, more Goddards by the score. Foreigners came and went as they did, in silence.

He called Renner "Cur" every once in a while. They tilted hats at a similar angle.

1909. 1910. 1911. The seasons smeared into one another. Captain Ketch's last pleasure was the wild high country they found. An arctic swamp, the air noticeably thin. Headwaters turned black and boggy: bracken fern and cranberry, huckleberry and azalea, sphagnum and reindeer moss. He hunkered to touch pitcher plants and sundews—flesh-eating plants, these. Twitching flies disappeared down slick green gullets. Quick for a fat man, he scrabbled up bruise-blue salamanders with constellations mapped on their backs that coated his hands in gluey slime. Then dry shale barrens, minute rocky prairies. He found the Roaring Plains and the Dolly Sods, the winds cannon-loud where no plant can grow and birds are blown in all directions, no foothold in the sky. He turned up his collar, to bid defiance to the roar. A crew located the largest tree ever found in that state, a white oak fourteen feet in diameter, sixteen feet up the trunk. Captain Ketch didn't see the felling himself, but he did count the rings. The oak was over seven hundred years old, and its rings bore the mark of fire and flood, mast and drought.

Captain Ketch said, "The Wandering Jew, behold it move." Unstack the buildings. Load the cars. The Cheat—a brawling river in Helena and Parsons and St. George—was a different matter where Blackpine now roved. It lost water to forks and branches, the main stem less and less, a middling trout stream. A man could jump it with a running start; a fox would cross it without pause. In low water summer, coons grabbed trout from the pools and ripped open their bellies as they squirmed and flapped square tails. There, ahead. At the sight of fresh timber, Blackpine paused. Stack the buildings back, fit the pegs, make the corners true.

On an appointed day, Captain Ketch stood atop Spruce Knob with a surveyor whose hair was shiny as bear grease. They took turns with the looking glass.

"Twenty-eight hundred acres. That's where Company lands peter out."

Captain Ketch gazed at the black delta of woods that ran aground at a stand of salt-white cliffs. "That it?"

"You're in better shape than most," the surveyor told him. "I was in the tablelands, and there's hardly a stick of wood left standing you could prop a table with!"

"Might favor west."

"Where to?"

"Oregon," Ketch said, pronouncing it like *octagon*. They spoke of that place—rain, jack salmon, Indian tribes—as the surveyor studied the strip of land through his theodolite: a swatch of forest called Gaudineer Point. The surveyor's craft is a matter of degrees. He made a mistake that day—thinking of Oregon—and, doing so, allowed a fifty-acre wedge that outlasted the saws, lost in a meddlesome gulley. The generations would drive their children here, as people visit ruined cathedrals. The surveyor closed the glass against the heel of his hand. He tossed it into a satchel full of tools; his instruments were curiously like a mariner's.

"Well, put the saws to it."

Summer of 1912, word came down that Cheat River Paper & Pulp was hiring no more. Rumor of "the halt" was passed from the commissary train to cook's helpers to the cook and so on. Captain Ketch gathered the fellows he esteemed most, herded them into his office, and asked them to come to Oregon. They said they'd think on it. The timber wolves circled the last great woods, bellowing as the trees fell. They were working themselves out of a job, but if you slowed you'd be fired. Better be cutting eight thou' a day. With the fever of hoarders, wolves began to hold back pay. Four taverns closed in a week's time. The camps pitched into high stands where corduroy roads did not reach. No one spoke of what he'd do next.

Different camps began to run into one another in the woods and bashfully shared their tobacco. A dance floor with too many partners. Their timber-shouts wove in the air. Renner and Truax crossed a field of slashings to a final pine rising from the waste, a pillar of green. They found a pair of cut-men from Camp Three dousing kerosene on a saw. They looked askance.

Truax said, "You go on and take it."

"No, you go on," the Camp Three men told him.

"It's all right."

"Please do!"

"Hurry up or Cap'll fire you in your last minute. 'Put the rollers under you, I don't mind! You'll get no letter of welcome from me!'"

They laughed. This polite dance took several minutes, and finally they rolled bone dice on a stump. Renner and Truax won the pleasure of sawing the last spruce to drop in Tuscarora. They weren't the ones to fell it, though. That went to Henthorn the axman. It occurred with no more fanfare than you'd grant the birth of a stillborn colt.

Knotbumpers had to sit around waiting for buckers to measure the log so they'd have something to do.

Next morning, Cheat River Paper & Pulp disbanded operations. Captain Ketch took inventory as the bunkhouses were disassembled, ax and peavey confiscated, last meals divvied out. They tossed the tarpaper roofs on raging bonfires and tied their meager belongings in dusty flour sacks given out by the cook. They'd become miners and carpenters, preachers and fathers, soldiers and postmen, jailers and jailed. None would farm here, because rain had washed the topsoil away. Some earth went north to the Monongahela, some went south to the Kanawha, but it all found its way to the Gulf of Mexico, the delta of Louisiana, the sickman's bung of the continent.

There were rumors of cuttings in the Canaan Valley to the north or Leatherbark to the southwest, the latter unlikely. Some spoke of Canady. A band of West Virginians planned to ride to Davis on the next train, but some would trek west, to the continent's ragged edge where orcas roll and seals throw themselves on beaches of stone.

They climbed Mare Camp Knob, just because. Captain Ketch stood on a stump. "We done something here and don't you forget it, we cut enough timber to reach the moon and back thrice over. That is the honest truth! Even if you measure it with that goddamned worthless Doyle Rule. I said it a thousand times, ought to use us a Scribner Rule like them northern boys do. Takes a better account of your saw kerf. Scribner gives you a quarter-inch kerf. What's that Doyle? Five-sixteenths. See, it don't match up to the saws realistic. I believe it underestimates your small log and overestimates your bigs. Anyway."

The men laughed politely at hale Marty Ketch.

"We'll be remembered. Just like the Egyptians, a-building their mighty pyramids block by block. We accomplished."

Viewed from that peak, the land was a mutilated sea. Naked Mount Spruce in the distance, biting clouds, highest in the state. They saw no deer, no livestock, not even a carrion crow. The horrible tranquility of it all. No birds sang. Nothing but the sound of their own voices, their own thoughts. They had emptied their world like a jug.

THERE WERE OTHER FIRES. In Helena, where the mill now stood empty, Edden Hammons, a brag fiddler walking the track, was first to see. He thought it a red fox dancing in the underbrush, the way they pounce after field mice with infernal glee.

A thin cursive of smoke marked the evening. That night the fire came ripsawing in one red curtain. All of Helena—beggar and lawyer, postman and nurse—stood in the street, murmuring to one another without a care to class or convention, as they would to see a comet come round once in a lifetime.

One great shimmer of heat. The fire vaulted the river and climbed the ridges in waves, driven on with whipcracking sounds. Creosoted ties flared and gave off a black smoke that tasted of oil and coated the tongue. The land hissed out there in the dark. At midnight, you could read a paper on the stoop of Grayab's store.

Incredibly, the morning came. The town smelled of scorched sap and turpentine. The fire stopped shy of Helena, and snowy inches of ash settled on the roofs. Where the last few deer caught fire, they left greasy smears upon the ground.

But the fire kept burning, favoring west and south. Three million acres gone. It smoldered though November, then a wet snow fell slapping.

Helena's decline was inevitable now: bare slabs, boarded shops, clashing walls of honeysuckle. The barber pole faded—the floor inside was covered in balls of dry hair no one bothered to sweep up, and they skittered on drafts that came in through the broken window. It took years of rain for the new Helena court to quit smelling like a smokehouse; the continual floods helped—it was built too close to the Cheat. The mill was auctioned piece by piece. The railroad office was staffed by a dozen cats that lounged among desks and overturned chairs.

FOR REASONS THAT WOULD REMAIN MYSTERIOUS to Cur, the warden called on him just seven years into his sentence of fourteen. He never appeared before a parole board. A guard merely took him from the slop line and led him to the office. It took a dazed moment for Cur to realize the warden was not the same man who'd signed him in to the prison. The smiling warden said Cur must have special friends somewhere. Cur didn't know what to say. He was handed a folded suit of cheap twill and an envelope stuffed with twenty-nine dollars, the money he'd earned trustying. No paperwork accompanied Cur's release; he does not exist in state records.

The penitentiary gate opened with a wince, and he was outside on a watered lawn.

Endless miles to Helena, even on the new highway, but Cur waved off truck and coupe alike that pulled along to offer a ride. He couldn't think of where else to go. Maybe he lacked imagination. He walked the pike—pavement now, with its astringent smell—but then decided to catch a train in Clarksburg. This was just too far. He wasn't in the shape he used to be; his head tended to list to one side. He had money enough, but buying a ticket was a new thing, and new things he feared. He had never been on a passenger train. It was nice, especially the way the cushions cradled his ruined back. A great relief, as long as he didn't look out at the black char of the world. He shut his eyes and slept. His stale breath silvered the window glass. Outside, the earth was cracking beneath a relentless sun. He could have stayed up north in the Ohio Valley—pottery works and steel mills, cigar and nail factories, the employers known to be kind and fair, especially in the glassworks. The city of Wheeling was said to be a workingman's joy, with a socialist mayor. But so near the penitentiary, to remind him of himself.

Arriving at the Helena depot on a dusty evening, he saw that even the common's decorative oaks had been cut. Draft horses had jerked out their stumps, and boys had quartered them with whipsaws. He stepped down. Other passengers flowed around him. He was unaccustomed to moving quickly. There was a new shyness in his motions—prison had given him that. He no longer had strong passions, not even upon entering this place. He was a cold swamp.

But he did have regrets—cussing the preacher, threatening Sally Cove—and they could make his cheeks burn. These moments were fixed in memory, as one pins butterflies to a board, pushing through the bodies, feeling that sweet and sickening give. He doubted Sally Cove was here—look at that abandoned office—but surely Seldomridge was. You couldn't imagine him anywhere else. Surely he still had ideas. Surely Cur could talk to him and learn how he was supposed to live now.

Cur booked a room in a Fishamble Street boardinghouse he recognized from years ago, though the name on the sign had been painted over with another, and another. He woke before dawn, as he had all his life. The japanned lamp would not light.

Leaving the boardinghouse, he made for East Bank. Something was odd about this place—something beyond the scabrous landscape around. The trouble was silence. The mill did not scream. A day in Helena always meant gnash and whine, but if a newcomer clutched his ears against it, he was quickly told, "It sounds like money to me."

The clapboard parsonage stood shyly in the shadow of the stone church, as it always had. He knocked. Even through the glass of the door, he knew it wasn't Seldomridge. The skin was too welcoming and smooth. No, the new pastor said, he didn't know where Seldomridge was.

"How long's he been gone?"

"Let me think. Five years now. At least."

The people left in town hardly remembered Seldomridge. While the new pastor was inviting him to services, Cur rudely walked away. He couldn't know that, to Seldomridge's own amazement, he had been given a large healthy church in the southern part of the state. This promotion was in consideration of Seldomridge's seniority, pushed along by a new paper bureaucracy. The latest state bishop, a reformer, didn't care for the old handshake deal to keep Seldomridge in Helena forever. Down there, Seldomridge took part in the mine wars, and in consequence he would be defrocked in May of 1919 by the American Council, with a vote of 8–1. Cur would never see the famous photograph: Seldomridge in a jail cell, sunlight cutting through the bars. The jailers gave the old man a rocking chair. Another prisoner cropped from the corner, only a leg and a brogan showing: Asa Neversummer, a miner so long he hardly remembered that other life in Helena, consigning his past to oblivion, hoping for better. Seldomridge would be there at Shanks Mountain, where the miners threw vigilantes down wells, dug rifle trenches, and claimed for themselves a hundred miles of ground for weeks on end, only to have their camps machine-gunned. Bombs whistled from hired planes. The leaders went to prison, and the rest were pardoned. When he was forced to appear in front of the council, Seldomridge recited the Social Creed in protest, and the bishops blithely responded that they heard the creed each Sunday and didn't recollect a call for violence. "Did you enjoy seeing yourself in the paper?" one bishop asked.

Cur had nowhere to go, nothing to do. He couldn't believe Seldomridge was gone—Cur's life had been expunged. His past was fantasy, even to him. He stumbled into a shop, like a man drunk on tanglefoot. A pot metal bell announced him. The establishment was threadbare but meticulously kept, smelling of liniment and buckets of fresh nails. To steady himself, he looked over the shelves, empty for the most part, but the essentials—fishhooks, packets of seed—would be there till judgment day. Cur recognized the shop as what used to be Barabbas Poling's, where he had sold off his carpenter's gear. He found a beauty behind the counter with sandy skin and blue-black hair. For something to say, Cur asked her to cut him a wedge of hoop cheese and slices of bread from the case. Afterward she smiled and wiped her brow with her wrist, the knife dangling.

"Hot," she said. She tallied his receipt on brown paper with authority. Clearly the shop was hers. "You look like you would ask me something."

Cur blushed. "Not at all."

"You aren't from here."

"Used to. I was a tree cutter."

She clucked her tongue. "One of those bad men. I have heard all about you."

Something faintly exotic to the twist of her mouth, to the wry leaping brow, and an accent he couldn't place. This was Lis Grayab's wife, young enough to be the man's daughter, sent across an ocean to him. It was not at all what she expected. This was a boring town, now that the mill had shut down, but the county courthouse brought lawyers and witnesses here, so the store scraped by, just barely, between that and a postal contract.

"Yes," he said with a smile. He hadn't spoken with a woman in so long. "I did it all."

"No, you didn't."

He grinned, asking, "Would I lie to you?"

"There's some you missed. Up on Gaudineer." That strip of land the surveyor overlooked, the last scrap. She told him of some ninety acres. All that was left of the old forest. "The trees are nice there. Often I went with my fiancé. You should go."

She sketched him a map on the back of the receipt, and he leaned down to study her drawing hand, their heads dangerously close. Her hair brushed his cheek, and brushed it again. He wouldn't see Gaudineer. He just wanted to lean in beside her. Perhaps he didn't look so poor, so criminal. He flared like a coal, alive again, as he turned back at the door.

"You went up there alone with a man? What would Mom say?"

"Times have changed."

He stepped out of Grayab's store and onto the place where, twenty-odd years later, a fussy WPA sculptor would watch the men crack open a crate of flashing bronze. Months the sculptor worked on it in stifling rooms, his one standing commission, a cast of three boy soldiers in uniform gazing out at strange new lands, with looks between canniness and curiosity, like cats at play: the absentees. The labor was on loan from the work camp, and could they bolt the statue to the pedestal? Yes they could. They left handprints behind. The men were muddy to the shoulders from a day of planting seedlings, reclaiming burnt-over mountain land the government bought up for five dollars an acre under the Weeks Act. No bunting, no band, not even the mayor to watch—the sculptor claimed he hated such, but missed it all the same. His creation would gather no more attention here than green rime, bird shit, and the occasional lesson of a precocious schoolteacher, asking her charges, "Would you someday be a senator, too?" Each question seemed to answer itself. He made them shift it to the right, then to the left. To catch the light of jogging suns.

Cur walked back to the boardinghouse, noticing that the absentees never had sprung for those cobblestones. It was eight o'clock in the morning. The thrill of meeting the woman didn't last. He considered what else he would do with his day and reclined on the mattress beneath a water-stained and buckled ceiling. This was all you could hope for: a place to lay your head.

He fiddled with the lamp and teased it into working. A newspaper had been left to skate the floor on intermittent drafts. The banal dispatches of weather and election gave him a small measure of comfort. He plumbed President Taft's mangled sentences:

THE DAY IS NOT FAR DISTANT WHEN THREE STARS & STRIPES AT THREE EQUIDISTANT POINTS WILL MARK OUR TERRITORY: ONE AT THE NORTH POLE, ANOTHER AT THE PANAMA CANAL, AND THE THIRD AT THE SOUTH POLE. THE WHOLE HEMISPHERE WILL BE OURS IN FACT AS, BY VIRTUE OF OUR SUPERIORITY OF RACE, IT ALREADY IS OURS MORALLY.

He dropped the paper and returned his key to the bewildered clerk.

PANTS BLACK TO THE KNEES with ash and char, Cur finished the walk he began seven years prior. He saw, in this symmetry, no beauty. He tried not to think of it. This time, no vision—not even a great fire—would draw him off the road.

He saw the cabin on the horizon, with a larger catalog home built alongside it. These few acres. Sarah Greathouse hadn't let them cut her trees, the ones belonging to her sons. Where they could shoot a deer if they wanted to and run foxhounds. The neighbors thought her insane, to leave good dollars rotting on the hill. She wouldn't even sell her mineral rights! But now the trees stood dead and stone gray and leprous, the bark falling away. Cur's half brothers had been waiting on their mother to die. When the time came, they could sell their coolish grove to the Company. They didn't wish her dead, exactly, but the money would be a boon. They weren't spurning her gift, they told their wives, only converting it to another currency. They didn't have much laid away. Everyone in Three Forks could use another dollar. But fires came, and they never got the chance to sell the place.

Dogs snapped to the gate, and Cur offered them tea-colored hands. In a minute he charmed them, feeding them tufts of bread from his pocket. He let himself in. A woman was standing beside the well.

"It's you," she said.

Sarah Greathouse took his hands. She was still a startling woman, and stunning. She had crow's feet, and her eyes were bright, feline, a river-water gray. Her back straight, her bearing slightly martial. But smiling. Morning glories lifted on the wind. They had replanted around the house and cabin, flowers, a vegetable garden.

Sarah let go. His heart was racing. Hummingbirds droned. At first he mistook the sound for his pulse.

She said, "I wasn't expecting you. I'm so glad you come."

She made him walk with her to the big house and waved him inside. He didn't know what to say. Sarah bid him sit in the new kitchen, saying, "I'll be back in a mite. I'll get you some eggs." The dress clung to her body, a wet place on the small of her back the size of a bootprint. He watched her go, remembering the stale honeysuckle taste of her mouth. Her teeth on his hip, his collarbone. Her hair still was dark, with stray shots of iron. Or was that the sun playing upon it? He wasn't sure. He remembered the cursive of stretch marks that shimmered in the skin of her hips. A realization made him blush—Sarah looked a good deal like Sally Cove—or, really, Sally looked like her. He had tried to replicate his own life. He could laugh a little at that. He had that talent. But then he told himself to forget and live in this one moment.

Cur sat at the table. Time heals all wounds, he wondered. It was true, the trite lessons he'd read of in novels and newspapers, it really was true. He waited ten minutes, twenty, but it felt an eternity.

Finally, he found her on the back porch gazing into the middle distance. Smiling, she turned and said, "I wasn't expecting you. I'm so glad you come."

She had mistaken him for Nathan, her son.

Her mind was gone. Whether disease or disquietude stole it away, it was beyond anyone's understanding. Cur waited for someone else to come.

With wary looks, Nathan and Jude welcomed him back. His half brothers were married now. They had trouble explaining Cur's return to their wives, for they had never told of his existence. Lilly especially did not like it.

"He'll work," Nathan assured.

She found little comfort in that.

Sarah Greathouse was a burden. She had to be watched every moment, to be kept from cutting her own hair, from letting herself go unwashed, from walking off—and Cur would do it. This warmed the wives to him. No more call to hang at Three Forks for stifling hours on end, tending the madwoman. The wives would have their lives back; they could dote on their children, be themselves. They made Cur the present of an army cot and a suit of clothes. He slept like a servant in the passage behind the kitchen. The Greathouses were nervous—it took him awhile to learn why. Jude and Nathan had worked in the tiny Low Gap sawmill until it closed. Now they had patronage jobs working on a county road crew, but they expected their party to be voted out in the next election. Meals were thin. Nathan cussed Cur for giving Sarah too much to eat through the day, then apologized the next day, opening his wallet. There was some talk of going to Marion County, a hundred miles west, where a zinc mine was opening.

Old Neil Greathouse was three years dead. Cur's long-ago premonition of his father's end had been far off. Had he mistaken a wish for divination? Nathan respectfully pointed him toward the burying ground, but let him go alone, in case he would weep. It was up in a rocky cove, and Cur walked through chamois-soft ferns and jagged greenstone. The graves had been placed there, Old Neil said, because fertile land can't be spared for the dead; they have no use or claim on it anyhow. Old Neil's was a limestone obelisk, pointing the way to heaven. It would fall to the soft persistent teeth of lichen, which hoarded calcium, chewing the names. Cur touched the chiseled letters, shallow to his fingers. It flaked a little to the touch. He felt nothing at all, no love, no hate, only the end of something, or the shadow of a feeling, easy to perceive but impossible to grasp. Some claimed that, in death, no one's so heavy as a dead preacher, but Cur thought of this weight upon them, his father's life, like a meteorite fallen to earth: not large in its dimensions but dense and burdensome. He couldn't know Old Neil. No one could. Sarah would have been the one to clean his father's body, running the comb through Old Neil's hair for the last time, fixing the buttons on his shirt. Or had she lost her mind by then? Had Cur driven her mad? He never saw the scars until, one day, Sarah tipped back a glass of water and her sleeve fell. On her arm, the flayed scalloped skin, purple and puckered. It reminded Cur of the dead men, of boiler explosions, of the safehouse ripped apart. Old Neil had held her bare body against the stove, marked her so everyone would know. In the thoughtlessness of youth, Cur hadn't considered the ways she would suffer—another thing he'd grown into, this way of thinking of others. When she set down the glass, her sleeve covered it over.

Nothing so lonesome as a hillside grave, only rain and snow to visit you. There were other stones, flecked with rose-colored feldspar, tongues and fingers of it. It was hard work, burying bodies in rocky ground. Sometimes they would pull up a good stone during interment, then use it as the marker. They had poured blood into this seam of earth: Josef and Marie Grothausen, Mathias and Judith and Dare, the second wife American and the anglicizer of their name. They had come here before America was a nation, and in their own country, the Greathouses would feel increasingly foreign, here in their mountains, far from the centers of commerce and printing press and power. They would be thought backward and worthless by those who had profited from them most.

Old Neil had lain a chock for Cur's twin brother Jesse, marked with an angular J, for only adults earned full names, the way a tortoise accrues its shell. Two of Cur's half sisters there: Daphne and another called Nell, of whom he'd never heard, for she'd been born with a face like a wilted flower. Cur left them there. This was their land. This country always belonged to the dead. The living rented upon their memories. The living looked embarrassed to be here.

SO HE SAT WITH SARAH GREATHOUSE. Morning begat noon, night, and dawn. Cur spoke of nonsense in the papers; he played word games in the corners, chaste with her as a child.

"I wasn't expecting you," said Sarah as he carried the tray to her room each morning. "I'm so glad you come." After he set it down, she would grasp his rough hands, and he would smile. One day was just like another. It was like paradise, it was like death.

Acknowledgments

I WISH TO THANK the following institutions and people who helped make this book possible: the University of Iowa, the Fine Arts Work Center, the Michener–Copernicus Society of America, Lookout Books, the St. Botolph Club Foundation, the Jentel Foundation, Tal Zamir, Janet Silver, Emily Louise Smith, Beth Staples, Anna Lena Phillips Bell, Lan Samantha Chang, Connie Brothers, Deb West, Jan Zenisek, Elizabeth McCracken, Allan Gurganus, Roger Skillings, Salvatore Scibona, Jaimy Gordon, and Greg and Mary Beth Null.

In this novel I take great liberties with history and geography, but in spirit the work is true. Inspiration was partly drawn from the following sources: Barbara Rasmussen's *Absentee Landowning and Exploitation in West Virginia, 1760–1920*; Philip V. Bagdon's *Shay Logging Locomotives at Cass, West Virginia, 1900–60* and *West Virginia's Last Logging Railroad—The Meadow River Company*; William Warden's *West Virginia Logging Railroads*; Ronald L. Lewis's *Transforming the Appalachian Countryside: Railroads, Deforestation, and Social Change in West Virginia, 1880–1920*; Mary Beth Stenger's "Lebanese in the Land of Opportunity: The Michael Family of Clarksburg"; Nancy Svet Burnett's *Slovenes in rural Appalachia: an oral history* and "Where the Rails Turn Up: Slovenes Come to Richwood"; Carl Feather's "Go See Sonny: Hedrick's Store in Hendricks"; Arthur C. Prichard's "Two Hundred Pounds or More: The Lebanese Community in Mannington"; Andrew Gennett's *Sound Wormy: Memoir of Andrew Gennett, Lumberman*; and Roy B. Clarkson's *Tumult on the Mountains: Lumbering in West Virginia 1770–1920* and *On Beyond Leatherbark: The Cass Saga*. To all the authors, thank you. I am in your debt. You do the hard work of making the vanished world real.

—MN

Lookout Books

Lookout is more than a name—it's our
publishing philosophy. Founded as the
literary book imprint of the Department
of Creative Writing at the University of
North Carolina Wilmington, Lookout
seeks out works by emerging and historically
underrepresented voices, as well as overlooked
gems by established writers. In a publishing
landscape increasingly indifferent to literary
innovation, Lookout offers a haven for
books that matter.

TEXT ADOBE CASLON PRO 10.5/13.8
DISPLAY THE WALDEN FONT CO.'S TYPE NO. II 20